NESTED EVIL
The Scourge of Witch'Bane

MJ Grothoff

T5I Publications

Copyright © 2026 by MJ Grothoff

All rights reserved.

No part of this publication may be reproduced, distributed, or transmitted in any form or by any means, including photocopying, recording, or other electronic or mechanical methods, without the prior written permission of the publisher, except as permitted by U.S. copyright law. For permission requests, contact MJ Grothoff at mjgrothoff.com.

The story, all names, characters, and incidents portrayed in this production, are fictitious. No identification with actual persons (living or deceased), places, buildings, and products is intended or should be inferred.

Cover & Maps by Miblart.com

Editing by Philip Athans — reedsy.com/philip-athans

Follow MJ Grothoff — mjgrothoff.com

ISBN — 978-1-971902-00-5 (paperback)

ISBN — 978-1-971902-01-2 (ebook)

THE SCOURGE OF WITCH'BANE

The Scourge of Witch'Bane is a trilogy, presented in the following sequence.

Book One – Nested Evil

Book Two – Wretched Evil

Book Three – Eternal Evil

CONTENTS

Glossary / Location / Character / Masuran Clans List	VII
1. Chapter 1	1
2. Chapter 2	11
3. Chapter 3	27
4. Chapter 4	41
5. Chapter 5	57
6. Chapter 6	73
7. Chapter 7	89
8. Chapter 8	103
9. Chapter 9	117
10. Chapter 10	133
11. Chapter 11	147
12. Chapter 12	161
13. Chapter 13	175
14. Chapter 14	187
15. Chapter 15	201
16. Chapter 16	219
17. Chapter 17	233

18.	Chapter 18	245
19.	Chapter 19	259
20.	Chapter 20	275
21.	Chapter 21	289
Coming Soon		301
Maps		303

GLOSSARY

Barkapes — created by the god Nathe, fierce fighters & thieves set into an ape's mind.
Cave-dwellers — humans living deep inside caves.
Crowl — green humanoid beings, live with shamans as leaders.
Dulisar Elves — forest elves living in the northwest forest of Dulisar on Briev.
Grangrul — lizard humanoids, taller than humans and live in caves or domed cities.
Masura — elvish type beings with wings & talons for feet, live in forest tree loft cities.
Sakti — energy allows you to cross short or great distances through the ethereal.
Scroll Keeper — keeper of the scrolls, called by wizards when they need help.
Thunderblood — clan mercenaries, original keepers of the Three Sisters.
Tontar — spiritual beings from the island of Anayana.

LOCATIONS

Anayana — one of five islands. Home of the tontars & prison for demigoddess Winna.
Asmodea / Witch'Bane — Masuran Forest.
Bathhh — western city of the Shale Mountains, run by the Wizard Stanton.
Breiv — one of five islands. Home of the masuras & prison for demigoddess Malum.
Eden — eastern port city, sits before the Dree Sea.
Eptiwuh / Epti Kingdom — human kingdom.
Esor — mountain range & home to the Esor Dragons.
Horfa — holy city on the island of Ihandra.
Ihandra / the Mystics Island — one of the five islands, home to the Seer of Seers.
Lotrs — one of the five islands, home of the druids, prison to Druiss.
Manawe — port city on Lheter lake, sits west of Witch'Bane.
Mudra — northern port city on the Cree Sea.
Róta — one of the five islands.

CHARACTERS

Arul II — King of Witch'Bane, father of Flued & Shapía.
Ati — Ethereal Being, Member of the Order of Lucidity.
Aza / The All / the One of One / the Great of Great — god of the in-between.
Bahg — Duke of Witch'Bane, father to Gavee, brother to Arul II, Witch'Bane's Thunderblood.
Crea — Mistress and Shaman of the Crowl.
Crym — thunderblood tontar from Anayana.
Dakii the Wanderer — scroll keeper.
Datta — thunderblood of BataRaul.
Druiss — demigoddess imprisoned on Lotrs, sister to Malum & Winna.
Flued / Asmodeus — Prince of Witch'Bane, son to King Arul II, King of Kings.
Gavee — Earl of Witch'Bane, son to Bahg, thunderblood trainee.
Grunt — shapeshifter weasel, honoree clan member of Witch'Bane.
Malum — demigoddess imprisoned on Briev, sister to Druiss & Winna.
Phawa — Queen of Witch'Bane, mother to Flued & Shapía, Rath Warrior Princess.
Rhile — Lahd to Prince Flued, leader of the Witch'Bane army.
Sattva — the Seer of Seers, Head of the Oracles.
Shaki — elfman oracle, aid to the Seer of Seers.
Shapía — Princess of Witch'Bane, daughter to King Arul II, the Blood Seer.
Taronquel — head council for Witch'Bane.
Trogan — Dragon from Esor, Prince.
Winna — demigoddess imprisoned on Anayana, sister to Druiss & Malum.

MASURAN CLANS

the Ancient Ones
La'Darium, Lohr, Ramus, Ranois, Rath, Torem, Tryolic
the Young Ones
BataRaul / Bata, DasaRaul / Dasa, Fens, Manawe, Witch'Bane

Chapter One

Gavee felt a chill run down his spine at the idea of visiting the far southern forest. Its ancient spaces and whispering trees painted danger in his mind. Higher into the air, the two masuras ascended, pushing dry air into their wings to understand the open range and distance from things hidden in the thick grass. The rolling hillside and wild wheat swayed beneath them in the warm breeze as they followed the dips and rolls with each hillcrest. They reached a ridge overlooking the Lower Lake's shoreline, and the queen halted in flight. It surprised Gavee and forced him to withdraw. She pointed, and at that spot on the water's bank, three mighty Esor Dragons bathed. They carried dark green scales and long faces. Their eyes had a sinister stare, and they had long, pointed tails. Two seem to bathe in the water with the third sunning itself.

"It's an odd scene," said the queen. "I don't believe I have seen dragons bathing."

The younger masura had never seen dragons, and with the panic on the queen's face, fear covered his thoughts.

"Dragons this far south?" questioned Gavee.

Queen Phawa's quiet voice held a ferocious edge.

"They do not travel together. I'm not fond of seeing more than one. We need to fly low and head back to Rath, and fast."

"Will they follow?" asked Gavee.

"If they spot us, yes. My father fought these evil beasts and taught us that Esor Dragons are wicked," said the queen.

"The Great Masuran War?"

"History holds more than books reveal, my nephew," Phawa said. "You'll soon come to understand the truth."

Turning, they flew over the open field, allowing their talons to drag across the tall grass. Gavee's mighty wing strokes pushed him along with unstoppable force. He was a proud masura, elvin beings with wings and talons as feet. They were masters of the skies, and through his training, he could out fly most masuras. He had yet to encounter a dragon.

A sudden gust pushed the masura ahead, almost causing him to tumble as he faced the queen, who had her sword in hand. Trees hung just beyond when a dragon dropped between them and the forest. In the air, it roared, sending the masuras tumbling back. They each caught themselves, powering their wings to hover.

"This way! Hurry, Gavee!" said the queen.

They moved left, heading for the field.

"Let's double back and return to the Crescents. I know a place the dragons cannot reach!" she said.

"We'll never make it!" said Gavee.

"We must and will!" said the queen.

The masuras burst into a frantic flight for the mountains. Their mighty feathered wings pushed their elflike bodies into increasing speed, and with their eagle eyes, they monitored the sky. The queen's slender royal scimitar caught Gavee's eye as it held firm in her grip. Etched onto the ivory handle of the family sword was a crested serpent arched on one side and an eagle with outstretched wings bent on the other. The Rath clan's crest wrapped around a mithril blade holding an ancient masuran saying: My strength shall be as strong as my wisdom. The interwoven gold and silver glistened on the wingtips.

Gavee loved the sword and realized he flew without his blade in hand. From its beautiful gold and silver sheath, the masura drew a simple moon sword. The leather-wrapped handle led to a small Witch'Bane shield and climbed to the silver blade. It was not magnificent, but it felt comfortable in his grip.

Even as the mountain range drew near, the very thing they sought to prevent took place. A dragon lowered in front of them, blocking the pass. The beast's maw opened wide, and it belted a roar, with flames engulfing the sky. The heat tossed Gavee back, and the queen's eyebrows furrowed.

Gavee searched for the dragons and stopped short as a sudden, gruesome pain tore into his side and yanked him skyward. Caught in the dragon's talons, Gavee's thin armor had not withheld the razor-sharp claws. He glanced to see the beast's scaly underbelly flexing under each wing flap. The creature's long neck twisted, lowering its enormous head with a sinister smile while the claw tightened.

The earl struggled for a breath as they approached a large open space high in the mountains. He felt each talon dig deeper, piercing his ribs. The blood dripped from the torn flesh, and Gavee grimaced in pain, trying to lift his sword. He caught sight of the queen, too, hanging from a beast's claw.

The dragons reached a mountain clearing and dropped their struggling prey in a heap. Gavee lay face down and watched the dirt kick from each inhale as it stretched his wound. He winced and turned to find the queen motionless.

"Mother?" he whispered.

"Be quiet," she said.

The last dragon landed, circling its victims.

"Are these the ones, Trogan?" questioned the most massive of the dragons.

"Yes, Crage, they carry the Witch'Bane symbol," answered Trogan, the middle-sized beast.

"Are we to scorch them as we did the others?" questioned the shortest. "Or may we consume them?"

"No, Bhronic, leave them alone. These are royals, and I have other intentions," answered Trogan.

"You haven't shared why we had to come to the lake," said Crage.

Trogan thundered to the creature and roared, forcing it to cower.

"I am the Prince of Esor. I have my reasons, and you are to follow. You do not need my plans."

The dragon whipped its tail through the tall grass and shot flames into the open field.

"You shouldn't be here!" he said.

Gavee opened an eye and watched the dragons continue their dance. He held on to his sword and wondered how to use it against such a giant beast. The dragons seemed more interested in their conversation than the masuras as they passed their victims and allowed them to study their slow and heavy-footed movements.

"Do you see their ears?" whispered the queen. "It's where we aim our swords."

"How do we get there?" he asked.

"Once the smallest one turns its back, I'll reach its backside and finish it."

"You can't attack the dragons, My Queen," said Gavee.

"Trained as a warrior, I have a few tricks up my sleeve as an oracle," she said.

"If we do nothing, will they leave?"

"Their intent is our doom. Do you see the scorched rocks behind us? I see a Witch'Bane Latuery shield in the ash mound. I think we've found our guards."

Gavee searched back, his heart raced, and his body shook from fear.

"Easy, Gavee. Concentrate. The warrior's truest enemy is their own mind. Focus on your sword and its location. It will forever be true. Prepare to cover your eyes and move."

As the dragons continued to circle around their prey, the masuras waited for the opportunity to expose the smallest dragon's back. The timing had to be exact, or a quick tail from the beasts and it would end the masuras. Gavee's heart continued to race.

He watched the queen stalk her victim with a deathly stare when she snapped her left hand forward and a white sphere formed in her palm. From the dirt, the proud Rath warrior princess, queen of Witch'Bane, lunged, targeting the smaller dragon's neck. The orb held a glow as she grew near the dragon's eyes. The queen muttered words Gavee could not hear.

Gavee shielded his eyes in amazement as the orb exploded. Surprised, the dragons stumbled from their chanted walk, leaving them unable to react. The female masura dug her talons into the tiny dragon's scales near its head, and it belted out a roar.

Time slowed for Gavee. With the orb's rays bouncing off the Rath family's sword as the queen raised the weapon, Phawa took a solemn breath and unleashed her attack with all her might.

The blade hit its mark, penetrating the beast's small ear, and blood gushed from the wound.

With blank eyes, the dragon dropped its lifeless body, while the queen flipped clear and landed in a defensive stance. The dead beast crashed with a thud. The sudden wind and dirt blew her brown hair forward, but her eyes remained stone cold, fixed on the ensuing target. Gavee marveled at the power. The other dragons snarled in disbelief.

The queen thrust onward and lunged at the next dragon. She caught its neck, and blood splattered.

Gavee could not wait, so he engaged in the fight. He countered, expanded his great wings, and leaped at the last beast. The side wound throbbed, but he ignored the ache and pushed for the dragon.

Trogan must have perceived the masura and rolled, surprising the Earl as it landed on all fours. Flames erupted as the beast roared.

The thunderblood trainee came to a stop in the dirt, staring down at death. Then Gavee swooped into the sky and bellowed a scream. He pulled his sword and lunged forward. The blade's aim snapped short, for the dragon had been ready, and it whipped its tail against its chest.

The masura winced and tossed over the clearing into a grassy field. He skipped twice on the ground and slammed against a boulder. His vision faded in and out but caught the queen in the distance, covered in dragon's blood, then things slipped into darkness.

* * *

The dragon used the momentary distraction and snatched her leg with its tail. The female masura dangled as her eyes glowed, and she conjured a second orb in her free hand. Fire-like energy swirled in the blue ball as she plunged it into the creature, causing it to fizz and spark. It roared and threw the queen toward the tree line.

"Do not hurt the queen!" said Trogan.

The beast bellowed at the field in anger.

"You filthy Masura!" it said.

"I need her alive!" said Trogan.

"The other one?"

"It may be important to her, so leave it."

* * *

The queen rolled to a stop and snapped behind a large tree. Gavee was in the field, but she couldn't search as she needed to kill the beasts. The warrior queen created a plan and advanced when the dragons separated and began their hunt. Crage skulked along the tree line, and Trogan proceeded to the opposite side. It gave her the opportunity, and she tracked the giant beast.

"Where are you, filthy masura?" roared Crage.

The dragon stayed near the forest's outskirts, and Queen Phawa followed through the trees. She sized the beast for an attack when she caught Gavee lying motionless against the lone rock. Despite the inner warrior's urge to end the hunt, the queen defied her instincts to gain a better vantage point. The motion drew the dragon's eye, and the giant beast whipped its tail, snapping at her with significant force. Phawa bounced and smashed into a boulder near Gavee. The creature didn't notice where the masura landed, but felt her beating heart.

"I'm not through with you, Masura! Do you think you could kill my brother and escape? Do you think you could burn me and live?" asked Crage.

Trogan peered over to see his companion rushing through the field.

"No, you fool! You're out of control! I need her! She must remain alive!"

* * *

Gavee awoke with the thunder. He glanced over in a haze to discover the queen covered in blood from a fresh wound on her forehead. He had trained as a thunderblood, fierce fighters and tactical negotiators, but none of it prepared him for dragons. This foe was different, and he felt a failure resonant through his thoughts.

His queen. His aunt. The one who adopted him as her own son after his mother had died, lay on a boulder next to him, gasping.

"Son," she said, "take my sword."

"Mother?" he cried.

"Carry it." She coughed and spat blood.

"No!" Gavee said.

Gavee could not comprehend the queen's words as she relinquished the sword. He took a knee, trying to stand.

"Mother!"

The blast was loud and sudden, and the heated air sent him sprawling. Putrid sulfur and ash filled his nose and lungs, and he gasped for fresh air. The last image Gavee saw through the smoke was Queen Phawa's body engulfed in flames, burning from the dragon's fire. He crashed to the ground.

"No, no!"

The young earl lay in the dirt, eyes upon her sword and its beautiful ivory handle. He was moments away from losing consciousness.

"That's what you get for thinking you can kill us!" said Crage.

Trogan landed next to Crage and stared at the smoldering ashes. "I needed her, you fool!"

He stalked closer, searching for the missing masura.

"You lost control," he said. "You don't know what you've done. Return to Esor, and I'll gather what I need from the remaining masura!"

"I should stay and help find the younger one."

"No! Allow me to clean up this mess," said Trogan.

The enormous dragon retreated. "As you please, Prince."

The ground shook as the massive creature sprang and swooped its enormous wings.

Trogan glanced again at the smoldering ash and groaned. "The witch wanted her dead, and it came true. This other one carries the Witch'Bane crest. I guess he'll have to do."

Gavee, dazed, met the dragon's gaze. Trogan gave a slight flick to Gavee's forehead. As the masura's ears popped from the jolt, he watched the green dragon go blurry until darkness again took hold.

* * *

Gavee soon awoke and sat in an open field. The sky held a green hue, and a low vibration stung his ears. The masura could not recall his past or future, unaware of the vast plain beneath swirling thunderclouds.

"Hello?" Gavee's voice rippled.

A murmur came from the distance.

"Is someone there?"

Above, the clouds turned a darker shade, and the low vibration rose louder, forcing him to cup his ears. He attempted to rise, but his body was heavy. Dizziness took hold, and the faint sounds grew louder, piercing his ears.

"Chrssshaahh," floated a whisper.

"Mighty Chrsshaahh," it repeated.

"Who calls..." a dark voice echoed.

"Who's there!" rippled Gavee.

"He's not a dragon!" an ancient voice boomed.

"He's needed, and I say Chrssshaahh!"

Gavee held his ears against the painful echoes.

"Who are you? Where am I?" asked Gavee.

The whispers grew, and the noise made him sick. He curled into a ball and heaved in agony. A rolling storm sound filled the air.

Then the whispers disappeared, and the green hue brightened. Pain subsided, and he tried looking up, but the brightness hurt his eyes.

It went dark.

Suddenly, light pierced the darkness, and lightning struck him in the chest. It sent the masura spinning into a tumble, and he came to rest, face down, with his chest burning. The sky returned to its green hue, and Gavee pulled himself up, screaming from the pain.

He stood with great effort and found his clothes tattered, his chest revealing a scorched mark. It held a glow and pulsed.

Gavee gazed at the sky and found nothing but a green expanse.

"Where am I?"

His voice echoed, and he searched, finding only rolling hills.

The thunderblood deep inside grabbed hold, and escape filled his thoughts. The masura flapped his wings to hover, but discovered they would not move fast enough for flight.

Gavee groaned and walked when he noticed the distant hill grew lower as a wave in the sea. The motion reached him, and it knocked him to the ground. He screamed in anguish and attempted to stand when a second wave hit, but more rigid and prominent.

The green clouds unleashed a torrent, and the rain pelted his skin and wings. His feathers tore from the impact, and he curled into the deluge. The field filled with water, and he sank into the abyss before he could react. Gavee attempted to swim up, but his arms would not move, and he fell deeper, farther from the crest. He waited for death to consume him as it became dark.

* * *

The masura awoke to pouring rain with a swollen face, a sore body, and a burning chest. His head pounded, and he attempted to look around. The queen's sword lay at his feet, and the Latuery surrounded him with his father, Bahg, holding his head.

"Wake up, son," said Bahg.

Gavee coughed.

"Where am I? Where's the queen?" he asked.

"We are by the Lower Lake, and for the queen, I pose the same question to you."

Gavee sat as the rain poured on the small valley.

"Sire, we need to get to safety," said the Latuery guard.

Bahg nodded and stood, bringing Gavee to his feet. The masura looked around, remaining in a daze when his chest throbbed. He pulled back his shirt, revealing a sizable, swollen burn.

"What happened?" asked Bahg.

"Dragons from Esor were waiting for our arrival here. They took us somewhere in the Cresent Mountains. The queen attacked and slew one beast. Then they killed her," he said.

Bahg's eyes widened at the words. "Would you take us to the location?"

Gavee lowered his head.

"The Latuery were missing as we exited Rath, and the queen insisted we continue without guards. The dragons lay waiting. They drove us over the field until they snatched and carried us to the mountain."

"How did you get the mark?" asked Bahg.

"I can't remember," answered Gavee.

Bahg gazed across the lake. The two remained motionless.

"I'm sorry," said Gavee.

He glanced at the waiting guards.

"How long have I been here?" asked Gavee.

"We've been searching for three days," said Bahg.

"Three days?" questioned Gavee as he looked around.

"Where are the dragons?" questioned Gavee.

The Latuery guard eyed the thunderblood trainee with hesitation.

"Gavee, dragons do not spend time in our lakes. It will be unknown until your memory returns," said Bahg.

Gavee tried to take a step, but his legs were powerless, and he dropped to a knee. Bahg lifted his son to both feet, and the many Latuery guards watched him stumble in a daze as he struggled to understand.

"Three green dragons appeared!" said Gavee.

Scowling, the guards waited for the Witch'Bane duke.

"Where are you?" questioned Gavee.

The masura slumped, and the rain mixed in with his tears as he studied the Rath blade.

"I will... I will have my revenge," he said, and dropped to the ground, unconscious.

Chapter Two

The Witch'Bane earl darted through the thick fog, smacked into a boulder and knocked the wind from his lungs. His adrenaline surged. His heart pounded in his chest like a drum.

Where... where is she? He thought.

He soared through the fog-shrouded mountains. The wind whipped past him, and he spotted the queen, her form barely visible against a distant boulder. He stretched out his arm, attempting to grab hers when she whispered something he could not comprehend.

What are you saying?

The massive shadow engulfed them, and a mighty Esor Dragon roared. Gavee threw his fists up in defense, shielding his eyes from the flames. The sulfur taste hit his tongue and burned his lungs. Her charred remains fixed in Gavee's thoughts.

No!

The earl snapped awake in a cold sweat, sitting in the dark. The tragedy hung on him, and the disbelief in his story from his loved ones was painful. He had removed his presence from the clan after the horrendous incident on the mountain. The memory returned after many moons, and the struggle to convince the royal family exacted its toll. The inquiry about Gavee becoming Witch'Bane's next thunderblood was now in question.

Gavee hid within a small cave, living a monk's existence in the Nathe Mountains, sitting on the southern tip of the Witch'Bane forest. His father, Bahg, Duke of Witch'Bane, continued to train his son as the next Witch'Bane thunderblood, but Gavee fell deeper into his own scrambled thoughts. The morning sun breached the cavern floor as it entered the opening, with the masura roosting on a small top shelf, allowing safety within the wild.

The small cave was a slit in the ground, deep in an open field, heading east, known to a few, with his father being the lone family member knowing the whereabouts. It blended into the wheat field from the sky, and it demanded an expert thunderblood to find it.

He observed the dust in the morning light and stepped down from the perch. The masura approached the opening to allow the sun to warm his face and the rays to hit his shirtless chest. He flinched when the warmth touched the scar. Gavee looked down and ran a finger along the raised mark, recalling the green field's dreams and voices. He had no explanation or memory of the wound. The battle's location remained gone in thought and, in the search, not yet found.

"Why were you there? What did you want?"

The scar throbbed with its usual fiery intensity, but beneath the familiar pain, a new, almost electric tingle vibrated. As it swelled and grew, the fist-sized mark shifted its shape. The marred skin throbbed under his touch, sending a white-hot shock through his body as he applied pressure. Gavee sank to his knees and drifted into a trance. His eyes shifted to bright green, and his vision landed within a dark cavern with blackened inscriptions scattered across the floor, walls, and ceilings, all in green.

He spoke in a low voice. "What does this mean?"

The walls had markings in an unknown language, with strange sigils crossing each other. He leaned in to read when things blurred, and it forced him to his hands and knees. The shock sent him back to his cave when Gavee slumped to the ground. He pulled himself up against a rock and sobbed.

An outside voice woke him from the spell as the afternoon deepened. The masura attempted to rise to his feet, but his mind spun, and his legs failed to stand. Unable to speak, he heard the voice call his name again and again. The spinning ideas made it difficult for him to think, as he hoped it was all a dream. He blinked several times until he could see his father lifting his face to give him a drink. Gavee sat and leaned against the wall with the outside light shadowing Bahg's stature.

"Come outside. You need fresh air," said Bahg.

Upon seeing his father, the masuran son smiled, his face alight with joy, and followed the request. Bahg donned his usual thunderblood attire: a long dark cloak, and a broadsword secured to his waist. His father, the clan's greatest warrior, bore the thunderblood symbol—two crossed swords branded on leather and sewn onto his left sleeve. The family's only duke was an elder, with some facial wrinkles and a scar above his left eye. The black thunderblood bandana on the forehead covered the small, receding, long black and gray hair and hid the remaining mark left from a past battle. He had seen many clashes, making him the lead ranger and tactician. Gavee remained in awe of how sharp and confident his father's demeanor carried him into a room.

"Why, in all the realms, are you lying in the dirt?" questioned Bahg.

Gavee dropped his head. "I should have saved her."

Bahg laid a hand on Gavee's shoulder. "The past is not here to keep you prisoner. Are you still having nightmares?"

Gavee nodded as tears fell.

"Yes... the dragon."

Bahg hesitated, selecting his words. "How could you even assume, my son, you could take them on? To face such a creature solo surpasses anyone's capacity, even with thunderblood training."

"Why don't you believe me?"

"This isn't about belief. The king and I understand you couldn't defeat what destroyed the queen. The biggest concern is the motive for the killing. Why? Why would they attack our queen?"

"I let my queen die," he said.

"The queen was a warrior who fought many battles in faraway forests. You say she defeated one of the vile creatures? This action alone would be a magnificent feat."

Gavee's focus shifted. "Wait, do you believe the dragons had a purpose? What purpose?"

"The details of the queen's whereabouts were given to those with a purpose. They struck."

"Why would they strike?"

Bahg stood, leaned against a tree, and gazed at the beautiful forest.

"The Great War, my son, the Great War."

"How are the dragons involved in this? They did not fight in the Great Masuran War."

Bahg sighed, then explained, "What I tell you next is not found in our history scrolls. The Great Masuran War landed in Esor. The mountains erupted into chaos, pitting the barkapes and masuras against the dragons and their orc minions. We destroyed many dragon halls dating back thousands of years. The truce allowed us to take the Upper Realm as our reward, leaving Esor to the dragons."

Gavee was stunned by the statement. "Why wasn't this included in our books or training? Is this the reason you avoid talking about the war?"

Bahg's finger slid down an old scar over his eye. "Yes, never documenting or speaking about it was decided by all involved. It is a forgotten war. The defeat affected both sides."

"Your scar?"

"From a dragon's tail, and a reminder of our failure."

"Do we not dare go to Esor for revenge? If we have beaten them once, could we not do it again?"

"There are other reasons we won the war."

"Reasons?"

Bahg paused.

"What happened before is difficult to explain. Now is not the right time, so we forget it for now."

"Forget it!" said Gavee. "How can I forget? They killed my queen! This hidden past tells the story and gives our clan reason to go after those beasts."

The rage drained from the masura, and his chest burned. His head dipped, and he gazed upon the foliage, his mind racing with the new information Bahg had revealed. Gavee sank into the brush, pulling up his knees and wrapping his arms around in a sigh. Bahg grunted at the action. Gavee's vision snapped bright green, and he fell into a trance. It wasn't the same, but a dark, tunneled passage with a distant voice.

"Father?" questioned Gavee.

The mumble changed to a whisper, and Gavee strained to hear Bahg.

"If she controls the dragons, why not attack? How did she free herself? I must find her location. I cannot allow her to destroy the clan or start another war."

Gavee snapped out of the deep daze and raised his face, unsure in the confusion. The vision returned, and Bahg straightened his stance.

"We must attend council. My brother wishes to discuss the upcoming Reflection Day for the queen."

Disoriented, Gavee struggled.

"Has it been a year?" he asked.

"The moment for our tribute is upon us," said Bahg. "We celebrate on the one-year anniversary of her death. It has been a year."

"It's still… difficult for me to face King Arul. I sense he holds me responsible for the queen's death. That moment's dread weighs over me."

Bahg rested his hand on his sword's hilt. "Your uncle does not hold you responsible. Nobody does. Nothing more you can do except move on from the past."

"Flued holds me responsible. I hold myself responsible. I shall train harder than ever to uncover the truth."

"Trust me, young warrior, we shall continue our training so that you are ready to locate the answers you seek. We should proceed to the council."

Gavee wondered about the whispers.

Was it Father? Should I tell him about the trance? *The green tunnel?*

He pulled himself together.

"Father?"

Bahg turned with a smile, but Gavee paused, withdrawing his remarks.

"Let's go to council," said Gavee.

* * *

They flew without incident and arrived within the city limits, traversing the main square, with hundreds of masuras flying here and there in their busy market. They reached the hall's large balcony, where the red-clad Latuery stood guard, showing His Majesty was inside. The red armor was the king's guard: warriors trained in hand-to-hand and close-quarters weapons. Second, only because of thunderblood's abilities, these dedicated soldiers were lethal, efficient, and loyal.

Upon entering, Gavee observed King Arul surveying his kingdom. The golden crown had the Witch'Bane symbol etched into the metal, and he wore the royal red robes with pride. His bright white wings and solid build appeared as strong as ever. The king, reaching the elder age of six hundred, was older than Bahg by fifty years, and his hair grayer. Masuras lived an extended mortal life of eight hundred years, with the last two hundred in the elder age transitioning their roles to the younger generation.

Shapía sat in her chair at the long council table, eating a blue dukina fruit. Gavee studied the fruit as it had an apple's texture and sweetness. He wondered how she had found such a treasure, not in season.

"About time you showed up, W.B.," said Shapía, crunching into the near-flawless shining dukina.

Gavee grinned. W.B. was his nickname among friends and those closest to him.

"Perhaps I sought a magnificent dukina, such as you conjured."

The princess winked and continued to eat.

"Guess we'll never know," she said.

Shapía, an oracle-in-training, wore the customary white robes. Most considered her beauty equal to the queen's and expected her to live up to her magical skill and prowess. Her long hair, fastened with a floral metal clip, contained a brown tint. It flowed against her white wings with their tan speckles among the feathers.

Shapía was under pressure but never revealed it. Her complete oracle instruction would begin on the mystical isle of Ihandra. She was quite prepared, as her whole life had readied her for the moment. As a young maiden of a hundred years, the five-year gap between Shapía and Gavee made her older and wiser in her years. She was neutral with her family members and loved it when she could irritate her cousin. Growth in this magical power always spurred Flued to better his skills.

King Arul smiled as he stared into Gavee's eyes, which bore Bahg's blue tint with a green hue. He embraced his nephew and then addressed Bahg.

"Where's Flued?"

"He'll be here soon, My King," answered Bahg.

Lord Taronquel, Witch'Bane's head council, limped with a cane and grimaced as he entered the council hall from a farther room. The masura donned the official head council red sash with the clan's symbol sitting center. The royal attire, though noble, did not establish a direct lineage to the monarch. Taronquel's family served the Witch'Bane royals for hundreds of years, and his father was head council before his death. Taronquel, a few years Gavee's senior, was smaller because of right-sided deformities. A single wing proved shorter, his right knee rigid, and a talon absent from his right foot. The impairments made the masura weaker, but his intelligence outweighed his physical faults.

"The preparations are nearing completion." He coughed. "Just beyond their forest, the Lohr clan is creating a memorial location."

"And agreed to by all clans?" asked His Majesty.

"Yes, my sire, it fits everyone's requirements," answered Taronquel.

Bahg adjusted his weapons.

"I never thought we would witness the Raths and Witch'Banes side by side again, my lord," said Bahg.

"We are not there yet, brother," said King Arul.

Bahg raised an eyebrow.

"This is Reflection Day for their warrior princess, our queen. It would be an unforgivable act."

"I'm certain they experience the same," said the king.

Flued stepped through the double doors into the hall. He adorned the Witch'Bane's royal gold and red robes over a woven tunic fashioned with a strap showing the clan's emblem. The black hair pulled tight revealed a thin jawline and a pointed chin. Like the king, the white wings possessed a slimmer build than Gavee, yet the tips fell lower. He carried himself confidently. The throne always made him smile, for the son, ten years older than Shapía, was considered the most intelligent and brightest Witch'Bane royal. Gavee agreed his cousin made wise decisions and understood the family's role. He was born a natural strategist.

Shapía hugged Flued.

"Good afternoon, my sister," said Flued. "My family."

He walked in front of Gavee and dropped the smile.

"Cousin," he said.

King Arul embraced Flued and addressed those present.

"The clans have agreed on Lohr as the location," answered the king.

"Outside of the Lohr forest, sire," said Taronquel.

"Good choice. Has the Lohr clan spoken of how we intend to gather?" asked Flued.

Taronquel glanced up. "Yes, they built an amphitheater into the hillside. It will allow us all to be part of Reflection and how the oracles connect with the stars."

Bahg worried about the idea.

"Being in the open makes everyone vulnerable."

Taronquel sensed the apprehension and said, "Each clan should have their Elite guard for protect—"

"Does it give the dragons an opportunity?" asked Gavee.

The chamber fell silent. Gazes shifted to the masura.

"We shall ensure field scouts are active," answered His Majesty. "It will be safe, Gavee."

Gavee said nothing else and fixed his eyes on the wooden table.

"I'll complete my mother's marvelous story tomorrow," said Flued, breaking the silence.

"I wish to read it," said Shapía.

"Once I have given the speech, you may read it any time," said Flued.

Shapía rolled her eyes.

"Reflection is in five days. Where is the statue?" asked the king.

"It shall be finished today and ready for your review tomorrow, sire. Rath will be thankful for such a gift," answered Taronquel.

The king gave a slight, uncertain grin. "In life, she broke down barriers. In her death, I hope she destroys it."

"I doubt we will ever get beyond that hill soon," said Bahg.

Ignoring the query, the king returned to the throne. Carved into the mighty chair's tall backrest was a massive thunderbolt, the symbol of the god Nathe. The red fabric-covered armrests, and following standard protocol for a masura chair, a gap at the back to accommodate the king's mighty wings. Gavee gazed upon the small, stoic Nathe statue at the far side of the room.

"Grunt is welcome at the memorial, correct, Father?" asked Shapía.

Bahg spoke before His Majesty could answer. "The shapeshifting weasel isn't Witch'Bane, nor a masura, his wishes notwithstanding."

Shapía snapped with some authority, "His name is Grunt, and he's family. His mother was there when our mother became an Oracle Conexus. They disciplined together at the holy site in Horfa. And we see him as family."

"Father?" questioned Gavee.

"He seems to always be with you anyway," said Bahg to Gavee.

The trainee ignored his mentor's snide comment.

"There would be others besides masuras at Reflection. The Lohr elves plan to attend, and even a human delegation from Eptiwuh," said Taronquel.

"All clans?" asked Flued.

"All but one," answered Taronquel.

Flued's pleasant demeanor shifted to ire, and Bahg slammed the table.

"May Nathe strike down the DasaRaul clan!" said Bahg.

Flued clasped hands and rose from the chair. "Ah yes, of course, it would be Dasa. What was their response?"

"They reject the idea," answered Taronquel.

"They reject Reflection Day?" asked Shapía.

The king responded with solemnity. "They refuse the idea with a Witch'Bane Reflection as we get set for battle with them."

"The war is their direction. Dasa can't attain peace during this time?" asked Shapía.

"There's no peace in war," said Flued. "They continue to assume we're involved with the pirated Breiv wood shipments."

"We don't grow this timber in our forest. How could we be involved?" questioned Shapía.

"We shall not answer these questions today," said the king. "For now, we concentrate on Reflection Day and the glory that was your mother. Flued, I'll need you to lead our delegation and work your intelligence into conversations with Rath. It is necessary to build a new relationship with the masuras in the south. Your mother started the bridge, and we will continue its work."

"I'll pursue it with great fervor, Father," answered Flued.

The king looked at his brother. "We'll need the thunderblood alliance working together over the next few days to uncover any possible interference."

Bahg straightened, and the king turned to Gavee.

"Your father's commands are mine. Follow them without cause."

Gavee returned a respectful nod.

"Consider it done, My King," said Bahg.

The king's attention shifted to Shapía, and eyes seemed to soften with a steady tone. "My daughter, it is almost time for you to leave for Horfa. Please call your own Oracle Conexus and help with the stabilization. We need our oracle."

"I've made the call, Father. When shall you have me set off for Horfa?"

"You'll leave with the oracle delegation after Reflection Day as they return to Ihandra."

"But?" is all she could squeeze out.

"I understand your confusion, my dear, but we must have our oracle. We begin a new chapter with Witch'Bane, thus exposing ourselves to untrustworthy individuals."

She ended her questions as the room became silent.

"You may go if you wish or stay as we work on additional plans for Reflection," said the king.

Shapía whispered to Gavee, "Come, let's find Grunt."

They gave a courteous nod and left the hall. Flued remained alongside his father in all clan-life aspects as training to become king.

"Where do you suppose he is?" asked Shapía as they came to the balcony.

"When we arrived, I saw the crow just outside the window," said Gavee.

Shapía frowned. "He must've heard your father."

"Follow me. I know where Grunt went," said Gavee.

The two masuras flew west toward Lheter Lake, the largest lake in the Upper Realm. Four masura clans shared its shores, and three rivers flowed from its waters. Three major ports broke from the lake, with Manawe, the original shipping port for trade throughout the Upper Realm. The lake bordered the northern section of the Nathe Mountains and contained the Dead Falls at the farthest western portion, where the third river rolled north toward Dulisar, home of the wood elves. The Dead Falls' rocky shoreline contained dangerous inlets and hidden coves, perfect for those wanting to disappear.

With odd ships and assorted characters roaming the vast water system, the lake's flight would be precarious. The shipping lanes hold random attacks from small boats lurking along the Nathe Mountains. All masuras flew with concern.

"Gavee," Shapía said.

Anchored on the far left, a ship with an unfamiliar flag awaited the return of its scows. It contained many odd creatures, with two grangruls watching the masuras fly overhead with their eyepieces. The grangrul, a vicious lizard folk, originated in the far reaches of the Lower Realm. Their beady eyes, razor-sharp teeth, and leathery, thick reptilian skin made them dangerous adversaries. They dwelled in caves and often hunted masuras, viewing them as food or servants. The giant lizards stood double the size of masuras, with long slithering tongues and camouflage-colored skin covering their skinny torsos.

Gavee and Shapía understood the alarm and flew higher to avoid any stray attacks. The flight carried them far from the danger, farther west, when they reached a beachy shore close to the Dead Land Falls. Gavee pulled his sword, and Shapía grabbed her bow.

"Do you expect problems?" she asked.

"I always expect problems," said Gavee.

Shapía peered down at Gavee's grip. "I see you still carry my mother's sword."

Gavee's smile faded as he looked to Shapía and back to the distant scene without an answer. She rested her hand on his shoulder as they hovered.

"You did not fail, cousin. What else do you imagine you could have accomplished?"

"I should have died protecting her, and I don't understand why the king gave me the sword."

"She always wished for the sword to be given to a warrior, and she mentioned you many times. My mother loved you as a son," she said.

"I wish they believed me about the dragons."

"I believe you, W.B."

"Why?"

"I know you, and if you lied, I would catch it. You're not a good liar." She smiled. "Besides, before mother disappeared, she mentioned an uneasy vibration was released, which carried a potential disaster to our world. It worried her, and she thought the dragons were part of this coming doom."

"Have you mentioned it to your father?"

"He and Bahg know yet remain silent. The information has an order of silence placed on it."

"You just broke the order," said Gavee.

"We have a pact, and if you spoke of it, I would feed you to the grangrul," said Shapía.

Gavee drew a deep breath and smiled.

"Let's track down Grunt. Prepare yourself," said Gavee.

The female masura pulled a quill, laced it within the bow, and Gavee pointed to a thicket of trees reaching out into the lake. They lowered into the tallest tree and landed to search with their eagle eyes for their friend. The thunderblood trainee scouted the shallow water and pointed farther out.

"Grunt gathers similar rocks in the swamp and uses them for sitting inside," said Gavee.

"What about the barkapes?" asked Shapía.

Gavee did not break the gaze.

"They're here, so ready the arrow," Gavee commanded.

The barkape, created by the god Nathe, protected his vast riches and stole to build his wealth. Nathe extracted elements from a fierce fighter and brains from a thief and set them into a monkey's mind, creating a lethal weapon. The beast had fangs jutting below the lip, a fighter's sense, and nimble fingers to aid in the treasure hoard. The devious monsters always traveled in skillful packs, making them dangerous, with high speed and vicious attacks from all directions. Unlike their brethren in the Esor Mountains, the Nathe barkapes no longer possessed intelligence or reasoning.

"He always puts the rocks in the same spot, correct?" asked Shapía.

"No, he moves them each time. I think they are deeper in," answered Gavee.

Shapía sighed. "So, he can be anywhere?"

Gavee surveyed the area. "Yes, we'll have to spread out within these tall trees. The canopy obscures the water, hindering the barkapes' abilities. You know how much those little creatures love to use masuras as target practice."

Shapía's eyebrows lowered. "You're not funny, Gavee. The Nathe barkapes are ruthless."

"I've been here many times in my thunderblood training. I'll span west. Just remain in my line of sight."

"Fine, but the first beast I spot, I take down," she said.

"I would," he said.

The masuras split to cover the swamp and search for their family friend. The weasel-type creature hailed from the island of Ihandra. Old forest magic created Grunt's kind, known for their heightened senses. His mother had been a sage before becoming a part of the Witch'Bane queen's constant consort.

Grunt was years younger than Gavee, but the two grew together. During an unfortunate forest raid, raiders killed Grunt's family, including his mother. The dark day happened when he was just a babe, so he carried no deep stain within his memory. He viewed Gavee as an older brother and loved the thunderblood lore.

"Grunt!" yelled Gavee.

"Gavee!" said Shapía. "You'll attract the barkapes," she paused. "And anything else hunting us?"

"If he knows we're here, he'll locate us," said Gavee.

"Cousin, we find Grunt and make it out alive."

Gavee sighed. "It'll take longer."

Shapía whispered, "We search in silence."

Gavee shrugged and nodded in agreement. The search continued in the thick swamp, with dark water looming below and the unknown hidden in the shadows. Shapía held firm to her weapon and tried to calm the fear, with Gavee creeping farther out of sight. Fear of the unseen kept her from shouting at him when the masura lowered herself for a better view.

A hoot broke the silence, and an angry howl came as a response. It continued from the front and then from the rear. Three more yells beckoned forward, and a loud screech surrounded her location.

"Gavee!" said Shapía.

More hoots ensued. The princess's arrow changed direction with the bow flitting in her hand, and several howls called out again, showing the beasts came in closer.

"Gavee!"

As she prepared for the next upward movement, a large stone struck the masura's left shoulder with unexpected force. She cried out in pain and lost her footing. The princess fell from the branch, and her wings caught her fall before she hit the water. While hovering, the sudden impact of an unseen stone, cold and heavy, knocked her from the air. The blow sent her into the tree and plunged her into the water. The sudden icy cold shock jolted her from her daze as a thick net enclosed her body, pulling her from the murky abyss.

Shapía hung in front of three small, knee-high barkapes, holding a staff and poking the masura. More barkapes arrived, amplifying the swamp's chaos. She tried to search for her lost bow when a crow landed above the apes in the distance.

Shapía recognized the bird. "Grunt! Help!"

The crow cawed and changed into a weasel with a wooden staff in hand. A magical wooden staff that once belonged to his mother. The unique ancient weapon gave its owner the power to shapeshift, teleport short distances, and release small magical energy blasts. The weasel became an expert with the staff and shapeshifted into different animals with little concentration. He winked with a wave at Shapía, then whistled. The barkapes turned to the distraction as the weasel lifted the staff, popping it onto the limb and sending a white shockwave through the forest. It flung the creatures off the branch and into the water.

The wild beasts floundered in the murky deep, screeching and clawing, trying to reach a tree.

Gavee landed in front of Shapía with a broad grin.

"I found Grunt," said Gavee.

Grunt waved the staff and dropped to all fours. His weasel hands became black paws with long nails, and a tail popped from the back end when he fully changed into a black panther. The shapeshifter jumped lower into the foliage, chasing the barkapes into the distance. The bedlam moved farther away, with Grunt releasing a deep growl, showing he had them on the move.

Shapía glared at her cousin in disgust. "Get me out!"

"Easy, let me see how," he said.

"Just wait, Gavee. I'll have my revenge!"

The masura hovered in front of Shapía, pulled a hidden dagger from the talon boots, and cut away the thick rope. Shapía avoided a watery plunge. A precise cut allowed them both to land on a branch.

"I was calling you!" said Shapía.

Gavee tried not to laugh. "I found Grunt when you started yelling. We worked our way here. Sorry for the delay."

* * *

Shapía found Gavee's attempt to cover his tracks unimpressive. She glanced down at his leg. "Where did you get the dagger?"

Gavee pulled the blade from its sheath and handed it over to Shapía. "It's something I gathered on a recent trip to Dulisar."

Shapía studied the exquisite craftsmanship. "Is it elvish?"

Gavee nodded. The black blade curved away from its point into a silver shaft with leather wrapped around the handle. The knob contained a crimson stone and elvish lettering etched in the blade.

"From a friend, I'm hoping?" she asked.

"Yes, it was a gift from the elvish princess, Lamír, for a thunderblood mission."

Gavee sheathed the gift, and a crow landed in front of them, shapeshifting into the weasel.

* * *

"Princess," said Grunt with a slight nod.

"Thank you for the help," said Shapía.

"When you follow your cousin, always expect him to lead you into a trap."

"Not true," said Gavee.

"Do we care to discuss these adventures?" questioned Grunt.

The earl appeared uneasy and answered, "Grunt, we came here to check on you."

Grunt's smile vanished. "Yes, I'm fine. It's just…"

Shapía went down on one knee, facing the weasel. "Uncle spoke only for himself. He went too far."

Grunt stared at the dirt.

"Reflection Day… am I allowed to go?"

Shapía's voice softened.

"You are family. Of course you're allowed."

Grunt's shoulders slumped. "I'm confused as to why Bahg dismisses me as such."

Gavee flipped the dagger in the air. The blade made three rotations, and he caught the handle.

"He trusts nobody outside my father," said Shapía.

"He trusts W.B."

"I'm his son, and trust must be there. I've spoken on your behalf. He remains stubborn and does not trust how your mother came to be along the queen's side."

Grunt stared at them with sadness and leaned on the staff. "This is something unknown even to me."

Gavee smiled, and Shapía stepped to the water's edge.

"Not to interrupt the moment, but I lost my bow in the water," said Shapía.

Grunt extended the wooden staff. "I shall make you a new one. Stronger and better."

"Mother gave me the bow when I began my oracle discipline. It is irreplaceable, and so is your mother's staff." Shapía's eyes welled.

"Horfa is impossible without her," said Shapía.

Grunt coughed, catching her attention, and popped the cane. He dropped into a snake and slithered into the water. Gavee kept watch for any returning barkapes as Grunt slithered from the green deep with the bow wrapped around his tail. He slipped back into his weasel form.

"Now you won't," he said.

She hugged her friend.

"Princess, I desire to help you reach Horfa. I'm not a sage, but it runs through my veins. I have studied from my mother's books, which has taught me some disciplines needed to get there."

Grunt continued to hold Shapía's hand and grinned at Gavee. "I am here for you both."

"Thank you, Grunt, but I depart for Horfa as soon as Reflection is over," said Shapía.

"Can we still attend the Reflection Day dinner? If I'm risking my life going to Horfa, I need some good eats!" said Grunt.

The three laughed.

"We need to return. You need to prepare for Horfa," said Gavee.

Grunt tapped the staff on the ground and transformed into a crow. He took two big flaps and lifted with the masuras trailing. They followed their friend homeward to prepare for Reflection and honor the queen.

Chapter Three

The hooded Taronquel soared in the dark hours before the sun rose above the Crescent Mountains. To avoid recognition, he flew low and undetected, following the Raul River north to the Cree Sea. This river flight would drag between two warring masuran clans, the BataRaul to the north and the DasaRaul to the south. Centuries of warfare between these clans bred deep hostility toward trespassers in their woods. Despite his gentle nature and somewhat lacking tracking skills, the masura took daring risks each time he ventured into the BataRaul forest. It would allow safe passage for the weakling struggling among the branches.

Along the river, BataRaul fighters maintained lookout perches with SkyRiders waiting in the treetops. The slower masura kept a keen eye on all threats as the flight struggled with this known presence. Hidden, Taronquel circled the guarded campfires until he reached BataRaul's far corner. This section presented the greatest travel danger, lacking tree and field cover. Fixed in the night sky, the moon allowed the Bata watch to see into the vast clearing below. The timing would require patience, as the masura had done it many times before and understood the steps.

The moon drifted south until it withdrew its light from the sky and fell behind the mountains. Darkness fell, and the masura slipped from the shadows into the field, his black robe blending seamlessly with the desolate terrain. The masura remained on the move, working to reach the Cree Sea and its shores before sunrise.

Taronquel's talons carefully traversed the giant rocks, resulting in the knees enduring frequent missteps. When he descended behind the large cliff boulders overlooking the sea, the light began peering into the far horizon. The Cree Sea crashed against the rocky terrain, and the masura lowered within the boulders until his black, feeble wings allowed them to expand. He descended from the edge, skimming across the water and sensing the salty mist on their face.

"Where is it?" he questioned.

The morning sun rose, and daylight would soon conceal the opening. In a panic, he drew closer to the cliff below a lone bush.

"There it is!"

With his wings, the masura forcefully dropped through the side opening, entering a narrow passage. He would wait there, as an invitation is required to enter the lair. The moment in the darkness adjusted his sight and revealed the rock maze. From behind, a slight poke in the leg followed by one on the right shoulder as the hooded guest gradually advanced along the path. The tiny gremlin creature, dressed in military garb, clutched a tiny spear and stood on a ledge at eye level. The tiny creature kept a warrior's mind and lived a militant life. Its slim body armor flexed under each little breath.

"Madame Malum does not expect you," it said in its graveled, high-pitched voice.

"I must see her," said Taronquel.

The masura snatched the tiny gremlin from the rocks and squeezed.

"Tell her I insist on seeing her now."

The leader nodded to the others, and they disappeared among the rocks. Focused intently on the gremlin, the masura held on tightly. With a final, desperate heave, the tiny creature tried to free its arms, but the pressure intensified, silencing its struggle.

"You shall enter," echoed a female voice.

The gremlins returned, and a smile crept from Taronquel.

"I knew she would see me."

The masura, still clutching the gremlin, slapped it against the rock, killing it instantly. The others hissed and growled when the masura grabbed another within his talons, crushing it in its grip and tossing it into the small gremlin band.

"Next time, you bring me to her immediately."

The ruthless masura stepped forward through the long, dark corridor, making their way around the rocks. It led to an enormous cavern hovering in a purple glow from the many cave mushrooms giving off light. The space made the limping masura uneasy, with the smell of rotting flesh permeating every rock and crevasse. Muffled voices came from the far left, where three naked female masuras chained to the wall hung limp at their knees. The middle one slumped in her chains and appeared to have the skin on her legs and arms flayed. Under the mouth restraints, the other two women cried out, each missing a foot and a hand.

"What brings you here?" a female voice echoed from the shadows.

"Reflection approaches," he said.

"Where?"

"Outside Lohr. They built an amphitheater on the ground."

"Out in the open?" she questioned.

"Yes, there is a constant watch."

"Watch?" she curled a laugh. "Our exercitus shall defeat them all."

"Exercitus?"

Silence fell on the cave as a broken masura body limped forth into the purple hue from the blackness. More feathers were missing than present on the black wings, and a tattered black robe, extending from her shoulders to the floor, covered her torso. The lavender light hued her milky white skin as the female leaned forward from the dark, revealing the lesions on her pocked face. Her missing teeth kept a black maw under the smile, and a cane sparked with each hit on the stone floor.

The broken masura reached out her bony hand, placing it upon the hooded masura's face. He squirmed under the hood from the presence and experienced the icy touch on his bones. His face stung where her hand had lain when he withdrew from the witch.

"My dear head council, why do you think I am gathering masuras?" She said, pointing to the chained prisoners.

"Madame Malum, I do not desire to kill them. We shall need them as we take the clans."

Malum choked with a laugh.

"None will die if they join our exercitus."

"Our?"

"Yes, you are the King of Kings, and we shall rule them together."

"How?"

Malum's bony finger pointed to a basin on the ground, surrounded by glowing purple mushrooms. Water dripped from the ceiling into the pool.

"Maybe we should stick your head in the basin to read what it says," she said.

The hooded masura groaned.

"No, madam, I am your trusting servant."

"Good."

The masuran witch sought to stretch her broken wings but failed, then crept forward to the prisoners. She grabbed the female masura's hair and pulled her head up. The masura snapped out of her unconscious state and screamed through the mouth restraint. Agony held her eyes, and the blood dripped onto the stone floor. Malum dipped her cane into the bloody mess, licked the fluid from the end, and curled an echoing laugh.

"Shhh, my love. Endure the pain. It should bring you closer to me," said Malum.

"Why do we have three today?"

"I've been watching them, and they are true masuran warriors. They'll show me the way to freedom from my entrapment," she said.

The cloaked masura limped alongside Malum and lifted the flayed masura's head.

"I believe she's dying," he said.

Malum hissed at the comment.

"It seems you are correct."

The witch took her bony hand, pressing it into the female masura's chest with ease. She yanked out the pumping heart, then crushed it within her grasp. Malum released a high-pitched screech, forcing the masura to hold his ears and cringe at the sound. The organ fell to dust within her claw, and she stamped the rock with the cane. Gremlins came forward from their hiding places.

"Remove her and find me another!" she said.

The new gremlin leader bowed, dropped the dead masura from the chains, and dragged her into the abyss. The hooded masura stood in front of another victim, raising her chin. She squirmed.

"She's a Fen," he said. "You'll have a hard time breaking them."

"She'll break or die," said Malum.

"You said they would not die."

"Why yes, if they join the exercitus, they live," she laughed.

Once away from the prisoners, the masura surveyed the cavern.

"Madame Malum, this is a waste. We must move forward with a new plan."

The witch snarled and hobbled her way to the masura, raising her bony hand along his cheek.

"Call me Mother, my beloved head council," she said.

He struggled to pull away, as a force kept him still.

"You are correct, and it is not the way, my son. I have experimented again with my spells and incantations from the gods with nothing but failure," she said.

She squeezed tighter.

"I created an escape before the masuras existed," she said.

She pulled her hand away, and his cheek returned to flesh.

"Come, my dear."

The witch hobbled back into the shadows and stood above the basin. He hesitated to move away from the light.

"Come, my son," she said.

He pulled the hood down farther, stepping alongside Malum. The cold grabbed his bones, and he hid his thoughts as whispers whirled around his ears. She rotated a thin finger over the water, and it spun when she pulled a red vial from within the tattered cloak.

"May this blood of a masuran king call upon my homeland plane and show us the way."

She released a red drop, which hit the basin with a sizzle. It swirled within, turning it dark until the light showed from its depths. The light cleared, and a vision appeared: a flat ebon stone with a milky center rippled in the small waves.

"I need my stone. It was taken from me and contains what we need to control the island," she hissed.

"Where is it?" he asked.

"The blood will reveal nothing to me, but I sense it's close," she said.

"How does this stone bend the knee of all masuras?" said the head council.

Malum raised her thin hand and placed it again upon his cheek, causing the masura to cringe.

"Trust me, my darling," she said.

"If it gives me the island crown, I'm your trusting servant."

Her mouth opened into a grimacing smile.

"Mother," she said.

The masura drew in a breath.

"Mother."

"You, my son, shall reign as the greatest king and vanquish the thunderbloods. Now go before they find you missing."

She released her hold, and he could feel the ability to move again. Taronquel moved back from the darkness. The witch slithered, following, as sparks popped with each step on the stone floor.

"Go? I can't fly through BataRaul in the morning light. I'll be questioned," he said.

"You shall leave, or I'll have you chained alongside the others," chuckled Malum through a cough.

Taronquel growled, limping through the path with anger. He traversed the dark passage as it led him out of the darkness, reaching the cave opening. He raised his arm against the bright sunlight.

"Great, it'll take me until the evening to get through Manawe."

* * *

Gavee followed close to Bahg, who settled within two large bushes. The masuras reached a dark section of the Fen forest. They were on a thunderblood mission, but Gavee did not know the exact details. Often, he was to observe and learn versus take part. It was early morning before the sun rose, where the forest was in its deepest sleep. They used shadows and darkness to reach their location without being seen.

The trainee settled alongside his mentor within the thick brush and drew in slight breaths, calming his presence. Bahg raised his hand to ease his son's discomfort. With sweat dripping from Gavee's forehead, the black mud on his face was being erased as he wiped. Bahg shook at the indiscretion. The elder signaled to remain silent, and they waited.

* * *

Night had finally fallen, with Gavee resting his eyes longer than he expected. By midday his stomach ached for nourishment, and he found the raisins in his pocket somewhat refreshing. The small amount of water in his water pouch was now empty, and his muscles ached from being locked in place for so long. Bahg woke him from his sleepy daze and pointed. A large fire had been lit in this circle of trees with the Fen king pacing and several of his guards remaining posted behind.

Bahg signaled masuras approaching.

Gavee kept his head still and moved only his eyes. A watchful guard could see even the slightest movement. Because their guards were easily outwitted, they often used Fen to train, but this time they had an actual mission. The sound of wings whipping through the trees came first, then several masuras appeared wearing DasaRaul garb. It was Dasa's

Thunderblood Chromic with the Dasa Prince Rim. They flew with a small guard. The party landed, and arms were embraced.

"Welcome, Prince," said the Fen king.

"Glad to be recognized," answered the Dasa prince. "Thank you for meeting us under such measures."

"A war is brewing, and we see fit to be on the winning side," answered the king. "Do you know when the attack shall occur?"

"We must honor Reflection, though my father wants to invade while everyone is away," said the prince.

"We will not take part if it happens during Reflection. You will have all the clans coming at you. It would be suicide," answered the king. "May we suggest five days after?"

"Indeed, Your Majesty. This is when we calculated it would be the best fit for an attack. The Raths have given their blessing and stated it must be at least five days," said the prince.

"Where do you need Fen?" asked the king.

"Attack from the east while we attack from the north and from the west, over the lake," said the prince.

The Fen king turned to a table and lifted a stein, downing the drink. He snapped his fingers as a servant ran forward and refilled the cup.

"What if I told you there is something else brewing, and this planned attack may not be needed?" said the king.

Both Dasa Prince and Thunderblood approached the table and whispered. The words were hollow to Gavee as he tried to read their lips. The frustration was mounting as the shadow of the raging fire continued to hide their lips. Bahg, too, grew frustrated in the moment with neither mentor nor trainee understanding the conversation. Vital information was being said, and Witch'Bane was deaf to it.

The party chuckled, and they had more drinks. Nothing else was being said, but the initial information was what they needed. Gavee broke the code and signaled when they would leave. An alarm triggered throughout Fen, and they lost the moment. Bahg's shoulders dropped, with the Fen King not waiting and flying out, away from the fire with an escort. The Fen guards remained to search through the trees. The DasaRaul group did not hesitate and took to the sky, reaching above the forest, disappearing in the night.

Bahg shook his head and pointed at several Fen guards approaching. Before Gavee could react, the mentor tore from the bush and flew hard and fast. His trainee followed when the Fen guards blew their whistles, with more fighters appearing in the forest. The Witch'Bane pair had to remain low in their flight, working to use the shadows and the darkness to help keep them disguised.

The mentor steadily handed his trainee a water pouch after taking a swig.

"You must follow me and remain tight. We have used this strategy before in training. Again, stay tight," whispered Bahg. "We head to Dasa's forest."

Gavee's eyes widened. "Our enemy?"

"Yes, we will use them for our escape."

Before Gavee could add to the questions, Bahg bolted from the brush in a low run. The young masura took after his father and kept to the same speed. They reached beyond several trees when Bahg launched into the air, tapping a tree with his talons and pushing off. The trainee recognized the pattern as it brought him back to the early days in training.

* * *

"Remember, use the forest as a shield to hide and the wind as your guide. Use the tree's momentum in the wind to hide the shudder from your movement," said Bahg.

They flew from tree to tree within the northern forest of Witch'Bane. This was their normal location for tree training. Gavee took notice of Bahg's rhythm, mirroring the flight.

"Look for the trees with deep foliage running to their top and use them for complete coverage. Alternate upward and downward movements. Avoid repetition. Your enemies will never know what befell them."

Bahg landed beside a large tree, wiping green moss on his cheeks.

"Before venturing into enemy territory, dull your appearance."

"What of our wings?" asked Gavee.

"We use our bodies and small branches by folding them tight, hiding them within the tree's foliage."

Gavee loved to train with his father. He felt inspired by each move and worked to emulate his hero. For years, Bahg had prepared him well in masuran ways and history. His father had been Witch'Bane's thunderblood for five hundred years, which showed in each swing and movement he made during a fight.

"When fighting, keep low in the trees. It prevents their ability to spread their wings, and with our training, you know how to fly without a full spread. Learn to grip the tree trunk with your talons, using the entire tree, not just the limbs."

Bahg leaped through the trees as Gavee watched in amazement, with the thunderblood's talons spitting bark from each grab. The trees never moved, nor did a branch shake as his father catapulted through the sky. He leaped with each tree swaying in silence when he turned around, landing next to Gavee.

"I want you to move four trees down, using the trunks. Let the wind guide you on the mission. Use the eagle eye at night. It will show you the path."

Gavee stretched talons, digging them into the ground. He looked for the first tree to hit, released a deep breath, and leaped into its center. The apprentice grabbed and wrapped his arms around the tree, forgetting to dig in his nails. He slid, forcing himself to let go, and slammed into the dirt with a thud.

The trainee jumped to his feet, keeping his eyes away from his father, who laughed aloud. Determined to wipe the smile from Bahg's face, he leaped for the tree and dug in the talons, grabbing hold with one hand. He felt the soft bark beneath his feet and then studied the breeze. The masura used the trees' sway, leaping to the second and landing in its middle. He glanced back, smiled, finding solace in a quiet tree. He peered down at Bahg.

"Don't be so proud. You have two more," said Bahg.

Gavee sighed and repeated the exercises, reaching the last trunk.

"Continue until you sense it," said Bahg.

With another bound, the masura sped up, encompassing more trees within its circle. The movement's pace increased when a vibration took hold of the forest's rhythm, illuminating the path for him. With the aim lowered, the student, full of confidence, worked to get closer to Bahg. Inattention cost him dearly; a sudden pull sent him sprawling. He lay down, coughing, trying to catch a breath.

"I never said to add trees. Let's improve on our previous attempt. You're waiting too long to pull the sword. In battle, you don't have the luxury."

"Pull my sword?"

"You are practicing to attack, correct?" questioned Bahg.

Gavee brushed off the dirt and shook his head. His father's reaction was unsurprising to him as he understood that fulfilling each request required complete training, which was never fast, smooth, or accurate.

"Yes, sir, right away," he answered.

* * *

They reached the Fen forest edge, escaping through the trees, and just passing several Fen fighters. Bahg thumped Gavee on the arm as they landed solid against a tree.

"Where are you in your head? You seem distracted, and right now we need you fully focused," groaned Bahg.

"My apologies, I was reflecting on our training, and we just followed the exact course we had laid out at home," answered Gavee. "I will remain focused going forward."

The masura went to leave when Bahg halted Gavee before they flew into the open lea between Fen and DasaRaul. It would be a long stretch flight, and...

"Fen is close," whispered Bahg. "If we leave now, they will certainly see us."

"How then?" asked Gavee.

"We use the clouds and remain low. I want talons touching the grass," said Bahg.

Bahg sheathed his sword, surprising Gavee. "We will not need them through this gap. I doubt Fen even follow once we are beyond their border," said Bahg. "But we must get beyond their border."

"What about Dasa? Won't they be on the lookout?" asked Gavee.

"Always, but there is a small area in their southern forest where they have a gap. We will easily land in it without being seen." Bahg winked.

The night sky was full of clouds, with a storm brewing west. It would provide the perfect cover, as long as Fen didn't find them first. Bahg lowered in the tree, as did Gavee, when several Fen soldiers landed just a few trees away.

"Was it Witch'Bane?" asked a soldier.

"No, they had markings from Rath," answered a soldier.

"If it's Rath, who cares? They know our plans and intend to back Dasa after Reflection," said the soldier.

"Good point. Let's head back. We saw nothing," said the soldier.

The Fen soldiers vaulted from the trees and disappeared into their forest.

"Looks like this will be easier than I expected," said Bahg.

"Do we just fly home?" asked Gavee.

"No, we stick to the plan. Dasa's southern forest, then across the river and back home. Without being seen," answered Bahg. "Consider it a training session."

The forest turned quiet, and Gavee leaned against the tree. The next lesson was about to begin, and this one would place them in great danger. He took a deep breath when he felt his body vibrate, his chest scar throbbed, and a green-hued vision pooled. He felt his body collapse.

"*What do you want from me?*" his voice slurred.

"*Our minds have fused,*" slurred a deep voice.

"*Fused?*"

"*I need your help, Masura.*"

"*Show yourself!*"

"*An evil like no other is coming.*"

"*Show yourself!*" screamed Gavee.

"*In time, but for now we can easily communicate,*" said the deep voice.

"*These interruptions must end. I have placed us in danger with this connection or fusion,*" said Gavee.

"*Going forward, it will be different,*" answered the voice.

The vision disappeared, and Gavee snapped from the trance. His father held his head as they remained low within a massive fir. He tried to move, but his father held him and kept silent. Two Fen guards appeared from nowhere, and the two remained still.

"Where did the others go?" asked a guard.

"They must have returned," said another guard.

"Are you sure you saw movement?" asked the guard.

"Yes, I saw something at the base move at that far tree."

"Was it a squirrel? They are heavy here," answered the guard.

The Fen masuras remained still and searched the shrubs and the ground just beyond the fir. The one shrugged to the other, and the two Fen soldiers took flight, leaving their space. Bahg placed a finger against his lips, and the two stood. The elder pointed to the field, and they slipped into the tall field grass, on foot and running. Gavee waited for his father to leap into flight, but his wings never spread out as they kept to the run across the tall grass under the cloudy night sky.

As they approached the forest's edge at high speed when Bahg spread his wings and disappeared faster than Gavee could keep up. It surprised the trainee, for his flight was well behind, and the alarm in Dasa sounded when the masura reached the DasaRaul trees and disappeared from sight. Gavee searched for a thick patch to slip into when he heard the Dasa guards in the distance. He used the lessons just learned by zigzagging through the forest. The alarm became louder throughout Dasa, and he fought to slow the panic building in his mind.

"There!"

He groaned at his outburst and darted into the thick foliage, letting him slip from sight in time.

Eight Dasa guards landed just beyond the location, spreading out to find the intruders.

"Where did they go?" asked a guard.

"They disappeared," answered another.

Gavee balled a fist in one hand and pulled his sword in the other.

"Are they Witch'Bane?" asked a guard.

"No one got a look. The movement was too quick."

The words eased Gavee's mind, watching the guards span through the branches and the foliage.

"Easy, masura," came a whisper from behind.

"Father," whispered Gavee.

"How do we return home?" asked Bahg.

The student pondered the question and searched for the guards. They had gathered high in the trees, moving farther from their position.

"Follow me," whispered Bahg.

Before the elder could take flight, the young one darted from the shrubs, leaving his father behind. He knew the training, and he wanted to prove his skill. Gavee veered in and out of the trees, working to gain speed when the alarm sounded. He ignored the Dasa hunt.

The masura concentrated and allowed his breath to ease. The search for an opening in the foliage leading to the river was on. He tucked in his wings to snap through a tree grouping when he felt a sudden jolt and, before he could react, a net trap sprang. It wrapped him tight, and the masura crashed to the dirt floor, tumbling into a tree and hitting with a loud thud. The wind kicked out of his lungs, and his head spun.

He panicked as he clawed at the thick netting. The trees' rustle grew at pace, with Dasa guards closing in on the intruder. He sought to withdraw a sword, but was unable to get a hold of it when a blade nicked his cheek and cut through the thick rope. Bahg pulled Gavee to his feet as blood rolled from the cut.

"Dumb move," whispered Bahg. "Follow."

The thunderblood darted for the river, and the two followed the Dasa bank east to an open field, with arrows flying, just missing the masura.

"Faster!" said Bahg.

The field came into view as a sharp pain shot through Gavee's left foot. He saw an arrow lodged in his ankle.

"I've been struck!"

"Keep flying. You will not die from it!"

Gavee growled at the words, and they charged south, well beyond Dasa's defense. The path led to a distant pond within their woods. They landed, and Gavee dropped near its shore.

"Easy, we'll get it out. You're not dying."

"I've been shot!" said Gavee.

"As a thunderblood, it shall not be your last. Experience is what you need."

"Did you know this would happen?"

"No, but assumed as much knowing Dasa's temperament on their border," said Bahg.

Gavee sneered at his father's simplicity in the situation.

"Place the rag in your mouth."

"Why?"

"Because it's going to hurt."

The elder snatched the arrow and pulled it away before Gavee was ready for the action. The masura looked up with paused confusion, and then his vision narrowed when he attempted to speak.

"Father," said Gavee.

"Rest, young one. You've had enough for today."

Gavee fell into Bahg's arms.

Chapter Four

The next day, a knock came. Gavee attempted to recollect the events of the night before, but the haze continued to obscure his thoughts. In his small tree loft, the masura stared at the cobwebs covering most items. The knock came louder, and he stepped down when a pain shot through his left leg. The bandaged wound contained a red dot at its center, and he hobbled to the door.

"Did we wake you, cousin?" asked Shapía.

The princess pushed her way inside, and Grunt stood behind her with a smile.

"Good morning, twit," said Grunt.

"How'd you know I'd be here?" asked Gavee.

Shapía and Grunt carried apples, biting into theirs and tossing one to Gavee. The masura placed it on a table and sat to remove the bandage.

"What happened?" asked Shapía.

"A training accident," said Gavee.

"Should be swifter next time," said Grunt.

Gavee smirked and stood.

"I require a fresh bandage."

"Do you need our help?" asked Shapía.

"This place needs a good cleaning," said Grunt.

Ignoring the intruders, Gavee went back to the training room to treat his wound. He placed a small pail under the water fountain and grabbed a cloth to clean it. The masura reached a seat when the scar on his chest throbbed and burned. He touched it through his shirt and fell into a deep trance. He stayed motionless in the room, enveloped in a green light, as a slurred voice emerged from nowhere.

"Grab the wound," said a deep voice. *"You can heal it."*

"Who's there?"

"You finally hear me."

Gavee tried to stand but had no energy. The vision rippled.

"You have healing powers. Grab the wound."

"Who are you? Where are you?"

"Trust me."

"Why should I trust you?"

"I cannot harm you. The power to heal is within your mind."

Gavee hesitated.

"Grab hold. Yes, the healing runs through your veins."

Gavee covered the glowing green wound with a hand after a mysterious force pulled him. The room turned brighter green, and a searing pain jolted through his body. Despite his efforts to release, a mysterious force maintained its hold as he fell back and abruptly woke from the trance. The masura coughed and shook with dizziness.

"W.B., are you all right?" asked Shapía.

"I'll be right out!" said Gavee.

He looked at his leg and found the arrow mark had gone.

"What...?"

He panicked and bandaged the area to hide what he did not understand. Gavee faked a limp and headed down the hallway.

"Why are we here?" he asked.

He grabbed the apple and took a bite.

"We can't visit?" asked Shapía.

"Not this early."

"Your brilliance has no end, twit," said Grunt.

"No wonder Bahg dislikes you," said Gavee.

"I need to speak with the goddess Sora," said Shapía.

"What? Why?" asked Gavee.

"Do you recall the Sora statue in my room?" answered Shapía.

"Yes, the glass-eyed statue?" said Gavee.

"That's the one. Mother gave it to me after returning from the visit with the oracle who lives in the mountain."

"I don't recall you ever saying where it came from?" said Gavee.

"It wasn't something I announced," said Shapía.

Grunt tsked at the question, causing Gavee to bite harder into the apple.

"Anyway, the oracle gave information to Mother, and they were to share it with me prior to my departure for Horfa."

"What information?" asked Gavee.

"She never told me."

"It sounds dangerous," said Grunt.

"I agree, but why again?" asked Gavee.

"While training, Mother and I would journey to the mountain to offer tributes at the monument. It's a holy place for oracles, and we often find answers to questions. The statue enhanced the oracle's presence, and Mother promised Sora would contact me. This occurred last night. I must visit her before I leave."

Gavee and Grunt exchanged glances, and then looked to Shapía.

"Contact? What kind of contact?" asked Gavee.

"In my dreams. It is all I wish to say about it."

"I'll escort you, Princess, and continue to guide you these days in your discipline. I promise my previous mistakes will not repeat," said Grunt with a slight head bow.

"Mistakes? What mistakes?" asked Gavee.

"Your typical oversights in some incantations and potion mistakes caused severe burns. It was one time. I apologized to those masuras for the lasting wounds," said Grunt.

"Lasting wounds?" laughed Gavee.

"It's not something I find funny, twit!"

Gavee threw the apple core at Grunt as the shapeshifter turned into a rat.

"Enough! I'll spend the whole day reaching the mountain alone. I need to be there before the moon reaches it," said Shapía.

Gavee ended the laughter, and Grunt snapped back to his weasel self with his weasel tail the last to pop.

"What?" asked Gavee. "More explanation is required. I cannot disappear for a full day. Bahg will search for me."

Shapía took a breath.

"The entrance is hidden and reveals itself when the moonlight hits the ridge. We need to go now, or I'll miss it."

"Fly to Ellebasi before tonight?" asked Gavee.

"If the princess must, I shall travel with her," said Grunt.

"I've been on these tales as we've grown, and they have been rough. I've flown to Dulisar's far side before on such ideas."

"You cannot believe the princess is making it up, especially about the queen. I believe you are stubborn and foolish."

"Don't call me stubborn, you little ferret."

"Ferret? You grangrul loving...!"

"Grangrul!"

"Enough!" said Shapía.

She growled at the two squabblers.

"I'll travel alone. I don't need the two of you fighting."

Shapía walked to the door, but Gavee grabbed her arm.

"It's not a spun tale," she said. "Besides, I don't want to go alone."

"Stop. I'll go with you. I always do, regardless of the tale's length. Let me grab my sword and a few things."

Gavee went back to the battle area to prepare for a quick journey. He looked over the queen's sword and sighed, sheathing the beautiful blade. He grabbed the dagger, slid it into a boot, and rejoined the others in the main room. They reached the balcony, and Grunt popped the cane onto the wooden floor, shapeshifting into the crow. He let out a caw before they departed the loft, heading south toward the Ellebasi Mountain.

They followed the Witch'Bane River south, through the Epti Kingdom, home to humans, and onto Mount Lake, sitting before the mountain. The mountain trek normally occupies a masura's entire day, yet these spirited youngsters finished it in half. They did not stop to rest but ate and drank in flight. The trip was simple, and they reached the river's far end, where the lake popped into view.

"There it is!" said Shapía.

"I still think we should have told someone!" said Gavee.

Grunt cawed.

Shapía pushed her wings into the air and swooped down to the lake below, dragging talons, skimming the beautiful blue water. She could feel its coolness, for it fed on an open spring rolling from the mountain.

"They say the water from the lake can cure any ailment or disease," she said.

Shapía landed on the shore next to Gavee, who slumped in exhaustion from the day's travel. He admired the way the sun glistened with the mountain dancing along the water's edge.

"It sure is a beautiful sight," he said.

Grunt landed, shapeshifting back to the weasel.

"I'm exhausted. Does the oracle have any food?" he asked.

"Do you sense the power?" asked Shapía.

"Power?" asked Gavee.

"There's great power here, cousin. I sense it throughout my entire being. You should place your wound in the water to heal."

Gavee stuttered, "I-I'm not sticking my wound in an unknown water source."

"Princess, where's the secret entrance?" asked Grunt.

"There's a ledge above the trees. There, the moon illuminates the path."

Gavee felt frustrated. "How do you know?"

"Mother instructed me on it and said to watch when the moon hit the ledge."

"It better be up there," said Gavee.

Grunt kicked Gavee in the leg, and Gavee returned the favor.

"It's real. Dusk is coming soon, and when it does, I'll show you."

"Can we not leave now?" asked Gavee.

"No," said Shapía.

The princess took a breath and calmed down.

"It's cursed during the day, and our presence may prevent the doorway from showing."

"I'm hungry. Let's eat," said Grunt.

The sun sat atop the mountain, and the three visitors mingled near the water's edge. Gavee divided dried meat from a pouch for the group, and they rested from the day's flight. Grunt built a fire with fish cooking before Gavee finished a fishing rod. It unnerved the thunderblood trainee, yet he ate anyway, and the three ate together in silence. The sun reached the Ellebasi Mountain, falling behind it and fading into the day's light.

"The moon sits behind us. Time to proceed," said the princess.

"As you wish, Princess," said Grunt.

"Stop with the niceties," said Gavee.

"Your cousin deserves respect, unlike you."

"Enough. You two are like children," said Shapía.

Grunt groaned at Gavee, doused the fire, and popped into the crow. The three rose to the ridge.

"I told you it was real," said Shapía.

"I never said the ridge didn't exist," said Gavee.

The wide, rocky ridge ran until it reached the mountain wall, where the ground turned into a well-kept grassy garden with yellow flowers lining its length. Shapía stood before the green grass and gazed at the natural beauty that fell upon her sight. The stone wall had an etched scene containing a giant entry into a magnificent castle. The artwork stretched the ridge's length with images of windows, towers, and birds in the background. All cut into the stone. Above the oversized castle door, a beautiful woman lay lengthwise with tears on her face, turned to etched raindrops.

"I guess it opens at dusk?" asked Gavee.

"The scene turns real when the moon hits the ridge. It's where Mother took me on our first official trip and where we come to pay homage to the goddess Ellebasi."

Shapía pointed to a blank wall where the ridge remained desolate.

"The doorway is not the etching. It opens on the far right."

"The ledge is unnatural," said Grunt. "I sense a trap, and I am certain I've seen the etched scene before in Ihandra."

"Did it awaken upon the moon?" asked Shapía.

"She wasn't a goddess, but an ever-lively Erinys."

"A what?" asked Gavee.

"An Erinys. A female devil. You would think a thunderblood in training would know the name," said Grunt.

"Explain," said Shapía.

"The Erinyes come from the Hell plane," said Grunt.

"I understand their purpose and origins. But why Ihandra?" asked Shapía.

"It was along the path beyond the Great Trees of Ihandra. The path is called Doom, and it laments a song to lull you to it. Then it shall capture your spirit and entrap you as its worker," said Grunt.

"Why would a path like this exist in Ihandra?" asked Gavee.

"The path of doom is for those on a different spiritual quest," said Shapía. "I was unaware it contained the doorway to the dark plane."

"We cannot stay here," said Gavee.

"Mother declared this a haven for oracles. The siren sings when the wall awakens, and the far doorway opens. The oracle's chamber sits inside a hollow, and all oracles are welcome," said Shapía.

"I speak about what I know and feel, Princess. It does not feel safe," said Grunt.

"We have to stay. I need to speak to the oracle," Shapía demanded.

"No, you proceed to Ihandra and continue the discipline without being poisoned by a she-devil," said Gavee.

"Then go, but I'm staying. The moon is near, and the door will open soon."

Gavee sighed and pulled his sword. Grunt snapped the cane, turned into the black panther, and prepared for what might fall upon them. The panther's pupils narrowed as his night vision focused on the moon sliding over the remote mountain.

The cliff ledge, bathed in light, showed a colorful, simple scene. Shapía pointed to the tears from the siren raining on the swaying flowers. The stone woman sang a soothing melody in a strange language as it pulled Shapía into the song. She could not resist and stepped onto the green grass. The music captivated Gavee, although he tried to ignore it, drawing both masuras to the woman.

Grunt growled a warning, and Shapía could not hold back anymore as she reached out to the flowing water. The woman stopped and snapped at Shapía with wonder and confusion. As her hair waved in the wind, the siren glided along the stone, closer to the masura.

"Who are you?" a woman softly asked.

"My name is Shapía, and I am from the Witch'Bane clan."

"You are not familiar. Are you a new oracle?"

"No, my mother—"

"I sense danger around you. I sense a dragon is here."

The etched woman floated to Gavee.

"Are you dragonborn?"

Gavee glanced between Shapía and the siren.

"No, I'm Masuran."

"Dragons have marked you. I sense evil erupting within you. It is going to consume you one day. You are not welcome here."

The woman floated before Shapía.

"You're no oracle and not welcome here, and neither is welcome."

She looked over Shapía's shoulder.

"I am to speak with the Sora. She requested my return before leaving for Horfa," said Shapía.

Her hair streamed backward as anger gripped the woman's face. Shapía shook inside, trying not to let fear overtake her stance. She had to stand tall.

"Siren, please, I need to see the oracle, Sora!" she said.

The siren's anger grew as Shapía tried to answer another question, with the last words riddling her thoughts.

"There's the opening!" said Gavee.

Grunt released a roar, and the wall siren shrieked, jumping Shapía. The woman with etched features emitted a loud shriek before vanishing into the rock. The scene sank into the rock face, leaving the green grass and the open doorway.

"Let's leave before it closes," said Gavee.

Grunt prowled near the dark passage and released a low growl, showing the opening appeared safe. Gavee readied the sword, and Shapía remained close to her cousin as they entered the unknown. With his night vision, Grunt led down a long, dark tunnel, ensuring the passage's safety. The dirt floor remained dry, and the air turned cooler the farther they traversed the path. The large stone door slammed shut, startling the party.

"Be ready," said Gavee.

Gavee clung tight to the wall, and Shapía locked onto her cousin's shoulder until the masuran vision gave way to shadows and small images. The passage revealed a vast cavern with a distant drop and a land bridge leading to a larger tunnel. Grunt leaped across large boulders toward the abyss, and the masuras floated to the land bridge.

"How far?" asked Gavee.

"Mother explained there would be a smaller cavern beyond the tunnel. Only oracles are allowed inside the chamber."

"You're not an oracle," said Gavee.

Grunt growled, coming to rest upon the bridge.

"Sora urged me to return before going to Horfa. I must try it."

"So, the plan is to walk into the chamber?" asked Gavee.

"You may leave, cousin," said Shapía.

"The door closed on us. I have no other direction but forward," said Gavee.

Grunt's warning prompted the cousins to stop their staring match on the bridge. Shapía pulled her bow, ready for what may come as Gavee unsheathed the queen's sword. The masuras reacted to the echoed growl, and a light shone within the far tunnel. The cave rumbled, and the light became brighter, with a deep growl rolling forward.

Grunt's hunches rose, returning to a more resounding, louder roar. The cavern shook, and the torch flame came forward as a large, four-fingered, gray hand pushed it ahead. The giant beast bent forward and stood before the land bridge through the opening. Gavee's eyes widened in shock. Grunt leaped onto a boulder, and Shapía worked to keep the bow steady.

"What is it?" asked Shapía.

"I don't have a clue!" said Gavee.

The giant beast towered over the bridge and stood as high as a tree. It had no eyes, two mangled, large, pointed ears sticking through thin, dark hair, and a pushed-in nose above large, razor teeth filling its maw. Simple rags covered its broad torso, holding a large staff in one hand. The beast thundered another growl and popped the stone floor when the giant ball atop the staff opened, and an eye blinked. The creature raised the staff, and the eye fixed on the masuras as its head angled toward them.

"Did the queen mention a monster?" asked Gavee.

"No, she said nothing! What is it?"

Grunt continued to jump from boulder to boulder as he prepared for an attack. The beast roared again and dropped the torch into the ravine, bursting into flames. It crossed the bridge and stuck the staff into a hole. The eye watched the masuras, and the beast pulled forward a giant wooden boomerang and slung the wooden object at Gavee and Shapía.

"Fly!" said Gavee.

Shapía lifted, and the wooden weapon missed her talons. As the weapon looped around again, Gavee deflected it with a grimace, sparks flying from the impact. The beast roared, lunging toward the fallen object. Grunt's swipe connected with its hind legs. It angered in pain, and the eye centered on the black panther. The boomerang skipped atop several stones, and Grunt dropped between two boulders before the wooden weapon nicked his tail, forcing a groan.

The mighty beast gnashed its teeth at the group and caught the boomerang. Shapía released several arrows into its thick arms when it yanked the small sticks and crumpled them in its grip. The beast thundered and returned alongside the eye, sending the weapon at Shapía's head.

The princess hit the target twice more, but it didn't react.

Gavee veered sharply right and swooped behind the distracted beast as its eye focused on his cousin. The thunderblood trainee worked to get behind the creature, with the fire bellowing and protecting its backside. The orange glow covered the cave, and its enormity allowed the animal to use its weapon without worry.

Again, the boomerang flew and ricocheted off the sidewalls, nearly catching Gavee off guard. When the boomerang landed in its keeper's hand, the eye swiveled and stared at the masura. The distraction allowed Grunt to sneak to the beast and leap on its backside, digging in its claws. The giant creature snarled and tried to grab the attacker, but could not reach the panther. Shapía released several more arrows, and the monster turned and withdrew toward the flames. Grunt released and catapulted over the fiery drop.

"We need to pull it away so Shapía can reach the chamber!" said Gavee.

"Will it follow?" asked Shapía.

"We need to get you down the tunnel. We'll keep the thing chasing us!" said Gavee.

The creature bellowed at Grunt, and the black panther darted to the land bridge. The giant eye caught the action, and the creature kicked Grunt backward. He tumbled until he crashed into the stone wall. The shapeshifter hissed, moaned, and then darted to the distant corner.

Gavee swooped at the eye, and the creature chased him away, protecting the item and returning to its side.

Grunt shot for the eye, and the beast tried to track the panther. Wiser to the action, the shapeshifter dodged the boomerang as it skipped along the rocks.

"Keep the eye on us!" said Gavee.

Grunt growled.

"Shoot your arrows into the eye! Continue shooting the arrows and distract it! It'll give you time to sneak into the tunnel without being noticed. Wait until it throws the boomerang again," said Gavee.

Grunt moved in closer, and Gavee veered so the eye would follow his flight. The beast launched the boomerang, and the masura deflected the throw.

Shapía sent arrows at the eye with the hits bouncing off the hard shell. The lost creature ran into the wall and dropped with a boom.

The princess continued the barrage as she pushed the wind behind and flew at high speed into the tunnel. She landed in a smaller cavern with three different closed doors, two more significant than the third, and they all featured large latches.

"There was never mention of doors," said Shapía.

Again, the beast's roar echoed from the distant cave, making the boomerang's bounce resonate in the cramped space.

"Think, Shapía, which one?" she said.

The tallest door, the monster's size, had a rotten smell, and she stayed clear. She reached for the handle of the larger one, which had no clear markings, before hesitating and withdrawing her hand.

"What if it's a trap?"

Shapía jumped at the beast's echoing roars down the tunnel and rushed to lift the latch. The door opened, and the corridor rumbled with a stone closing off the tunnel. The masura became locked inside, and panic pushed her to the now-closed opening, searching for a gap.

"W.B.!"

She placed her ear against the stone.

"Gavee!"

Her voice echoed, and no sound filtered through the rock. Shapía leaned against the cold stone, slapping it.

"I need to press ahead."

She turned and discovered three chambers. The middle held a massive door wide open, with hay scattered throughout the room and a big pot in a far corner. She eyed the other door, closed, but moved past it to the smaller, standard door. It held a small gold latch, and she lifted the metal object. The door opened by itself, releasing a warm breeze scented with nectar.

"Enter, Princess," whispered a female voice.

Shapía hesitated to allow the door to ease open. The bright room with sky-blue walls and floor featured a woman in a shiny silver robe sitting in the center. Her skin was dark brown, her head bald, and she bore a smile upon a beautiful elvish face. The woman sat on an oversized chair with her legs draped over it. The large green rug circled the floor's center, with flowers in vases on the chair sides, and a green path led from the doorway.

"Princess, you are in no danger and are welcome in my sanctuary."

The princess tucked in her wings and entered through the arched doorway. She gazed at the domed ceiling and its floating clouds, passing onto the walls and then to the floor, disappearing behind large bookshelves. The door slid closed, and Shapía found herself at peace, with no concerns. The female oracle possessed deep green eyes, and a yellow glow hung above her head. She held out her hand.

"Come closer, Princess," said the woman.

Shapía's talons echoed on the hard path, and she stopped in front of the green circle.

"You hold your mother's eyes," said the woman.

Shapía blushed and bowed her head.

"Princess, do not bow your eyes."

"I'm unsure how to behave in her presence."

The woman laughed. "I am no goddess."

"You are Sora?"

"I am the oracle, Sora."

"How do I address you?"

"As if you are with your mother. I wish only the best for those living on the island, and I hold my heart closer to those who awake to the oracle path."

"I came because my mother had instructed us to come together, but…"

"The mighty queen's death has grasped your heart and has not released its hold. You need to be free of it before reaching Horfa."

"How I miss her so."

"Look into my eyes, and we will discover it together."

The Witch'Bane princess paused at the request, and the muse smiled. She leaned forward, staring into the deep green, and fell into its void. Her consciousness cleared, revealing a vast meadow as her surroundings. The woman walked, and Shapía followed alongside the oracle.

"Your mother's death has been hidden from the oracles."

"How?"

"It tells us there is a powerful source on the island."

"Are we in danger?"

"Even I cannot tell. The identity is hidden, but it used the dragons to kill."

"The dragons must be aligned with it. Could the oracles see through the beasts?"

"Mind tricks won't work. The dragons are too clever."

"Do you believe the dragons are helping?" asked Shapía.

"As an oracle, my dear, part with belief. It leads you to false truths and creates an ideology. A Seer of Seers will be liberated from having a self."

Shapía stopped as the muse continued onward.

"Seer of Seers?"

The woman turned, leaned into a tall flower, and enjoyed its aroma.

"Like this flower destined to produce a sweet odor, you, child, are destined to guide the awakened. If you free yourself from the self."

"Free the self? I'm confused."

"The answer is in Horfa. It will become apparent in your training."

"You requested my return before Horfa. Why?"

The muse's smile dropped.

"You must reach it before the Reflection for your queen. The truth awakens there, and our island holds onto despair until you arrive. Your mother understood and made sure you returned to hear my message. You are the key to the truth, and the island remains locked until you uncover the meaning. You mustn't wait."

"Why the riddles?"

"I do not wish to lead your thoughts or ideas. To understand your situation, you need to perceive it visually and mentally. Anything beyond riddles creates an idea without knowledge."

"So, confusion," said Shapía.

"I have something you have to protect with your life. The Great Seer offers further explanation, this necklace, a divine treasure. The power in it could control all the islands and their beings when you learn how to use it."

Shapía's eyes widened as she looked down into the muse's hands. It contained a milky white gem on a simple silver necklace. Shapía raised it and took notice of the pink center.

"It's simple yet draws me to it," she said.

"Yes, this is the Mazerth Stone. The pink center is its heart, the heart of the Five Islands. It has to return to the Seer of Seers as the darkness is searching and poses a threat to everything."

"How do I use it?"

"Use it?" said the oracle. "Keep it secure. It's not for use."

"Why not deceive the evil, revealing its origin, since you know it seeks you?"

"The island is blessed to have you, my dear," said Sora. "No one knows the Mazerth is beyond the Sovereign Hall, and we wish for this secret to remain."

"Why give it to me and take the chance?"

"It has never been safer at this moment," said Sora. "Hide it well and reach Horfa. The islands wait for your destiny to unfold."

Before Shapía could say a word, the female turned and snapped her fingers. Her vision turned bright white, then black, easing into the night sky. Alone on the outside ledge, the masura concentrated on the information before she realized it. The necklace lay on her neck, and she tucked it away from prying eyes. Moonlight on the ridge revealed an open door. She could hear Gavee screaming at Grunt.

"No, bring it to the far side!"

The princess eased down the passage toward the orange glow until she could see the enormous cavern. The floor continued to rumble, with Gavee hovering to the left and Grunt's hair on end, growling at the beast, who leaped at a ledge where its boomerang lay. Her eyes fixed on the scene, and she giggled at the sight.

"I met with an oracle!" she said.

Gavee's eyes jumped to Shapía and then back at the far passage. Grunt hissed.

"How?" asked Gavee.

"I'll explain later!"

The beast hurled the boomerang at Shapía, clipping her left ear. She dropped to one knee and winced in pain.

"Shapía!" Gavee called.

"I'm fine. Let's go!"

Grunt growled and tried to dash for the bridge when the creature kicked him past the fire opening and into the cave wall. Grunt moaned.

Gavee charged the beast.

"Gavee, no!" said Shapía. "It guards the entrance. We need to leave it. Let's head out!"

The thunderblood trainee cursed at the words, but dropped from the cave ceiling and soared past Shapía.

Grunt emerged limping from the tunnel. Then, before the princess, he became a crow. They flew through the darkness, following the river until they reached a tree cluster along the riverbank beyond the human city.

"I have to rest for a moment. My wings tire from the fight," said Gavee.

Grunt cawed.

"Not for long. We need to get back home tonight," said Shapía.

The two masuras landed beside the river, and Grunt shifted back as a weasel. He eased to the ground and sat against a tree, holding his right hip.

"How did you slip past?" asked Gavee.

"I didn't. I was placed on the ledge by the oracle."

"What did she say?" asked Gavee.

"Words for my ears. We should get home."

"I am too old for these battles and drawn-out flights," said Grunt.

Gavee drank from the river, and Shapía observed the lit human city.

"Does it need to be so bright?" she asked.

"Bahg says it avoids surprise night attacks. I disagree with it," said Gavee.

"It's a method to avoid unknown attacks," said Grunt.

"They understand the city better than anyone. Keep it dark and the sentry alert. Defend it better," said Shapía.

"It's their city. I'm certain they understand how to defend it," said Gavee. "I would do it differently."

Suddenly, an arrow thumped between Shapía and Gavee. Before they could react, several lanterns lit before them, and five men stood with swords and arrows pointed at the three in idle talk.

"You against the tree, don't move another finger!" said a man with a laced bow.

"How did I not sense their arrival?" asked Grunt. "This day has been a long one."

"Why are you here?" asked a human, pulling forward atop the battle steed.

Shapía took notice as her gaze fixed upon the man. He sat tall on the steed with armor fitting the stature and wore a shiny silver helmet with white and black feathers poking from its top. The man carried a large silver shield with a white bird in its center and a battle sword at his side.

"We have to rest our wings after a long flight," answered Shapía.

"Masura, you're trespassing. You must come with us," the mounted man said.

"We need to return to Witch'Bane…"

"Shapía?" asked Gavee.

Grunt used the distraction and popped the cane on the ground, shifting to the panther. He growled and took to the tall grass before an arrow could fly. The changeling roared, jumping the men. He growled again to keep them guessing.

"My suggestion, human, is let us fly out before our friend pulls you into the darkness, one by one," said Gavee.

Grunt growled.

"If we release you, Witch'Bane, then your changeling leaves us alone," said the man.

"Agreed," said Shapía.

Gavee sneered.

"He'll harm no one," said Gavee.

"Do not return to our land unless you have permission."

On his steed, the man wheeled the horse away into the night. The men on foot continued to move, searching for the big black cat. Grunt growled.

"Let's go," said Gavee. "And discuss why we never give our clan's name."

Shapía maintained her gaze toward the darkness as they took to flight, and Grunt continued to press the men with growls, keeping them on their toes. Grunt, now a crow, caught the royals while the masuras safely avoided arrows. He cawed.

"Yes, it was quite unexpected," said Gavee. "And yes, it is unfortunate they know our name."

Shapía ignored the comment and concentrated on the oracle.

"I must get to Horfa," she said.

Chapter Five

F lued landed in the Witch'Bane courtyard, greeted by red-clad Latuery. He walked through the double doors and passed the watch before being announced.

"Father, you requested my presence?"

The king waved his son to the table, continuing discussions with Lord Taronquel.

"I want us seated next to Toren. They were the only clan to aid us in the Great Masuran War."

"I understand, Your Majesty, but it might be a better fit if we sit near the Raths. It allows our continued efforts our queen had begun with the clan."

King Arul groaned and sat back.

"We are waiting for your sister and cousin. They have requested the gathering," answered the king. "We sit alongside Toren, and I send my eldest to continue to build a future with Rath."

King Arul smiled at Flued.

"Father, I'm honored to be the voice and ears for Witch'Bane," said Flued.

Flued had frequented Rath with his mother on several occasions, with each visit improving over the previous one. The prince stretched his wings and poured the mead from a ceramic ewer into a silver cup. He approached the window and looked at the sunlit morning into Witch'Bane. Several masuran children played in the trees, and a female masura flew with a basket.

"I'll do anything for our clan," he said.

* * *

Gavee zipped past the window Flued was looking out and landed alongside Shapía in the courtyard. The duo confidently charged into the hall with heads held high.

"Good day, everyone," said Shapía.

Gavee bowed to the king, grabbing a banana from a bowl.

"Where is Bahg?" questioned Taronquel.

"I am unaware, Head Council," said Gavee, sitting in a chair close to the door.

"I'm here," answered Bahg.

The thunderblood came up a spiral staircase, reading a scroll as he walked, not missing a step or breaking from the parchment. He positioned himself beside the smiling king. Bahg closed the scroll.

"We are here," said the king.

"Yes, we are," said Shapía.

"Please," said the king, giving the floor to his daughter.

"Over a year ago, Mother returned from a visit to the oracle Sora. She instructed us to return a year later before my departure for Horfa."

"Visit?" questioned the king.

"Only an oracle would know, Mother said, and I was required to keep oracle training a secret."

Shapía waited to see if he had other questions, but the king instructed her to continue.

"Yesterday, Gavee, Grunt, and I returned to the mountain as requested."

Bahg directed his attention toward the masura, and Gavee kept his eyes on the floor. Lord Taronquel frowned, and the king groaned. Flued leaned against the wall and shook his head.

"I met with an oracle, and she instructed me to go before Reflection. She stated, my future is in the scrolls, and I'll find expert knowledge explaining mother's death and preventing the masura's utter destruction."

Silence filled the room, with attention centered on the princess. She grasped the words' significance, then observed Gavee's downcast gaze.

"Destruction?" questioned Taronquel.

"Enough," said the king.

"I want to stay for Reflection, Father," said Shapía. "This is the Masuran Way."

The king stood, snatched his goblet from the table, and downed the drink.

"I will not explain the danger you placed yourself and the clan in by going alone. My frustration regarding the trip and mountain return shall remain unvoiced. If the oracle says you cannot wait, you must leave before Reflection. Your mother lived her life by the words of the goddess."

"I cannot miss Mother's Reflection," said Shapía.

"This isn't a choice, my daughter."

"I'll take her," said Bahg.

"Same," said Gavee.

"No," said Bahg. "We require a thunderblood for Reflection. You'll be assigned to ensure the king's safety during his absence from our forest. Besides, you've already taken the princess on an ill-advised trip."

Gavee held his tongue.

"And the Latuery," said Flued, "shall ensure the king is safe, too."

"Agree. The thunderblood of each clan must meet tomorrow to confer about Reflection. You'll represent us there," said Bahg.

Gavee bit his lip, fighting the excitement of performing an official thunderblood duty without his mentor. He swelled inside and could not find the words. He nodded his response.

"Your king gives you great honor, and you nod?" questioned Bahg.

Gavee snapped out of his distraction and stood.

"I'm honored, My King."

Bahg continued to smirk at Gavee, and the masura avoided eye contact.

Shapía broke the silence.

"If I must... when, Father?"

"You'll meet Horfa's longship at the Fen port. Give your name, and there will be no questions. Bahg, bring the king's mark for safe travel. Depart tomorrow using the Ihandra passage."

"We must prepare," said Bahg.

Shapía showed disappointment in the order, and the king went to his daughter. He embraced her in a sincere hug and kissed her forehead.

"It's going to be fine, my child. Your mother would have preferred you to be in Horfa than at the ceremony," he said.

She took a deep breath and smiled, stepping out the door.

"Shapía, wait," said Gavee.

"Thunderblood, we must discuss Reflection," said Bahg.

"Yes, sir. Safe travels, Princess."

"Excuse me, Sire. I must meet with the cooks to ensure the meal meets our standards," said Taronquel.

"Be certain the feast is delicious," said the king.

"I shall return after the midday meal, Father," said Flued. "I must fly to a northern post to tend to a Latuery matter."

"I guess it's just the brothers," said the king.

"For a moment, I must prepare to escort your daughter to Horfa and cover things with my son," answered Bahg.

"Indeed, everyone's occupied," the king declared.

* * *

Shapía veered from the council with no intention of her loft. The pressure was too much, with even a simple flight becoming difficult. With her heart pounding, she followed the familiar path where the queen and princess met for discussions and training. She approached the white birch and perched in her favorite tree overlooking Lheter Lake, and finally she could not suppress the tears. Her mother's death continued to fill her thoughts, and she wanted to have one last word. The loss left a hole, and she wondered how training could continue without a mother's loving touch.

The crow landed alongside, but she did not break her stare with a storm rumbling just before the lake. Grunt shifted and sat on the limb.

"You know what I'll miss the most?" he asked.

Shapía did not respond.

"How our mothers laughed together. What a bond they had."

"They were close," she said.

"I suspect it happens when you discipline together. A bond occurs," said Grunt.

"I've always been curious why mother brought you to Witch'Bane and raised you in the Masuran way."

"I caused an issue and had to depart Ihandra."

Shapía sat next to her friend.

"We always wondered," she said.

"Yes, I gave my mother trouble in those days. It placed her in a bad way with the Horfa, and when the village attack occurred, your mother pulled me in close, taking me under her wing," he said.

"Grunt?"

"This is something I'd rather not discuss, for your mother was kind enough to take me in and treat me as her son. I look to you and Gavee as siblings," said Grunt.

"We look to you as our brother. I know you and Gavee have become close over the years, and we also have our bond."

"You are correct, My Princess. I wish to escort you to Horfa and see its beauty together, but I'm afraid Bahg would not allow me to travel as a companion."

"Why doesn't he like you?"

"I'm not sure, but he makes it known," said Grunt.

"Maybe I'll ask on the trip?"

"No need. We stay at our distance. Besides, we're both on our chosen paths. I'll travel with Gavee, ensuring Witch'Bane's safety at Reflection while you become our oracle."

"I wish I could stay," she said.

"The clan needs its oracle, and the oracle insists. You must go."

"Maybe someday we shall understand the truth about why."

"It may be something you'd rather not uncover."

Shapía grunted in agreement.

"The once-distant storm is heading our way. We should return and enjoy the rain with tea before your departure," said Grunt.

"Yes, my friend," said Shapía. "Help me prepare."

Grunt popped the staff onto the branch, causing his body to bend and change with black feathers popping through. Soon wings slid where his arms were, and his feet turned to small talons. He returned to the crow. They left for Shapía's loft before the thundering storm moved into the forest.

* * *

The weak masura flew south toward the Nathe Mountains, where the forest met the cliff walls. With a distant storm rolling toward Lheter Lake, the Witch'Bane pushed his flight to a hidden location before the rain arrived. The forest against the mountain cliffs ran thick and unattended with ground clutter, making it almost impossible to land. He reached a branch worn from continuous activity and counted the mulberry shrubs dotting the ground. Moving from tree to tree, he landed in front of three giant stones where the cliff met the rocky terrain. The masura bypassed the first two, circled the third, then entered a concealed tunnel.

Three torches lined the tunnel wall, reaching inside a cavern with large fallen stones on the floor. He clutched the lantern, leaped onto a rock, peering into the cave below. The female masura, Rhile, the lahd, second in command of the Witch'Bane warriors, behind Flued, stood centered in ten tall torches sticking from the dirt floor to the far left in an open area. She stood between two chained masuras stretched across large rocks, opposite each other, with wings spread and anchored to the ground. The Witch'Bane masura held a whip in her right hand, and sweat dripped from her brow.

Rhile released a stinging snap, forcing the captive into a muffled scream.

"Are they still not talking?" asked the hooded masura.

"I don't think they know," answered Rhile.

The whip snapped against the other masura as Taronquel landed beside his accomplice and said, "I must have the stone."

He proceeded to the bloody masura, seizing his hair and lifting the head.

"Where's this seer?"

The whipped masura moaned under its mouth guard, and the hooded Taronquel unchained the restraint.

"She lives in a mound in the Dulisar swamp," coughed the Masura.

"And the stone?"

"We no longer have it."

"Manawe gave up the stone?" questioned Rhile.

"It resides either within the hall or with the seer," said Taronquel.

Taronquel released the hair, and the masura's head hit the stone, knocking him unconscious.

"Dare we?" asked Rhile.

"I'll consult with Malum."

"And them?"

"No survivors."

The muzzled masura attempted to cry out as Taronquel ascended into the cavern's tall ceiling. Rhile grabbed the masura's head and slit his neck, allowing the blood to fill her talons. She repeated the action with the other, then drank from a water bucket, waiting for the head council to return.

The feeble masura reached a high overlook within the cave, landed in a tunnel, and pushed the torch outward to show the way. The narrow corridor forced the masura to fold his wings, entering a chamber with a large waterhole. He touched the flame to the water's rim, and a ring lit around the basin.

From inside his shirt, the masura pulled a leather sack and tossed its powder contents into the pool. With a hiss and a bubble, the water spun and mixed with the magic. The flames danced around the whirlpool when an image rose from the dark mire. As the fire neared the center, wings appeared. The broken masura form came into full view.

"Mother Malum, the stone still eludes me," said Taronquel.

"It's on this cursed island," she said.

"There's a seer."

"Ah yes, the one in the swamp."

"How do I make her talk?"

"You'll hand her a precious gift."

The dark ooze rippled forward and lapped over its edge. It pulled away, leaving a black gem with a white dot in its center.

"Is this the stone you want?"

"In appearance, but it's much different. It shall make the seer speak," coughed the image.

"I just hand over the item, and she'll tell me what she knows?"

"No, you weak-minded fool. Negotiate a price, and the gem will pay it off."

Taronquel tried to fetch the gem.

"Don't touch it, you dolt."

She slapped his hand away.

"How do I give it to her if I can't touch it?"

"Improvise. It'll be the last thing the witch sees," laughed Malum.

He opened the sack and retrieved the gem within it.

"Leave. Find the seer," she said.

The black image fell into the pool as its fire extinguished, leaving the room in darkness. The masura fumbled through the darkness and arrived at the tunnel's end. He looked down to find Rhile eating from a bowl, waiting for him.

"When do we leave?" she asked.

"Now."

Rhile gave the bowl to the head council, and he ate the fruit sitting in it.

"Do we have time to eat?" she asked.

"As we discuss our trip."

"Listening," said Rhile.

"As you always have, my dearest," said Taronquel. "We travel to the swamp for the seer. She holds the information we need."

"What about the scouts who trailed you?"

"They'll relay that we met secretly and leave us at the Dead Falls. This should confuse the king," he said with a smile.

"The tricks you hold are dark, and I draw to it," she said.

"Trust me. There may be trying times, but don't give up faith in me."

Rhile took a knee and bowed her head.

"I am your faithful servant and do what you require. Remain hidden forever, and I would still follow."

The broken masura grinned.

"Let's go."

They followed the Nathe Mountains along Lheter Lake, taking on heavy rain and lightning strikes. The head council ignored the trailing watch, holding the mission in mind and finding the seer to uncover the stone. Madame Rhile had a stern face and did not question the flight as large droplets pelted their wings. They made it to the Dead Falls, where the current overflowed its banks and thundered onto the rocky buildup. The far-distant Manawe port appeared abandoned, with rational beings avoiding the horrible storm. They did not stop.

"Do they still follow?" questioned Rhile.

"No, the spies turned back upon the first lightning strike."

Silence fell from the head council as the masuras pressed onward, following the Dead River toward Stalk Lake and the swamp beyond. The wind howled hard as they entered beyond the Manawe land, where Dulisar and the Dead Lands themselves met. The howl over the lake pushed against their flight as if the island had fought their arrival. They avoided the far Dulisar banks where the wood elves held their territory, and Witch'Bane was less than welcome in the realm.

The Dead Lands, a lifeless wasteland, were home to slithering creatures daring to live in the desolation. Lightning strikes forced the masuras to fly in random patterns along the shore. The push made it difficult for the weaker masura to reach beyond the wicked storm, and a fog had settled upon the swamp.

As they flew onward, the lake, initially filled with dead tree stumps, gradually transitioned into a marshy swamp. The unsettling silence did not stir the masuras from their mission, and they settled upon a barren tree. The hooded masura shook the excess water from his wings and looked over the foggy landscape.

"If you're a seer, where's your home?" questioned Taronquel.

"The fog does not help."

"We must separate and communicate through our secret call. The silence should allow us to maintain a suitable distance. When you find the lair, continue the call until the other shows."

"Aye."

Rhile left the branch, causing the misty air to funnel around her trailing wings as she slipped beyond sight. With a heavy sigh, the head council lifted his wings into the haze. The dense mist forced the flight into a slow glide, missing unseen trees stripped of life. In the silence, he kept his sword at the ready, with the dimming sun darkening the search. Taronquel landed on a broken tree extending over the water, atop fallen trees.

"I believe I've been here before?"

When Rhile called, the hooded masura groaned in response. From behind, the bird's sound grew stronger after first echoing around. The masura ascended, tracked the sound, and then, after landing to better hear, changed course. The call captured a firmer tone, and the clouds dissipated with Rhile standing on a sandy shore, pointing to a large mud mound in the water.

Taronquel found the lahd and contemplated the large mud dome. It was an island without a tree or limb near the moated land. Wooden planks encircled the mystery mound and stopped at a large, flat stone.

"I think this is it," said Rhile.

"It's not natural," he said.

"How do we get in?" she asked.

"Unknown. Did you fly over?"

"No."

"Let's try."

The water around the mound began to bubble and sizzle as it rose, covering the wooden planks.

"You are not welcome, masuras," boomed a female voice.

Crows cawed in the distant fog, forcing the masuras to pull swords. They did not say a word and waited, but nothing else came.

"Show yourself!" said the head council.

Darkness rolled in as the silence lingered. They stood poised, anticipating conflict, as daylight faded. Mist again filled in around the water's edge, and the masuras eased, sheathing swords.

"How long do we wait?" asked Rhile.

"If the woman is anything like Malum, she'll arrive in the dark. Let's build a fire."

They piled wood, with Rhile taking out the flint and lighting the fire. She kept stacking the pieces until the swamp carried an orange glow. Taronquel gave his friend dried meat, and they filled their stomachs. The fog retreated, and the stars sparkled above.

"I'll take the first watch. You'll grab it when the moon reaches beyond our sight," said Taronquel.

"As you wish."

Rhile perched on the dead tree and closed her eyes. The hooded masura focused on the mound, alert to the surroundings. The moon traversed the night sky, and the weaker masura struggled with sleep. He shook his head and prevented his eyes from shutting. The head council could not fight the urge when a boom shuddered throughout the swamp. Taronquel jumped with a sword drawn, and Rhile fell backward.

"Look!" said Rhile.

Four long torches circled the mound, accompanied by four barkapes, each holding a staff. Light shone above the flat stone where an opening sat, and two crows perched upon the metal rod formed in a cross. The crows cawed.

"One may enter," boomed the female voice.

"It's a trap," said Rhile.

"I carry Malum's protection. There's no concern."

Taronquel worked his different-sized wings and floated. He flapped twice, then came to rest upon the flat stone in front of the mound. The mud and thatched twig doorway lay open, and a stone stairway led down the thatched hall, lined with torches. The masura glanced at Rhile, tucked in his wings, and entered the seer's mound. He descended five steps, proceeded to a short hall, and then to a room.

Before him, an unknown being sat hunched beneath a black robe. The room remained dark, with an orange hue from the hall torches, and a small fire sat in front of the mysterious creature. Bones from arms and legs lined the rear wall, and a pot stirred atop a flame with a green ooze popping from the heat.

"Why have you come?" asked the female.

"I've been told you could help with my search."

Her ashen hands emerged from the dark robe, pulling back the hood. Smooth and white as a cloud was her eyeless face. Her black hair flowed down her shoulders. The nose was missing, and the upper lip curled beneath itself, with breath crackling under each heave. She dropped a small bone into the pot.

"Do you offer anything in return for information on the Mazerth Stone?"

Taronquel, unsurprised, reached into his cloak. He pulled out the small leather pouch, dropping it in front of the seer. She sniffed the air and fixed her mute eyes on the masura.

"This is your trade?" asked the seer.

"You haven't opened it."

"It contains Malum's mark. I smell the evil."

"You'll take it as payment and tell me the stone's location."

"Pick it up, Masura. I do not desire the death gem. I sense it's evil."

She stirred the pot. He placed the sack under his cloak.

"I have news about the stone you seek and will share it, but not for what lies inside the sack," she said.

Taronquel waited.

"I want the masura waiting on the beach," she said.

The question confused the head council.

"Explain," he said.

"I want a masuran to protect me, and she is a powerful fighter. Will you sacrifice your friend for the details?"

Taronquel growled. The thought angered him, and then he calmed his nerves.

"If it gives me what I need, she's yours."

The room fell silent when the seer chuckled.

"There is something about you, Masura. A foul odor permeates you. I'll give you the information you seek. Then I want you out of my swamp."

"Agreed."

"The disc you want is secret, beyond any eyes. There is one who may know its history and whereabouts," she said.

"May?" he asked.

"There is no record. If so, your Malum doesn't require your aid," she said.

The sorceress laughed and coughed at the words.

"Enough with the delay," said Taronquel.

She kept stirring the cauldron, dropping in roots.

"The wandering scroll keeper named Dakii possesses history's knowledge and should know its whereabouts."

"Where is this Dakii?" asked Taronquel.

"The keeper was last seen near Eden."

"Last seen? Is he still there?"

The witch stirred the thick ooze and wafted its aroma to her absent nose. She gurgled in a breath.

"He is still in the pirate city."

"We'll find him."

"I sense something else is stirring in the Upper Realm. It will change the course for masuras. It covers you," she said.

Taronquel did not answer.

"Your hand, Masura."

The head council hesitated and turned to the exit, finding a barkape standing between him and the hall.

"You won't leave until you give me your hand," she said.

He gritted and did as she demanded when she took her white bony hand, forcing his palm open. She leaned in and licked the palm of his hand. He grimaced at the action.

"If you don't deliver the masura, you'll not make it from my swamp," chuckled the seer.

The masura jerked his hand away and stared at his palm. A black dot sat in the center, entering his veins. He curled it into a fist and watched it travel his arm.

"How do I stop it once you have your servant?"

She held out a vial.

"This is going to stop it from killing you. My new servant will deliver it on the shore."

She smiled.

Taronquel cursed the seer and shoved the barkape to the side. He hit the stairs and jumped into a flight, easing beside Rhile.

"Did she tell you?"

"Yes," he answered.

"And?"

"She requests your presence."

Rhile gave a confused stare. The head council looked to his palm, and the inky blackness penetrated every vein on his arm. He hissed at the sight, and a smile rose on his face. "I know the way."

"Way?" asked Rhile.

"Here's your task. You must follow my directions if we wish to get out alive."

"I'm still confused?"

"The cost was high," said Taronquel.

"Whose cost?" questioned Rhile.

"She desires a masura as a guardian."

"What masura?" questioned Rhile.

"You."

"And you agreed?"

"I have a plan to free us from this request," he said.

"By leaving?"

"We cannot."

The masura grasped his hand as the black veins throbbed under the fire's glow.

"It means if we leave without a fulfilled agreement, we both die," said Taronquel.

Rhile's anger rose.

"Here is how we escape," said Taronquel.

He pulled out the leather sack.

"When you get in front of the seer, ask her for the vial. It is imperative that you have it before, or else we're finished."

"Understood," said Rhile.

"Inside the bag is a gem. Take it out and shove it down her throat," he said.

Rhile took the sack and opened it.

"No."

He stopped her hand.

"You must take it out before her, then... shove it... down... her... throat," said Taronquel.

"At your command."

"Go," he said.

* * *

Rhile, without another word, pushed to the mound and reached the open door. The brave soldier, her heart pounding, glanced over her shoulder, glimpsing the hooded masura's shadowed face. She descended the stairs into the small, thatched hall. Seated and hooded, the seer was still as a statue. The only movement was the slow rise and fall of her chest. The scene surprised the masura as the woman puffed from a pipe in her white, bony hand, and smoke drifted out from her missing nose.

"My new servant," she said.

"Indeed," said Rhile. "The vial."

The seer tossed the yellow vial to Rhile, and the lahd's anger grew, dropping it into a pocket. She retrieved the leather sack and seized the gem. The white center spun, and her hand turned black. A searing pain caused her to scream, and its sudden grip shocked her. The wicked woman laughed at the misfortune when Rhile's anger thundered forward, grabbing the woman's jaw and forcing it open. The female masura jammed her fist into the seer's throat as the witch gurgled and tried to retaliate when the lahd released the gem. She withdrew her hand, remaining tar black and hard as glass.

The eyeless woman grasped at her throat, foaming at the mouth as the mound shook. The veins in her neck turned black as she spat and jerked from the reaction. Rhile ran down the hall as it closed in. She fought through the muck and then tore through the opening, screaming her way from the destruction. Amidst the sinking mound, the barkapes howled and hooted. The fanged monkey beasts dropped into the murky deep and disappeared into the muck. The lahd landed beside the head council, holding out her hand.

* * *

"What did you do?" she cried.

Taronquel grabbed Rhile's shoulders in shock at the smooth black hand.

"Malum will fix it."

"Did you know? Is that why I had to wait?" panicked Rhile.

"I told you to wait because the seer refused the gem. I wanted her to eat it as punishment for her ignorance. We head to Malum, and she'll fix it."

"The pain!" cried Rhile.

"It does not appear to be moving down your arm."

"Take me right away!"

The lahd grabbed him by the throat and raised him from the ground. Taronquel squeezed Rhile's legs, forcing her to drop the grip. The lahd fell to her knees.

"I'm sorry. The anger took hold," cried Rhile.

"We'll fix it," worried Taronquel, touching Rhile's head. "Do you have my antidote?"

The lahd raised her hand, and the head council took the vial. He looked at his hand, and the black streak disappeared into his shoulder beyond his vision. The masura downed the sour, warm liquid and felt it fall down his throat. He fell to his knees beside Rhile and gagged on the potion. The heated substance ran through his arm, and he watched it run down the arm and spew from the spot on his palm. It sizzled as it landed among the dead leaves and dried the muddy ground.

"We go to Malum," he said.

"The... pain," she groaned.

"She'll fix this, or I'll end it. I promise."

Chapter Six

Shapía looked over her loft, and the queen's touch rested on each item. With its thunderbolt, the red sash draped the tables, walls, and chairs. She smiled in its warmth and provided haven. Although her mother's chair, brought from Rath, remained at the table, she never used it. Today was Reflection Day, yet she would not take part. The masura stepped before the Sora statue. She watched the water falling from the ewer.

"Stay with me, my oracle, no matter how far I may drift."

Shapía gave a slight head bow as she studied the Mazerth Stone. The gem had little sparkle, and some weight carried around her neck when she wore it.

"I must hide it."

She closed her eyes and concentrated on the simple spell she had learned at a young age.

"Bring the stone into my mind, where a soul shall never find. Hide it from prying eyes so no being can unmask its prize."

She placed the necklace around her neck, and it disappeared.

"The next time I come through these doors, I'll be a changed masura."

She tightened the belt on the satchel and suppressed tears as she glanced around the loft. Shapía pulled out of the drawer a silver necklace she had received as a gift from her mother. With its thunderbolt, a symbol of Nathe, and talons, a symbol of Rath, meshed together in a circle. It showed the union between the Witch'Bane and Rath clans, running through her veins. It was the one item bonding the three with hope for a future masuran blending. Reflection Day would have permitted her to keep discussing the union with the Raths, but her destiny was elsewhere, and she could no longer disregard the call.

"Shapía?"

Gavee's voice, muffled through the balcony door, jolted the princess from her thoughts, and she stood for a moment in silence.

"She must be at council," said Flued.

"I'm here!" said Shapía. "For now," she mumbled.

The masuras entered with smiles.

"You're headed to Horfa. Why the tears?" asked Gavee.

"I'll be a new masura upon my return. It will all be different."

"Yes, and wiser. It'll be different in a better way," said Flued.

"Plus, you'll have ideas on updating the loft," said Gavee.

Gavee lifted a sash placed on the table, and it crumpled in the middle. Shapía groaned and fixed the piece, returning it to its spot. Flued moaned at the action and straightened the sash.

"Why are you so happy?" she asked. "Today is mother's Reflection, and you lost a family member to Horfa."

Shapía couldn't stop the tears from falling, and Flued held her close.

"I smile because today is a big day. You leave to fulfill your destiny. I am going to become a full delegator and our eventual king. These reasons have overshadowed the true purpose," answered Flued.

"I'm sorry for flipping the sash. It was insensitive," said Gavee.

Flued released his hold as Shapía wiped her tears.

"Another thing I'll miss," she said.

Gavee placed an arm over Shapía's shoulders. "We'll always be together as long as we carry your mother's gift."

The earl pulled forward the same necklace and grinned, forcing Shapía into her own, when Flued pulled out his chain, surprising Gavee.

"I harbor no resentment toward you, my future thunderblood. I want our union as strong as our fathers," said Flued.

The three smiled.

"You must promise me something, though," she said to Flued.

"Name it," answered Flued.

"Forgive Gavee."

Gavee dropped his shoulders and lowered his head, trying to pull away, but Shapía would not let him leave the tight circle. Flued stared at his cousin.

"I harbor no resentment," said Flued.

"That differs from forgiveness," said Shapía.

The room remained silent.

"There is nothing to forgive. I don't hold my cousin responsible."

Gavee looked up, confused.

"Why the silence? Why the glare?" questioned Shapía.

Flued pulled back.

"I'm angry at myself, and he reminds me of how I failed our family. Our queen. My mother. There was nothing further we could have expected, given all he did."

"How did you fail?" questioned Shapía.

Flued sat. "I had planned to accompany Mother, but Father requested I attend to some business in Manawe the day before. It was possible for it to wait until we got back, but going to Sovereign Hall heightened my ambitions and self-interest. I, instead, asked our cousin to escort her through the danger."

"And you would be dead," said Shapía.

"Why do you think that?" questioned Gavee.

"He's the next king. You would either kidnap or kill him, yes?" questioned Shapía.

Gavee pondered the thought.

"Yes, it had to be me," said Gavee.

"I had not considered it," said Flued.

"Neither of you can stop the dragons. We must move forward, and I need my two brothers to be united while I'm gone."

"I've never left your brother's side and shall always be his thunderblood," said Gavee.

"And I, your trusted king," said Flued.

"Why the bandage on the hand?" asked Shapía to Flued.

"Oh, I grabbed the wrong branch when doing some work around my loft. It's dumb," answered Flued.

"Good, let's go to council and eat something before you leave," said Gavee.

Before leaving, the masuras hugged and embarked on a short flight past Flued's loft and to the council rooftop. The morning food brought the clan royals mingling, eating, and discussing the day's events. Seated on his throne, the king conversed and dined with Bahg. The two brothers engaged in a deep conversation and were unaware their offspring had taken a seat at the table. Flued, Shapía, and Gavee exchanged smiles, then smiled at their father and uncle.

"When do we leave, Uncle?" asked Shapía.

The king and thunderblood remained locked in their conversation. Laughter erupted, pulling the pair away from their intense discussion. The brothers shared a laugh and gathered as a clan to have the morning meal together. They discussed the queen, and the morning sun illuminated the room.

"My wife and queen are near," said the king.

As the meal continued, the table remained lively, and the stories being shared repeated as the morning sun rose higher, signaling that it was time for Bahg and Shapía to depart for Horfa. The room fell silent. The travelers stood before the king, and all rose for the departed.

"Be safe, my daughter. I leave you in protected hands and await your return," said the king. "I send you on this path with my love."

The two embraced, and he kissed her forehead.

He turned to Bahg. "The mission's clear. Follow it with the highest regard and urgency."

"I shall, My King," answered Bahg with a head bow.

Flued advanced while they both gazed about the room. "Safe travels, my dearest sister," he said. "We wait for our oracle to return."

They embraced, and Gavee came forward, pulling her close and placing his forehead against hers.

"Be safe, my Witch'Bane sister. You travel with the one I would follow to the end of time. He'll be your light."

Shapía fought the tears, grinned, and placed the pouch on her back. Silence fell.

※ ※ ※

Bahg embraced the king, then pulled Gavee aside.

"Stay in the trees at Reflection and observe the open field. I distrust DasaRaul with their ignorance of protocol. I also do not trust Rath, so when the thunderblood gathers, remain on the outer perimeter. Things are happening within our guild, and we appear to be on the outside."

"Outside?" questioned Gavee.

"Yes, I'll explain when I return. I believe in you, son. This is your time," said Bahg.

"Be safe, Father, and take care of my cousin," said Gavee.

Bahg hugged his son, and the action shocked Gavee. His father's display of physical emotion was surprising to him, as he had never seen it before among other masuras.

Bahg gave another nod to the king, and the two flew from the council hall, heading west through the Witch'Bane forest to reach the far tree edge.

* * *

In-flight, Shapía watched the many masuras waving as they passed, and she returned the honor. The clan awaited her return, understanding her new role.

"We're going to take a fresh path to the fields. There may be some among us, not with us," said Bahg.

"These are our folks?" questioned Shapía.

"Things are changing, niece, and we must get you to Horfa."

The princess followed the thunderblood, who, to avoid detection, took a winding path through the trees. The forest remained dotted with masuras, carrying out their daily routines until they went beyond the busy trees and thick overgrowth. Its garden made flying or traveling into the clan's woods difficult. It prevented vagabonds from roaming, setting up camp for the night, or accessing the masuran city center without being noticed. Each clan had a similar section, with traps built into the hidden foliage.

With a powerful thrust of her wings, cutting through the still morning air, the princess matched the rhythm of her uncle, weaving between the trees, the rustling of leaves a constant whisper around her. Bahg never looked back, pushing the masura to understand her strength when they approached the forest edge, landing behind the last tree line. The rushing Witch'Bane River poured past, and just beyond it, an open field rolled forward with a distant tree westward, showing the DasaRaul forest. Sweat dripped from Shapía's brow, and her breath deepened.

"Why are we rushing?" she asked.

"We must reach the pier before midday, or we'll miss the ferry."

"When is the next boat?"

"Not until the moon is at midnight," answered Bahg.

"Oh," she said.

"We need to stay hidden among the wild grass and make sure the Dasa southern watch is kept far from where we are heading. We need no trouble from that clan."

"Why don't we follow the Fen Spring? It's lower in the valley."

"I trust the Fens less than Dasa."

"We're using their port?" she asked.

"We need to watch ourselves until the Ihandra ferry departs."

Shapía was confused. "I don't recall the travel through the field between Fen and us to be so treacherous."

"My dearest niece, since your mother's death, our lives have become treacherous."

"Why didn't we bring an escort?"

"It brings too much attention, and we would be stopped well before the port. We fly alone. I suggest you drink and prepare a quill before leaving the forest. Our flight must be a fast, low flight with long wings," said Bahg.

"Faster than what we just flew?"

"And lower."

Shapía glanced at the field filling before them while taking a drink from her waterskin. She didn't mind long wings, but the distance would be painful. Long wings demanded a powerful downward thrust for a successful glide, resulting in days of shoulder pain from the extensive journey. The masura searched the sky and found several vultures in the far distance, circling the lea, and sounds from behind surrounded them with bird tweets and caws echoing through the forest.

Bahg pulled his sword and nodded, lifting from their position and swooping just above the field grass. The low flight bounced the tall, tan, wild grass off the talons and under each wing flap. Shapía's teeth gritted, forcing the wind to take her farther. Moving over the open field, the Witch'Bane masuras kept a keen eye on the remote Dasa forest and another on the Fen Spring for an unknown passerby.

The princess worked hard to stay close to her uncle, with the Fen forest coming into the picture. Compared to most masuras, the Fens have a unique clan structure. The king represents a council, and the council votes on how the clan moves, with the king not having the overall authority. The Fens' central city is within what the Fens called the Fortress Mountain, connected to the Crescent Mountain range, pouring skyward from the Fen forest. Unlike most clans, they live as miners and mountain masuras versus farmers and forest growers. The Witch'Banes and Fens had a unique history, often at odds, from bad trades on both sides.

"The deadly forest approaches," warned Bahg. "Keep an eye on the sky."

Shapía clutched the bow tight and the arrow quill even tighter, her neck aching as she tried to monitor all directions. The cloudless sky allowed the sun's heat to build as they entered farther into the field and away from the cold spring. As Bahg drew near the lone tree, he drifted toward its shade. The large baellerin tree towered alone in the open lea, used as a meeting point for treaty signings between the clans. It represented peace and a haven for travelers. It sat between the Fen and DasaRaul forests, with the Raul River at its north. The masuras came to rest in its middle to escape the sun and relax the wings.

"We'll cross and follow the Raul River, keeping Fen at a distance. If needed, we are to fly westward to BataRaul."

"Are we still in danger?"

"Yes, I fear we've been spotted and followed."

The Witch'Bane thunderblood glanced back with Shapía doing the same.

"Do you see them?" she asked.

"No, I feel their presence. We should get moving and stay low. It'll be difficult for anyone to track us throughout the field."

Bahg dropped from the branch and swooped along the tall grass when the ground before him snapped open, launching a net across the thunderblood's body. It curled around his wings, and the masura tumbled through the grass.

"Uncle!"

Shapía pulled up her bow and snapped from side to side.

"Easy, Princess," came a deep voice from behind.

"This is a haven. You cannot touch me here!"

"And we shall not," said another, landing before the tree. "You mustn't use the bow while in the haven. Else, the pact is null."

She growled and lowered her aim.

"Princess, come out of the tree," said the Fen guard.

"Uncle, are you okay?" a panicked Shapía asked.

When she received no answer, she turned to the Fen. "What do you want from us?"

"Come down, and we'll discuss everything you ask."

Shapía froze, not knowing what to do, as Bahg lay motionless, wrapped in the net. She maintained the bow as it trembled in her hand, now surrounded by many masuras. Three hovered above with arrows pointing down, four surrounded the net, and three stood in front of her, swords ready. The Witch'Bane masura wanted to scream with nowhere to turn and her protector lying silent in the dirt.

"We must get to the Fen port. I must get to Ihandra today," she said.

"You need to come with us. We'll discuss what happens next."

The largest masura pointed a sword at Bahg's head, and Shapía stowed the bow, floating down to the soldiers.

"Where are we going?"

"Follow in peace, and nothing should happen to your thunderblood."

Shapía agreed, and the three soldiers rose in the sky with the Witch'Bane princess following close behind. Looking back, she saw Bahg was still in the net. She wondered how they would transport him as they approached the Fen forest. Her stomach tightened as more guards came into view among the trees as they moved deeper into the unknown. The trees and bushes appeared darker, with the silence holding its own against birds or wild animals. They reached a small tree loft painted black with a tiny window and a plain door holding a balcony ledge. They approached, and the three guards hovered, pointing at the door.

"You'll stay here for now until we call for you."

"What about my thunderblood? What happened to him? Why am I being held? We did nothing but fly across open land. I demand answers."

"You'll get your answer soon enough, Princess. For now, you must wait."

Shapía hovered in front of the door and scowled at her captors. They should be at the port preparing to leave for Ihandra.

"Not prisoners," she groaned.

Nobody knew their location, and she could not break free from the fear clutching her hand. She pushed the door forward, opening to a simple roost containing a single table, chair, no hallway, and a door leading to a smaller bedroom. The masura paused, entered, and closed the door. The room turned darker, with the window letting in a single light. She peered out the opening to endless trees and thick bushes.

"What do I do now?"

* * *

As the day moved forward, her stomach grumbled. Perched on the roost, fear and anger overwhelmed her, uncertain of her escape. The anger drove her to the window, where she yelled at the Fen guard she couldn't see but sensed nearby.

"I demand to see your king!" she said. "I am a princess of Witch'Bane!"

No response was given, and she sat in the chair. The heat within the loft became thick and silent as the afternoon rolled on when she heard the motion on the ledge. Shapía, sitting and staring, heard mumbling, followed by a knock.

"Princess, come with us."

Shapía took a deep breath and composed herself before opening the door.

The wind rushed in, carrying with it the scent of rain and the sound of distant thunder, but she remained silent. Farther into the Fen forest, the guards stumbled before successfully reaching the Witch'Bane. She never looked back and waited to be guided to their next location.

The tree lofts came into view as masuras flew about their daily business without paying attention to the Witch'Bane. Moving closer to the center, the flight continued through the trees. The Fen masuras did not break their stride, pushing Shapía, veering left and right over and over until they reached a distance from the forest's edge. She noticed a circular clearing with smoke rising from its center and guards posted within the trees. The three masuras floated into the opening and landed in front of a roaring fire.

The tallest masura the princess had ever seen stepped from a table and approached, drinking from a stein. His wings and hair were dark black, with a patch over the left eye where a deep scar drifted down his face and onto his chest. The muscular masura handed a cup to Shapía.

"Drink, Princess, and eat from our table," the masura said in a dark voice.

Shapía did not wait and gulped every drop as it trickled down her throat. She rushed to the table, grabbing bread and biting into its soft core. The food slammed into her gut, and she exhaled, continuing to eat when she noticed the stillness.

"Bahg!" she screamed.

The princess ran to her uncle, who slumped against a tree, chained at the feet. He had a beaten and bloody face, and he struggled to lift his head. She took him in her hands, and he opened an eye, trying to smile.

"Well, hello."

"What have they done to you?"

"I suspect they aren't friends with Witch'Bane anymore."

The thunderblood smiled through a busted lip, and Shapía glared at the large masura.

"He will be avenged!"

"Princess, things are changing within our lands, and you know nothing of what the future holds. We've been paid a mighty gem to stop you and this thunderblood from leaving the island."

Shapía tried to understand, looking over her uncle's wounds. She returned to the table, grabbed a cup, and went back to Bahg.

"Why, why do it?" she yelled.

"It's a simple return for something you would not understand. Correct, Bahg?"

The tall masura finished the stein and wiped his mouth. Bahg spat blood, holding his tongue.

"Why would the Fen King do such a thing?" demanded Shapía.

"Losha, come here, my sister," said the tall masura.

An older female came from the dark forest with a heavy limp. The white-haired, fair masura pressed her right arm against her body and struggled with each step. Her gray wings lacked feathers, and her talons dragged across the dirt. Her right eye had a white pupil, and her lower jaw was askew to the left with an overbite. With an arm around her slouched shoulders, the towering masura positioned themselves before Bahg.

"Sister, here's your hero."

The broken masura tried to laugh, coughing until tears fell.

"Look at you now, Witch'Bane," said Losha. "My wounds are now your wounds."

She spat at him, balled a fist, and stood between Bahg and the Fens.

"Enough! I demand answers!" growled Shapía.

The tall king stepped toward the Witch'Bane princess, and she faced her fear. He took a hand and brushed back her brown hair.

"My beautiful sister was whole once until she was left to die by her hero. The one masura who was to be her protector during the Great Masuran War. The one who promised to protect her and bring her home. Instead, Witch'Bane did what they did: protected themselves and ensured Witch'Bane was safe. Your hero uncle was betrothed to Losha before the war, before the great move from Rath."

He moved and squatted next to Bahg, lifting his face.

"Your clan's unity and protection with our clan is no longer. Clan unification is complete. Past crimes demand retribution. I, King Torum, denounce you, Witch'Bane, and curse the day you led us into the Upper Realm destruction."

The king tossed Bahg's face to the side, pushing the thunderblood's body. He took Losha by the hand and led her to the center. As he observed the trees, more Fen masuras appeared, emerging from the dense forest.

"There they are, the great Witch'Bane, the mighty Bahg, and his sweet Princess Shapía. She wishes to know why we would treat her thunderblood with such discontent!"

The Fen masuras laughed, and the king returned to Shapía.

"I'm unsure what you know about your lineage, but it has been brutal and selfish. This newfound agreement has Witch'Bane returning to its roots, back to a sub-family with no forest of its own. Also, payment is due for its past offenses."

"My father and brother intend not to allow this injustice to our thunderblood to pass without consequence. They meet today with all clans, and when word reaches them about what has happened, you'll find your forest in war," said Shapía.

The king laughed. "Take her to the workers' quarters. She'll learn her place soon enough."

Shapía glanced in all directions as Fen masuras approached, trapping her. She looked back at Bahg.

"Get to Horfa," he spat.

"I will, Uncle! I promise!" she screamed.

* * *

Gavee reached the Lohr forest and scouted the new amphitheater, an impressive theater dug into a large hillside facing the woods, with a massive field lingering behind it. The forest, horseshoed from left to right, had Gavee in awe with its immensity. It would fit all clans, remaining close enough to the woods to safeguard the ceremony. In the Upper Realms' southern section, the Lohr forest sat, and the theater, near Lohr's west side, was also close to Rath for visiting. The proximity did concern Gavee.

Following the Nathe River south, the Witch'Bane royal flight would pass the Ellebasi Mountain into the Lohr forest. Further to the southwest, butting Lohr against Rath, was where the queen and his mother learned their warrior skills. The Lohr and Rath clans, along with La'Darium, Ramus, Ranois, Toren, and the extinct Tryolics clan, are regarded as the Ancient Ones. The Young Ones are the Witch'Bane, BataRaul, DasaRaul, Fen, and Manawe clans.

An ancient presence lingered in the forest, where the deep green trees covered the southern expanse. The thunderblood trainee had completed a few missions with Bahg in the Lohr forest, but today they only stayed to study its growth. Thunderbloods could travel through the outer stretches to ensure their clan's safety and understand the forest's edge. The Lohr posts dotted before the massive field, but the rolling downward hill concerned Gavee.

He settled onto the biggest tree, and the scent of pine filled his nostrils as he leaned against its sturdy trunk. With his entry, the mighty Bellow seemed to sigh as he inspected the field of swaying tall grass. The thoughts of being the lone thunderblood and its responsibility for the clan's safety built into anxiety. He cherished the family's trust in their protection with high regard, even if it started weighing on his shoulders.

"I wish I had his mind. He would see the things I should," said Gavee.

Gavee wrestled with his thoughts and drew a long breath.

"Relax, employ your training, and observe how the grass moves in the wind. If there are traps, it'll tell the truth."

The masura took flight, soaring over the expanse and finding its position rolled beyond sight. Thunderbloods from many clans he recognized, but didn't know the names of, filled the quiet area. He hoped to meet up with the one he watched float into the amphitheater. Datta, the BataRaul thunderblood, known throughout the masuran clans, wielded a skilled sword and a history following the name. It seemed strange she wasn't a BataRaul yet worked on protecting royalty. The history taught about her escape from the grangrul arenas, where Datta fought daily to remain alive. Gavee desired to know this masura and to train to fight the grangrul. It would be difficult to complete because she was a hardened warrior and had few conversations.

Datta floated higher than the others as she circled the area and hovered above Lohr. Gavee began a slow climb, hoping Datta would take note and move to meet him. The earl leveled at her and floated closer in her direction. His attention shifted to the theater before realizing Datta had moved from her spot.

"May I help you, Witch'Bane?" asked a female voice.

Gavee turned to find Datta floating behind him.

"Um, I was just trying to get a better view. I saw your position, and I thought..."

"You're Earl Gavee, correct?"

"I am," he said. "You're Datta?"

"Why are you following me, Witch'Bane?"

"Oh, I wasn't, um..."

"You are, and it's ugly."

"I just wanted to talk to you and—"

"I choose not to train with others," she interrupted. "Besides, if your subtle climb is an example of your measure, I'd say I've trained beyond your knowledge."

"It was a sloppy way for me to—"

"I'll catch you later, Witch'Bane. I'm sure I'll see you coming."

Datta winked and smiled, drifting down toward the Lohr trees. Gavee looked at her auburn wings fluttering in the wind and the swords crossed on her back.

"Um, oh? What's wrong with you? You're a confident thunderblood. Show her where your training skills have landed, you fool."

The horn sounded from the amphitheater, calling the thunderbloods to gather on the stage. Gavee lowered alongside the others to a lone masura standing before them, twirling a sword tip into the wooden structure.

"Welcome to our beautiful amphitheater and home to the Lohr clan," said the Lohr thunderblood. "I'm sure you desire the protection plan we've established. We enlisted the Rath Elite to secure the field, and we'll have protection throughout, from the mountains to the trees. We hold this honor in high regard and thank the families for their support. If you look behind, to the theater, each section is clan colored, marking where your families shall sit."

The party turning saw the vast theater emerging from the earth. Gavee noticed Rath positioned center with his clan third to the left, next to Lohr. He turned to the masura, who smirked, and the thunderblood group stared at Gavee.

"Question, Witch'Bane?"

"My clan's location is unacceptable. Reflection honors our queen, yet we're positioned so far left. We sent how and where Witch'Bane would be seated."

"Your request was received and considered by my King. We celebrate a Rath warrior princess who led this southern area during a great war. Her direction saved these forests from falling into wretched hands. Rath has lost its warrior princess, and under your watch, I believe. Witch'Bane is to be seated where it's appropriate."

Gavee gritted and clenched his fist at the words. Eyes redirected to the Witch'Bane, and he continued to stare at the masura, who wore a smirk.

"You speak as if you understand what is happening today. Reflection is for my queen, and respect is for her family. She fought to unite, and we wish for Reflection to continue to build this unification," said Gavee.

"We respect her family, and the rightful masuran clans are united."

"The move does not go unnoticed. It degrades everything the queen stood for: a united masura."

"The arrangement remains, Witch'Bane," said the Rath Thunderblood.

The other thunderbloods surrounded Rath, including Toren. Gavee was alone except for a lone elf, Princess Lamír, the thunderblood of the Dulisar elves. The Dulisar grinned at Witch'Bane and stood next to the masura. Datta remained on her own.

"Dulisar is not to take part in masuran politics. We have a long-standing peace accord with Witch'Bane, and it is to continue," said Lamír.

Gavee glared at the Toren Thunderblood beside Rath, but kept the peace.

"Continue," he said.

The Toren Thunderblood turned to the group. "When your families arrive, they'll go directly to their locations. You'll find Toren and Rath Elites hardening the perimeter upon the full seating and the guards filling into the fields behind for additional protection."

"Are we expecting an attack?" questioned the Ramus Thunderblood.

"Word of this masuran gathering has reached as far as Eden. Many groups are going to advance to make use of this opportunity here or in your forests. I'm ensuring we have taken measures to protect us."

Gavee listened, working on his own question, but not finding one to bring forward. The group mingled, keeping the side conversations among those close, thus keeping the family connections intact. Gavee, Lamír, and Datta all remained apart from the pack.

"I thought Dulisar was not attending," said Datta.

"It was my belief when we spoke last, but my king became interested in the ceremony when we received information on its location," answered Lamír.

"How's your training, Gavee?" asked Lamír.

"It must be well if he is here representing the clan already," said Datta.

Gavee caught the eye roll but ignored it. "Reflection has our clan moving in many directions, and I'll take on the full thunderblood role next autumn."

"Even after the queen…?" questioned Datta.

"And you have fought dragons before?" Lamír asked Datta.

"Always Witch'Bane's protector," said Datta. "Besides, there's no proof."

"Enough," said Gavee. "I need no one to protect or defend me. I appreciate and honor our friendship, Lamír, but anyone who places their questioning eye on me for the queen's death will never have their minds changed, even when it is proven true."

The three stood looking at the theater.

"I'm surprised, Datta," said Lamír, "that you would side with these masuras. After all, I believe the Raths tried to have you removed."

Datta released a long sigh.

"This is why I need you in my life, Lamír. My mouth overtakes my senses, and you pull me back to them. Gavee, I'm sorry for my ignorance. I know the truth will finally allow you to be free of this unkindness."

"At least BataRaul will sit along our outer side," he said.

"I find this whole thing disrespectful. It appears it is more for the politics and insults to your clan than for the Witch'Bane queen," said Datta.

"It's been this way since I can remember, being the outside clan, even though we brought balance to the Upper Realm."

"Dulisar recognizes it and stands with you at any cost. Witch'Bane has our trust."

"Same with BataRaul. I know little about the Upper Realm War. The Tryolics, my lost clan, had their fight against the grangrul in the Lower Realm, and Rath ignored our plea for help. This righteousness from the great clan ended us, and my family is lost forever. I would never trust a Rath or a Lohr, yet their Elite surround us," said Datta.

"Be alert is what I'm hearing," said Gavee.

"More than alert, Witch'Bane. Something bigger is developing. I'm concerned about the open disrespect and the other masuras siding with Lohr and Rath. I must prepare," said Datta. "After Reflection, Lamír and I are called to Eden for a treasure hunt. You're welcome to come along and partake."

Gavee received their approving gaze; he felt good, confident.

"I'm in," he said.

"I'll see you both after Reflection."

Datta floated off, sticking along the eastern tree line, disappearing beyond sight quicker than Gavee expected. The simple way her wings moved kept him in awe. When he searched the eyes of the other thunderbloods, they deliberately redirected their gaze away from the masura.

"You are welcome to sit with my family," Gavee told Lamír.

"No, I've found a location. Thank you, W.B.," said Lamír.

"Good. I must focus and understand the seating. My king will be angry."

"It would anger any king. Be safe, my friend," said Lamír.

"Thanks again for the dagger," he said.

"The baellerin wood allowed my forest, our protection, to grow because of it."

"Keep that low," worried Gavee.

"I'm sorry, nobody knows, and we have kept it a secret. My king was surprised by the kindness and had the smithy specially make the dagger for the finder," she said.

"It would bring certainty to the war with DasaRaul. They already suspect it was us."

"They stole it themselves," said Lamír.

"We know this, and the thunderbloods know this, but do you think they'll come to Witch'Bane's side?"

"Dulisar shall," she said. "Take care, my close friend."

The elf departed, vanishing into the tall field grass. Gavee ignored the prying eyes of the others and lifted with anger, drifting to the amphitheater's top and then coming to rest on the grass overlooking the deep field. The distant Sora Mountains kept him staring as he focused on his clan. He looked toward the wild field and waited for his family, cursing the situation. He played the words over and over and wanted to scream but maintained composure, not giving them the satisfaction.

"They will all pay for the disrespectful display. If not now, in the future. I will never forget."

Chapter Seven

The day carried forward with Gavee remaining at the theater's overlook. The thunderblood encounter soured his mind on the guild, and he watched them disappear within Lohr. He observed Datta fly in a repetitive pattern before the mountains. The urge to train with Bata's thunderblood became a necessity.

"Focus," he said.

He dropped the thought, concentrating on the distant masuras flying toward his location. They came into view, showing the black and blue of the Ranois clan, easing Gavee's mind as he watched them march through the clear sky. The seating change and the thunderbloods' actions would surely anger the king, and Gavee would shoulder the blame.

"Did they make a mistake?" he mumbled.

In his thoughts, the masura continued to struggle. *This is for the queen. I am strong enough.*

Gavee rose higher in the tree until he reached the top. He took deep breaths of the cool air and understood it was too early for Witch'Bane's arrival. King Arul intended to make a statement with their clan arriving last and flying in before the other families. The masura watched the thickening clouds, patiently waiting for the day's end. His thoughts wandered to his family during happier moments, when his eyes closed and his body trembled. The bright light drew him in, and it all slipped into a green vision.

The landscape before him moved forward with snow-capped mountains and a snowy vale. He drifted without control, and the view turned on its own as it scanned the hills. The wind muffled any sound when a low rumble rippled in the distance. As the mountainside sloped down, the view extended to the tree line. His sight focused on a distant, dark object moving amidst the clouds, heading in his direction. The rumble came again, and a giant dragon popped into his vision. Facing doom, he panicked at the soaring view. Unable to speak or act, the view's sudden disappearance startled him awake, causing him to break out in a sweat.

Gavee took a gasping breath and tried to grasp the current vision. He shook his head to erase the confusion when a bellowing horn disrupted the silence. He peered north as the royal clans showed for Reflection.

What are these random dreams? he thought.

The Witch'Bane thunderblood focused on the mission and searched behind him with Lohr already in their position.

"Where are you?"

The amphitheater filled as the sun rose, extending into the afternoon. He fidgeted, rising, then lowering, waiting for his clan, when a familiar black crow landed beside him on the treetop.

"Where have you been?" asked Gavee.

The crow cawed.

"Yes, I recommend remaining as the crow. What I experienced could place you in danger."

Grunt continued to caw.

"I'll explain later. For now, thoughts on the area's security?"

Grunt cawed.

"I agree. It is more open than expected, yet Lohr has hidden dugouts to stop any oddities."

Grunt cawed.

"Yes, there are SkyRiders."

Grunt cawed.

"I'm certain. It's a masuran trick. I recognize the ploy. We're safe."

Gavee ignored the next few caws with nerves growing thin, when a distant sparkle grabbed his attention. The Witch'Bane shields appeared in the closing sun's light, with the royal court building behind them. They flew in dress armor, with Flued leading the march flight and the king in its front center, enclosed by the Latuery. The royals lined up behind, while the Witch'Bane troops fell in around them with wings flapping in synchronization. Honored and deeply moved, he smiled widely and gratefully as he gazed upon the majestic sight. The sheer scale and beauty left him breathless. The earl looked at the venue where the BataRaul, La'Darium, Lohr, Manawe, Ramus, Ranois, Rath, and Torem clans awaited their arrival.

"Just as the king planned."

Conscious of the king's presence, the thunderblood inhaled deeply. His heart pounded in anticipation of the surprise with the seating. Wondering about the king's reaction left him in a position he had never experienced. Fear and shame were all he could conjure as the Witch'Bane entourage lowered and approached the seats without incident. BataRaul sat right, Ranois left.

Gavee and Grunt reached a sizable empty tree, affording a side view of the stage and a refined look at King Arul. Flued stood with a scowl. The king made no remark, and Lord Taronquel stewed with the change. The Witch'Bane's civil reaction surprised Gavee.

A sea of faces surrounded the royal clan seated in the center. Their section ten seats across and twenty rows back, the air thick with anticipation. The group remained silent as all eight clans settled, studying the stage. Before them, the simple scene contained a large item underneath a draped cloth with the Rath crest on its front. The ceremony would begin once the sun disappeared, and dusk was upon them.

"Where's Rhile?" Gavee questioned. "Why isn't the lahd next to Flued?"

The missing expert fighter was an oddity. This moment would allow Rhile to show the essential position in the clan. This was a special masuran occasion, and her absence was a concern.

"The majority are here and sitting together. Why would such a distinguished warrior miss it?"

Grunt remained silent.

The sun fell closer to the horizon, and torches were lit throughout the grounds and the Lohr forest. Two enormous cauldrons at the far ends torched high with a blue flame at their tips. Giant drums pounded from the woods, and torches danced in and around the trees with their rhythm. The dancing torches lit the stage where a smiling female masura floated to its center. Dusk settled, and Gavee noticed several thunderbloods appearing behind the assembly, returning to the fields. The open field, forest, and theater offered complete protection, and the desire to watch Reflection kept his eyes on the stage.

"My King, royal court, and wonderful guests, I am Lord Ster, head council for clan Lohr, and we welcome you to our amphitheater as we hold Reflection for the warrior princess and queen, Phawa."

The announcement brought polite applause from the audience.

"Her presence in all masuran forests is well known, her the ability to bring us all together to build a great bridge for the clans shows here, now, as we sit united today." She smiled. "The Reflection ceremony shall end with the monument's unveiling, crafted by Lohr artisans, then a feast, where we may enjoy each other's company."

Grunt returned to his weasel self, staying close to the tree.

"What are you doing?" whispered Gavee.

"I must. There is a crow in the distant tree, staring, and I'm afraid of its intentions."

"I need your crow's eyesight to see through the shadows. Dark clouds appear north of where the moon should be shining."

"I still maintain my night vision," said Grunt. "I'll keep a watch."

Gavee directed his attention to the far distance as lightning rippled across gathering clouds. Thunder had yet to reach their location, and he hoped it would remain north.

"Our forest?" questioned Gavee.

"We have masuras to secure our home," said Grunt.

"Those clouds are moving fast, Witch'Bane," said a female voice.

Gavee pulled his sword, and Grunt readied his walking stick as Datta floated down and landed on a limb. The masura, frustrated, sheathed her sword, her gaze fixed on the weasel.

"Have you ever seen a storm move like it?" she asked.

"Who's this?" questioned Grunt.

"Datta."

"The famous Bata thunderblood?" questioned Grunt.

"Yes," said Gavee.

"We should investigate, Witch'Bane," said Datta.

"We? Why are you pulling me with you?" questioned Gavee.

"I thought you were different, Witch'Bane. Or am I mistaken?" asked Datta.

Gavee studied the clouds with another lightning strike, then a slight rumble.

"I think we should go," said Grunt.

"It's moving fast," said Gavee. "And south."

"Let's go, Witch'Bane," said Datta.

Datta rose and flew into the darkness. Grunt snapped the stick, and the crow followed, not waiting for Gavee. The earl's attention turned to the stage, where a fresh masura captivated the audience. He could no longer see Datta or Grunt in the dark sky and raised his wings.

"Just go already," he said.

The thunderblood pushed the breeze against the downdraft, catapulting him toward Grunt. Reflection continued, even as the thunder grew louder and the wind howled through the expanse. He floated alongside Datta, who showed the storm's rolling edge.

"None of this is normal!"

Gavee nodded, pointing to Lohr, where hidden Lohr field fighters appeared from their hideouts as the gusts tormented the field. The storm clouds were on the move, and they had to alert the clans.

The amphitheater had changed. Its many torch lights were now blocked, with a massive cover pulled over the audience. Lohr had prepared for severe weather with a long canvas wrapped around a sturdy wooden frame and sides covering the masuran seats. It stretched toward the woods and secured among the trees.

Gavee and Datta came to a hover, awed by the massive protection.

"I've seen nothing like it," said Gavee.

"It still won't protect whatever is creating the storm," said Datta.

They landed before the theater, and Datta leaned down, touching the fabric.

"It'll be destroyed."

Gavee followed, and Grunt turned into the weasel.

"I sense possessed magic headed in our direction," said Grunt. "I can taste it, and my staff vibrates with a warning."

The storm swirled, and the darkness came closer, with the rain hiding everything within as the two thunderbloods readied their blades.

"Let's move them!" said Datta.

"It's too late. The madness is here!" said Grunt.

The downpour moved like a solid wall, pressing the wild grass as it mowed the field, and it came upon the masuras, stalling short of the theater. Gavee's eagle eyes focused beyond the rain, taking in the many shapes headed at them, bounding forward in an endless run. When lightning lit the landscape, the hidden figures came into view.

"Barkapes! There are barkapes!" said Gavee.

The storm surged, its deluge hitting Reflection and pouring into the Lohr forest. Blackness filled the space in front of them. The only sound came from the thunder. Gavee looked to Grunt, and the weasel clutched the staff in front of him as a blue light glowed on its end. His friend leaned into the wind with a white orb in his left paw. Then Gavee looked at Datta, holding both blades and concentrating on the faraway images.

The evil lurking on the island noticed the masuran gathering and promptly unleashed its wrath.

Far in the distance, the lightning continued, and the violent winds raged. The masuras could not fly in such a wind, keeping them to a fast ground run. It would be a natural attack, holding the flying fighters grounded and trapping the clans under the tarp. Grunt raised the white orb and pushed its light farther out, giving them a wider view. Field fighters had created several lined barriers in front of the seats, and the outside group fought the enraged apes. The massive tarp whipped in the wind, and the trees swayed back and forth with the thunderous clouds stalling overhead.

"What is it?" asked Gavee.

"It's magic unleashed!" answered Grunt.

The weasel wheeled, its orb flashing across the amphitheater, deep into the trees. The light revealed a horrifying scene: masuras battling each other and grangrul attacking in the woods, a chaotic mess of clashing steel and guttural roars.

"DasaRaul's colors!" said Datta. "The clans are under attack!"

"Have they formed an alliance with the grangrul?" questioned Gavee.

The battle raged in front of and behind them, with the thunder clapping at every turn. Gavee turned and shoved the sword into the canvas, slipping through the top. It was chaos as the Dasa masuras and grangrul infiltrated the stage, fighting to reach the masuran kings.

The Latuery and Witch'Bane soldiers created a solid wall around their king and etta, preventing an attack.

"Where is Rhile?" questioned Gavee.

Grunt lowered and sent an orb above Witch'Bane, grabbing their attention. Gavee alerted Flued about the barkapes in the open space, leading them to move from the death trap. The prince pointed ahead, showing they had no place to go forward.

"Dare we go up?" asked Gavee.

"If we remain here, the barkapes are going to topple overhead and come down on us!" said Grunt.

Lightning struck a giant Bellow tree in front of the stage, felling the massive object and smashing the wooden platform, sending grangruls flying into the masuras. United against the lizard folk, the clans fought fiercely throughout the amphitheater. The grangruls' body armor covered their torsos and provided little protection on their legs and arms, giving the sword a simple target. The silver sling was helpful in the strong wind, with the archers useless. In front of the stage, a thick battle raged, leaving King Arul trapped but safe under the tarp. Gavee worked toward the king.

"We must leave! The barkapes, they'll tear into the tarp soon enough!"

"The current situation has us blocked from all sides!" answered Flued.

"Witch'Banes!" said Grunt.

The Lohr and Rath clans disappeared through a hidden exit and funneled their way from the attack. Flued signaled for them to charge behind Lohr, remaining close, hoping to follow their lead.

King Arul pointed to King Bereet, BataRaul's leader, and the clan remained locked with Witch'Bane. A furious storm roared overhead, and the tarp ends flapped in the strong wind. The cover bowed, and its moorings strained against the pull, with rain flooding the stage.

Grunt touched the ground and read its vibrations. "The rain is easing, and I perceive wings in the air!"

"Wings? What wings?" questioned the king.

"Masuran, but they hold a distinct vibration. The barkapes have entered the Lohr forest, and I believe those tunnels might lead us into a trap!"

"What direction do you suggest?" asked Flued.

"Up," answered Grunt.

The weasel pointed to the opening Gavee had created, cutting into the fabric to make the hole larger. They looked to their ruler, who agreed with the Witch'Bane clan marching to the top. The Witch'Bane thunderblood, coming upon a charging barkape, popped through the easing rain. The beast gnashed its teeth and howled as it charged in one long bound at the masura. He waited for the creature to arrive and then rose in time for the animal to miss its target. It rolled across the tarp and slipped from sight, with Gavee turning and ready for the next beast.

Grunt sent a fiery orb through the opening and lit the area, showing the thick clouds remaining and masuras flying overhead.

Witch'Bane soldiers reached the opening when another rip formed at the distant end, and Datta popped through with swords at their ready. The two clans poured into the open field, attacking the remaining barkapes and Dasa masuras, dropping in from their flight. Gavee met the attacking masura headlong and in mid-flight, and the exchange sent sparks from the swords. Yellow skin and smoky white glazed eyes marked the masura, though it wore the Dasa colors. The odd masura foamed from its mouth, and its sword throws fell limp and uncontrolled. The thunderblood parried the initial jabs before thrusting the tip into the chest. Gavee repeated the same steps as the masuras fell from the sky.

Grunt sent orb after orb into the rushing barkapes, electrifying the beasts and sending charred ape hair wafting into the downpour. The weasel twirled the cane and broke the crazed ape's jaw, crushing the knee of another and ending their lives with a red orb. The magic rolled from Grunt's tongue, and the shapeshifter's power poured down on the screeching apes before they could bound for the smaller creature. Gavee remained close to Grunt, using the magic to help fight.

"The clan has moved beyond the tarp and onto open land. The king may be in danger!" said Gavee.

Grunt sent a small red orb into a barkape when a sizable blue explosion tossed barkapes and masuras in the far-distant field. Another crashed and shattered in an oncoming attack. Gavee and Grunt grappled with the source of the help as another explosion ripped through the trees.

"There!" said Grunt.

The Witch'Bane thunderblood squinted in the light rain and waited as clouds faded from the moonlight. In the rainy distance, a blue energy ball formed, then hurled toward the lea by a horned being riding a spotted pegasus. It repeated its pattern and gave a path for the royal clans to continue their fight north.

"It looks to be Crym," said Gavee.

"A what?" asked Grunt.

"Not a what, but a who! It's Crym, a TonTar. He's a friend and one I trust. Make your way to the king and offer help at the front!"

"As you command!"

Grunt took to running, sending orbs into the path before him, surprising Gavee, since his friend limped when he walked. The weasel went to help with the king's protection, with the DasaRaul masuras and barkapes striking the party.

The thunderblood's sword vibrated with each swing, striking a Dasa fighter with identical white eyes, lost in a distant realm.

Datta landed next to Gavee. "We need to move our kings!"

"We have Crym helping!" said Gavee.

"Why is he here? The tontars don't come to Breiv unless requested. Traveling from Anayana is a long journey," said Datta.

"My father requested the tontars come for Reflection. He did not trust this day of alliance with the Ancient Ones," said Gavee.

"I understand. I trust none of the families except the two I fly with tonight," said Datta. "Why would the tontars even help a masura, much less a clan? What else is going on here, trainee?"

The last word embarrassed and angered Gavee. He finished an enemy with a roar and turned to Datta.

"I owe you no explanation! Both clans are out and rushing as fast as they can through the fight!" said Gavee.

Datta did not press.

"They have to move faster. The clouds are gaining in strength, and it'll be impossible to fly!" screamed Datta. "Head to your king and push the party onward! Crym will lead the way!"

"I'll direct the clans to Crym. Let's fight as one!" said Gavee.

"Without haste!"

A thunderous roar muddied the expanse, with a sliver of moon giving some light. From the northeast, the storm approached while the meadow illuminated, filled with barkapes, and the sky opened for flight. Gavee reached Flued, who battled the Dasa fighters in a dull skirmish. The future king ducked a lunge from a sword, then rolled, missing another and returning to a hover. Flued danced the blade against his enemies until he brought a backswing, sending the head of one on a roll. The second roared in response, yet Flued's sword ended the fight. The prince, now covered in masuran blood, took notice of Gavee.

"We have to hurry, for the sky ahead gives us flight forward!" said Gavee.

"Once we reach the ridge top, it'll give us a better view going north!" answered Flued.

"We have a tontar helping," said Gavee.

"I saw it on the pegasus. Why is it here?"

"It's Crym, and he's here to help."

"What is a tontar doing on Breiv?" questioned Flued.

"He's on a mission for us, and I requested his return for Reflection."

"What mission?"

"We'll discuss this after we reach our forest. Let Crym fight for us."

"I need you to get beyond the ridge and help lead the line to Witch'Bane," said Flued.

"I shall," said Gavee.

The thunderblood parried another Dasa fighter, sending the blade through its side. He battled amidst the drizzle, facing one masura after another appearing from different directions. He grabbed a Dasa by its neck and found it was a young girl, eyes glazed and not carrying a weapon.

"Something's wrong. These masuras cannot be DasaRaul."

He reached the hilltop, and the long valley stretched alongside the Nathe River. Scattered throughout the tall grass, the barkapes clamored toward them, and fewer Dasa fighters than expected were in the sky. The sky to the northwest rumbled and roared, coming toward their location. The human city, Eptiwuh, glowed in the darkness, while the Witch'Bane forest lingered far away.

Two masuras attacked the earl, but he countered, dropping one with a gut shot and the other in the head, knocking a barkape from its run. He pushed forward, seeking the king behind him, and Flued near to reach.

The king thrust his blade into the lifeless Dasa fighter as the Latuery fought to protect their king, slowing the progress of the never-ending onslaught and reaching for the forest's safety.

Below, Grunt defeated the barkapes after shifting into the panther.

"We'll be hit by the storm before reaching home!" said Gavee to a Witch'Bane fighter.

"Our army waits for us on the river's far side, sir," said the fighter. "We just need to get there!"

"Keep pushing. I see the fight growing in our favor! Use these ten—forge ahead!"

"Aye, sir, we'll fight through it!" said the fighter.

Gavee watched them rip through the Dasa horde, and he flew back to Flued.

"These are not normal Dasa fighters!" he said.

"We're aware. The unknown masuras wear Dasa colors, so they are all the same, our enemy!" said Flued.

"Something else drives them to their death!" said Gavee.

"Whatever Dasa sided with shall be their death!" said Flued.

The storm swept into the field with precision lightning strikes. Its crack and rumble vibrated the plain and moved through the billowing clouds. The air filled with electricity, and the strikes rained down upon each other, pushing the troops apart. The masuras weaved through bolts, entering the fray. Gavee protected the king's backside, downing any arrow strike or thrown dagger.

The river was approaching, and the Witch'Bane's army awaited their arrival. The lead group reached the flowing water when static in the air made Gavee glance behind him. A sudden energy pulse threw him forward and tumbling end over end and taking down fellow masuras. He hovered above the screeching barkapes, working off the dizziness. Grunt maintained a blue orb over them, and the Latuery deflected the crazed apes with Flued crouched in the center.

The king lay on his wings, and Gavee panicked, veering down to the group.

"My King!" he said.

Flued held the king's head and Lord Taronquel's hand. King Arul's eyes glazed to a smoky white, and a black mark smoldered on the metal chest protector. The Latuery formed a protective layer around their king, with the riverbank just beyond the last row. Arul's body convulsed, and his hands grasped wildly above him.

"Lightning struck him in the chest!" angered Flued.

"We have to get him to the medicus," said Taronquel.

"This is sorcery. I doubt the medicus will know," worried Gavee.

"We have no other choice," said Flued.

"Sir, Bata's king was also hit," said a guard.

Gavee stood, and both formations reached the ground, spreading to the hillside.

"Latuery, king formation!" said Flued. "Gavee, return to Bata and tell them they shall seek refuge in our forest."

"I shall!"

"Grunt, keep the light from the king. We want no more attention on his location."

"Yes, Sire." Grunt shifted to the black panther as lightning continued to strike, launching its victims skyward.

"We move now!" said Flued.

Gavee stormed from the party and engaged an enemy, severing its torso. A sideways force sent him rolling down a small hill, landing him on the riverbank. The masura jumped to his feet with a sword ready when a barkape pounced before he could take a swing. Piercing the top armor, the ape bit into Gavee's shoulder. The thunderblood grabbed his dagger and jabbed into its leg. The ape released its hold and slapped the masura to the ground. With a roar and chest-thumping, the fanged beast charged the masura again, whose head still rang from the blow. He waited, rolled forward on the barkape's lunge, and thrust upward, ripping into its torso and spilling blood across Gavee's body. The ape was dead before it hit the ground, and it lay covered in its blood. The thunderblood sat, shaking the thumping in his head.

"Come on, Thunderblood!" he said.

The earl of Witch'Bane leaped into flight and headed to the BataRaul party. The batarōhn surrounded their fallen leader, who lay in a similar trance. Datta met him in flight.

"Our army is fortified beyond the river. Take refuge with us until you may safely reach your forest," said Gavee. "Our king is in the same state."

"Come, let us talk to Prince Mahtri," said Datta.

They lowered within the batarōhn, and Prince Mahtri tried to wake his father.

"Prince Mahtri, you will never wake him," said Gavee.

The Bata prince looked up with despair.

"My king lay in the same manner. Come and take refuge at Witch'Bane."

"King Arul has fallen the same?" questioned Mahtri. "Let's move past the chaos and set a plan for revenge against Dasa!"

"These are not Dasa fighters," said Gavee to Datta.

"Regardless, they are involved somehow," said Mahtri.

"We can discuss it later at Witch'Bane. For now, we need to get away from the storm," said Datta.

The storm raged forward, and the party moved across the river. The Witch'Bane's army stopped any further attack and stood firm against the Dasa masuras. Both kings flew to the forest's shelter, and the chaos continued to thunder overhead. The Witch'Banes' home was under attack from the evil wind, with barkapes and Dasa fighters in their forest. Gavee found the guard general, Saor, and grabbed him by the arm, causing the general almost to strike the earl.

"My apologies, Sire," said the general.

"None needed, General. I would have followed through with a strike," said Gavee. "Maintain the line here and prevent the evil from reaching the first trees to our home."

"Upon my death would be the only way they ever reach our tree line, our home!" said the general.

"The king is not in good health. Prince Flued is required to take over," said Gavee.

"The king is injured? When, how? Where was the Latuery?" asked the general.

"I was there. It was a lightning strike. No way to avoid it."

"My post remains until word comes from my king."

"Thank you, General."

"Thank you, Thunderblood. May Nathe be your guardian."

"As yours."

The Witch'Bane looked out at the dark field through the soft drizzle and tried to understand the fight and flight, taking them from the deepest part of the Upper Realm to their home. Even in the faint moonlight, one could see the many dead bodies with the curse befalling his homeland. The widespread carnage left him wondering if his visions had foreshadowed his new danger.

Chapter Eight

Gavee struggled to hear, with arms outstretched, trying to reach the queen. Her voice was a whisper, and he could only read her lips. "My sword" is all he understood. The violent end swept across the field. He felt the flame tip burn his fingers and snatched them back, screaming in terror. The dragon's flame scorched the surrounding dirt, and he coughed in its heat. The queen's ashes lay in a heap as he cried out her name, when an echo came crashing back.

"Gavee! Gavee!"

He jumped from the dream, and Flued stood in front of him with a drink.

"Time to wake, cousin."

Flued handed Gavee a goblet, and he looked over its contents. His persistent dreams had varied conclusions, culminating in an evil deed and a desperate attempt to comprehend the queen's dying words. The dragon fire drew fierce anger with each dream and a hatred for the filthy beasts. Following the attack, thunderblood slept beside the royal chamber, and the king remained unconscious. The condition worsened, with eyes glazed black, skin white, and fear gripping his mouth. Gavee swigged the drink in one gulp, placing it on the floor and entering the king's chambers. Flued sat in a chair alongside the bed, and the king's breath raced, raising his chest in a scary scene. Gavee grabbed his hand.

"His breath is erratic," said Gavee.

"It started a few moments ago," answered Flued.

"Has the medicus been called?"

"No,"

"Why?" questioned Gavee.

"What is she to do? Nothing has worked. Even the little magic potions conjured from the unknown have done nothing."

The future king sat back and dropped his head on the seatback, with wings falling between the side holes. The clan's attempts to save their king failed. Would they ever find a cure?

Lord Taronquel entered, pulling back the drapes and allowing the sun to awaken the dull.

"Good morning, my prince. How is our king?"

"Still the same," answered Flued.

"Not the same! Look at the breathing!" said Gavee.

"It started yesterday, sirs," said the female medicus assistant.

Both snapped their attention to the assistant.

"Didn't the medicus tell you?" she asked.

Gavee curled his lips and stepped to the window.

"I hope Shapía has made it to Horfa," said Gavee. "We need Bahg back in our forest."

Grunt stood outside the king's door.

"Excuse me, my lords, Earl. May I speak with you briefly?"

Flued groaned at the weasel's appearance.

"I'll meet you outside," answered Gavee.

Gavee paused at the doorway and said to Flued, "We need a king to decide on Dasa-Raul's actions in the field."

He left without waiting for a reply, descending the wooden spiral stairs to the city courtyard. Two Latuery stood guard. Unknowing, the weasel reached the king, and it made Gavee chuckle how Grunt defeated all the watches. The shapeshifter sat against a tree, twirling his walking stick.

"What is it, my friend?" asked Gavee.

"The tontar states he must speak to you immediately," answered Grunt.

"Crym? Where?"

"I am everywhere," said the tontar, coming from the shadows.

Gavee smiled, and Grunt pointed with his staff.

"I believe you were requested to stay at the forest edge until welcomed into Witch'Bane," said Grunt.

"I'm welcome here, and by an actual Witch'Bane," said Crym.

The two embraced forearms and traded greetings. Grunt held ire over the intrusion, and the tontar smiled at his friend. The tontars are large creatures with horns curling up from the upper forehead and straightening into a point. His eyes, dark red, pointed cheeks and teeth sharpened like knives. He wore a long, dark maroon cloak, dragging on the floor, and shiny black boots with dagger hilts sticking out from their sheaths. Grunt groaned, overwhelmed by burned ash.

"You should have waited," said Grunt.

"You have no say here, changeling, and this business is for Witch'Bane."

Grunt tapped the cane and scowled at the words.

"I want to say I'm glad to see you, but I was hoping it would be many moons later," said Gavee.

"Yes, I believe the agreement was for forty moons unless I had news or understood something bad was truly festering," said Crym.

"You're a bit late for that," said Grunt.

"I've been collecting information on the island since the queen's death, shapeshifter, and when I came to return, they held me at the island's TB Guild."

"What?" questioned Gavee.

"We must speak in private," he said.

"Grunt, please leave us. Stay close. We may need to leave," said Gavee.

"As you wish," said Grunt.

The weasel limped with his cane without removing his eyes from Crym. The tontar ignored the tiny creature.

"Speak, my friend," said Gavee.

"The masuran thunderblood guild is working to remove you from the Order."

"What?" questioned Gavee.

"Your clan faces island danger. Where's your father?"

"He's with Shapía. They had to leave before Reflection. She had to get to Horfa."

"They're both gone?"

"Why?" asked Gavee.

"Is the prince still here?"

"Yes, he is inside with the king."

"I must speak to you both. Flued is the current king, and I have details on what attacked and how to awaken King Arul from his nightmare."

"What about our guild? How can you be certain they are working to remove me?"

"I must speak to Flued!" demanded Crym. "King Arul's life hangs before us. Some are pushing for this removal, though it remains unapproved. We'll discuss this later. Your king's life is what we must attend to."

Gavee stared into the trees and wished his father were there to help.

"Let's talk, but I need to understand where you found this information."

"I'll explain upstairs."

Gavee and the tontar followed, making their way to the council hall. Grunt pursued, avoiding the tontar's long, thin tail and holding his breath from the metallic stench. Flued sat on the king's throne with Taronquel standing alongside.

"This is Crym," said Gavee.

"He's your king. Where is the head bow and respect?" asked Taronquel.

"My apologies, I am still adjusting," said Gavee with a slight head bow.

"Welcome, Crym. I assume you had business with Bahg and Gavee before helping us escape the attack. A tontar from Anayana often brings a surprise," said Flued.

"I did, Your Majesty," said Crym.

"Majesty?" questioned Flued.

"Yes, in masuran code, if the king becomes unable to hold the chair, the next in line is king," answered Crym. "You're king and deserve its recognition."

Flued sat higher, and Taronquel fixed his crooked stance. The new king took a deep breath and folded his hands.

"What information do you carry?" asked King Flued.

The tontar held a hairy hand with a metal ring stitched in the palm. He lowered the middle finger to the black center, and a giant blue energy ball grew in its place, twirling in his thick, pale hand. His red eyes brightened, and he stared into the ball as its glow shunned out all the other lights.

"The Esor Dragons carried out the queen's death."

The scene carried a dragon, and the queen, arm shielding her face, lay upon the ground. It popped to the dragons, flying north, disappearing into a dark cloud. Gavee's eyes widened in shock.

"Another forced them to commit the murder, for this is not their cause, and I could not uncover the force controlling them, yet it exists."

The smoke-filled ball dropped into a fresh picture: an older man near a cave fire.

"The scroll keeper, Dakii the Wanderer, knows how to find what's unknown. He's beyond the Upper Realm and rests in Eden's swamps."

The room fell silent, with Crym staring into the ball as its energy shuttered and distorted the picture. Flued glanced at Gavee, then at the tontar.

"A scroll keeper will carry this information?" questioned the king.

The tontar eyed the orb.

"They can read scrolls written in many forms and different languages," said Crym.

The scene changed to the older man holding a parchment over the flames as words appeared.

"Most scrolls hold demons from entering our world. True. A few written in secret, telling the island's story, hiding items the scroll keeper could understand and read," said Crym.

"There are many scroll keepers besides Dakii. Why would this one carry the knowledge?" asked the king.

"Yes, there are many on each island."

The ball changed again, with several beings holding their scrolls.

"There is one who holds the island's secret. One who keeps the many Breiv stories as his own."

The picture swirled back to Dakii.

"Why would the scroll keeper just give us the information? Why would he hand them over if he writes them secretly?" questioned the king.

The ball turned red, and the Witch'Bane crest floated in its center.

"The scroll keeper desires something this family holds. He will tell you anything for the old token and follow you to the island's ends to help you if you'll help him," said Crym.

The three masuras puzzled over the thought.

"Ancient token?" questioned the king.

The ball, filled with smoke, turned blue.

"It is a token created before Witch'Bane existed," continued Crym.

The scene remained filled with smoke.

"The history is hidden in the scrolls. It's a secret, and Dakii, the Wanderer, understands its importance," said Crym.

The scene held the older man again, sitting beside a fire, smoking a pipe.

"What is the token?" Flued again asked.

"The scroll keeper knows the answer."

"Why hasn't the unknown force captured the scroll keeper?" questioned Flued.

"Another question I cannot answer, Witch'Bane King."

"When do I leave?" asked Gavee.

"Leave?" questioned Flued.

"Yes, we require the scroll keeper. He'll be aware of how to free your father from the trap. We must find him before this... unknown does."

"Why is this information unfamiliar to our thunderblood?" questioned the king.

"My training had just discussed the scroll keeper. Bahg is still our thunderblood, and his actions are his own," answered Gavee.

"Bahg and Gavee sent me to find the keeper and bring him here," interrupted the tontar. "But I was taken prisoner and placed inside the thunderblood guild."

"Taken? I don't understand," questioned Flued.

"To access the other islands as a foreign thunderblood, you must possess a local thunderblood coin. When I handed the Witch'Bane coin to the arresting thunderbloods, they laughed and took me away," said Crym.

"How did you escape?" asked Gavee.

"Don't interrupt the king," said Crym.

Gavee lowered his head.

"I am sworn to secrecy about my help. One day, I will explain," said Crym.

Flued frowned.

"Why should I trust the tale? DasaRaul attacked us at Reflection, breaking a masuran code with the grangruls and using barkapes in the attack. My father remains trapped in pain. You arrive and hold this odd story of being taken prisoner, and we must find a scroll keeper," said Flued.

The tontar pulled a silver coin from his cloak with the thunderblood stamp. He placed it on the table and stepped back.

"This coin was given to me by Bahg. It allows me passage as an extension to your clan and safe travels through all forests upon return," said Crym.

Flued leaned in, grabbing the item. He stared at the red thunderbolt, recognizing Nathe's crest, and flipped it. Two crossed scimitars with the letters TB above the swords: the Thunderblood symbol. The thunderbloods carried such items and would hand them to those hired for information.

"I am here to continue my service under Bahg's call. I will help you find the scroll keeper," said Crym.

Gavee stared at the coin, feeling his father's awareness and disappointment grow upon his shoulders.

"Have we received word if they have arrived in Ihandra?" asked Gavee.

Flued flipped the coin and handed it back to the TonTar.

"No, we should not expect a word for many moons. Bahg stated he would send a message with a kite hawk once they settled into Horfa."

"When do we leave?" asked Gavee.

The Witch'Bane thunderblood glanced at the tontar and then at the king. Flued stared at the tontar.

"We need a cure," said Gavee.

"The war before your forest still battles hither and thither. We must leave at night, providing cover, and with the clouds providing the shadow advantage," said Crym.

Flued nodded.

"I would agree. Gavee, find the scroll keeper and bring him and his information back to Witch'Bane. Take the shapeshifter to help search."

Gavee gave a head bow.

"Now, Lord Taronquel, we must begin our buildup for war with DasaRaul. Call the royals and bring in our generals. Once we have our plan, we must send word to BataRaul, for they live in our current state."

"We must save our true king!" said Flued.

"Crym, follow me. We will get food and prepare," said Gavee.

"I continue to be your trusted servant," bowed the tontar.

* * *

Shapía lay in the damp, dark hole, shivering from the cold air. Along the long cave hall, a distant sparkle foretold the passing days and nights. The far wall in front of her cell fell beyond sight, and the small prison kept her unable to stand. The straw-covered mud floor was where she stayed, and she went outside twice to get rid of the little water and food she had eaten. Bahg was near, in a hole with guards hidden in the dark, keeping communications silent. The masura scraped the sidewall with her talons, angering the guards, and they jabbed her with a stick to stop the damage.

They stripped the Witch'Bane from her belongings. She wore tattered linen, barely covering her skin. Her prison was cold and damp. She did not want it all to end here. The posted armed guards would give no escape, and she hoped the blackness would allow them to go deeper into the mountain. The rigid dirt walls held many roots, telling the masura she did not sit far from the topsoil.

"Uncle?" she whispered.

"I'm here, Princess."

"I have roots in my prison."

"Yes, if you speak with the tree, it shall tell you its location is in a large courtyard made from stone. The roots are from one of the four trees in a giant garden surrounded by Fen guards."

"Why did they do this? I was unaware Fen was an enemy," said Shapía.

"They've never been an enemy, but not a friend, either. Their actions are about me and not you, and I'm sorry they dragged you in to punish me."

"How long will they hold us?" she asked.

"We will not find out."

Shapía paused. "I don't understand."

"Word has been sent."

"How will anyone discover our location?"

"I had the unseen follow us into the field, and they reached just outside. They'll return soon, and we'll get you to Horfa."

"What about home?"

"You must get to Horfa. It's more important than at any other time in our history."

Shapía shivered from the cold, pulling the straw over her body.

"Uncle?"

"Yes, my princess."

"When?"

"Soon. Very soon,"

"Quiet," charged a guard.

The princess stared at the distant sparkle, placing a hand in front of her face and allowing it to disappear, then moving it to find the dot. She continued to play in this fashion when it dimmed until it no longer sparkled. Darkness engulfed the prison, and the lone masura pressed against the dirt wall and metal bar doorway. Shapía waited for

Bahg to share thoughts about Horfa and the future ahead. The dream became vivid, with the massive dead volcano looming over the island. A long dirt path in the open green field zigzagged into a narrow passage where the rim had collapsed. In the vision, the masuras marched on, their ranks unbroken. She turned, and her mother held her hand with a smile.

"Mother?"

The queen, squeezing her hand, remained silent. Together, they followed the wings in front of them, working toward Horfa. The smells and sounds filled her senses, and the most massive tree Shapía had ever seen fell into the picture as it sat centered inside the rim. Its canopy leveled to the dead volcano with tree lofts peppering the mighty branches. Singing lamented within the crater, and she felt joy filling her heart. Her skin vibrated from the low hum hanging in the air, and she held tight to the queen's hand.

"You belong here," said the queen in a slow-drawn voice. *"Masuras everywhere await your arrival."*

Shapía smiled, trying to speak, but had no voice. Her mother stopped and took her other hand. The queen's smile grew until it pulled back, and her eyes widened. The wind swirled around them, their hair snapping in the gusts.

"If you do not make it, destruction will fall upon them all."

Shapía's body shook, and the ground trembled when she snapped from the dream. Bahg kneeled over and smiled, shaking her shoulders.

"Uncle?"

He placed a finger against her lips.

"Don't speak," he whispered. "Our friends have arrived to save us."

A giant creature, struggling to grin, loomed to Shapía's left. The humanoid snake stood to Bahg's shoulder height and had a human head with its cobra hood hovering over the top. Its torso with hands and feet blended into the snake's body with a long snake's tail reaching into the darkness. The princess knew the creature was a hood, though she'd never encountered one before. She hid the fright and nodded an answer.

"We must go," said the creature. "We cannot hold back the Fens for too long within their cave."

The snake's body folded around the torso and slithered away from the tunnel entrance into the darkness.

Shapía stood, grabbing Bahg's hand when he grimaced, and she eased up on the grip. Although battered and beaten, the strong masura advanced with a steady charge. More hoods came from the dark, slithering before them with information for their leader.

"I cannot see uncle," she whispered.

"Light is coming," said Bahg. "We will see forward soon enough."

The blackness soon fell to a purple hue, and a hood slithered forward, holding two sticks with glowing mushrooms atop, showing the way. The hood bowed and handed Shapía the purple item, then to Bahg.

"Lord Senith awaits us before the chasm. Our force will get you to Mudra and the waiting boat at the Discovery Rock, Duke of Witch'Bane."

The hood slithered forward, not waiting for the masuras.

"Who are they?" whispered Shapía.

"They come from the island of Róta, and Lord Senith is their thunderblood. My Princess, more is occurring, and it has been escalating for a while. Your mother's death was the start across all Five Islands. The many lores and legends are awakening."

"Why are they here in Breiv?"

"Let's keep moving. I'll explain once we reach the boat to Ihandra."

Bahg held up the stick and pressed toward the large, open tunnel. Wooden slates covered the cavern floor, enabling masura's talons to dig in and gain foot speed. The hoods grew in number, now surrounding the two Witch'Banes, and charged deep into the underground passage. Shapía held tight to Bahg, with the injured thunderblood bleeding from a head wound and grimacing under each limping step. As they descended, the air grew cooler. Many overhangs featured hoods lining the distant walls. The passage opened into a giant cavern where a taller hood waited for the masuras. The leader held out their sword, saluting Bahg.

"I am sad to see you this way, my friend," said the leader.

"We've both had days like it and sometimes together, Lord Senith," said Bahg.

"I would have our medicus tend your wounds if it were not for the trouble coming our way from Fen."

Looking back, the group heard the echoing sound of marching talons coming from the darkness. Hood guards barreled out of the shaft, approaching their leader.

"Fens are pushing our way. We must go now, sir!" said the hood.

"Surround Witch'Bane! We will charge through the tunnel, connect and get them to the awaiting boat!" said Lord Senith.

"Tunnel connect?" questioned Shapía.

"It's where Fen and the dwarves meet to trade, and both guard types are often on watch. It will bring on a fight," answered Bahg.

"We have no weapons?"

Lord Senith tapped his tail on the cavern floor when two hood soldiers slithered forward, holding swords.

"This will help," said Senith.

Bahg saluted with the new weapon, and the party slithered forward with the masuras amid the Hood army. With the walls and ceiling closing in, the tunnel drew the charge closer. The sound of the slithering hoods filled the air, and Shapía held tight to Bahg. The fighting from behind grew closer, with the hoods pushing Bahg into a running limp.

Shapía held back the fear, focusing on the creatures and saving them from an enemy. Her thoughts fell onto Gavee, Flued, and her father, wanting them near with Bahg alongside, where she felt safe.

With a sudden stop, the party's charge into the purple tunnels grew faster, as a battle ahead engulfed the path in chaos. The hoods built a wall around the masuras, and Lord Senith remained alongside Bahg.

"The dwarves are battling the connection, but we outnumber them."

"Behind?" questioned Bahg.

"I've ordered a wall, and the Fens will find it hard to pass."

The walls around Witch'Bane squeezed in, and the tunnel behind pushed against them, with the fighting becoming closer.

"Be ready. The Fens are not letting us go easy," worried Bahg.

Shapía looked at her uncle's face, and anger grew. The thought of her tiny cell and the change against her clan created a fire inside. She gripped the sword and readied it.

"Ease your grip, my niece. You'll tire if the fight lasts," said Bahg through his bloody mouth.

The push forward moved, with dwarves charging into the packed hoods. One spun and reached just beyond Shapía when Bahg ended the charge with a sword lunge.

"Charge forward!" shouted Senith.

The party roared forward, pushing against the one before them, and the hoods mixed into the fighting dwarves. Shapía soon found herself separated from Bahg as they reached the connection. Crisscrossed stone walkways spanned a vast chasm, dropping into an unknown abyss, while swords echoed through the walls. The princess stretched her wings and hovered above the fight as an axe brushed the right wing from the melee. With Bahg's sword, the defenseless dwarf fell as the battle below consumed the cavern.

Bahg rose, pulling Shapía to the far tunnel when the Fens broke through, and the enemy masuras took flight, sending arrows into the hoods. Lord Senith sent a low hiss, echoing through the chamber as the fighters grew their hoods and the arrows bounced off their protection. Shapía met the first aggressor, and the pure swordplay ended with a quick slash to the throat by the Witch'Bane princess. She had trained with Bahg and held the sword with high confidence.

In the tunnel, the fight swayed back and forth, with Shapía encountering another fighter. The complex sword clash forced her into a spin to avoid hits. Two Fen fighters pressed the masura against the cave wall. Her eyes widened in fear as a sword tip burst through the Fen's chest, causing the being to drop and the other to flee back into the tunnel.

"No more fighting," Bahg insisted. "Let's move on!"

"They surround us!" worried Shapía.

"No, Senith has made an opening."

The hood leader waved the masuras to him, and Shapía grabbed Bahg's arm as they darted into the passage surrounded by their protectors.

"The tunnel's end is near! We have a trap to keep them from coming forward."

"And the Fen watches at the entrance?" questioned Bahg.

"You have more friends awaiting your arrival outside," hissed the hood leader.

They ran with tucked wings, fighting back the battle from behind. The connection opening's struggle continued to come into the passage when the outside air pushed down the corridor. Shapía took in the fresh air, and determination for freedom grabbed her mind. They ran faster, passing through two giant stones when the last few hoods slithered in, and a rock slab slammed the far passage closed. The princess spotted two massive tontars, unfamiliar creatures, sporting horns on their foreheads. Their red glowing eyes tinted the air, while a few more arrived breathless. The sight brought concern to Bahg's busted lip.

"Tontars here? This is bad," Bahg said to Senith.

"It is as you predicted," answered Senith.

Bahg looked at the one being. "The island is no longer safe. We must get her to Horfa," he said.

"Your escort has arrived," said a smiling tontar.

"Lord Burn, thank you for coming," said Bahg.

"Witch'Bane requires help, and we still owe a debt. We would be nowhere else," replied the tontar, still smiled.

"Shapía, this is Lord Burn, a friend of Witch'Bane."

She wondered why the tontars had never been to their council, but smiled anyway and gave a head bow.

"It's as if I am looking at the queen," the still-smiling tontar said.

The princess grimaced a bit at the pointed teeth, but remained cordial. "Uncle, I must speak to you."

"We must keep moving," he answered.

"No, we stay here," said Lord Burn. "The trip beyond the cave opening brings danger. I wait for my troops to arrive."

"Fine," said Bahg.

He pulled her to the side.

"What worries you?"

"All of it. I've never seen hoods or tontars, yet our family and I are recognized by them. How could I have been so unaware of both the opposition and our allies?"

Bahg took a deep breath and shook his head. "You, your brother, and your cousin are just coming of age to understand these things. The genuine history will soon show, and you'll discover where to trust and fear."

Shapía fought back tears.

"Yes, Uncle. I'll follow without question."

He lifted her chin.

"No, never stop questioning. Your mother never gave it up. Why should you?"

Chapter Nine

Taronquel stared at his hand with the black dot now spread to his fingers and curled a fist. The dark lahd's quarters sat in grim silence as they sat in a remote location, with the cloud-filled night giving the head council a chance to get to Malum and repair the damage. He eased onto the balcony and listened.

"Rhile?" he whispered.

The loft held an eerie silence as Taronquel eased to the door.

"Rhile, are you in?" he asked.

The masura pushed open the door, finding the small main living area empty.

"Rhile?"

He entered the loft and moved down the dark hall to a closed door. Taronquel stepped closer and placed an ear against the door, then knocked.

"Rhile?"

He heard mumbling from the opposite side, prompting him to push it open. There, he found Rhile seated in the far corner, gently rocking while holding her hand. The color in her face turned gaunt, her skin stretched. Dread pierced Taronquel as he watched saliva drip from her open mouth.

"We must go to Malum," said Taronquel.

The masura strained to pull her vision to Taronquel with a heavy breath.

"You did this," she said.

"I was unaware. Malum remained silent regarding the stone's capabilities. You must believe me," he said.

The lahd pulled her stare back to the floor. Taronquel eased down to lift the masura to her feet.

"You'll need to gather your energy. Our flight will take us to the far shores beyond BataRaul."

"To the Raul cliffs?" she asked.

"Yes, Malum's lair."

"BataRaul allows you safe passage?" she questioned.

"No, we'll follow the Raul River, then cut through Bata onto the field between the forest and cliffs."

"I'll never make it in my condition."

"We'll figure it out as we go. We must depart before sunrise."

Taronquel assisted the broken masura to the main room, grabbing a water jug. Rhile poured the liquid over her face, gulping the drink. The head council held an orange and handed the fruit to the lahd, who tore into the object, eating it whole.

"Feel better?"

"No, let's go."

Upon arrival on the balcony, the pair flew north toward the distant borders of Witch'Bane. The moon remained hidden, and Taronquel pushed Rhile into a fast pace, needing to get to the Witch'Bane River to avoid contact with the Latuery. The flight took them into a thick forest overlooking the fast-paced river spun from Lheter Lake.

They flew beyond Dasa's lakefront and headed north to the Raul River, running between the two Raul clans. Rhile's flight was slow, forcing Taronquel to take her hand and drag the masura across the sky. The fishing on the lake was heavy, keeping Taronquel's attention ahead and avoiding eye contact. The lahd's face held a new bony feature, and anyone close would question her health. Taronquel followed the same path, getting duplicate stares from both Raul's sides. He ensured they kept closer to BataRaul, knowing they held a peace accord with the clan.

"We must fly faster," he said.

"I'm flying as fast as possible with the curse I've been given!"

The late night faded as the masuras followed the tree line along the open field, continuing north with most foot movement. Taronquel stopped.

"Wait," he whispered.

On the distant shore, the crashing waves gave him a profound determination. The dawn remained hidden when they darted from the trees on foot across the open field. BataRaul's arrows whizzed past the masuras.

NESTED EVIL

"Intruders!" said a watch.

"We must fly!" said Taronquel.

"I don't know if I can!" she cried.

The head council grabbed her hand, pulling them into the sky. The arrow barrage followed until they reached beyond the cliffs and over the sea. Rhile held onto Taronquel as her wings failed, with the BataRaul search party ending in their pursuit.

"My strength," she said.

"Let's move closer to the cliffs. We need to search for the three large protruding stones."

"The cliff is filled with rocks," gasped Rhile.

"We'll find it!"

The delicate masura's wings dropped to the side, forcing Taronquel to tuck under her arms. They plummeted toward the water while Taronquel fought to gain control. Each wing flap was a struggle for the broken head council as he pulled the lahd forward. The flight became almost impossible when he caught the opening.

"There!" he gasped. "Rhile, you must... flap... your wings!"

With a shudder, the weakened masura inhaled, her breath rattling slightly.

"I'll pull myself up," she said.

"Are you sure?"

"Yes!"

Taronquel released, and Rhile pushed her wings to soar forward. They flew to a small landing in front of the large rocks and dropped to the rocky base. Taronquel lay on the rock and stared at the starry sky, exhausted, but he pushed up from the ground. His wings ached from the flight, and his arms went numb.

"She's inside. Come, let's get healed," he said.

The beaten masura returned a moan, and they pulled through the tricky opening. The darkness soon disappeared as torches lined the walls, lighting the path. Taronquel expected a gremlin watch, but none came as whispers filled in from behind. Rhile drooled and moaned with Taronquel's pull through the rocky maze. The giant cavern filled with a fiery orange glow, and he soured at the stench. The whispers grew louder.

Taronquel leaned Rhile against a large rock and turned to a scene he had not expected. The cavern center roared with a massive flame, its center burning blue, green, and orange. It tipped the ceiling, holding no sound to its intense fire. Nine masuras with wings spread wide and eyes blackened sat near the fire, naked and covered in inked runes. Each held a significant scarred mark on their chest and whispered in a locked, unknown chant. The head council approached the scene with caution.

"Enter, my son." Malum's voice echoed through the cavern in its whisper, and Taronquel stepped to her known hole.

In the shadows, the black mass circled in the darkness. "What did you bring to me?"

"I have come for your help," he said.

"She is weak and damaged."

"She is how I know where the stone sits. Will you save her from the evil?"

"Come into the dark, my son."

He hesitated.

"It's your mother. Do not fear," she said.

The masura stepped forward, with the darkness engulfing his body. It wiggled around the wings and then passed into the throat.

"She poisoned you," coughed Malum.

The darkness engulfed his hand.

"A weak poison," she said.

The hand throbbed, then released.

"Who has the stone?" she questioned.

The darkness wrapped around his head.

"Ah, so the scroll keeper has the information. I don't know its name. It's unfamiliar," said Malum.

The masura held his tongue.

"You had the damaged one kill the seeker. Good, she was too close to the elves. They would have sensed our presence through her," said Malum.

Darkness enveloped him, entering and then leaving his nostrils.

"Your friend is not lost. She will be the leader of our new exercitus," said Malum.

Taronquel stepped out of the dark. "I need her for Witch'Bane."

Malum slithered around the masura. "The damage is irreversible. It is the way."

"Your king is under the spell?" she hissed.

"Yes, but I need Rhile," he demanded.

"Where is the uncle?" she hissed.

"With the money I paid, he should be held in Fen, along with Shapía."

"And the cousin?"

"I have it arranged. Are you not concerned about Flued?"

Malum smiled. "The kingdom is coming under your control."

Taronquel became uneasy with the silent answer.

"I will need Rhile," he growled.

She chuckled. "My son, the Exercitus, your army, sits before the eternal flame."

Malum raised an arm, and her thin finger pointed to the fire. Rhile stood naked before the massive flame, her wings and eyes ink black, body covered in the same runes and with a mark on the left breast. She whispered the same chant with raised arms, calling out to the flame.

"They will follow your every command, even to their deaths."

Taronquel's eyes widened at the thought, and he built power within his body.

"My son, it is time," said Malum.

From the fire, the entranced masuras moved toward Taronquel and Malum. The lahd, with unblinking eyes, stopped the group in front of the masura. Gathered in a circle, the others stared into the beyond, whispering.

"Here is your leader. Make him whole," hissed Malum.

With a collective heave, the group closed in, their hands gripping the masura as they lifted him aloft.

"Release me! Release me!" he said.

Oblivious to his struggles, the tranced masuras gripped his legs, arms, and wings tightly, their grip like iron.

"Mother Malum, why!" he yelled.

"Ease, my son, the power I give you shall bring down the thunderbloods and any masuras in your way," said Malum.

The group marched to the massive fire, still stuck in the whisper. They stood before the flame with Taronquel kicking and screaming, trying to escape. Malum moved from the dark and floated down before them all, her thin arms raised, and eyes glazed white. She wailed as her broken black wings pulled outward. The massive fire released its roar, drowning out the whispered chants, with Malum's high squeal pitch towering above it.

"The curse is called upon its flame,

"To take the body as a claim,

"And free the rows from the condemned,

"By placing their souls into the gem!"

Upon the last word, they tossed Taronquel into the flames. The surprised masura screamed but remained protected within the green center. He floated in its depths, with the masuras circling the fire, locked in their whispered chant. He watched Malum rise to hover in front of him, now with her eyes black.

"Show us your truth," she hissed.

The high scream blasted through his body, and he grabbed at his ears, trying to release the screech. His body distorted, arched in pain, and he screamed with fists clenched. The masura snapped from the agony and hovered before a grinning Malum.

"You'll bring me the item allowing you to hide as another," she hissed. "It is something I require."

"Hide?" he questioned.

"Yes, King Flued."

The words shocked Flued. He glanced at himself, then at Malum.

"Did you really believe I wouldn't recognize you from our initial meeting?" she asked.

"I hid my identity for a reason," he said.

"I know, my son, and the trick was successful," said Malum.

Flued stared into Malum's darkness.

"I am ready," he growled.

"You are chosen. Bring me my victory!" shrieked Malum.

Malum opened her maw, and a bee swarm thundered forward, slamming into his left hand. He screamed from the pain and could not move as they entered his body. They ran under his skin and across his arm, with the vibration shuddering his vision to bright light. Agonizing pain surged from his spine, bees buzzing through his throat and out through his mouth. The white light dropped, and he could see Malum hovering. Her bright purple eyes now matched the flames, which popped against his body, causing him pain.

"King of Kings, my power runs through you. Now rise and lead my army to win back my island!" she screamed.

Searing pain shot through Flued, sending the limbs straight when it all ceased. His mind went blank.

***

Time passed when his eyes snapped wide, and he coughed, finding himself on the dirt floor. A sudden silence fell over the cave as the masura jumped to his feet. Glowing purple mushrooms provided the sole light, and he stood where the fire once burned. The

Exercitus waited in formation before him, donned in the Witch'Bane armor. Rhile stood at attention and awaited the command.

The prince experienced a sharp pain in his left palm, making him jump out of the vision. Embedded in the center was a small black gem with a white center. He touched it and experienced a power surge, then a pain in his left chest. When he pulled back his shirt, his attire startled him. He donned the king's armor, with the thunderbolt centered upon the chest plate, but colored a deep purple.

"Malum?" called Flued.

"Yes, my son?" answered Malum.

The witch hovered forward from the hole.

"You now hold the power of a thousand exercitus. Take your new soldiers and conquer the island for me," said Malum.

"How?" asked Flued.

"I have given you some of me," she said.

Flued held out his left hand.

"Experience its strength. You are one. Call it forth," demanded Malum.

"How did you know it was me?" he asked.

"The fire revealed the truth. It removed one of the many items I need to find my sisters and be free," hissed Malum.

"The mask?" asked Flued.

"Yes, where did you collect it?"

"I found it buried behind the Dead Falls. It was inside a copper box," he said.

"A copper box? Are they all this way?" she questioned.

"All?" he questioned.

"Yes, the other items. The copper is why I cannot locate them. What a devious trick! I curse thunderblood," she said.

"How does this mask hold such ability?" he asked.

"The Mask of Lynul!" she curled a laugh. "It was a gift from a demi in his great divinity. It allowed us to hide within the peaceful realm until my sister dropped hers into the water of awareness, and our time was over."

"I don't understand," he said.

"Do not bother knowing its history. We need this mask. It is a required piece to help us take the island."

"I found another item alongside it," he said.

"Was it a mirror?" she questioned.

"Yes?" he answered.

"Those fools!" she shrieked. "I must have it. Keep it safe."

"It remains hidden in my loft. No one is allowed inside."

"Many more remain," said Malum.

"The pain!" he screamed.

Flued grabbed his hand, burning as if on fire. The embedded stone and its white center glowed. The hand vibrated with a black sphere spinning in his palm. He looked at Malum.

"Use it, my son."

The masura instinctively looked at a large rock and sent the black orb into the stone. It exploded, and the power sent Flued to one knee. He coughed, struggling to catch his breath.

"You must learn how to use it."

He tried to stand, but his knees buckled.

"How can I use a power that weakens me?" he asked.

"Begin smaller."

He stood and formed the ball. It floated to eye level and sent a finger into the center. The surrounding energy grew, and he flung it across the cavern. It exploded into the wall, and the masura remained on his feet.

"How do we grow the exercitus?"

"Come with me."

The witch slid forward, and Flued followed when they came upon two large stones and a path leading between and beyond the rocks. There, a chained masuran male lay against a rock wall. He was unharmed and was a well-known Latuery.

"Prince Flued, my etta, help me," he gasped.

The masura's lips had dried, and he had not eaten for some time.

"Bring him into the exercitus," hissed Malum.

The prince eyed Malum, then his own hand. He took a deep breath and concentrated on the white center. The power surged, and the energy sphere appeared, spinning in his hand. He approached the latuery, and fear rose on the masura's face.

"No, My Prince!" yelled the masura.

Flued's eyes darkened purple, and he floated the sphere, allowing it to engulf the captive. The masura screamed in pain, convulsing as the orb spun faster. He jerked back and forth when he went limp and came to one knee. The sphere disappeared, and the now unchained masura found himself covered in inked runes.

"Are you ready to follow?" asked Flued.

"I am here to serve My King."

"The power lives within you. My power is now our power," hissed Malum.

The evil smile slid to Flued's lips, and the mind built on the idea.

"The island will be ours," said Flued.

She slid next to the new king.

"Bring me the stone and your father. It is through him we shall lead together."

"As you wish, Mother."

Her thin hand reached out from the darkness and placed it upon his face. Her touch created warmth as the mass floated back within the hole. Flued approached Rhile.

"How are you, my friend?"

"We are ready to follow our king."

He stared into her eyes and found them blank. Lifeless. His inner thoughts embraced her pain, but the power sitting at hand brought a focus to the throne.

"Follow me."

The exercitus fell into a single formation and marched beyond the cavern, taking flight over the sea. The night held steady, and Flued pushed them over BataRaul with no fear for what might lie in the path.

* * *

Gavee watched the clouds pass over the morning seascape. Near the fire, Grunt and Crym watched as the Lost Sea rolled onto the Upper Realm's shores. The party sat just beyond where the Lower and Upper Realms came together, and two days traveled south from Witch'Bane. The chaos prevailed west, pushing them to move along the southern sea, landing in front of an area filled with danger for a masura.

From the Lower Realm, they would cut across and reach Eden faster. The hunt for the keeper of the scrolls kept him focused. A break was necessary, for the next few days demanded constant vigilance in the desolate land of the grangruls. The tontar quenched the small fire, infuriating Grunt, who prepared fish.

"Why?" asked Grunt.

"We've been camping long enough. Eden's journey is long. The scroll keeper may be on the move," said Crym.

With a snarl, the shapeshifter slid the fish from its stick and ate it whole, ignoring the tontar. The Witch'Bane earl spread his wings and latched the satchel upon his back, unsheathing the sword. The queen followed him in his dreams and in every action with the blade. He neared the truth concerning her death, fueled by his desire to solve the mystery.

"Our path gives little cover, and with the cloudless sky, we will have nowhere to hide," worried Gavee.

"I could conjure a cloud formation?" questioned Crym.

"I think it would bring more attention as a lone visible cloud," said Grunt.

"No, we fly on alert and prepare to fight what may come ahead," said Gavee.

Gavee sheathed his sword.

"As you wish, W.B.," said Crym.

Grunt, tapping his stick, transformed into a crow as Crym blew into a small device. Gavee smiled, waiting for the spotted pegasus, Dreamus. The masura became fond of the flying creature and loved its beauty. Its brown spots on the silver body sparkled against the sunlight, and the moderate wing flaps made no sound. The connection between Crym and Dreamus held as the tontar sat upon the mighty beast, and formed them as one being in the sky. The pegasus floated into sight and landed in front of the tontar.

After crossing the dry field and following the dirt path, they sailed into the Lower Realm. The lizard folk, Grangrul, devastated the Lower Realm during the First Age, taking it for themselves and destroying the land and its creatures. From the Upper Realm, the path followed the tree line where the Lohr masuras protected the upper field against invading beasts. The many posts ran thick with the masura watch, taking notice of the pegasus rider, lone masura, and flying crow. Gavee understood it would be an odd sighting, but they would pass without issue with his black cloak hiding the Witch'Bane colors and the thunderblood emblem upon the left pant leg.

With the grangrul mounds peeking on the horizon, the trail veered into the desert. The lizard folk live in underground cities within large dirt mounds. One entrance and exit existed in the underground town. Adobe buildings led to the back of the dome where the secondary quarters and the grangruls' hunting birds, the devil hawks, lived in training cages. The foul creatures had glowing red eyes, horns jetting from their skulls, and talons as giant as an eagle's. They trained to hunt and kill masuras. The devil hawks would hide within the open, flat, rolling lands, striking without sound. Each masuran child learned how to evade and escape danger while alerting others to the threat.

Grunt cawed as they flew farther into the Lower Realm, and Gavee pulled his sword for protection. Crym held little concern for the danger, with his staff secured to the backside. The low hills rolled forward, and the path zigzagged across the land. Gavee, with an eagle's sight, could see the far-distant grangrul mounds, and his body shivered at the view. He pushed harder against the warm air when a loud ringing halted the flight. The loud noise turned soft, and his vision faded to green with his chest mark burning. The green fire roared before him, and a low heartbeat rang in his ears. His mind was not his own, experiencing a connection to something yet remote.

"Chrsssannnthhh," faintly echoed, with a rattle each time it repeated. The fire thundered higher and spun, brightening the green scene with cave walls towering all around until it opened to the sky. The flames whipped behind, and soon he found them encircling, blocking the cave.

"Chrsssannnthhh," beckoned again when the fire molded into peering eyes and a sinister grin emerged. Gavee panicked as a sudden jolt shot through his chest, then another. He woke to Crym hovering with the staff in hand.

"W.B.!" shouted the tontar.

He shook off the spell, and Grunt hovered before him, cawing. When Crym raised the staff once more, the masura found his balance difficult to regain.

"I'm fine. Just give me a moment," said Gavee.

The masura shook his head, still in a hover.

"No, Grunt, I don't know why my eyes turned dark green," said Gavee.

The crow cawed again.

"My skin, too?" questioned Gavee.

"Explain yourself, Thunderblood," said Crym.

Gavee squinted against the sun. "I don't know what it is."

Crym lowered the staff. "Can you continue?"

"We must," answered Gavee.

"I go no farther until I know what you possess or what possesses you," said Crym.

Gavee hesitated as he stared at the dirt. Crym kept his scowl, and Grunt floated in the warm breeze as the three hovered in place.

"Something happened to me after the dragon killed my queen. I still do not understand it, and I am unsure why it occurs or how to control it."

"It's powerful, and I sense the dragon's breath on you, masura," said Crym. "It's dark and cruel."

"When we get beyond the open danger, we'll discuss it more, but for now, we must move forward," said Gavee.

"I agree, but more is needed," answered Crym.

Crym pulled the reins, and Dreamus turned, pushing forward into the sky. Grunt continued to caw, but Gavee did not answer, thrusting the air between the feathers and flying on.

"I still don't know, Grunt. I have hidden nothing and don't know what it is or how it happened."

The three continued with a required focus on the danger growing as they entered the grangrul territory. Gavee could not shake the flames and eyes with its sinister smile. The thought sent shivers through him. His chest mark pulsed. Grunt stared at Gavee, who became annoyed at the action and pushed ahead to focus on the path. The tontar in front of the group never looked back, following the dirt road. The trail dipped and then dropped into an open fissure where the ground split wide. A tall waterfall veered to one side, its stream flowing directly to a pool, which plunged into a cave. Thirst fell upon Gavee's tongue, and the water sparkled in the sunshine with the danger lurking too close.

Crym pulled back and pointed into the opening, where a grangrul caravan pushed enslaved beings forward: masuras, dwarves, halflings, and many other beings shackled between the many grangrul chariots pulled by sabercats marched across the desert. Grunt cawed, and Gavee cursed the scene.

"I agree with Grunt. We can't pass without helping," said Gavee.

"Our mission has nothing to do with those poor beings, Thunderblood," said Crym.

"My mission has everything to do with those beings," said Gavee.

Crym murmured at the comment.

"This is foolish. Your king remains in horror, and you want to stop and save the unknown?" asked Crym.

"Are you not a thunderblood?" questioned Gavee.

Crym pulled the reins back on Dreamus. "Gavee, we have been friends longer than we have been thunderblood trainees. If we stop, the keeper of the scrolls gets farther away."

"I take my oath and place before my own needs," said Gavee.

Crym gritted at the words. He took a long breath and released it.

"What's the plan?"

"We'll come in from opposite sides," said Gavee.

"Attack the rear first, and I'll come straight on. With the sun in their direction, we'll stay out of view just before we strike," said Crym.

Grunt cawed.

"Yes, shapeshifter, I recommend the black panther strikes quickly, but watch those sabercats. They'll release once we attack," said Crym. "You must attack when they pass beyond the cave if we wish to avoid anything hiding in it. Your attack will drive the front faster, and they'll focus on the ridges."

"Once we hit, the devil hawks will be alerted," said Gavee.

"Indeed, start by freeing the back masuras. They'll help in the fight," said Crym.

"Weapons?"

"They'll have to find a way."

Gavee nodded and looked at Grunt. "Let's split up. I'll signal when we attack. Be safe, my friend."

"I must repeat, I believe this to be a bad idea, and it delays our mission."

"We have an oath before we have a mission," answered Gavee.

Grunt did not answer, and Gavee dropped straight down, allowing the glide to reach just above the hardened dirt, soaring for the ridge. He watched Grunt do the same with Crym, no longer within range. Whips echoed from the crevasse, and the chariot wheels squeaked across the hardened rocks, followed close behind. The heat from the ground and sun swelled around his wings, making it challenging to keep a quick flight.

The shallow drop into the cut allowed a low flight, hiding them from the evil awaiting in the valley. Near the cave entrance, the caravan paused. The grangruls congregated at the small pool, where the water flowed into the unseen. Gavee came to rest in front of the ridge and lay flat, watching the scene. He counted six grans, with each riding a sabercat pulling a chariot.

"Those poor beings," he said.

The subordinate count held fifteen masuras, twenty halflings, four dwarves, and a creature he had never seen before. The being's yellow skin with black stripes covered its long, thin stature. It had enormous eyes, no mouth, and two slits for a nose. Alone behind the final chariot, the creature captivated the earl. The sabercats groaned when a grangrul stepped to the yellow being, pulling it to the chariot and handing it a bucket. The creature wasted no time dipping it into the water and moving toward the back of the two sabercats. Its white eyes turned orange, and it held out a hand as it approached. The sabers purred, lowered, and lay on their sides, dropping into a louder purr as the yellow being poured water into a large bowl.

Gavee followed the creature as it repeated the steps twice and then returned to its rear position. Ignoring the movement, the grangruls continued to bathe in the cold water. Severely beaten and showing signs of prolonged mistreatment were the captives. With the sabers at rest, the earl intended to ambush the unsuspecting evil creatures. But the damp, echoing cave betrayed their presence. The grangruls' alarmed shrieks pierced the silence, warning the thunderblood.

"It could be a trap. Stay alert."

The evil beasts finished their bath, and the front grangruls sent a whip upon their captors as a game. Their hissed laughter echoed behind the pain from the bonded. Gavee searched the far ridge, and Grunt hopped along, waiting for the opportunity. The caravan was moving, with the temporary stop making the grangruls' awareness dull. Gavee waited for the yellow being to pass the cave when he signaled Grunt. Two boulders acted as a doorway, giving them the proper distance and time to strike.

Gavee's senses sharpened with each wheel turn as the tortured yellow creature crossed the gate, overtaken by the thunderblood mind. His eagle vision spotted Grunt, who returned a wink. The two soared into the gorge as Gavee pushed hard against the heated air. The silent flight brought the yellow being closer when Grunt lowered, shifting into the black panther and striking into a fast run. With a swing of its blade, the thunderblood decapitated the first grangrul. At that exact moment, Grunt leaped onto a lizard's back and bit down into its scaly neck, flipping the chariot.

The masura veered forward, with chaos blowing across the caravan. Blood from the grangrul stained his blade as he flew above the enslaved group. Grunt's growl echoed, and a sabercat thundered as Gavee focused on the next lizard. The second gran suffered the same fate, its head bouncing off the sabercat. Three grangruls prepared for the masura as the thunderblood hovered. An arrow zipped past his head, and he dodged a spear thrown to the side. The far lizard released a high-pitched whistle when a blue orb slammed into its chariot, tossing its lifeless torso into the far wall.

Crym and Dreamus swooped in, and as the tontar headed for the second grangrul, a red orb hit him, sending both crashing to the ground. The lizard held its staff, turning to Gavee and sending a ball of light. The thunderblood avoided the blow, sliding to the floor. Grunt groaned and moaned behind, fighting with a saber as the yellow creature unhitched more cats, allowing them to circle the shapeshifter. Outsized, Grunt shifted to the crow and darted between the enslaved, remaining low and away from the grangruls.

The far lizard aimed its staff, sending a red orb into the rock cliff behind Gavee and dropping rocky debris onto the masura. He hit the ground hard, gasping and shaking with dizziness. Dreamus landed between him and the grangrul, with Crym sending a blue orb into the abandoned chariot. The lizard leaped from its post and disappeared behind a large boulder along with the others. The area went silent, and Grunt cawed from overhead with a confusing statement.

"What do you mean they're gone?" said Gavee.

"We need to leave!" said Crym.

"We must free them first!" said Gavee.

"This isn't the moment for heroism. Your king has directed us to find the keeper of scrolls, not save the enslaved."

"I'm not saving them. I'm freeing them, and there is always time to do such things." Gavee said, "True to thunderblood principles, it reflects sound judgment."

Hissing and growling, the sabercats surrounded the two remaining captors within the gorge.

Grunt cawed with panic, settled into Gavee as he searched from right to left.

He asked, "Where are they?"

"I cannot see them," said Crym, who had risen above the ridgeline.

Gavee flapped his wings when something caught his leg, yanking him to the ground. Before he could move, a net fell upon him, strapping itself to the rocky floor. Crym hurled blue orbs when red ones shot from two sides, and the sound Gavee feared echoed. The devil hawks had arrived, and they had fallen into the trap Crym had warned them about, with Gavee unable to move and Grunt shifting back, working to cut the large netting.

"I'll get you out! They won't take you!"

Gavee struggled and fought the netting when it tightened under the struggle.

"Stop, Grunt! It is getting tighter!"

The shapeshifter stepped back and shifted into a black panther, jumping beyond Gavee's vision. Then Gavee spotted Crym fighting back arrows and red orbs, trying to stay within striking range. The barrage overwhelmed the tontar, and Gavee heard Grunt screech and snarl, understanding the sound and knowing his friend was outnumbered.

"Crym! Grunt! Go! Find the keeper of the scrolls! You must get him back to Witch'Bane. I'll fight my way back. You must save the king!"

"I cannot leave your side!" yelled Crym.

"You must!"

The grangrul surrounded Gavee, hissing and poking the masura.

"He's an excellent catch," hissed a lizard.

"Yes, we will use him as a trainer."

Grunt bellowed a growl.

"Grunt! You must find the keeper of the scrolls!"

"I won't leave you! I can't leave you!" yelled Grunt.

"You must!"

The net wrapped around his legs and tightened around his wings and arms.

"Go—*please!* Find the scroll keeper!"

The grangruls dragged the net between the chained prisoners, and Gavee gritted over the loose stone. The grangruls' cruelty had broken the prisoners' spirits, leaving them as mere shells to perform their labor. Upon their faces lay anguish and pain, while fear mounted on the netted masura. He fought the despair and focused on his thunderblood training. The surroundings became clearer, and he worked on the possibility of an escape. As they dragged behind the large boulder, Gavee screamed one last time.

"Find the scroll keeper! You must find him!"

Chapter Ten

The open field lay just beyond the shadowy cave, and Shapía longed to soar. The hoods' journey through the Fen caverns and dwarf crossroads proved taxing for the masuras. Bahg continued to mend the cut under his eye, stitching the wound to stop the bleeding. The princess grimaced as the sharp metal looped in and out, with its thread closing the gap. Lord Senith kept a powerful divide between the darkness and their location with the field's watch.

"Fens have been seen above the cavern, waiting for our arrival," said the hood lord.

"We should not have stopped," said Bahg.

"There was no choice. My warriors had to rest," said Senith.

"I understand, but they gather more and more the longer we stay. Guards would have been the only ones chasing us through the wide-open space. I would take my chances with them, not the Fen army waiting to attack," said Bahg.

Bahg crouched beside a boulder, watching the far field.

"We must hold for Tarm. He should be here soon and push back the Fen," said Lord Burn.

Bahg lowered his gaze to the dirt floor.

"Tarm?" questioned Bahg. "Something happened at Reflection."

"Reflection?" questioned Shapía.

"As you expected, there is some evil lurking, and it sits before Witch'Bane. It fills the southern fields like a plague," said Burn.

"We have to return," said Shapía.

"It has not entered Witch'Bane?" asked Bahg.

"No, it remains on its own and in the fields," said Burn.

Bahg looked upward with a nod.

"We wait for Tarm and continue to Ihandra, then get you to Horfa," said Bahg.

Shapía knelt beside Bahg.

"How do we know our family is safe?" she asked.

He smiled and turned.

"We should trust the skills and training of our warriors. With what Senith and Burn revealed, you must get to Horfa. We shall turn this tide at the most critical historical point for Witch'Bane," said Bahg.

Bahg looked outside, beyond the cavern.

"Our location does place us in an uncharted direction. We leave from Mudra, not Fens port," he said.

"The holy city?" asked Shapía.

"Yes, it won't be lengthy, but it is dangerous. Tarm can ensure our safety in the sacred place where they await our arrival," said Bahg.

"Why? Why is it so important to other beings that I reach Horfa?" asked Shapía.

Bahg redirected his attention toward Shapía when Senith interrupted, "Princess, the portents have predicted the one imprisoned would be the one who sees the truth for all beings from all the islands."

"Portents?" she questioned.

"It's not something easy to explain," said Bahg. "Your mother was more than a warrior and queen. She came from a lineage deeper and further than the masuras. This blood waits within, ready for discovery."

Bahg brought her in close for a hug.

"Trust me."

Shapía took in the embrace and exhaled. A bloodline more ancient than the masuras themselves, she pondered. She attempted to release the words as a hood guard appeared from the field. It unwrapped its protection, coming to a stand. Lord Burn moved to the exit.

The hood saluted. "Sire, we have word of the tontar being near."

"I sense other dangers," said Bahg.

"Benndis," said Burn.

"Yes," continued the hood. "The Fens have spread through the trees and carry the enormous weapon."

"Benndis!" said Bahg.

Shapía braced against the wall on the word, seeing firsthand what damage the weaponry creates in a forest. The weapon is a massive, hollow wooden ball, sometimes bigger than a simple, single masuran loft, with metal bands crisscrossing the sphere. It vaulted forward by tree catapults, spinning as it flew, ejecting small metal darts with its descent in the sky. An explosion would send metal shards upon impact, ripping apart everything around it. The benndis would plow through trees and forests, creating destruction. Bahg observed the princess's concern and returned to her side.

"We'll get through it without a scratch. Between our hood friends and the tontars, Ihandra is in our grasp," he said.

He embraced the princess, hiding his concerns. The thunderblood returned to the cavern entrance when a horn blasted from outside, with additional horns responding to the announcement. Bahg ran back and grabbed Shapía, pulling her deeper into the cave, when an explosion thundered at the entrance. The two masuras tumbled down the tunnel, and the hoods crumbled atop with falling rocks, filling in around the echo. Shapía's ears rang as she lay curled against the stone wall. The collapsed cave entrance bellowed dust, showing a faint glow, as Bahg swooped up the young girl, going deeper into the tunnel at a bend in the path.

"Are you hurt?" asked Bahg.

"No, my ears are ringing," she answered.

"It'll go away," he said.

"Benndis?" she asked.

"Yes, but it didn't collapse, giving us a way out," he said.

"Do they plan to send another?"

"No, the horns are the tontars warning us about what's coming. They've started their attack, and the Fens intend not to endanger their fighters," said Bahg.

"You're bleeding again," said Shapía.

Bahg clutched his right ear with blood smeared across a hand.

"I'll be fine. Prepare to leave in a rush."

The rubble and dust hovered as the living tended to the wounded. Shapía had never seen such a sight and could not stop the tears. A scene of carnage and death, a brutal price paid for their protection, lay before them.

"Wait here," said Bahg.

The elder left the bend and rejoined the gap, where he worked to move large stones from injured hoods. The hood lord, Senith, pressed an arm to his chest and grimaced as he fought to lift rocks from the damage. Shapía watched the hoods use their long tails to help remove the wreckage, and Bahg dug out the entrance. Lord Burn pushed large rocks to the side and made a passage forward. The rumble of a hit deep out in the field shook the cavern, causing dust to powder from the ceiling. The horn blast came again, and the far-off roar from fighting reached the tunnel.

Hoods slithered from the opening into the unseen fight, with more rumbling from benndis slamming the ground. Shapía eased past the bend, wanting to help and attend to the injured hoods. The fighting grew closer, with hoods forming a barrier between the outside and the cave, when Bahg pulled Shapía toward the bend.

"Should we not fight, Uncle?"

"Beings are fighting and dying for our safety. It would be reckless for us to enter and risk death, wasting the lives of those who have died. Some battles are not meant for us."

The daylight faded with benndis ending its surge in front of the cavern entrance. Torches were soon lit, and the guarding hoods made a path for Lord Senith and a guest. Shapía noticed a new tontar. It stood well above the masuras, with the hood leader growing in its stance. The tontar had thick, black horns that grew from its skull, and it pulled back its long ebony hair. His eyes glowed red, and he gripped a long black spear with black leather armor covering the torso except for the thin black tail shaped into a red arrowhead. Shapía grabbed her nose as the stench of burning metal filled the air.

"Tarm, my friend," said Bahg.

"Bahg, I'm glad to see you alive, yet bruised?" questioned Tarm.

"A gift from Torum," said Bahg.

"He still holds you responsible for Losha after all these years. Her injuries are her own, and their failure is on Torum's shoulders," said Tarm.

"King Torum now," said Bahg.

"King? They made him king?" asked Tarm.

"Or he made himself king," said Bahg.

"I am more positive about this attack," said Tarm.

"We must go, my friends," said Senith.

"Yes, the ship awaits in Mudra for this one," said Tarm to Shapía.

The tontar's teeth possessed sharp points with a bright red tongue. She smirked and then lowered her gaze, with Bahg smiling at the interaction.

"I think you forget how ugly you are," said Bahg.

"And your feet are something to behold," answered Tarm. "It's time for us to go."

The hood fighters surrounded the masuras and used the broken entrance to escape under the cloak of night. Shapía wanted to break free, but the powerful push into the field kept the hoods close. The tontars kept themselves in rank, waiting for their leader to return, with several hovering above on their pegasus. Shapía again covered her nose with an overwhelming odor more pungent than the cave. Tarm's ride awaited, and the tontar stopped in front of the flying horse.

"I want the unit to stay along the Fen tree line to keep those masuras from leaving their forest. The warriors will follow us until the poppy fields. There, we'll have an escort by the Mudra guardians into the city," said Tarm.

"Yes, my lord," answered a tontar. "The benndis?"

"If they try those again, attack the position until they are destroyed."

"I'll spread the word," said Lord Burn.

The tontar saddled the pegasus with a command.

"Shields!" he thundered.

The tontars flying army extended their right hand as a blue orb appeared and spun, creating a bright blue hue. Each fighter snapped their hand, and a see-through blue shield appeared. The protection crackled and zipped with an electrical charge, surprising Shapía. She looked to Bahg, who smiled.

"I'm glad they're on our side," he said.

The party rose into the evening sky and fled to the awaiting ship.

"I still don't know who they are?" questioned Shapía.

"They are tontars from the island of Anayana, and Tarm is their elder thunderblood." Said Bahg. "He's my closest ally, and I trust him with my life. His son, Crym, is on a mission for us."

"Why have you or anyone ever spoken about the tontars working with our clan?" puzzled Shapía. "Why have we been kept in ignorance by our allies? You kept us guarded, and now I am struggling to survive!"

"As a young royal, it's your job to learn about our internal culture and how important your position is in the family's existence. When you come of age, we introduce the islands outside our forest, and you learn how to structure the clan into the islands. There is a reason behind it."

"The truth should never be concealed to protect or pretend. We've been led wrong, and it stops with us," said Shapía. "We move forward."

"As you wish. The tontars only come to Breiv if necessary. There is a misunderstanding and prejudice against the tontars. They are loyal companions and never bring their convictions into any interactions," said Bahg.

"Convictions? What religion does one follow to create such hidden secrets?"

"It is an old, mysterious way, and you'll learn it in due time at Horfa. Stay alert and be ready to hit the dirt to take cover. Flying without a weapon leaves us vulnerable," said Bahg.

"I'm hungry," said Shapía.

"The ship is scheduled to host a feast. Stay silent."

Shapía groaned at the words, monitoring the river, then again to the far Fen forest. The Raul River continued north out of view with a hillside rising, hiding what lay beyond. The Fen Mountains continued to the east, with the danger remaining real and deadly.

"It'll be a long flight," she said.

"Our fight is not over," said Bahg. "It's imperative to keep a fast pace."

Moonlight provided a safe direction toward Mudra under the clear, dark sky. The explosions continued with the hood battle raging, letting the tontar escort and masuras flee the captors. Stars fell into a spring formation, giving off a chilly evening as the moonlight led the way. The tontars on the pegasus kept a tight structure around the masuras, and Shapía caught hoods slithering in the tall grass.

"There's a charge coming!" yelled a tontar.

"Troops, come with me! I've had enough of the Fen disturbance. Bahg, if I don't see you before you reach Mudra, be safe, my friend, and get her to Horfa!" said Tarm.

Before Bahg could respond, the party veered to the right, leaving the smaller group following the river. Bahg nodded to the lead tontar, and they flew deeper into the shadows. The hilltop made its way and descended with the Cree Sea in the background. Mudra, a holy city, was at the water's edge, with poppy fields forming its border.

Arrows continued their assault on the small group. Purple shields dissolved the wooden shafts and melted the silver tips. Shapía glanced over to witness Lord Tarm and the tontars engaged in battle against the relentless Fen attack. She pushed harder, flying down the hill and arriving at the poppy border, when the Witch'Bane thunderblood grabbed the princess's hand and diverted her attention. The tontars halted and hovered in front of the line.

"We go no farther, Thunderblood."

Shapía stared at Bahg.

"I understand," said Bahg. "May your return trip to Anayana keep the tontar clans safe. Thank your king for the sacrifice made today."

"The demand was required, and the hope for all lies upon our seers' shoulders," said Tarm.

The tontar stared at Shapía, and her eyes widened.

"In time, we are all destined to understand her might," said Bahg.

The tontar pulled out a large conch and blew, sending a low vibration.

An answered conch returned, with Tarm hovering at the hilltop. The Fens fled to their mountain protection, while the tontars waited for the group escorting the Witch'Banes. Bahg bowed, and Tarm followed suit as the Anayana visitors vanished into the night.

"Are we safe?" asked Shapía.

"Yes, as we step into the poppies, we enter Mudra and the city boundaries for protection. War and those who bring it cannot enter," said Bahg.

"The tontars?" questioned Shapía.

"No, their kind could not enter," answered Bahg.

Bahg said no more and landed in front of the barrier's small brick wall.

"Come down. We have to walk from here," he said.

"Walk?" asked Shapía.

"Once we enter, it'll be known, and the Mudra Keep shall meet us."

Shapía landed.

"Where will they meet us?" she asked.

"I don't know," said Bahg.

Bahg hopped over the wall, and Shapía followed when energy grabbed hold, taking control of her body. The sensation dropped her to one knee, and the sudden rush blinded her. She blinked against the waning light, experiencing a burn on her left wrist. A symbol embedded in her skin with deep red ink. It was not bigger than a petal from a rose, and it raised a smile, for her mother had a similar marking given to her upon acceptance at Horfa.

The mark was different, holding a thick, curved line running like a river from the wrist and ending at a short straight line, stopping its flow mid-forearm. At the curve's center, a line emerged toward the left and curled into a tail with a similar tail hanging free above the straight line. She expected to uncover the symbol's meaning.

Her head spun, and darkness grabbed hold. Then, a dazzling light came and faded. A being hovered, offering a head bow, and Shapía returned the gesture. She floated, approaching the glow where a ghost figure in a blue hood, carrying no legs, waited. Shapía started when it raised the blue garment with its invisible arms.

A soft female voice rippled, "Welcome, Princess of Witch'Bane. We have been awaiting your arrival. When word arrived about the misfortunes among the masuran clans, a worry grew about your loss. The great seer assured your arrival in Mudra, and the excitement built inside our city."

Shapía stayed locked on the flowing blue cape and the white surroundings. She attempted to speak, finding no voice.

"Princess, your physical voice is useless in the ethereal. Your mind needs the proper training."

"Why did you expect me?" she asked.

The being, surprised, hovered without an answer.

"Do you know how my family fares in our forest?" continued Shapía.

"Your gifts are greater than the scrolls have revealed."

"Mother and I have been speaking in this manner since childhood. I questioned the words, not the method. Do you have information on Witch'Bane?" asked Shapía.

"This information has yet to arrive. We are here to welcome and help you get to Ihandra."

Shapía stared at the fresh mark.

"When do we leave?"

"My dear one, you have already left."

The being spun until it disappeared, and the bright light again blinded her. She sat straight, finding Bahg standing at her feet, looking out over the ship's side and smoking a pipe. Evening lingered, and the saltwater filled her senses. The ship's aft towered overhead. Sweat covered her forehead. She pushed up her sleeve and examined a strange marking.

"They said you would wake up at sea. I didn't realize it would be when we arrived at Ihandra."

The thunderblood took a puff and waved her to his side. Shapía hid her wrist and stood to find Ihandra and its port humming in the darkness behind Bahg. She gazed at the distant scene, then settled beside the rail.

"I cannot find an expression to explain what I experienced."

"Whatever it was, you fought it every step."

She wiped the sweat from her brow. "It tells me I'm ready."

"Watch the confidence, my loving niece."

She smirked, questioned her readiness, and wondered if it was all a mistake. She panicked at that moment, built on the thoughts when the mark on her wrist ached, dropping the fear and releasing a long breath.

"I am ready," she mumbled.

* * *

Flued slouched, sitting in front of the portal inside his room. The mirror he had found locked in an unmarked safe inside the Sovereign Hall featured a hidden quality, producing a portal. He worried Malum would discover his many lies about the mask. Through dreams, she began to speak and show him how to make the gate between her cave and his room. He peered into the glowing center, with the remote cave system at hand.

His right index finger followed the black ring formed in the left palm. Silence filled the room, with a violet tinge pervading the space. Black mold under the walls and floors created a fine dust that hung in the air. The masura's eyes sank in, and dread lay upon his lips when he balled his hands into a fist. His thoughts built with anger, and his body grew in strength from the fire. The change was immediate in hearing and sight, improving with each breath, with skin, charcoal, and talons, dark black. He sensed the painful transformation and desired more, grimacing with a smile.

"Mother?" his voice echoed.

The space remained silent.

"Mother?" he said.

Malum slipped into the vision, hovering in the pool and coming through the gateway. She remained in its grasp.

"Yes, my son," she said.

"I'm moving the portal to the council hall. My father remains in the cocoon, and I plan to control it all from the mightiest tree," he said.

"What do you ask?"

"How do I shut the passage down? I no longer control its force, and it remains open," said Flued.

"I've placed a spell upon it, my dear. It will not move," answered Malum.

"It must and will, else I shall not return," he said.

"Do not threaten me," she hissed.

"Old Crow, you need me more than I need you. The exercitus is under my spell, and this is growing in influence. We must be united to lay revenge on this island," he said.

"Ease, my child. Our connection goes beyond the fire, and we shall control the entire island, sending Lohr's children to the depths for which he sent me," she said.

"Then shut down the gateway so I may move it," he angered.

"For you, I shall. Do not leave it closed for long. Your abilities grow with it open," she said.

Malum floated down to the pool, disappearing into the darkness. The radiance spun, and Flued could hear her voice.

"Curse this land. Curse this island. Curse the beings who formed his way. Close the gate and restore the power. Be quick before it's too late." Thundered Malum.

The black fungus crept along the floorboards, snaking its way back to the portal. The energy sucked back into the abyss, sealing the portal with only the mirror remaining on the floor. It bounced a bit from the dramatic closure. The chamber lay in darkness, and Flued stood, stretching his violet wings. He popped his neck sideways and sensed the surge through his fingers. He grabbed the mirror and smirked at the force he wielded, leaving the room.

The Witch'Bane forest possessed an eerie silence, with no masuras in the trees and the night darkening the shadows. The exercitus kept a close watch on the once-peaceful clan, overseeing the families' move into a large loft until their transformation into naraka. Unlike exercitus, they are death beings who hold an evil touch with a simple breath. They looked to the exercitus as their masters and Flued as their god.

The darkened masura landed on the council hall balcony, covered in fungus. He moved swiftly into the hall, where Taronquel continued trapped and pinned to the ceiling. The broken masura sat unchanged, and his mouth sewn shut.

Flued ignored the head council and reached the far side, where Rhile stood protecting the former king, enclosed in a large lavender cocoon. The thick webbing hid the body, but random kicks showed he had struggled in pain. The chamber contained a few candles, maintaining a gloomy presence, and the female masura standing guard possessed sunken, glowing amethyst eyes, lost in a trance.

"My Etta," said Flued.

Rhile snapped to attention.

"Clear the room's table and chairs. The gateway is moving in its place," said Flued.

Flued stepped below Taronquel.

"Watch and see the great force fester before you. Bear witness to its greatness," he said.

Flued flicked a finger in Taronquel's direction, and the thick thread zipped across his maw, allowing him to open the mouth.

The head council was quick to snap an answer. "The evil I warned your father and mother of has seeped into the clan. May Nathe strike you down to the deepest of Yama's holes!"

"With this opening, I control those holes!" he laughed.

"You control…"

Flued flicked a finger at the words, and the thread shut the mouth. The focus returned to Rhile and several narakas, taking an axe to the mighty clan table and demolishing its Witch'Bane history. They sent the broken pieces over the balcony, where a fire roared in the town square. Flued dragged the king's chair in front of the cocoon and faced it to the room's center. He placed a large, black, rectangular cloak over his shoulders and stepped into the room's middle, setting the mirror down. The masura retreated and pulled forth a scroll. His eyes darkened, and a deep purple hue saturated the surroundings.

"Mirror, mirror, shall you find,

"The gate to Malum and her mind.

"I seek the strength to extend my length.

"To make them cower and grow my strength.

"Open, Open, Open the door!

"Open, Open, Open, for I say no more!

"Jaka! Yama!"

The glass turned ebon black, and an ooze fell from its center, crusting over and spreading across the wooden floor. It seeped around Flued's talons and then rose onto the king's throne, creeping upward and forming a purple crest, replacing the Witch'Bane lightning bolt. In the middle of this new symbol stood a sword pointing down, flanked by two angled daggers, forming a Y shape. The amethyst gem on the sword's hilt gleamed in the dark, resting next to a fresh throne. As the black liquid crusted, it formed the king's chair, with faces squirming in the muck.

The black, crusty spores spread along the walls, encasing Taronquel's web prison in a thick, ebon shell. Filled with hate and anger, the masura wept in pain. The mirror hardened, the center shattered, and light thundered through the portal, with Malum emerging from the shadows. The powerful witch hovered and then slid across the floor in front of Flued. Her bony hand reached from the violet cloak, and its evil affected his face.

"Asmodeus, my son, let us begin your reign. Sit on your throne and call forth your exercitus," she said.

The masura paused on the fresh name and stretched his blackened wings. He withdrew his pallium and stepped up to the throne. Feeling its energy, his vision took on a purple shade with a red glow coming from the surrounding beings. Malum aimed her crooked staff at the rock floor, with her other hand hovering near the gateway.

"Open a gate and allow the exercitus to join our home," said Malum.

Energy from the gateway shot through the witch, her staff, and into the rocks. It cracked and shattered until a chasm appeared.

"Come forth, my children!" she cackled.

Wind burst through, and the exercitus soldiers entered the gateway leading from Malum's hidden lair. They ventured into the Witch'Bane's forest, taking posts as guardians of their new home.

Flued, now Asmodeus felt their energy, and his thoughts controlled their movement and placement. The forest filled his mind with red lights dotting the trees as they served as a fortress before the Witch'Bane River. Malum hovered over her regal throne and sat upon it, clutching the cane.

Rhile stayed by Asmodeus, raising her ebon arms.

"Fighters for Asmodeus, protect the great forest home, and let us prepare to grow our might," her voice thundered.

This recent age opened the door with Asmodeus leading the island forces. His skin was a purplish hue, and his pupils were black as the most profound chasm. Behind him, the Witch'Bane king, trapped, jerked in agony, causing the cocoon to bow in and out.

"It is imperative we find the disk, my son," hissed Malum.

"I have sent scouts. They'll find it before long," said Asmodeus.

"It answers everything," said Malum.

"No, it answers nothing, yet provides the ability to fulfill what I see through my fresh eyes. I have the answers, and these paths lead to full dominance beyond this world," said Asmodeus.

Malum squeezed Asmodeus's hand.

"You see him," said Malum.

Asmodeus gazed into the center as his fresh insight answered many questions. One vision repeated, and in it, he felt the answer blocked. He sent this insight outward in search of Gavee, finding it on the energy plane. It emitted an odd light, one no other masura carried. The green pulse appeared stable, forming a barrier with the mysterious green, not allowing the vision to enter and giving pain when he tried.

It angered Asmodeus, showing his path and destruction if he did not break into the green light. Somehow, Gavee maintained a key and would have to stop his cousin from entering the door. He reached out to Shapía when a bright white light forced him to cringe and shut his eyes. The pain shot needles into his brain, and he screamed.

"Your sister holds a power even I cannot uncover," hissed Malum.

"She will bend the knee," said Asmodeus.

"The plane tells me it may never happen," said Malum.

"Then she dies!" cursed Asmodeus.

"Her death grows your power," said Malum.

"Death indeed," he said.

Chapter Eleven

The morning arose like the previous days, with a water bucket drenching the small, barred cell. Gavee restrained his reaction, learning the grangruls enjoyed his discomfort, and drew the whip harder on his anger. A head injury causing some memory loss and blackouts succeeded his capture, making it difficult to distinguish one day from another. The lump remained a throbbing, painful reminder, sensitive to even the lightest touch.

The grangrul are slave drivers who fill arenas and pockets for the gamblers. They use masuras to train the devil hawks for attacks and entertainment in the theater. Gavee found himself trapped in a practice facility with no escape. The large domed wooden cages connected to a more significant section, where a groomed forest and designed course trained the birds. The caged masura would teach the birds how to hunt as the grangrul trainer observed and sent whistled commands.

A new view of the city came from the sun's light. Gavee, when atop the largest tree, studied the massive city of endless adobe buildings stacked from one side to the next, higher than the tallest tree. Opposite the cages, and towering over the town, was the single entrance to the grangrul city. The endless enslaved moved behind their masters' whips with halflings, imp humanoids, and other creatures stumbling from building to building under shackles and chains.

With a touch to the cell door, the trainer's staff popped it open, freeing Gavee to crawl from the muck. The straw and mud thickened his body and wings as he forced them to span open into a stretch.

"Today, slave, you train, then go to the arena to make me rich," said the lizard in a gurgled laugh.

Gavee stayed silent with his stomach in knots while he waited for the gruel. The lizard's blue tongue slithered between its sharp teeth and overbite jaw as it raised its whip. He cowered from the pain when it hissed a laugh.

"Eat."

The creature pointed its thin fingers to a bucket on the ground, and the thunderblood trainee dug a hand into the gray slop. He gagged at the putrid smell, forcing a swallow against its bile slime as it slid down his throat. Gavee ate daily, ignoring the stench, anticipating the whip's impact on his back. The grangrul commanded through the lashing, showing when to sleep, eat, and train the birds. He scooped the fourth handful when the snap grimaced his face, and he oozed the gruel through his fingers. His wings bore the burden, with feathers missing and unhealed scars replacing the skin.

His tattered black, now gray shirt and torn pants kept him covered. His captors seized the queen's sword, the Thunderblood dagger, and the Witch'Bane cloak sewn by the queen, losing them forever to the open market. The caravan staged, and his imprisonment planned, with the masters slipping, calling him by name.

The whip snap awoke him, and he winced at the pain.

"Time to train," it slithered.

The grangrul pointed to the far gate, entering a small tree patch where the devil hawks roosted. The horned hawk stood half a masura tall with a wingspan the same, and long claws protruding from its wingtips. Flying in a group of five, the lead beast had branched horns with an elongated beak protruding from its skull. The holding area contained countless flocks as they all peered down at the masura. The well-trained creatures never moved without the lead and held their position until the high-pitched whistle drew them.

With their red eyes staring, the pair moved through the foliage until they reached the ultimate locked gate. With a rusty groan, the grangrul opened the small door, as it did every morning, following its established routine. Gavee crawled onto the practice field when the lizard pulled a lever, triggering the wall to drop the top quarter. The opening allowed the hawks to enter once the whistle blew. The masura stood before a tree grouping thicker than the devil hawk roosts and unfurled his wings. From the dim grangrul dome, Gavee heard the rain, the whips on slave backs, and their painful moans filling the silence. It made Gavee aware that the day had begun for the entrapped beings.

The masura took flight, rising to the cage top and gliding past the apex until he reached the tallest tree. It became a cycle, giving him a view of the streets to study the routine guard change and patterned day in the lizard city. The distant waterfall filled the surroundings as the water landed in its pool, and the wild creatures who made the prison home moved about the floor. The well-maintained woods contained the hand of imprisoned masuras hidden from Gavee. He expected the whistle and the incoming thumping from the devil hawk's wings fluttering through the open gate, cursing its sound.

The whistle blasted, and a screech beckoned from the leader. Gavee had to wait for the birds to catch his presence before making the flight into a drill pattern. He found the double lash from not following instructional procedures too painful and allowed the evil creatures to come close enough, often missing the trailing talons. From the branch, the thunderblood opened his mind, hearing the trees speak as air built under his wings. The masura soared through the trees, following the same pattern as he flew daily. With a split flock, the hawks screeched, calling each other during the hunt as the leader continued toward Gavee. The masura sensed the trees' concern for his safety.

With two birds veering from the far right, clipping Gavee's talons, the first obstacle's protruding boulder closed, forcing the masura into a tumble. The thunderblood trainee rolled and went into a full run as he slid behind the boulder, sprinting down the hidden embankment toward the pool. Two additional birds plunged from the waterfall while he endured leg wounds. He got to the water, and then the whistle blew twice, calling for a strike.

Fear grabbed hold. The grangrul had not used this attack in training.

As Gavee came to the pool's rocky shoreline searching for defense, the birds repeated their calls in distinct sounds. The grangrul emerged from the tree line, blowing a whistle, and the devil hawks gathered at the cage roof. In the pool's center, a protruding stone was the masura's destination.

"There," he gritted.

The grangrul piped again, and Gavee did not pause for the beasts as instructed, pushing his wings into the air to reach the falling stream. The hawks pursued him as he thundered into the rushing water. He hit hard, propelling himself onto a hidden cliff behind the waterfall. He rolled and slammed into the rock face. Gavee coughed from the impact and tried to come to his knees, holding his side.

In the soft mud lay talon prints leading to a carved-out hollow with straw and bedding, waiting for its owner to return.

The falls' roar muted sounds beyond, as the masura searched through the water. The devil hawks would wait in a roost with the grangrul, angry about the training change. Gavee observed the footprints, deciding to stand and fight against the foul creatures.

"Despite the cost, I'll do this for them."

Focused on the cascading water and its rhythm, the trainee relaxed until awareness faded to darkness. His chest burned at the marking as Gavee's body drifted from the falls. The black faded to green, and then a green image emerged into the cavern of symbols and unknown words etched in stone. He couldn't shake the dream, and his body became heavy and slow.

"*What is this?*" he slurred.

"*We are connecting,*" said the deep voice.

"*Who are we?*"

"*I cannot tell you yet. It would disturb your mind. We must first grow our connection and trust.*"

"Without being acquainted, I have no wish to form a bond. It may be simple mind control, similar to what has imprisoned my king."

"*I assure you, masura, I had no part in it. I wish to grow the trust between us.*"

"Why?"

"*I need your help. We need your help from the same harm that covers your king.*"

"How?"

"*You once carried what it wanted, but it's now hidden. You shall come across one who can help find it, but you must escape. We are short on time.*"

"What is it? If you have the information, why not retrieve it yourself or come rescue me from this underworld? I'm trapped within a hole, holding one way out and guarded."

"*It follows me, so I couldn't search for it or even save you from the wretched. My only way is through our connection.*"

"What's the item?"

"*In the ancient scrolls, it's called Lonn. In my language, it goes by a different name. You identify it as the queen's sword.*"

"Lonn? Why is it called Haven? Why name it? I don't understand."

"*You must break free from your prison, Masura, and find the one who knows where Lonn is located. Go follow the path. It'll end the nightmare.*"

The green broke into gray, then black, bringing the rushing water sensation, and then his prison. Gavee closed his eyes, contemplating the unknown voice, with thoughts drifting to the queen and the year since the dragon encounter. The green dream grabbed his attention, and the voice in his head held his tongue.

The thunderblood's eyes popped open, focusing past the cascading water, and the attack plan rolled into action.

"We must find the scroll keeper."

Deep into the water, the thunderblood trainee searched, finding the grangrul with a battle staff standing on the water bank. The gate key straddled its hip, while the devil hawks perched on the tree behind their master. With energy built into strength, the masura smashed through the waterfall, heading for the grangrul. The grangrul released its whistle, and the lead hawk squealed its kill command. From the haunted roost, a bird assault began, but Gavee preempted them, getting to the grangrul first and snatching the staff, then seizing the grangrul by the throat. He crushed the lizard's windpipe, ending its fight.

The lead devil hawk swooped in, meeting the spinning staff, and its head cracked, finishing the bird. The flock slid past Gavee and then roosted in a distant tree, concluding their fight. Lost without their leader.

He searched the woods and did not find the second grangrul, which often lurked near the leading trainer. Gavee headed to the top opening, dashing through the roosting trees and landing in the prison yard. He made his way to the small prisons and unlocked each one, releasing the few halflings, changelings, and lone humans from the cells. They burst through the shack's gate.

The trainer stood there, with whip and sword ready. "You'll pay, masura!"

It sent a whip to a halfling's legs, and the tiny creature curled in a scream.

Gavee took the distraction and landed the staff in the lizard's right eye, twirled, and cracked its head. The beast dropped its sword and curled up on the ground. With the loose weapon in hand, the thunderblood trainee gave the staff to the human and unlocked the gate. From the shed, prisoners surged into the grangrul, then melted into the city's streets.

Gavee slid the little dagger the lizard carried across its throat, ensuring no alarm.

The adobe buildings towered three stories high, and the narrow streets would allow a single drawn cart to ease through the tight roads with small balconies and simple windows. As they entered the city center, whistles blew, alerting the city to the escape. Gavee slipped through an open door and found a young male masura sweeping the floor. He placed a finger on his lips and shut the door. The lad peered out a side window, then waved for Gavee to follow him up the wooden stairs.

The stairs spiraled past the second and onto the third floor when the boy smiled, waving Gavee to a dirty old tapestry. He pulled it and pointed to a door. Gavee worried about what awaited them beyond the tapestry. The boy shook his head in disgust and opened it to a black, windowless room.

"My room, they never go. It's slave quarters and forbidden to be touched."

Gavee did not understand.

"You be safe until we both escape," said the masura.

"Slave!" thundered a grangrul.

Horrified, the boy pushed Gavee into the room and closed the door.

The thunderblood trainee stood still, listening to the talons hitting the wooden planks until they faded, and he kept silent. The place gave no sound, and the darkness broke from the small light coming through the door frame. He eased against a dirt wall near the entrance, closing his eyes to allow the energy to slow and bring in the surroundings. Gavee waited in the darkness, not knowing his next move, and wore a smile from the little freedom he had found in the foul city.

* * *

Shapía roosted in a meditative state in her Horfa living quarters. A simple loft, blankets for warmth, a single candle for light. Her first oracle session at the Horfa's Oracle of Oracles was soon to begin during the Sattva period, as the day ended. As soon as they arrived, she touched the glass figure held by the rainbow-colored being, feeling warmth and comfort as she landed in front of it.

Maintaining a feminine vibration, the oracle shapeshifted, disguising the truth concealed within the identity. Shapía's presence swept the island with a silent murmur of the new Seer of Seers. She brought hope and balance to the Five Islands.

From the silence, the princess rose, opened the door, and gazed upon the immense Mighty Tree. At Horfa, on the island of Ihandra, the Mystic Island, a dead volcano overlooked the land with the Waterfalls of Silence hanging against its backside, falling into the sea. The collapsed southern wall made its way to a lush forest where the tree of trees, the Mighty Tree, lay in its center. It towered, reaching the same height as the volcano's rim, and its limbs, themselves the size of trees, branched together in a network, creating a city within and throughout the branches. The port on the far side carried a bustling town, and the path to Horfa rose from dirt to stone passages, narrowing to allow four across as it met a bridge over the fallen volcano wall leading to the mighty tree.

Protected under the goddess Sora, the island developed into a sanctuary, balancing the Five Islands. Ihandra vibrated in low tantras and soft melodies, sweeping over the basin with a misty rain. Near the Mighty Tree, a single ray of memory fell from peaceful days and bright stars. The Mystics vigilantly guarded their knowledge and secrets about the island's past and future.

The masura descended, passing the stairs and circling the mighty tree's trunk before landing by the outside dining area. Level with the canopy of the beautiful, lush forest, the platform sat inside the rim. She looked forward to dinner with Bahg before the evening session. The Witch'Bane thunderblood sat alone, staring at the tabletop, holding a cup in both hands. Shapía beamed with delight, her joy overflowing during the cherished family visit.

"Uncle," she said with a smile.

Bahg drew his attention to Shapía, and a forced smile.

"My niece."

Shapía worried about the pretend action as the two embraced and sat.

"You look well," said Bahg.

"Aware," she answered. "Your wounds seem to heal."

"When you stay in a place of healing, things go well."

They laughed.

"I take it your development is coming along," he said.

"It's overwhelming and yet comfortable. I sleep so deep amidst the exhaustion," said Shapía.

She grabbed a cup and downed the fruit drink. Shapía had become accustomed to the flavor, which held a sweet cinnamon taste with a spicy kick. She savored each swallow.

"Any word from home?" she asked.

"Are you telling me your training has not awakened you to the information?"

She stared at Bahg.

"What's wrong?" she asked.

"There was an attack at Reflection, bringing war to the Upper Realm," said Bahg.

"This clarifies the emotion," she said. "I'm surprised you haven't returned."

"There's more." He rose and moved to the railing. "Flued is the cause."

He gripped the railing.

"What?" questioned Shapía.

He turned with tears in his eyes, and panic struck.

"Your brother has sided with the darkness. He controls Witch'Bane and DasaRaul, with Bata soon to follow. Our family and clan are now something,"—he paused — "not normal."

Shapía failed to find words as she listened to Bahg continue with the tale of Reflection and the battle, all coordinated by Flued. The money he paid Fen to kill Bahg and take her as a slave made the stomach curl. Then he said something stunning and painful.

"He hired the grangruls to capture Gavee."

She could not believe it. Flued had anger and a twisted mind, but never hatred for his cousin.

"I don't understand. The grangrul?" she asked.

"It appears none of us understands."

A sudden panic set in around her father.

"What of father?" she asked.

"No one knows. I'm unsure whether the king is dead or alive."

"And the other clans?" she asked.

"Flued wields evil magic, forcing them to fight in their forests for survival. The Upper Realm is burning, and it's because of our family," said Bahg.

He faced the forest, his head bowed. She attended his side.

"I don't sense Father is deceased, and Gavee remains within my heart, which tells me he's alive," said Shapía.

"You sound familiar."

"Familiar?" she asked.

He forced a smile. "Your mother would say similar things when you three would be missing from one of your adventures."

"I perceive her presence inside me, and tranquility amidst the conflict," said Shapía.

"Anger is my emotion. How could your brother be so foolish?"

She returned to the table, quenching her thirst. "Flued has always been about Flued. Father never saw it or ignored it, and Mother tried to hug her way through it. Gavee and I saw him as he was, and it would lead to a fight."

Bahg returned to the table. "Your parents did not ignore it. The problem is known, and we tried to guide him from the clan history. Your grandfather's illness is hereditary, and talks about excluding Flued lasted a considerable time."

Shapía was stunned mid-drink and lowered the cup. Food arrived, and Shapía gave a bow to the maitrins with their kindness. She took the fruit, bread, and rice to eat with the sun beyond the rim, and training bells echoed within the trees.

"Exclude Flued?"

"There is much to learn, but it's not my place to tell. Be aware, the things your family has done, we did for a better life," said Bahg.

Bahg picked a few pieces of fruit and stood. "I'm to leave Horfa."

"Leave?" she questioned.

"You are safe, and beyond anyone's grasp. I must return and save our king."

Shapía rose, and they embraced.

"I shall see you again, Uncle," she said.

"In these times, all we have is hope," said Bahg.

"My mind is becoming clearer. I cannot wait to see you again."

Bahg did not wait, opened his wings, lifted, dropped, and flew into the forest. She watched him disappear, and she grabbed some bread. The platform remained with many followers, and most looked at her with pride. Those allowed to mingle within the Mighty Tree understood what Shapía represented and carried excitement for what was to come. She took a sip when a fairy settled on the table. The small creature, standing no taller than a monarch butterfly, wore similar robes as the others, with long black hair and pointy ears peeking out. Her wings were see-through with sparkles, and sparkling dust trailed behind her flight.

"Guru Lin awaits your arrival," said the fairy.

"I am on my way," answered Shapía.

She took flight. Shapía touched down on the second-highest platform on the Mighty Tree's north side and met her guru, a female human in traditional saffron robes. The masura bowed as she approached and went down on one knee. The female placed a hand atop Shapía's head and slid it to her chin, raising her sight.

"My child, I see your mother whenever you land," she said with a smile.

"My Guru, I am here as requested. May I learn more and be less attached to my presumptions, so my mind is not bound to my ideas," answered Shapía.

"Don't overthink it, my dear."

She patted Shapía and proceeded to her spot on a saffron cushion, with the masura following and sitting on a white pillow. The two stayed silent while Guru Lin stared at the wood-planked floor, and Shapía struggled to maintain a similar concentration.

The smell of honeysuckle settled upon everything, with the night silence holding a light tune from a distant sitar. Shapía followed the mentor, maintaining the pose until the princess experienced heavy eyelids and succumbed to slumber.

A bell awakened her.

"When we met the first day you landed on these shores, I stated, as the past, present, and future became one, it would be the moment for you to sit and become what you already are, allowing the awakening to begin."

Guru Lin stood and popped her cane on the planked floor. The candlelight dimmed, and white orbs hung overhead, sparkling as if alive. Pictures appeared, swirling into each other and folding, creating new ones.

"Sattva awoke and sensed the ripple across the continuum. This calls upon you to join the order, to become the leader, and to usher us into a new era. Our order holds the reality of where we come from and how we awoke. It depicts a reality demanding release from the familiar," said Guru Lin.

Shapía's mouth gaped, and she marveled at the images. She closed her mouth and found Guru Lin appearing to wait for an answer. The princess struggled to speak through a dry mouth but found the words. "I am ready, My Guru."

Guru Lin snapped her fingers, and the light sources curled, whipping around until they formed five large individual light forms.

"The Five Islands, as you know, are a gift from the creators. These lands teem with life, conscious beings, and dreamers," said Guru Lin.

Light images appeared from the dots, showing animals walking on all fours, standing, and then in clothes. Small groups turned to towns, cities singing in some and war in others, bringing chaos throughout the orbs.

"Some awakened to the dream from these dreamers and are called oracles."

The light images fractured and rotated in a slow, spinning circle. Guru Lin raised the walking stick, pulling down one light source, and it hovered in her hand.

"Then we have one who transcends the oracle."

"Sattva?" questioned Shapía.

"Yes, but her light is dimming."

The light source dimmed yellow.

"When this source ceases to be, we face dark times."

The circling lights shattered and charged at each other, exploding.

"A new light has been found. A light, Sattva, did not foresee until..." With a lift of her walking stick, Guru Lin caused a light to appear from the dark. She pulled it onto her palm. "Until the light brings in a new age for the Five Islands."

The light flitted with the stray balls, flowing into a rotating circle. Guru Lin remained before Shapía and caressed the masura's face.

"The light is you, my dear. You are the hope for the next age."

Shapía frowned at the words, and the guru's expression changed. The princess fought the tears as they rolled down her cheeks.

"My dear, you're prepared, and during the true awakening, the truth with the life you believe you lost is realized. The unknown is scary if you believe it exists."

"The unknown exists, Guru Lin. I am uncertain about what the future holds in these words."

"It exists because you choose to take part in existence. Sattva transcends existence, yet takes part in helping guide and direct."

Shapía failed to contain her anxiety and jumped to her feet. She paced the darkened space with jumbled thoughts racing through her mind. The words offered no meaning, and the panic about never seeing home again filled her with fear. Guru Lin came to Shapía and grabbed her left wrist. The hidden mark scorched forward, causing Shapía to yelp. The guru snapped her hold to show the wrist where the once-hidden pattern appeared as a burn.

Guru Lin smiled and said, "Your mother is here."

"Why does it burn?" she asked.

"The power makes its mark permanent."

"Power?" she questioned.

"Sit. We must train. Then you'll meet with the seer."

The princess froze at the words. "Sattva?"

"Yes, I intend to train you in Oracle skills and history," said the guru. "With matters unseen by me, the seer guides you."

For learning and focus, they returned to the cushion. The ideas surpassed Shapía's conception, forcing her to listen to the guru.

"Over these past days, the centering has become the core of your energy. In the core, you're destined to grow, to move without moving, travel without traveling, and reach beyond your island without sailing. The force carries your full energy and the many incantations, spells, charms, and weapons," said Guru Lin.

Guru Lin rose and winked at Shapía.

"We call it the Settling, which created the Sangkohr, or protective center."

From inside the robe, the mentor produced two hand fans adorned with lovely Horfa symbols. The robed woman released a deep breath, snapping the fans open and sending them into a twirl, rolling them over her hands. A light cloud formed at her feet as the markings sparked into a deep blue, dimming the area. As the guru twirled the fans, eyes shifted to match the colors of the symbols as the arms inter-crossed and snapped them in a repeated pattern. The mentor's pose made the boards vibrate, fans whirling in both hands.

The scene before her caused the princess to wonder. Guru Lin's position held firm, and her eyes sparked deep blue. Her body faded until a hollow image remained.

"The energy allows you to cross short or great distances, depending on thought."

Guru Lin's words echoed from behind, causing Shapía to jump from the apparition, and her teacher now stood on a distant branch. Between the hollow and solid images, the princess snapped, working on wrapping her thoughts concerning the magic. With a snap of her fingers, the Horfa mother grinned and disappeared. Her eyes turned dark green as the bright image snapped alive and the fans closed. In a slow dance, the teacher spun, arms raised high, before lowering them. She cracked the fans.

"When mastered, you can snap in and out, protecting both energies."

The guru's energy sat on a limb above Shapía, and the hollow image fell into the same form. The woman removed a sword and sliced down a large tree branch.

"In this state, you possess more than your physical power. You hold the full energy from reality and, when wielded, can cut anything in its path."

The guru returned to physical form, standing before Shapía, using a hand fan to cool her body. The woman snapped a fan against the broken limb, and it raised, restoring itself into place.

"It drains your source, but you'll learn how to move it into other forms. Now, what object would be your connection to the outer being?"

"Object?"

"Yes, my fans are my connection to my physical being and my heritage. What will connect you to your mother?"

"You mean my clan heritage?"

"No, your mother. Witch'Bane does not have a clan heritage."

Shapía experienced some confusion.

"It is not for me to foretell," said the guru. "Sattva shall explain. Let us sit in silence and prepare for the meeting because, in it, I believe the truth will awaken."

"I find it impossible to sit in silence after your words. Why is my clan not worthy of an object?"

"I've spoken more than I should have and above my ability. It is your turn to see the seer."

The mark on Shapía's wrist stung again, and this time, emerged as raised skin.

"The seer awaits," said Lin. "Follow me."

Lin went to the balcony, snapped her fans open, and twirled them around her hands. Shapía watched the woman's energy drift from the body and smiled, waving the masura to follow. She pushed her wings into motion and remained behind the drifting energy as it rose and floated to the backside of the Mighty Tree. They climbed, reaching higher until they arrived at the mighty tree's top. The most prominent white flower Shapía had ever seen lay bloomed. Its center possessed a white glow, explaining the aura visible from below. A being in a thick yellow robe was sitting in its center. A spot on the large petal showed a place to sit before the being.

"She waits," said Lin.

The female energy drifted away, and Shapía continued hovering, hesitant. She surveyed the night sky, detected no sound, and discovered her enclosure. Sattva did not move.

"Mother, be with me," muttered Shapía.

The masura lowered and sat with legs crossed on the indent. The petal was soft and emitted a light flowery aroma, with the light appearing to be a hard shell. She concentrated on the yellow hood, awaiting direction from the mysterious figure. The oversized robe showed a body within, but with no movement, Shapía worried.

"You must release the hold on this identity," said a soft voice.

"This is outside my understanding," Shapía replied.

"The raised marking on your left wrist continues to burn until you realize it is but a mirage, a compulsion created by indulgence."

"Why does everyone speak in such a way?" questioned Shapía.

Sattva raised her gaze, and the masura suppressed her surprise. The being was a glass figure with a myriad of colors flowing inside. Her face had beautiful blue eyes and soft lips, which blossomed into a smile.

"Your mother tells me you grasp what I am saying," said Sattva.

"My mother is dead."

"Yes, she has departed from this life, but her energy remains. It guided you this past year and sent you to visit Sora's oracle."

"Her presence?"

"Yes, it's not just about being there. The concept of 'more' clarifies the indulgence I am discussing."

"I grasp, so it becomes?" questioned Shapía.

"Ah, you were listening when you sat on the ledge years back."

"Mother stated that the grasp makes it real and creates the world. If I release the idea of grasping, creation doesn't exist."

"Mmmm, if it were that simple. It takes all the grains of sand to stop seeing an end, but only a moment to recognize it."

"I'm not ready," said Shapía.

"The knowledge you hold is greater than you realize. The Mazerth Stone is an example of indulgence. I am happy you have it."

"Its nature is a mystery to me, but its weight pains my shoulders," said Shapía.

"Yes, it controls or destroys, so it holds a negative mark. We intend to remove it and keep it safe here in Ihandra. We sit silently and allow our energy to hover at the Mighty Tree."

"As you wish, Great One."

"No one is great. All are equal."

Chapter Twelve

From afar, a whip cracked, awakening Gavee. The recipient's grunt penetrated the thick walls. The masura remained motionless, with an ear against the dirt. Since going into hiding, the first incident Gavee had overheard was the mumbled hisses and wood breaking between the grangruls. The door to the room outside the slave quarters slammed shut as the masura entered with a small lit candle. Dal, cornered, snarled, his ragged shirt whipped to shreds.

"City angry with escape. All slaves pay the price," said Dal.

"I must give myself to them," whispered Gavee. "I cannot have anyone tortured for my cause."

"They kill you. You stay."

"I expect them to search homes," said Gavee.

"It started. I plan to move you, and then we return."

"Why are you doing this for me?" asked Gavee.

"I want to flee, but life has been in the city. I need help beyond the door."

Gavee wondered how many would want the same chance. "If I had my sword…"

"I saw it," whispered Dal.

Gavee's eyes widened. "Where?"

"Master had it, then sold it. He got a second home, which is where my friend went. It's still within the city limits, though."

"Do you know where it is?"

"Yes." Dal shook his head at the thought and gazed at the floor.

"If you get me to the sword, I'm able to free us both."

"My friend?"

"And your friend."

"I'll come back."

Dal jumped through the entrance before Gavee could request food, with his stomach moaning and dry throat yearning for water. The masura lost count of the days, yet his body showed several had passed. He longed for more than the dim light peeking through the door, and his wings were sore from their confined position. He settled against the clay wall, concentrating on the outside, when he fell into a trance. The scar on his chest throbbed, and his body vibrated with his breath intensifying. Thoughts shifted as a green fog filled his subconscious. He sensed his body drifting until he reached a hillside.

"Masura," came a deep voice.

"What do you want from me?" asked Gavee.

"The evil power is growing. You must find the scroll keeper before they do."

"Before whom? Who is searching?" questioned Gavee.

"If he is found by 'the one,' the few will determine the fate of all beings on every island. They will remove the freedoms and bring their own to rule all."

"Why don't you stop them?" asked Gavee.

Gavee's sight looked out across an open field, a field Gavee recognized.

"Why are we atop the Crescents?"

Gavee gasped.

"Why did you bring me here?"

The clearing remained unchanged, with the burned landscape enduring from the fateful day. The spot where the queen died contained a female masura statue with flowers planted and blooming in a circle.

"Who placed the statue? The flowers? Who knows about this?" asked Gavee.

"If you do not reach the scroll keeper first, her death will be tragic. It would be a failure to know what she knew and not to stop. We're destined to rue the moment lost."

"We? Who are you?" asked Gavee.

"You would not understand. I will share this information at the right time. You must trust me. I am not deceiving you. A war is coming, and there is one way to avoid it."

"The scroll keeper," said Gavee.

"Yes, you must reach him first."

The green vision narrowed until Gavee fell into darkness. He awoke. Dal entered.

"We head out now."

"Where?" asked Gavee.

"At our private place."

Gavee groaned at the idea. "Private place?"

"Place, my friend, and I go to plan. We need to leave."

The younger masura opened the small door, waiting for the elder to leave. Gavee squinted in the harsh light and stood with some pain. Since his arrival, he had squatted or remained on the ground, and the few days in hiding kept his body cramped. Dal did not wait, dashing down the dirt stairs and passing through a hallway. They proceeded down and onto the second floor, with the curtains drawn in front of rounded rooms. The stairwell descended directly to its end at a closed wooden door. Dal darted into a distant unknown as Gavee stopped at the last step.

"Dal," whispered Gavee.

The boy did not answer.

"Dal," he said.

The masura returned to the room, handing Gavee bread and a banana. He smiled and downed the items, enjoying their taste. Dal only received small food scraps. This treat was therefore very welcome. The bread offered a sweet aroma and flavor, with the banana just ripe and quenching the thirst. Dal handed him a glass filled with honey mead. Gavee did not hold back, allowing it to pour from the sides.

"We go."

Dal handed Gavee a brown cloak, the slave's garb, and the two entered the street. The narrow passageways offered enough space for a slave-pulled cart. The tall adobe buildings lined the street, with slaves moving, keeping their eyesight on the ground ahead. Gavee took the same posture and clung to Dal's brown cloak as they approached a town square with a large water fountain. It contained little significance, with the multitude moving about their business.

"Where are the grangrul?" whispered Gavee.

"The masters talk about you. They set a plan to search all homes and slave places."

"How are we going to exit through one gate?" asked Gavee.

"There's another way, but I must get my friend."

Dal pushed ahead. Gavee observed the dirt path and avoided eye contact with the street urchins. The city homes widened in different ways of interjecting along the path. When a loud siren sounded, they had arrived at a smaller house, and the slaves began running.

"We must vacate the street. Trouble. Friend is close."

The masura pulled Gavee forward, navigating a thick crowd before Dal abruptly turned left into a small room. It featured a round brick well in the center, with a locked wooden cover and a broken bench.

"He meets us here."

The outside rush grew, and Dal placed a wooden dowel, securing the entrance. "How does your friend enter?"

"He knocks," said Dal.

"What is this?"

"Old water hole. Not used. It has no more water."

The thunderblood trainee moved to the cover and worked around it, trying to discover how to remove the barrier. The steel bars crossing each other locked it to the brick foundation, flush with the edge.

"How do we get inside?" asked Gavee.

"Friend has the key."

"And you trust your friend?" questioned Gavee.

Dal frowned.

"What about my sword?" asked Gavee.

"Oh, it's no longer in the city."

"Can you tell me where?"

"No, we flee into the hole. We don't need it."

"I need my sword."

Dal pressed his ear to the door, waiting for a knock. Gavee groaned, and the two remained silent as the siren blared. Feet pounded past repeatedly, with the outside disturbance echoing in the small room. The thunderblood trainee braced against the mud wall and eased his breath, listening to the sounds creeping inside the silent room. The noise fell further still when three raps came to the door. Smiling through the missing teeth, the lad raised the wooden bar. There stood a happy halfling, missing two front teeth. The short, stocky being wore a torn vest with a tattered brown shirt and gray boots. He stood to the height of Gavee's chest.

"Dal, my boy," said the halfling.

"Benny, come," answered Dal.

The halfling popped through with Dal slamming the door.

NESTED EVIL

"Keys?" asked Dal.

"Aye," said the toothless halfling.

The halfling attempted to climb the brick but failed. The masura helped him and kept a sharp eye on the new creature. With a ring full of keys, the halfling struggled to open the well.

"We need to go now," demanded Gavee.

"One moment, one moment," answered Benny. "Hey, you're the masura."

Gavee said nothing and kept his stare on the locked lid. The lock flipped open, and the halfling stowed the keys in his pocket. He jumped from the well, and Gavee removed the heavy bars, lifting the circular lid. Fresh air lifted from the darkness, and the masura tried to see into the black.

"How far down does it go?" asked Gavee.

"Far enough," answered Benny. "Why is he here?"

"He needs help too, Benny," said Dal.

The halfling groaned and removed several loose bricks from the floor. He withdrew a long rope from his pocket. Securing one end to the door, he tossed the other into the well, heeding Gavee's warning.

"Where does the tunnel go?" asked Gavee.

"We are going to uncover it together, masura," answered the halfling.

"Wait, are there tunnels?"

"It stored water at one time, and then they moved to a different source. The water comes from somewhere," answered Benny.

Gavee glared at the well.

"Indeed, I've witnessed water pooling in from the ground near the wells. There are no tunnels," said Gavee.

"Help me down, doubter. I'll show you."

The halfling grabbed the rope, and Gavee lifted Benny to the well. He dragged himself inside, climbing into the dark. Dal joined Gavee as they listened to the echoes and the struggling creature working down the rope.

"Are you close?" questioned Gavee.

The door slammed open, releasing the rope into the well. A thud followed. Dal's eyes widened as several grangruls stood with whips and long staffs. They burst into the small room, unleashing fury. Gavee attempted to move from the barrage, unable to evade the torrid cracks, with Dal howling through each hit. The two masuras curled into a ball as the grangruls cursed with each blow.

"I treated you with fairness, slave!"

The lizard snapped a hit against Dal's shoulders.

"You lied and brought shame to my house!"

Snap!

"I sell you with this creature!"

The whip snapped twice on Gavee's back as he curled in his feathers. The knotted leather end tore at his wings, with feathers popping from their place.

Dal cried out, begging forgiveness, but the grangrul disregarded his pleas, raising its whip. The lizard folk at the door hissed with laughter, encouraging their comrade to continue the barrage and building its rage. Blood collected under the thunderblood's feet when he rose, caught the whip's ends as it fell, and let it coil around his arm.

"Enough!" Gavee thundered.

He yanked the whip free and stood before his captors.

Dal shivered from the pain as his wings suffered deeply from the hits.

Fury filled Gavee's face and body. "You will no longer hit the boy or me!"

The lizards withdrew from the scene as Dal's owner looked down the well.

"How this open?" asked the grangrul.

Gavee gripped tight to the whip, with Dal remaining on the floor, quivering from the pain. The lizard snatched the torch and dropped it into the well, searching in its light.

"Where did you find the rope?"

The lizard came at Dal, and Gavee raised the whip.

"Take me where you need to. Leave Dal alone!" growled Gavee.

The lizard's tongue slipped in and out as the others watched the masura.

"Both are heading to the arena," growled Dal's owner.

"He had nothing to do with my escape."

"It is done. I've sold you both."

"Both?" questioned Gavee.

"You've been in my home for more than a day. You become my property," it hissed through a smile.

"Master, no," whimpered Dal.

The grangrul grabbed another whip.

"No more!" said Gavee.

The lizard snarled through an upper lip.

"I'm going in peace, but Dal stays with me. There will be no more hitting."

The grangrul extended its green, bony hand for the whip. "No, it stays with me until we leave."

"No slave has a weapon in grangrul city," hissed another grangrul.

"I do today, or you share the keeper's pain in the cage." Gavee pushed out his chest and overlooked the blood trickling down his forehead. His chin pushed forward, and his eyes remained focused on the lizard folk.

"Come," said a voice from behind the group.

The giant lizards moved aside as a hunched elder came forward. The old lizard walked with a cane, and its skin had faded to a darker green, with its tongue slithering between its broken teeth.

"No one has stepped against my fighters and lived." It took a deep breath. "Your warrior stance will fetch an acceptable price for our town."

Dal's owner smirked at the remark.

"We have no more damage to either slave," said the elder.

As Gavee helped Dal to his feet, the elder turned, and the guards followed. The boy held his right leg, and blood dripped from his back. The masura wiped the tears from Dal's eyes, then pulled the lad forward, glancing at the well. They stepped down the dirt street, and two grangrul guards followed. Silence reigned until they discovered a large town square filled with lizard folk watching the escaped slaves. The buildings towered four stories, and lizards stood staring at the silent parade in each window, balcony, and door. Young and old, lizards and slaves, dared to glance filled the packed streets.

Dal pressed against Gavee, and they marched from street to street, getting closer to the exit. They came to the steps, towering upward, and the elder stepped away. Two guards emerged from behind and shoved Gavee. The masuras stepped onto the dirt stoop and then proceeded to the top. The thunderblood turned, seeing the lizard folk staring from their adobe homes.

"It's my home," spat Dal. "I'm glad we go."

"We shall discover a way out, young one."

Dal tried to smile through the gash cutting his mouth, but gave a grimace instead. The masuras stepped through the steel doors and entered the sunlight. Gavee raised an arm to the brightness and sensed the heat upon his chest. The domed city kept a constant coolness and never heated from the sun's rays.

Dal limped onward and gasped. "First time," he said, squinting.

Gavee realized the words and anger grew with the beasts who pushed them to a waiting caravan. The shackled slumped in their stance, waiting for the incoming slaves to be added. Gavee blocked the beating sun with an arm, counting thirty prisoners, two to a row. With little care for the creature hobbling nearby, the unfortunate, chained prisoners maintained their hidden, downcast stares. The halfling, orc, and masura, the punished grangrul, human, and elf, chained alongside each other, dried in the heat. Shackled from throat to feet, the dwarves lay in an open cart with parsnips.

The thunderblood trainee had to save these poor souls one day and get them to freedom.

Gavee's memory of the caravan deception highlighted the inescapable and untrickable nature of many grangruls. Burdened, the lizard folk guarded their cargo with great concern. The desert-surrounded mound contained a rocky path leading beyond a dune and to the east, farther into the Lower Realm. They dragged Dal along, shackling the lad to an angry grangrul who hissed at the enslaved.

"Shut up, prisoner! Next time, you don't steal from the high guard."

"I don't want to be chained to a slave," it hissed.

Dal whimpered after the guard ignored his plea. The chained grangrul yanked back, causing the masura to slam to the surface in a puff. With a hiss, the grangrul guard pulled Gavee to the rear, reacting to the action. They picked up a long chain where Gavee would find himself alone, behind the caravan, with a lone grangrul atop a large battle bird. The giant flightless bird featured a stout beak, thick neck, and enormous claws. The grangrul rode them into battle, and these creatures could outrun most land animals.

With a piercing squawk from the bird, the lead cart pulled ahead, hauling the slave train to its next stop. Gavee picked up the chain and wrapped the links around his wrists to help keep the cutting to a minimum. Propelled by the sun, the push continued, driving the party down the path. The roasted march proceeded onward under the heat, lasting the entire day until the sun was directly overhead. On their battle birds, the grangruls quenched their thirst, readying their long whips. The random snap and lizard gurgle kept the slaves awake and the train on the move.

Gavee felt the immediate steps from the giant bird. The threat of further whipping prevented him from looking back. Under the cloudless sky, a lone devil hawk swooped along the caravan line, destroying any false sense of security and escape. The thunderblood shuddered its wings to keep a breeze upon the body, hovering just above the head to keep the sun's rays from the face. The keepers did not bother with the motion, as the other masuras in line had given him the idea.

As the march continued, the thunderblood trainee recognized the area, passing Lake Oht. They had reached outside the Lower Realm and into Oht, a realm considered the between, as it ended at the far city of Eden, a city of indifference. They would settle in Bathhh, home to a dirty wizard selling goods and beings. The far dune came into view as they climbed the rocky path and paused at its top. The city below bustled in the distance, connected to an oasis that was lush green, glistening in the sunlight.

"There's your new dwelling, Thunderblood," said the grangrul.

It snapped its whip against Gavee's wings, and his talons curled from the sting. The lead hawk squealed, and the others followed suit, with the grangruls all snapping their whips together against their captives. He took notice and wondered how it would end. A full day's journey was implied by the march's length. The weary, far-traveled slaves found no rest upon reaching Dal and Gavee. Despite the effort, W.B. couldn't break through the thick metal and lock securing the chains.

"Think, W.B.," he mumbled.

Gavee clutched a stone within a talon and tossed it into his hands without the grangrul noticing. He attempted to work it across the shackles, but failed. The hard rock did nothing to the lock as the city grew closer. The cheering became louder, with the city center holding a large arena. Gavee had seen a similar scene on a travel outing with Bahg and understood that these cities kept as a central trade, a slave market. The cheering came from the battle arena, where slaves fought to stay alive while their captors bet on their deaths. The gates approached, and the caravan stopped its death march.

"I plan on betting big on you, slave," hissed the guard from behind.

Gavee disregarded the beast as they steered to the side. The thunderblood trainee took a deep breath to focus and remain alert. The surrounding energy flickered, and the insight took in each object, tent, and creature muddling outside the city walls.

"I will escape," he gritted. "An escape for all."

The day's breeze soothed his face, momentarily easing his hunger and thirst. A sudden tug on the chain anchored him firmly to the ground, bringing back a sense of peace. The guard pinned the chain with a steel stake, anchoring the slaves from running.

"Welcome to Bathhh, slaves! Your new home!"

The grangrul's deep voice echoed, and the hissing laughter from the guards followed.

"We camp here till morning. Gates closed until the next sunrise."

The guards all worked in unison, performing the camp duties countless times before, as they each gathered wood, started a fire, and prepared a meal. Gavee sat in the dirt when a one-eyed halfling came over with a water bucket, handing the masura a ladle. He dropped his hands into the warm water and grabbed a fistful, tossing it over his body. The halfling cursed at the action.

"Water for a drink, not a stupid *bath*, Masura!"

Gavee slapped the spoon into the bucket and took two large gulps. He threw it into the water and watched the halfling drag the wooden bucket to the slave line. The masura pulled his wings over his head, with the sun slipping to the west. He watched the dirt when hissing laughter drew his attention. The vile creatures opened a sack and removed several tiny fairies chained together as they struggled to break free from their agony. The lizard clutched one by its leg, dangling the other two, with drool falling from its gaping teeth. It spoke in a language Gavee still did not understand, then it dropped the three beautiful beings into the boiling pot.

Gavee looked away from the appalling scene. Their screams echoed through the open valley until they faded away. The lizards continued to defile any decency their kind may have had. They cared nothing for others or nature, sitting at their front door, taking everything for themselves. He gazed at the ground, working to drown out the nasty noise of the lizards eating their cooked meal. The lizards noticed his disgust and threw their bones at him.

"Eat, slave," they chuckled.

They devoured their meal with the night's cooling relief, arriving as the lizards took turns watching their prisoner, and the crackling fire filled the night air. Gavee savored the taste of bread and mutton to fill his belly.

"We can't use you weak in the morning," hissed the guard.

The masura chewed on each piece when the one-eyed halfling approached, handing over the spoon. He peered up, dropping the vessel into the bucket to find Dal inching into view as the city noise carried on behind the walls. The young masura remained unimpressed, not worried. His years spent serving must have dulled his sensitivity to such events. A grangrul crawled past as the boy waved, then lowered his hand to the dirt. Gavee failed to smile, then faced the rolling field. He hoped to be beyond the chains when home popped into his mind.

"The king."

Home rushed forward with panic filling his head. The tragedy remained in his forest, and being locked away, with no one knowing where he had landed, started to build on his shoulders. Escape became paramount. Return was the sole aim. Nighttime thoughts persisted, drifting into dreams. The starry night kept him awake as he struggled in the heat, trying to get some sleep.

Early dawn finally arrived when a leg kick and a guard's hiss had the masura sitting. With little time to brush the dirt from his worn clothing, the lizards yanked the masura ahead, linking him to the others as they rejoined the line to enter the city.

The devil hawks roosted out of sight, and the chariots remained outside the walls. The grangrul leader grabbed the chain tight and drew the slaves close in step as they came through the gate.

Bathhh, unlike Khrakin, was above ground with a wall surrounding the city and guards posted throughout its several shady neighborhoods. They followed the crooked path leading downward into its center, where a massive domed colosseum sat at the bottom. The enormous dome, even in the morning, resounded with audience applause. The buildings, made with mud and thatch, pitched two or three stories high, creating a rising and falling shamble. Worn paths, barely wide enough for passage, connected structures.

They advanced ahead, snaking through the towering shanty mud town. They heard the slithering tongues as they passed the countless windows, a random snap echoing the whip. Several enslaved beings populated Gavee's view. None seemed preferred. The distant domed roof was always visible, looming in the distance. Lit torches lining the meandering path showed the way to the Colosseum. They walked past the same structures as they went deeper into the city, with the air becoming fouler and rotting fish filling the senses.

They reached the dome, stepped alongside its several arched openings, and staggered higher than two stacked trees. Inside, Gavee could see large, scattered Bellows and jetting boulders in sections, and a large waterfall sat in its center. Perched on the upper dome rim, the devil hawks observed the scene, keeping the "entertainment" from escaping their demise. The pull forward continued when they reached a long, dropped stone stair descending below the stadium. The lead grangrul grabbed a torch, then descended. They reached the bottom and approached a lizard with a whip at a large gate.

"We have new runners," slithered the lead guard.

The lizard, staring at the chained gang, turned and unlocked the gate, holding its whip in its left claw. The lead guard yanked the chain into the shadows as it raised the torch into their new home. Gavee was the last to enter, then they forced them to raise their hands to unlock the wrists and body shackles. The guards slipped to the other side, and the metal gate snapped into place, locking and trapping them in their new cell.

"Welcome to your new home, runners. Don't get comfortable since most are unlikely to be here long," it hissed and laughed. "Now, move before I come back in with my whip."

"How far?" asked Gavee.

The guard silently returned to its post.

The enclosed dark dirt path hallway gave no sign of an end. Dal returned to Gavee, and neither spoke as the party crept onward, easing each step and digging talons into the soft soil. With their hands extended, they moved, expecting to bump into a wall or something worse at any moment. Dal's breath grew rapid as he grabbed Gavee's arm and held it tight. The overwhelming darkness cut deep into Witch'Bane's own when he stopped the madness and allowed his thunderblood training to grab hold. He pushed ahead, leading the group along the wall.

W.B. pushed forward until his hands stopped on a thick, damp dirt wall. Roots crawled along the blockage, showing they stood below the bellows within the stadium. Gavee continued through the passage, which held many bends, and the soil became harder to move through as it became muck under the talons. Soon, a sparkling dot appeared, and cheers came from afar. The thunderblood pushed them forward when a gate became apparent, and a guard stood across from them with a whip in hand.

Gavee paused.

As the tunnel ended, doom awaited. The masura surged ahead, coming into the torch's light, bringing notice to the lizard. Its tongue slithered faster, tasting the cold, damp air. The gate unlocked, and the metal squeaked as it swung open into another passage.

"Move, slaves," growled the lizard.

Gavee embraced the impending pain as he slid past the disgusting creature, yet it did not release the leather, hissing as he passed. He eased the tension when pain raked across his wings, and the whip crackled, dropping him to the damp floor. Another snap greeted them and burned, causing him to scream in pain.

"Move faster," demanded the lizard.

The thunderblood trainee fought the agony and jumped to his feet. He reacted swiftly, avoiding the third snap as the lizard recoiled. The group ducked, and the whip's impact caused painful shouts. The torchlit passage led past wooden doors with small, barred windows in the middle, showing cell rooms. He dragged Dal close, wanting the lad to land with him in the same hole. The grangrul raised a lever, and several doors opened to empty rooms.

"In!"

They walked into the cell with two other masuras, and the doors slammed shut.

Gavee's eyes eventually adjusted, finding the room sealed with stone walls and a dirt ceiling with tree roots jetting out. One corner contained hay for bedding and old chains connected to the stone wall. The cramped conditions and the inadequate bedding troubled him in the overcrowded cells. Gavee moved to the door's window to search for the light, finding the far stone wall and nothing else in view.

Time to create a survival plan and teach the lad to make his escape.

Chapter Thirteen

Sleep for Shapía ran deep, with the queen's image flashing in her dreams. The dramatic scenes pulled at her heart, and she ached for her touch. The vision bounced from the queen to Gavee fighting unknown, massive darkness, and the king lost inside a cage. It jumped scenes, causing a rapid breath when the chaos dropped her from the sleeping perch and she awoke on the wooden floor. Sweat covered her body, and blackness enveloped the night sky.

The night training with Guru Lin and the brief sitting with Sattva ripped what she knew and understood from her heart. The truth leaked into every thought, reaching inside her conscience. Shapía, saddened, breathed deeply, then faced the night.

"I need food."

The masura wrapped herself in the saffron robe and stepped to the balcony. The sweet aroma wafted to her senses, and the calming buzz lifted her spirit. She floated to the banquet hall, where everyone remained silent, and a light tune repeated from a distant harp and violin playing a melody. The fruit, bread, vegetables, and grain offering made the meat she had desired fall away with each meal. The food satisfied the gut, and the steamed long rice from Lotrs removed the edge with sweet cherries and peaches, adding flavor.

Shapía sat alone, gazing at the food, away from the peering stares. Since her meeting with Sattva, word spread and respect for the next Seer of Seers fell on her shoulders, creating a loneliness Shapía had never experienced. She filled her gut and pushed the plate to the side when a male pixie landed on the table. The tiny being had blond hair with ears poking through and wore a silver vest with black pants. Its wings had brown and yellow spots and carried a bow across its right arm, but had no arrows in its quiver. They bowed and approached, making the masura uncomfortable with the gesture. They spoke mind to mind.

"Guru Lin requests your presence."

"I'm not training today. It's a day to rest?"

"I am the messenger, my Sweet Great Seer," he bowed.

"Sweet Great Seer?" questioned Shapía.

The pixie's cheeks turned red, and he lowered his gaze. *"Forgive me. The name we have given you is for the sweetness in your eyes and the smile that overwhelms our hearts. We are grateful you are here to take the islands into the new age."*

Shapía's vision widened.

"New age? What new age?" she asked aloud.

"Why, the age without Sattva, and the end to chaos building from Breiv? It causes a constant ripple among the islands, and the evil lurking behind it is burning the isles' equanimity."

"Burning its equanimity?" she muttered. "What have I missed since coming here?"

"It is to unfold, Sweet Great Seer, but for now, Guru Lin awaits."

"I'm not dressed to meet Guru Lin."

"This request is urgent."

Shapía collected the plate after the pixie flitted away—then a hand touched hers, and a smiling female elf then took it from her. The masura lingered in the uncomfortable attention when her thoughts jumped to Guru Lin. She had no leisure to muddle with the discomfort and looked at her robe, sighing, then going to meet her teacher.

The glow from the many white candles, illumined plants, and fireflies raised a beautiful aurora around the Mighty Tree. She pushed her wings forward, lifting into the tree's massive body and small living city throughout its limbs. Shapía had reservations about accepting the title of Sweet Great Seer, a title that prompted each robed figure she passed to show reverence.

The scene kept her in awe of the numerous seance levels, meditations, teachings, and simple gatherings. The Mighty Tree sections displayed respect for the next higher set, with the guru level, the highest order, sitting on top.

Shapía circled the tree and studied the dark, broken volcanic cauldron with its busy distant port bringing in fresh devotees. Although peaceful, the island was where she found a home, but Witch'Bane called from the south with worry for her clan.

The chilly night prevented the oncoming rain, and Shapía floated onto Guru Lin's dark meditation platform before the rain settled upon the area. The masura walked across the wooden floor, lighting the few small oil lamps to prepare the training room. She tapped the small gong and sat on the cushion. Entering, Guru Lin sat silently, and the vibrations ceased. Shapía kept her eyes on the platform and tried to end her thoughts and calm her mind. The practice required concentration and silence.

"It is our last training session," said Guru Lin.

Shapía attempted to snap out of her meditative state, not knowing how long they had sat together.

"I'm sorry, Guru Lin?"

"I have taught you the basics, the middle road, and the advanced understandings. It required a much shorter period than even Sattva expected."

"I'm not ready."

The guru laughed. "Keep this innocence, my dear. You'll always need more time to get ready. Just keep proceeding forward. The way ahead is a mirror. When walking the path, grasp nothing, and happiness shall grab your heart."

Shapía understood the repeated phrase, yet still did not trust the words. Guru Lin stood, giving a bow, shocking Shapía with the gesture, and the trainee remained with caution.

"When you leave the room, my dear, I bow to you for all eternity. You are the seer of seers and soon are about to understand what it means," said Lin.

Lin pointed to the wooden spiral stairs around the tree base, leading to Sattva's solitude. Shapía hesitated, for it would be the first occasion she rose to the sanctuary. As she touched the tree, the masura sensed its energy surge through her hands and wings as it took a breath. The power almost knocked her to the floor, but she remained firm, allowing the images to flash before her with her vision turning white and her body floating. Blankness consumed her consciousness, then she was floating amidst fluffy clouds, the gentle sway making her weightless and disoriented.

"Shapía," said Sattva's voice.

She couldn't overcome her tiredness.

"Shapía," said the voice, louder.

"Shapía!"

She snapped from the fog and settled before Sattva's seclusion, somehow making it up the stairs. The quiet space contained red-lit stones, creating a hue on the open platform. The sound from the distant, silent falls filled the background, confusing Shapía. Sattva kneeled in the far corner, facing north, with a large, flat stone sitting in front of her on the floor. Something moved inside the smoke as the light fog spun and hovered over the rock. With a final bow from the guru, the mist vanished as she rose, smiling.

Across the wooden slats, the feminine figure and saffron robe drifted. Sattva's glass-like skin swirled with a maroon cloud filling the void, and she offered a hand to Shapía. The masura experienced her form entering a daze through a slow and methodical movement.

"My dear, this moment reveals your readiness for truth."

Shapía heard the words float, similar to a dream.

"We are connected, and your mother understood it to be true. In her haste, though, she destroyed herself without realizing the truth."

Shapía struggled to grasp the words, and before she realized it, they floated from the great Mighty Tree and toward the distant falls, naked but without a chill. Her wings did not flap, and she remained hand in hand with Sattva, admiring the glass figure.

"The masurans' genuine history has been hidden, with the island's truth different from what you knew as a youngling. Now it awakens, a first sight for you."

They landed on a stone platform overlooking the falls as the water fell silently. The cut rock featured symbols in a large circle, and as they stepped into its center, the markings glowed red with five small flames jumping alive at the platform's corners. Sattva prompted Shapía to sit. Silence followed, broken only by Shapía's gaze sweeping the island under the night sky. The countless lights through the Mighty Tree's limbs created a slight glow with its occupants meddling at the base. From the right, the distant shoreline's waves crashed in a steady rhythm, punctuated only by the gentle breeze rustling through the nearby trees.

"The great Aza, our truth, waits. Its presence is sensed as a silent hum awakening your consciousness."

Shapía pondered the meaning. *"Aza?"*

Sattva smiled at the connection.

"The true god gives life to our world. The one who is loved by Ellebasi and honored by Nathe."

"Aza was never mentioned in our books or teachings."

"He was not, for his truth is kept in silence and honor, falling to the gods we know and adore. The All *is the One of One, the Great of Great."*

Sattva reached out a hand and snagged a water droplet from the air, cupping it in her hands. The droplet, growing in speed and size, twirled in the water. As it hovered above, the ball soon dwarfed Sattva's hands, revealing a scene.

"Those great masuran history books are lies. They deceive you and the young."

She waved a hand, turned a page, and the image flipped to her grandfather, King Arul I.

"As you know, the masuras dwell in Breiv's Upper Realm. The Great One, Nathe, created his creatures to tend to the forest and grow his lands. The families grew into a multitude, with the Raths leading them all, crowned as the Royals. Eventually, families split from the Royals, creating their own forests and names, such as the Lohrs, Ranois, and La'Dariums. Within these clans, lower clans wanted their forests and royal place at the table."

The water scene grew, and the waves flipped the views in and out.

"Witch'Bane was no different, and at the end of the first age, your grandfather set out to find a forest for his own. The Fens had secured passage across the Crescent Mountains and made friends with the Esor Dragons."

An Esor Dragon floated in the scene and swooped toward its cavern home.

"Your mother's grandfather, King Boran II of Rath, disagreed with Witch'Bane's exit from his royal clan, demanding they stay in the forest. The Rauls sided with your Witch'Bane grandfather, creating a rift and seeping into the various clan families. The lower clans demanded more freedom, and they wanted their forests."

Masuras argued with King Arul I and King Storhn of Raul at a council meeting.

"Your grandfather was locked in a dungeon because he refused to bow to King Boran II. King Storhn escaped with his sons, leaving the forest. Your father remained inside the city, hidden and planning your grandfather's escape."

Shapía's jaw dropped. The taught lore spoke of a peaceful break, with Witch'Bane fighting alongside the Fens to reach Lheter Lake, where the elves repelled the grangrul from making a home in fertile land.

Sattva smiled. *"I know what you've been told, but all families agreed to rewrite history."*

"Why?"

"Your mother."

The young Princess Phawa entered and carried a smile as she embraced Arul II. Shapía fought her tears.

"Your father and uncle fought in the keep, rescuing their king, but sending the forest into a war. Witch'Banes and Rauls united, liberating their families from Rath rule. They reached the eastern Crescent Mountains, where the barkapes had escaped from the dragons."

A fanged creature jumped into the picture, and Shapía leaned back from the foul beast.

"These barkapes are different, bred for intelligence and the ability to speak. The dragons enslaved them, raising them to garden their farmlands and maintain their dens while gathering jewels and gems."

Kings Arul I and Storhn, amidst the barkapes, shook hands, a gesture of unity and a newly formed alliance.

"The agreement bound both beings to aid the other in their battle for freedom. The barkapes resisted the Raths and Ranois, with many casualties, in the Great Masuran War, enabling your father to kill King Boran II before the king attempted to kill his granddaughter for betraying her clan."

Shapía's face fell in shock as the vision displayed Arul II and Phawa embracing in tears.

"Her grandfather tried to kill her?" cried Shapía.

"Within it, the truth was buried."

"Her father?"

"He wished to conceal his disgrace. Masurans never harm their kin. It is a crime against the gods. The insanity had grabbed your great-grandfather and twisted his ideas into thinking it was for the gods."

"Is this why our family is banned from Rath?"

"No, it goes deeper."

The water image showed King Boran III kneeling, weeping, to Queen Phawa.

"Your grandfather wanted his grandchildren raised in the Rath lineage. Phawa understood it contained danger, for her father showed similar markings as his father, and the clan still possessed Arul, responsible for the death."

Tears ran down her cheek, and she sensed the pain in her mother's eyes, with the scene showing them embracing when she was a child.

"For help with the Great Masuran War, Witch'Bane, Raul, and Fens found themselves bound to the freedom the barkapes desired from their masters."

"The Esor War."

"Yes, your mother begged her father for help, but he swore an oath about Witch'Bane's banishment and refused. He did, though, speak of a secret that controls the dragons."

The image turned dark, and a withered old female appeared with broken wings and a sunken, pale face.

"It saved countless lives and ended the tragedy before it began."

The picture rolled into a dragon nestled in a cave, eyes cloudy white.

"It's my father's gaze before we left," Shapía said.

Her attention flooded to Sattva, who kept a focus on the water.

"It is the same evil your mother discovered, plotting to enter Witch'Bane and do the same to her family."

Phawa found herself in the darkness, holding out the sword and screaming at something lurking beyond her sight. The picture switched to Flued, standing in a dark space, taking a knee, and bowing his head.

"Flued?"

Sattva dropped her hands, allowing the giant ball to explode on the rock. Her gaze rolled to Shapía, with pupils glowing red.

"He is now one with evil, which controls his mind."

Shapía couldn't believe it. Her loving brother had cared for their family.

"His ideas fall similar to his great-grandfather's, but far more twisted and lusting for power. The evil has been given safe passage from its lair and walks above ground now. Your brother ensured it, breaking the method that stopped it from happening before masuras flew the skies."

The princess found the story unbelievable. The world she knew crashed down upon her.

"It's time to place the Mazerth Stone in a safe location."

The seer touched Shapía's neck, and the necklace appeared, floating from her neck to Sattva's hands. She stepped to the glowing boulder as it lifted, revealing a safe pocket. The chain glowed as it entered the velvet safety. The floating rock lowered to cover the gem, sinking beneath the other flat stones.

Sattva smiled and approached Shapía. *"It's time."*

Before Shapía could think, a high-pitched ring stung her head, and panic took hold.

Sattva grabbed her arm, and the fear disappeared, sending her consciousness into a freefall.

The Mighty Tree, the island, the sea and the sky disappeared, with darkness surrounding all.

"Guru Sattva!"

"I still hold your hand, my child. Sight will return, and then your reality will shatter, revealing the true reality. Close your eyes until I tell you to open them to your fresh sight."

A rushing vibration roared past her ears, making her hair stand on end and the air grow cold and thin. The suffocation intensified as breathing became impossible, and her eyes flew open in fright. Sattva no longer maintained the glass-like torso as the multicolored tunnel thundered past them. The all-black entity's icy white hands gripped her arm. The bright, smooth tunnel pulled them through, and the dark, shallow cloak hid her face and body, muffling the surrounding sounds. She tried to grab Sattva's attention, but her lungs burned, and she found no air to breathe. A crushing weight settled on her chest. Her breath hitched, and the world dissolved into black.

Shapía perceived her body floating, and her spirit drifted into a soundless void. Numbness consumed the masura, yet her heartbeat saturated the silence. The thumping increased, and she wanted to yell, yet something grabbed her voice. She couldn't escape the torturous thump as the beat intensified. The agony tore at her soul when a snap awoke her awareness, and she lay crumpled on a flat stone. Her vision swam, the world tilting on its axis, and a violent headache vibrated through her skull. She tried to ignore the pain and stand, but failed to regain her composure.

"Wait, my child. Allow the transition to take hold."

Shapía shook her head. Then the scene drew attention to endless clouds in a silent void. She lay naked on a large, flat boulder, blacker than anything she had seen prior, surrounded by a light gray fog. The stone seemed to dip and rise when similar rocks floated through the clouds. Sattva hovered as a shadowy ghost, folding within itself where a face would be, and the figure shuddered with a distant high pitch. Shapía lifted a hand and saw her form remained unchanged. She appeared to remain as she was before the journey.

"Where are we?" asked Shapía, finding her voice.

"We are in the in-between plane from where we departed to where we go once our physical existence ends. It is where we pay homage and thank the one who has given us direction. It is the place where we meet Aza and the Ever-Light."

Shapía looked around and saw repeated dark stones floating in space. Some supported small, elevated platforms, and others crumpled into their pits. The different rocks bounced against one another without a sound, beyond their location.

"I have found your connection to the Knowing. They are to bring you here and to wherever your direction must send you when we leave this plane. It will keep your concentration and allow the light to glow."

Sattva raised her arms until they rippled with a rainbow, appearing as the lone color on the plane. It arched across, and she snapped it, flattening it straight. A deep voice chanted, repeating incantations.

"Smite the light, bring the fight."

The voice pitched higher until Shapía covered her ears with the static sound. The flat stone vibrated, and Shapía rose to hover above it. Sattva turned solid black, and the rainbow pushed forth a pair of items. It stopped as quickly as it started, and Sattva's ghost form returned, with two black leather bracers now sitting on the rock. The masura picked them up and gazed at the embedded gems and the imprint running its length.

"Put them on."

"May I have clothes?" she asked.

"You stand before me as a warrior."

Shapía looked down to find she was wearing black masuran battle armor. The dark protection seemed light, like she wore nothing, and its markings were foreign.

"The saktis," said Sattva.

She donned the left bracer, then the right, securing both tightly on her forearms. They each possessed jewels and markings on their sleeves. The left carried a green pyramid gem with a white slit down its center, near the wrist, and a blue pyramid-shaped gem with purple specks at the top of the forearm. On the right contained a brown pyramid gem with dark yellow streaks and a glittering purple pyramid gem at its top. They both had identical etchings in the leather: a triangle near the top with a straight line leading to the hand, dipped into the eternity loop. Two straight lines, one shorter than the other, ran parallel to the loop with tiny triangles on their ends. The etching held crumbled, buried ebon gems, emitting its glisten inside.

"These are your saktis, your energy source, and they wield might from Aza's plane. Representing the static metal charge, the left lower arm, the cat's eye, conjures what is needed. The lapis lazuli on the upper represents the water element, keeping the charge in balance. The right lower is the tiger's eye, representing the solid islands. And the upper is an amethyst, representing the healing nature of the elements. It would guard you against a sudden end to the experience."

"End?"

"Your current life, my dear, is an experience. Following your death, a fresh experience shall begin."

She looked them over and felt tremendous joy with the new items.

"They are not weapons," interrupted Sattva. "They are a connection to the above and should have the answers to the below."

The fit was perfect, a soothing comfort against her skin. Shapía tried sliding them off for a closer look.

Sattva chuckled. "They do not come off."

Shapía panicked at the notion.

"Ease, wise one. Allow existence to flow, embrace it, and welcome the All."

"The all?"

"You must learn to let them into your consciousness. They are going to protect and guide you with the answers. The All is in them and in you."

"How?"

"Concentrate on one."

The princess eyed the left bracer, studying the shining crushed gems within the carved symbol as the light bounced around the colorful gemstones. It was slow and meticulous as it traversed the black, crushed rocks, glimmering with purple specks when it entered lapis lazuli and returned to shimmer in the white slit in the cat's eye. It mesmerized the masura, and she grew closer to the light as it crackled and bounced through the crushed stone. The movement increased, and the ball became a beam, sparking a light inside the gems. Shapía withdrew into herself, watching the left bracer glow.

She flipped her view to her right, and the gems flickered and reached a full beam. The bracers pulsed with energy as they filled her, and the strength resonated in her bones. She felt herself becoming one with its energy.

"Concentrate on a shield for protection."

Shapía drew in the king's mighty Witch'Bane shield and the power it encompassed when it sat within his hand. The left bracer forced her hand into a ball, thrusting forward from the gems and building a large, glowing, clear shield with static light dancing around its edges.

"Now, the other side," said Sattva.

Shapía's thoughts gathered around Grunt and his long staff as the right bracer hummed. The skilled weasel captivated Shapía with its use, and the long staff appeared in a surge from the gems. As the electrical energy surged through it, Shapía realized its force in her hand. The staff twirled, and the shield was light and firm.

"The moment has arrived. Learn the saktis and become the seer of seers."

"What is the seer of seers?" she demanded.

Sattva raised an arm, and a black skeleton with a sword rose from the stone. It chattered its teeth and howled a guttered growl, lunging for Shapía, nicking her right leg. Her skin boiled from the cut as it seared and burned. The undead swiped at her face, and she blocked it with the staff, slamming the shield into its torso. The skeleton stumbled, chattering its teeth when it approached with a sword raised high, swinging downward. Shapía blocked the charge and jabbed the long staff into its skull, knocking it back again.

"Reaching Aza requires completing these challenges."

Sattva's blackness rolled into a ball at the words, disappearing, leaving Shapía alone with the undead. It chattered and stomped on the rock, bringing forth two more black skeletons armed with swords. With a loud shriek, the three undead rattled their teeth, gaped their maws, and charged at the masura. The shield blocked the first strike and the second with the staff. The third strike pierced her stomach as they fought.

Shapía experienced a pain she had never encountered, doubling over and onto the stone floor. Her form burning, the energy from her bracers dropped, leaving her defenseless. The three skeletons stood over her, and their teeth chattered when she watched the one shove the sword into her chest. The searing agony consumed her as the breath faded.

"Am I dying?"

The meaning thundered through her thoughts, and her mother's death clamored forward when a familiar voice echoed in the space.

"Death leaves behind the old and ignites the new," said Queen Phawa.

Shapía's breath became labored, and movement was impossible when a skeleton sent its blade in. She experienced no sensation and forced a long blink, catching the skeletons turning their backs. Her last breath came and went, leaving her with a sense of icy stillness.

The stillness took over when she popped open her eyes and inhaled a deep, painful breath. She was alone on the flat slab, still wearing the bracers and armor.

"Death is a stage to leave behind who you believed you were and allow a reborn lotus to appear."

Sattva's voice echoed in the gray clouds when Shapía noticed the talons and legs were black and rigid.

"You must continue forward, wise one, and become the seer of seers. Become the *All*!"

A pair of skeletons rose from the stone and chattered their teeth. Shapía shook her head and raised her arms, sending the energy through the bracers.

"Not again!" she thundered.

Chapter Fourteen

Asmodeus sat on the new throne made from the enemy's wings. The tall seat fanned four sets of masuran wings, three sets from the DasaRaul king and two princes, and the third set from Dasa's thunderblood, Chromic. The chair seat and arms and feathers came from Dasa's Elite Guard leaders, and the crafted feather carpet running from the opening to the chair came from Dasa's queen, princess, and the royal guard.

Asmodeus kept the eldest Dasa princess chained to the wall, alive, for his personal use.

Despite the sun's rays illuminating the forest, the space held a constant, chilling darkness. The air itself felt heavy and cold. The room remained sullen.

Asmodeus's flesh held a violet and white hue. His pupils had changed to the same color, and his wings were a gleaming ebony. The masura's stare transcended the room, with senses attuned to the forest and its vibrations. Now called Asmodea, the once Witch'Bane forest spanned the Witch'Bane River and into DasaRaul, creating one clan. The chaos turned the Upper Realm on edge, forcing the humans to reinforce the southern Lohr Mountains to protect their kingdom. The battle had been brutal, tearing apart Witch'Bane and DasaRaul, bringing one law across the combined forest.

With a thunderous roar, the king led the charge into DasaRaul's capital, the ground trembling under the weight of his advancing army. The conquering soldiers quickly imprisoned the royal court, silencing their terrified screams with triumphant shouts. This secured the populace of his future kingdom.

King Thwar and his sons, the princes Rim and Septar, fought with bravery and courage until the end. Asmodeus replayed the Dasa council loft battle as Septar perished before Queen Miyan. In defense of his sisters, the princesses Banyan and Beetwin, the sword killed Prince Rim when the Exercitus took the loft. They dragged Beetwin, screaming, as her sister died in front of her eyes with the Dasa royals piled in the room's center. The Witch'Bane's dagger found its mark, piercing King Thwar's heart with a sickening thud as his furious, despairing gaze remained fixed beyond Asmodeus.

With a raw display of power, Asmodeus obliterated the royal court in a searing blast, the deafening roar echoing through the palace, slaking an insatiable thirst for BataRaul's demise. The southern Bata forest, refortified along its borders, was effectively walled off against the Asmodean horde. The conquest sent off alarms throughout the Upper Realm, sending a notice to the far-distant Lower Realm masura clans in the Nalyan Mountains.

Asmodeus enjoyed the chaos he created.

He sat forward on the throne, spinning his sword as it dug into the wooden surface. He stared into the ruby gem Mother Malum gave him, as its force built his psyche and mental awareness. The ruby gave Asmodeus a strength he had never encountered, allowing him to create turmoil past his borders with simple thought and concentration. Malum's lair stayed open, resulting in a dark skin covering the council loft.

The Asmodean clan's concentration was war, growing the clan, and enslaving the Dasa clans to farm and maintain the forest. Rhile entered the darkened room. Her red eyes left a tint around the dark violet skin, and movement appeared painful. The lahd approached, dropping to one knee with a bow.

"My King, our scouts have breached BataRaul, and the forces continue to build within Lheter Lake. They are unaware we are building a nest along the Lost Sea shoreline," said Rhile.

"The Fens?" Asmodeus's voice had deepened with the change.

"They severed contact with us, sire."

The spinning blade stopped as a slight grin came to Asmodeus's lavender lips. "They escaped."

"Just as you proclaimed."

"Mother Malum's truth unfolds, and each piece falls into place," said Asmodeus.

Asmodeus stood, sheathing his sword and touching a hand upon the ruby hilt. He walked to the bound Dasa princess, lifted her face, and stared into its blank expression.

"What do you think, Princess? Should we invade Fen, or grow my army first?"

He laughed and dropped her head. The king gestured his lahd to ease, snapping his fingers. A masuran boy came in and poured drinks. The lad never looked up from the floor and cowered in a distant room.

"Where are we with transformations?" he asked.

Rhile rose, and Asmodeus handed her a drink. "Our clan has transformed," she said, "and the enslaved continue to be stubborn, and will be until they understand the other choice."

"And my exercitus?"

"We have four thousand troops and growing."

Asmodeus downed his own vessel and took Rhile's hand. "Mother would be pleased with your actions. You deserve to be next to my side as we take the island," he said.

"When did she discover you were not the broken one?" she asked.

"Well, in her own brilliant mind, she always knew, but I suspect not."

"How far do you follow her, my mighty king?" she asked.

"Until we rule all," he said.

Rhile smiled. "I will guard you with my life, My King."

Asmodeus released her hand and slid to the room's center, where the portal hummed. The energy grew as he drew near its rim.

"I must speak with Malum. Go to the altar, bring the five, and I'll meet you there with the Dasa princess. We are planning on taking the Manawe port. It must be part of my Asmodean kingdom before we move into BataRaul and approach the western elves from Dulisar."

"I believe they would not accept our authority."

"They'll accept it."

Rhile gave a slight bow and flew from the room, leaving Asmodeus standing in front of the portal. The king took a breath and readied for the pain he endured each time he stepped through the gateway. The ability to keep the door open each time he entered took strength. He gritted as the structure hardened when the talons passed into the lair. The cold cavern hit his face, and a low hum filled the chamber. A lilac hue brightened with the entrance. Asmodeus marveled at Malum's domain.

"My son," whispered Malum's voice.

It drew Asmodeus's attention to the landing.

"Mother."

Malum glided from the dark hole, and Asmodeus noticed her dusky violet skin with black eyes and face, fuller than sunken. It surprised the masura, and Malum remarked on the expression.

"Each step we take closer to my sisters, the island's power fills inside. My powers are gaining strength, and I desire to share them with you, my son."

A chill ran down Asmodeus's spine as Malum's bony fingers brushed against his cheek. The touch was cold and dry. His skin boiled at the touch, and the masura grinned through the suffering as the flesh darkened from the contact. Malum slid to the edge of the overlook, the wind whipping through her hair as Asmodeus followed, both gazing in awe at the vast, breathtaking panorama below.

"It's grown," said Asmodeus.

The cave walls extended far out of sight, and the ceiling was high enough to grow the most massive Bellow tree. Hammers rang, and chisels scraped against the stone as the builders worked hard to carve into the walls, creating the magnificent city. Malum slithered a smile to the creation and popped the cane onto the surface. The glowing mushrooms brightened, and the underground city's enormity made Asmodeus's jaw drop.

"Why do we need an underground city?" he asked.

"My dear, where do you think I would ever exist? It was once a magnificent domain, pushing past this vastness. It is our home," said Malum.

"Our home?" he questioned.

Malum chuckled with a cough.

"My sisters and I intend to share our life again in what was once the sisters' realm. It is growing as planned."

The dwarves, masuras, elves, and many island creatures worked alongside, chiseling into the stone and building the undercity. They all held blank stares, with eyes darkened and skin pure white. They distinguished themselves from the exercitus, who oversaw the workers, ensuring the job advanced without interference.

"Has the ruby shown its might to you?" she questioned.

"Yes, it comes to me when I sleep. I move about the island within the shadows. It has shown me the weaknesses and vulnerabilities we intend to destroy as we expand throughout the island."

"Good. Use it to create chaos inside, then attack when it reveals an opportunity to strike. It is to be a guiding force as we secure our island and find the one they call Dakii."

"I have scouts searching for the scroll keeper. BataRaul has sent their thunderblood to find him, leaving them as vulnerable as we need them."

"The opportunity to hit is now striking down any possibility of an escape."

"It shall be done, Mother."

"Go, I must feast, for my strength grows weak."

Moving to a far wall, the witch landed in front of several chained female masuras. The ones still alive screamed, knowing the danger coming for them when Asmodeus returned to the opening, never looking at the horror. The pain permeated his consciousness as he slid through the current, and the cave noise fell silent as the dark council room entered the view. Taronquel gazed from the hanging cage with his mouth free, and Asmodeus growled at the once head council.

"Why do you keep me alive?" asked Taronquel.

"My father must feed soon," answered Asmodeus.

"Evil never wins," groaned Taronquel.

"You have lost," said Asmodeus. "The island truths have come forward, and your gods shall pay."

"You think the witch would share her control?"

Asmodeus raised his sword, pushing it into the webbing and forcing Taronquel to wince.

"At the hilt sits a gem given to me by the so-called witch. I've been given immense power, her power. It increases with each moment, giving me foresight and where I sit in the future," said Asmodeus.

"What a farce," spat Taronquel.

The king stuck the pointed tip into Taronquel's foot, and the masura barked from the action.

"In the future, respect the giver of life," said Asmodeus.

"The giver of life?" scoffed Taronquel. "Listen to you. You've been deceived. May the heavens punish you for it."

"How little you know of your gods and the great books in your halls. Unfortunately, unless I change your mind, you're doomed not to be here when we sweep across the island," said Asmodeus.

"Change my mind?" questioned Taronquel.

"Yes, the sight is going to be very, very grand. You ought to be here for it," said Asmodeus.

Taronquel's eyes shot wide at the words.

"I've heard those words before. Where have they been spoken?"

Asmodeus chuckled. "These ideas are not new. The planned war is to be quick, with a few clans joining me at the great altar to begin the merge."

"Join you? At the altar?"

"Oh yes, it is a magnificent place, where wings can span... and Malum's influence fills its guests. It's the future home for the Great Masuran Hall," said Asmodeus.

"You plan to move to the Great Hall?"

"You poor soul, little do you understand the profound depths these plans have laid out these many years. The gathering has begun, and soon we're going to be a family again," said Asmodeus.

"One family...? This is nonsense."

Asmodeus returned to the throne and placed a foot atop the seat, leaning against the knee. He brushed the wings and chuckled at Taronquel.

"One family unless you stand in the way," said Asmodeus.

"You're a monster! How I wish to be there when Nathe strikes you down!"

"Taronquel, my old friend, I keep you alive hoping you see things in a fresh way. You are a brilliant tactician and would help us build our empire. What needs to occur to change your thoughts?"

"I thought you kept me alive to feed me to the king."

Asmodeus squeezed a hand into a ball.

"I am king!"

"Not mine!"

The king took a long breath.

"Guard! Bring in the special prisoner!"

Asmodeus smiled. "The moment has arrived, Head Council, to see if what I know is in you or if I am missing: your true self. I doubt it."

The exercitus guards entered the room, pulling a naked masura by its wings. The beaten male did not respond, with one eye swollen and bruises throughout the body. They dropped him before their king and waited, ready to obey. Asmodeus twitched a finger, and they drew swords, cutting Taronquel down from the web. The broken masura hit the floor and moaned.

"I think you know this creature," said Asmodeus.

The king smiled as he tugged Taronquel's hair, raising his head. Taronquel's eyes widened.

"Ranu!" gasped Taronquel.

"Yes, good job. Dasa's former head council and, I believe, your friend," said Asmodeus.

Asmodeus dropped his head and withdrew. He raised his left palm, focusing on the black ring embedded in his left hand. The force within spun until it became a bright white orb when Asmodeus sent it into Ranu. The electric bolt surged through the masura's body, floundering on the ground. Taronquel remained in his place with anger, watching his friend in pain. Asmodeus yanked the hand away, and the energy dropped, bringing the room to rest.

"You see, Taronquel, my ability is greater than I expected. I defeat them with a raised arm while standing here smiling," said Asmodeus.

Taronquel remained silent, keeping his angry eyes on Ranu. Asmodeus sent the orb disappearing into the body, releasing and crossing his arms. He gave a nod to the guard, and the guard dropped a sword in front of Taronquel.

"I want you to put the inferior being out of its misery," said Asmodeus.

The broken masura was silent.

"Fine," said Asmodeus.

He repeated, acting more intent, sending the masura's body into a painful jerk. Taronquel seethed at the scene and came to his feet, grabbing the sword.

"I intend to kill you!" angered Taronquel.

The frail masura came to Asmodeus, but the king was ready and froze him in an instant with his left hand.

"Tsk, tsk," groaned Asmodeus.

He kept the arm up, freezing Taronquel with the sword raised.

"The strength is unique depending on my mind. It can kill, send pain, or keep you suspended within my control," he said.

Asmodeus sighed.

"You shall do this with or without my help."

The strength surging through the masura forced the sword down and pointed at Ranu. Taronquel's eyes remained focused on Asmodeus, unable to speak.

"If you make me help you, it shall be a slow, painful death for your dear friend."

Asmodeus forced the sword to slice at Ranu's left wing, dropping half to the floor. The masura screamed in pain and balled up, begging for his life. Taronquel's breathing grew angrier, unable to free himself from the hold.

"What say you, Head Council? Oh, let's free your mouth."

Following the words, Taronquel uttered a scream. "Free me! I'll do what I must!"

Asmodeus smirked and lowered the arm, dropping Taronquel and the sword. The broken masura heaved himself up and grabbed the weapon. His concentration settled on the bloody blade, and he paused for a moment.

"Let's do it!" yelled Asmodeus.

Taronquel seethed at the demand and cried.

"My dear friend, forgive me. I do this to end the misery this devil gives you."

The head council drew the masura flat with a talon, raised the sword and sent it into his heart. Tears streamed as Taronquel dropped, holding his friend's head, weeping.

"Well done, Head Council, well done." Asmodeus clapped.

He waved at the guards, and they pulled the broken masura, fighting to remain with his friend, to the webbed prison. The black-crusted webbing sealed him in once more, and he curled, keeping his eyes on Ranu's lifeless body.

"Did you sense his might? Did you feel his power release and enter your body?" asked Asmodeus.

Taronquel held his tongue. Asmodeus placed a hand on the sword's hilt as it stuck through Ranu. He shuffled it back and forth.

"The anger it took to send the sword far into the wooden floor," said Asmodeus.

He moved to the webbing and eased where Taronquel's head lay.

"The surge is sweeter when you know the foe as a lover. I wonder if he knew how much you loved him."

The words pushed Taronquel into a sob.

"I guess you'll never know unless you experienced it at that bitter end you delivered."

Asmodeus proceeded to his father's cocoon and touched the throbbing entity. It jerked at the touch.

"How I yearn to know the power you possessed. I desire it," whispered Asmodeus.

Asmodeus stepped in front of the portal and touched the charge with the ruby hilt.

"I must leave you both alone. Remain with your lover for now. It's to be the last time."

With a flash and twirl, the passage changed the scene to a different cavern. The massive fire pit roared as its flames danced high into the center. The dome rose beyond sight as the walls vanished from view and, to the right, held the altar. Behind it, a drop into a vast chasm.

"Exercitus!" his dark voice echoed in the cave. "Bring the princess!"

Two masuran Royal Asmodean guards appeared in the council hall. Their eyes were black, skin and wings lilac, and they wore dark lilac metal armor. Asmodeus tapped the entrance, allowing the gateway to open.

"Take her to Malum and alert the guests."

The creatures unchained the beaten, weary Dasa princess, and she moaned with wrists bleeding from the tight shackles. A guard placed her on a shoulder, and they proceeded through the portal, bringing a sharp scream from the princess.

Asmodeus looked to his father, festering in the massive web, and then to Taronquel. "Soon."

The king braced for the pain and stepped through the gateway, enjoying the searing electrical surge. The masura's eyes widened as he perceived his powers growing, traversing the magic. He stepped onto the fixed platform overlooking the massive cavern. The enormous fire roared to the tall Bellow tree's height, and the many masuras mingled in front of the high altar.

Asmodeus raised his wings and floated to the party.

The king of Rath and La'Darium waited as they spoke with their royal court in front of the altar. The guests bowed their heads to Asmodeus and stared at the changed masura. Oblivious to their presence, the Asmodean king took his place in front of the altar; the murmuring prayers of the assembled masuras were a hushed backdrop to his arrival.

"I have many questions," said King Boran III of Rath.

"I have a simple question," said Asmodeus. "Where is the Mazerth Stone?"

"Why would you want or need it?" questioned King Danum La'Darium

"It's for our conquest and control. It leads us to a powerful clan," said Asmodeus.

"Tucked away in the Sovereign Hall," Boran said.

"Ah, the Sovereign Hall. What a brilliant choice and location. It's safe there," answered Asmodeus.

"What is your plan with it?" questioned Danum.

"None at this time, but we will decide on its path when we get there."

Asmodeus turned, stood on a step, and waited as Malum emerged from the shadows. He desired to watch their faces when they observed the powerful witch float before them.

"And may we trust these beings, my son?" asked Malum.

"Yes, Mother, they are ready," answered Asmodeus.

"Ready?" questioned King Boran.

Malum covered herself with a purple haze, gliding before them and reaching out a pure white, thin hand. They hardened their stance with each touch and became stone figures, unable to move or speak. The haze drifted to each member, performing the same action, then landed in front of Asmodeus. The smoke receded into the small jar Malum held in her right hand, and she corked its top.

"This is unnecessary, Mother. They had agreed to the deal, and are why the other clans' kings have fallen into the bottomless dream," said Asmodeus.

"Everything I do is necessary. I know how easy it is to persuade a masura and convince them to change course. We have come a long way, and under my control, will ensure their commitment," said Malum.

"I need their minds as kings," said Asmodeus.

Malum growled. "I'll free two kings. The others remain in my charge."

Asmodeus smiled. "Thank you, Mother."

Malum descended to the kings, opened a vial and tapped their heads with the cane. Lavender smoke slipped through their nostrils, returning to the jar where she corked it. Both masuras snapped from their sleep, looking confused and scared as Malum returned to Asmodeus's side. The kings could not move.

"I demand answers!" cursed the king of Rath.

"Complete loyalty is required," said Malum.

"What Madame Malum requests, King Boran, is loyalty to the new masuran way: one clan, one master, one king. The unification should spread our strength and abilities all over the island. Along with eliminating our foes and creating a better island way."

"One king? This was never an agreement," remarked King Danum.

"Look around you, La'Darium. The opportunity for negotiation has passed," said Asmodeus. "Time for compliance is required."

"Let me place them under thy spell," said Malum.

"What do you want?" asked King Boran.

"The same as before, a united clan," answered Asmodeus.

"But one king?" questioned Boran of Rath.

"Yes," answered Asmodeus.

"Which answers to Malum," groaned La'Darium.

"No, they answer to me! I'm the masuran king, and the island will unite under my control. If you disagree, you return to the spell and are sent to our regular units," said Asmodeus.

"Our clans?" asked King La'Darium.

"The clan members remain in their forests, living their daily lives as they do today. The royal families no longer hold the throne, but lead the forests under my reign. You remain at my side, helping defeat those in our way. After total island control, you'll return to the forests you came to and lead them from my command," said Asmodeus.

"And we have no say in the agreement," Rath angered.

"Enough!" thundered Malum. "These fools will not follow your lead."

"Mother, they intend to, and our kingdom will be grand in it," said Asmodeus. "With your history, knowledge, and afar treaties, the one masura clan is destined to be the greatest ever to exist."

"This is not an agreement, Witch'Bane. You hold us prisoner under dark magic and control it. There is no repentance for your madness," said Rath.

"Enough of this foolishness," cracked Malum.

The former kings held their tongues with the exercitus encircling the group.

Malum moved behind the altar, raising her thin arms. "In the mighty kingdom, the king needs a bride to bear him an heir. This marriage comes before the altar as a union for Druin, the homeland, and my sisters' plane!"

The voice rolled, and the cavern moaned with its power.

"If the council has forsaken this matrimony, the deceit is forever lasting time spent in the in-between. Their death, an eternity."

A loud clap bounced off the stone walls as they disappeared into the darkness.

"Bring forth the princess!"

From behind a large stone, the Dasa princess stepped forward, dressed in the traditional masura wedding garb. The beautiful masura's black hair folded into a long ponytail with a lavender lily sticking from the side. The bleeding scars on the wrist were gone, removed with no signs of torture. Her face and eyes, deep purple, with the eyelids black and drawn back, had lost their original appearance. The long black dress covered the talons, with the Thunderbolt crest encircled on the upper left chest. Purple lilies wrapped within her intense black wings and in her hair. The masura stood before Asmodeus, who could not escape the beauty.

Malum raised her left hand and dotted the area with small flames, lighting each spot. She turned to the chasm and closed her dead eyes. The demigod mumbled, spat, and gurgled when her neck snapped straight upward.

"Burn, burn, burn the fire!

"Grow, grow, grow it higher!

"I call out the one we named Flame!

"And charge you to show me your bane!"

From below, a roar resounded in the darkness until it ripped forward, and the shrill filled the cavern. Asmodeus covered his ears as the others kept silent when an orange glow formed from the drop. Flames from the entire rift rippled into the long tunnel, unseen past the altar's fiery height. The bulky Flame hauled its demonic torso from the depths and towered over Malum. The fire beast roared at the demigoddess, with flames bursting from its body. Malum did not shudder at the sight.

"Flame from the hidden mystery. I have returned, and you shall do my bidding!"

The massive beast thundered against the words and threw a fireball into the large pit, exploding the wood.

"Fire now, fire now! Else I shall turn you back into a cow!" she cried.

The demi-creature turned and sent fireballs into the open seam. The flames rose along the crevice, following the opening until they disappeared into the tunnel. It sent a small fireball into the awaiting princess, sending the body alive and eyes aglow.

"Go now, find the once deadly crevasse and bring it to life. It should guide us in our direction. Be ready for our arrival!"

The demon roared at the command and crawled into the rift as the orange hue turned red. The shrieking subsided with the sound of the fire, becoming a subtle backdrop. Malum floated to the altar and mumbled. The princess climbed the ancient stone altar, its rough surface cool beneath her fingertips, and lay flat upon it. "This mind and body are given to the island to bear an heir to the lone throne. Consummation is a must, and in the commingle shall be born the next sister to rule the island as I leave this plane and regain what I have lost."

Alarmed by the words, Asmodeus tried to talk, finding he could not move his jaw.

Malum looked at the masura and groaned at the idea when the fire within the drop roared higher. Her attention refocused on the altar. She removed the cork from the small vial and allowed the smoke to billow. It covered the platform and those standing around it. Asmodeus could no longer see Malum or anything farther than the smoke as the light popped into the haze. The flashes grew more rapid, with electrical charges zapping the air, causing discomfort with each burst. It vibrated and hummed, filling Asmodeus's ears.

"This pair is now forever wed before the mighty Flame, and their bond creates the seed to grow its force!"

The moment stretched his conceptions with confusion, and he noticed his body grow cold with his clothing falling to the side. The fire from behind sent its light into the haze, and he still could not move when he rose in the air and drifted until he came parallel to the princess, hovering over her naked torso. His head swam, and he could not focus when hands rubbed his body through the violet haze. The princess's eyes sparkled purple, and lips quivered under a chant Asmodeus could not hear.

"Become one, so the seed shall plant, and our future grows!"

Their naked bodies hovered above the altar, and the light bursts increased with hands now rubbing both torsos. The excitement swelled in Asmodeus's thoughts. The humming became more turbulent, and the rubbing shifted faster, catching the light burst rhythm. As darkness faded to pure white light, the charged air overwhelmed him, and his mind drifted into intense, silent thought.

The brightness dimmed until he found the young queen before him, naked, with wings covering her front. With a disconcerting stutter, the white backdrop changed faces. First, Malum's, harsh and imposing, then Rhile's, gentler and more familiar, finally focusing on the DasaRaul princess.

His body drifted, pulling him forward and into her wings as the scene continued to snap back and forth. Their naked bodies pressed against each other, and she whispered into his ear.

"We are forever one."

Malum's voice shocked Asmodeus as it echoed in his head, and their lips locked. He experienced a sudden thrust and electrical release repeating in the blurred vision. The new queen's expression held ecstasy and drew his mind deeper. Her wings thrust him tighter, and warm darkness enveloped him with a sudden light burst. He was numb and weary, with light coming through and Malum's face before him.

"We are to rule the island."

His mind wandered as he focused. Her face became dark and cold. He awoke in the cavern, covered in fur, lying on the altar next to the new queen, who was asleep. Naked on the cold stone surface, the royal family huddled together, the rhythmic crackle of the distant fire pit a low hum in the background. The chasm was dark, and Malum was gone as Rhile lingered over the altar. The female masura stood naked, with purple skin shining against the distant firelight. She ran a hand through his hair and onto his chest.

"She won't take you away from me and what we planned."

Rhile climbed atop Asmodeus and leaned to an ear.

"I am to bear the next heir to the throne, who will be our child."

The energy grabbed them both as Asmodeus sat, and Rhile wrapped her legs around the king. The others slept, and the queen lay on the side, away from them, as their bodies rose and lowered in complete silence. Her wings encircled them, and he drew forward, pressing his lips against her breast. He felt each grasp and body motion, her hands digging into his back, as the moment remained clear. She pressed a finger against his lips and one against hers until they both reached the ultimate release. His thoughts raced on having two heirs.

She released him, and he rested atop the stone altar when she lowered and kissed him, leaving the chamber without another word. He lay on the flat rock and pondered the events leading to the last moments. Did he just challenge Malum and her position on this plane? The truth had to be hidden where she could not penetrate his consciousness. The queen jerked in her sleep, and he drifted to BataRaul and farther, growing his empire.

Chapter Fifteen

The cell's damp chill clung to Gavee, preventing sleep, while a mournful wind howled incessantly through the small, barred window. Darkness perpetually haunted the dwelling. A ceaseless moan echoed from the shadowy hallway.

Dal remained in the same spot for days with his knees drawn up, lying on his side and facing the wall.

The humidity would not release. Gavee wiped the sweat from his forehead. The straw used for bedding made the mud thick as it absorbed water and caked his talons. He had counted at least three days since their arrival, with sunlight seeping in from the far right. The runners arrived and departed, yet the new runners for the day still needed to go to the course.

The room's silent murmur broke as a guard scratched their way down the hall, reaching their cell. Gavee felt its approach and descended to Dal. His gaze remained fixed on the ground as keys scraped the door. The dim light peeked in as the lizard held a whip. Its forked tongue slipped between its crooked teeth, and drool slid from its mouth. It raised and released its strap, sending an echo bouncing off the stone walls. The room jumped to their feet, stood in line as directed, and the foul creature entered the cell. It stood over Gavee and Dal.

"Slaves, come, for you must train in course," it cracked the whip.

Gavee stood, pulling Dal to his feet, and proceeded to the gate where they paused to the grangrul standing in the way. Its loose phlegm gurgled between its broken teeth as its grip on the whip twisted. The creature withdrew, giving space, and they crouched through to avoid the lash. They stopped at the wall and paused for the guard. The slow grind forward had the mud path thicken between the talons when the whip snapped across

Gavee's upper legs. It dropped him into the mud, and he growled at the captors, releasing a yelp. The pain brought a tear, and he fought to locate the thunderblood inside.

Dal tried to help when a snap just missed his face. Gavee motioned him away, flinging the mud from his body and pushing Dal in front to keep him from the vile creature. The corridor, unchanged, featured dripping water and a few torches. They reached the passage end and expected the lizard to unlock the gate, with Gavee's senses focused on the beast gurgling behind.

The rusted metal door squealed under the movement, and the lizard pointed with its long claw down the hallway into an empty, dark abyss. Gavee taped Dal's shoulder, and the pair moved into the warm tunnel. The steel trap closed behind them.

"Follow the path, runners."

With each step, the blackness choked their sight until darkness filled everything. The sound from the stadium roared above them. Gavee raised a hand to help guide the way. Dal whimpered, and the elder patted the shoulder with assurance, an assurance the thunderblood trainee was unsure if he could give the masura. The tunnel's commotion and darkness brought a shiver as they pressed forward, waiting for the end to show.

After many darkened steps, his hands landed upon a mud wall, feeling the roots poking through and following its turn. Gavee muttered the thunderblood line, "Center the energy," as the steps became longer and courage grew.

The light appeared, ending the timeless walk with the mud between their talons weighing each step. They reached the gate with arms raised, blocking the painful light, and the guard unlocked the door.

"Move faster, runner." It lashed the whip.

They pushed past, slinging caked mud to no avail and cringing through the gate. They awaited the snap when the guard slammed the rusty door, pointing its claw down another long, torchlit passage. Wooden planks made up the floor ahead, and loose stones formed the walls, which rose to a wooden cover. Wear on the wood allowed the talon tips to rip in, and the roof above gaped, revealing the dome. As the roars increased, the crowd's thumping grew louder for the new victims. A couple of oversized wooden doors without a guard awaited their arrival.

They approached an iron gate, where a room awaited beyond the entrance. It contained benches filled with others' heads in hands, and sitting in exhaustion. The grangrul appeared from a hidden passage and leaned against a giant club with its tongue lingering outside its gnashing teeth.

"Young masura? We've not had one like you for a long time," it hissed. "We make you primary course."

Gavee tugged Dal behind and pushed out his chest.

"He stays with me."

The lizard brought the club over its bony shoulder and stared. It slithered to a large metal door holding a smaller door. The lizard rapped on the gate, and an answering rap returned.

"You both run course on the other side. If you reach the end, you're given food and returned to cage."

"What if we don't?" Dal squeaked.

"No more runner," it rasped with a chuckle.

"How do we know the end?" questioned Gavee.

"Look for a red flag. It saves lives."

The small door opened.

"Or it may not," it laughed.

The small door squeaked open and revealed no picture of what awaited. The lizard slammed its club against the large door.

"Go!" it growled.

He grabbed Dal's shoulders.

"Stay within my wings. Search for the flag, ignoring everything. You'll be our eyes for it. You need to find it."

Dal's eyes widened in fear when Gavee took a breath, ducked through the small door, and gasped. The thunderblood gazed at the setting in front of him, an image only a grangrul would create, let alone enjoy. A small, dead forest filled with trees holding no leaves, shrubs desolate of a single blade, and a rocky dirt floor. They created a forest fit for their games, with nothing alive except the collected creatures to venture through it. He followed the tall walls, entrapping the hideous sight, with rows running left and right, rising to the top.

He caught movement heading for the lifeless forest's far reaches, flying over the top branches, soaring and lowering.

Dumbfounded and confused, Gavee stared at the masura with a grin. Datta's poise and calm in the dead forest shocked the Witch'Bane. She landed with a stern glare and dirt from head to talon, with her BataRaul armor tattered but firm.

"You don't know me," she snapped.

The spectators went silent and waited. Datta raised her hands to the audience. Her voice echoed, "I'm here to train you on the course, masuras. You compete for your life in three days. Learn, for you have a short time to understand the course."

The onlookers cheered.

"This is about surviving! Being alive! Greetings on another day! For anything else, the answer is death!" thundered Datta.

The arena erupted in cheers and chants.

"We train with the arena watching?" confused Gavee.

"The important point, Masura, is the more we stand and talk, the less time we have to learn!"

Datta turned, taking flight and soaring past the dead trees. The restless crowd chanted, "Hawk! Hawk! Hawk!" with Datta swooping into the lifeless forest.

"I know that masura," whispered Gavee. "She'll lead us out."

"If we live," moaned Dal. Tears dropped from his cheeks.

"You could still be locked in your home," said W.B.

The words surprised the lad, and he wiped his tears.

"You need to become angry at your captors, or they'll beat you," Gavee said.

"Training, masuras!" yelled Datta.

Gavee soared for the trees and found Dal still on the ground.

The masura stared at his wingtips and tried to lift them while Gavee circled back and landed.

"Dal?"

"I never fly. I fly just a few times here and there. Master wants my wings fresh."

Anger caused Gavee's jaws to tighten. He forced a breath and calmed his senses, embracing the lad.

"My training will protect us, and we'll escape with Datta."

Dal remained nervous. Gavee took his hand.

"Come."

To Dal's astonishment, they took flight and caught Datta hovering above the trees.

The arena stretched farther than he realized, shocking him to see the dead forest end at a giant drop into a rocky ravine. The detached section traveled far, nearing a dirt wall, ascending toward a mountain-sized hill, and attaining the dome top. They continued to float through the arena as the audience threw trash and other items.

Datta kept them close to the center and then hovered. "Crossing the ravine will prove difficult. The birds can lure you into a trap, so don't go down. Always stay up," she said.

"I don't understand," said Gavee.

"Once you enter the arena, a whistle is blown, sending out the devil hawks. They rise from the hillside and move your way, so the instant you come through the door, be on your way. Don't wait for the whistle," said Datta.

"Devil hawks?" questioned Dal.

"Do you not know them?" asked Gavee.

"Yes, but they kill masuras," worried Dal.

"Not just them," said Datta. "Watch the lizards near the ledges. They'll begin shooting arrows and aiming to take you down. They are rewarded for injury and for allowing the devil hawks to end it. If you make it beyond the rock valley, you need to rise above the hillside and reach the flag. The whistle blows and ends the chase."

"So, arrows, devil hawks, and a simple flag?" said Gavee.

"They throw more during the chase. It's more challenging than I make it sound," said Datta.

"Once we grab the flag, we're done?" asked Gavee.

"I wish to agree, but the final part is unfamiliar, and I encountered it once after I came back indoors," answered Datta.

"How long have you been here?" asked Gavee.

"Long enough," she groaned. "You must listen because the beast they are about to release, we shall be the first group to challenge it."

Gavee bit his tongue.

"They captured a creature not from this island. I know it from my travels, and I hope you have come across it."

"What is it?" asked Gavee.

"A brendentók, a dragon from the island of Róta."

"How did they get it?" asked Gavee.

"They stole the egg and raised it in a training arena. It has been fighting masuras since it hatched."

"I have experience with these dragons, and they are easily outwitted. They're mean, and fire melts metal," said Gavee. "How does it not catch the arena on fire or bring it all down?"

"They control it with a band on its neck. It's allowed to use its fire in the course and not outside the boundary lines."

"A dragon?" questioned Dal.

"Yes, a dwarf dragon," said Gavee. "The brendentók is a dwarf dragon."

"They are roughly the size of elephants and fit inside the course," said Datta.

"Ela-fant?" continued Dal.

"Just stay with me," said Gavee.

Datta pointed to the green poles outlining the arena course. The conversation broke off with a siren, and the crowd cheered.

"Here comes the hawk," said Datta

"Just one?" asked Gavee.

"Yes, in training, they send the one," answered Datta.

Gavee eyed Dal, then Datta. "Dal, stay between us and keep your wings pushing downward. It lets your tips catch the stream and keep within our speed."

The three expected the creature, observing the cheering crowd's eyes centered on the bird. Its horns first appeared as it dipped and rolled near the rock piles, then it shot up into the air and hovered, belting its call. The screech forced Dal to cover his ears, and Gavee gave him a nudge.

"I'll distract it and pull it in my direction. Head to the top and grab the flag!" said Datta.

She did not hesitate and darted at the devil hawk, screaming at the bird. It returned its call and aimed for the masura. Bellowing at the enemy, the thunderblood trainee's anger grew with a gutted growl. The hawk screamed again as Datta jumped her legs forward and reached out her sharpened nails. The bird appeared ready on the move, tucking in its wings, dropping, and swooping through the tree line. It aimed at its new victims in its cage.

"Gavee!" screamed Datta.

The thunderblood caught the red, beady eyes glowing in their direction. He pulled Dal into his arms and dived for the open valley. The spectators cheered at the move, the chant of "Hawk! Hawk! Hawk!" increased in momentum.

Gavee cut in and out, grabbing a large stone with a talon. He tossed it to Dal, and the boy returned it to the elder. The motion was quick, and the devil hawk was oblivious, in its speed growing closer. He could sense the creature closing in when he halted, turned, and rocketed at the stone at the bird. The crazed beast could not avoid the hit, and feathers popped into the air with it, bouncing across the rocky floor. Silence overcame the spectators.

"Retrieve the flag!" Datta's voice echoed when cut short, and the siren blasted its warning.

The audience broke into cheers, and the metal wall's top windows dropped, slamming its metal hinges with its sound overtaking the arena's excitement.

Gavee pushed Dal from his arms and shouted, "Fly with me!"

The duo reached the massive hillside.

Devil hawks poured into the arena—more than Gavee had ever seen.

The drag on their wings pushed them almost into the hillside as they tried to climb the hill. Giant wooden fans rotated on the rooftop, creating a loud wind. Gavee could hear nothing and was unaware of the approaching attackers. He remained focused and kept Dal within reach.

With a sudden burst, the birds split in half, creating neat formations that followed the perimeter markers. The cheers escalated into a frenzied noise, the guttural cry of "Kill!" booming through the stadium. Datta remained low for a chance not to be seen and mauled.

Gavee dragged Dal aside as the flag appeared from behind a boulder. They landed on a ledge, pushed by the wind as the thunderblood trainee looked over his shoulder, catching the formation, and the giant fans helped him. The devil hawk, with its smaller stature, could not enter the stream without risking being tossed to the side.

Dal struggled to stand and grabbed Gavee's arm.

"Remain hidden," Gavee told him. "I'll reach the flag!"

Gavee released Dal, and he flipped over, rolling down the hillside. The birds realized their misfortune and descended onto the lone masura.

Gavee's choice had to be the flag to end the cursed attack. He thrust his wings forward and down, fighting the powerful blast. Datta felt a growl rise at the sight of Dal's tumble. The thunderblood screamed at the hawks and bolted from hiding. The first devil hawk appeared when Dal turned and kicked the beast in the chest, grabbing and tossing it. It bounced across the dirt and rocks.

Just as Gavee was reaching the last boulder to grab the flag, a third gust of wind kicked in from the side. With the boulder in hand, the masura strained toward the edge. Against the rock, the gust pulled him away, forcing a stretch to his spine, and he grimaced. The wind drowned out all noise, and he could no longer see Dal or the course.

Dal took flight when a hawk grabbed the boy by the pant leg and yanked backward, waiting for its flock. The lad screamed with the hawk's talons digging into a thigh when another grabbed the other leg. Blood dripped through his pants, and the birds picked up the scent. More jumped onto his shoulders, grabbing his wings and pulling him from the sides.

Datta reached Dal and dug both talons into a bird holding its wings. She snapped its neck when the flock arrived. The devil hawks swooped, screeching and hitting them both, with Datta trying to fight off the attack. Dal screamed in pain when the horn blasted, and the birds ended the madness as fast as it started.

Gavee stood with the flag. Dal lay on the ground, whimpering from the pain and blood dripping from his nose. The cuts injured the masuras, but not fatally. Gavee landed next to Dal and tried to tend to his wounds when a second horn blew, sending "boos" from the crowd.

"It's done. Time to return to the cage," said Datta.

"Are we all in the same cage?" asked Gavee.

"Unsure. I've never killed a devil hawk. I'm uncertain about what's coming next."

* * *

It had been a few days since their test run, and Datta took the brunt of the hawk's death. She lay covered in matted straw and lost the battle to stay dry. Thunder boomed through the cell and drowned out the relentless dripping from the mysterious water. The repetitive boom kept its tempo, letting Gavee understand the time was near. He rehearsed the course in his head and noted Dal asleep. He repeated the steps they would need to follow to reach the flag.

"Datta," he whispered through the metal bars.

The masura remained facing away from the hallway.

"Come on, Datta. I need to understand your reason for being here. The grangrul could not have captured you and delivered you here," said Gavee.

She turned and moved to the bars.

"Grunt found me, and I understood where you would end up. I was here before. The dolts still don't understand it's me," said Datta.

"You've been here?" asked Gavee.

"Yes, my fighting and survival skills stemmed from here," said Datta.

Gavee tried to uncover the words.

"I was a runner for these monsters and understood their weaknesses."

"How do we escape?" asked Gavee.

"My previous exit has since closed, and I've been lying here thinking about it. I understand the method, but it's going to be challenging. It may even be crazy," said Datta.

"With a pair of thunderbloods, all is possible," grinned Gavee.

"When we do, we need to locate the scroll keeper."

"And heal our kings," said Gavee.

"Much has changed, Gavee," said Datta.

Gavee ignored the words and focused on the escape. "What is the plan?"

The squeaking from old metal now filtered through the boom, showing the runners had made it to the course. Grangrul guards appeared in the hall, and the masuras' private conversation ended. They both stood, brushing off the loose straw and peeling off the mud.

Dal remained next to Gavee, and the lad shook.

"We have a plan, and freedom is close," whispered Gavee.

The grangrul hissed at the cell doors and unlocked the metal, swinging it open. It stood with a whip in its bony claw between the gates, and its tongue slithered. It cracked the leather.

"Move!"

The snap startled Dal, and Gavee moved the boy between Datta and himself, growling at the lizard. It raised the whip, and the trainee did not flinch, maintaining the walk down the corridor. They reached the line and observed the many sad creatures awaiting their time to walk down the path. The goblin would be the first to run, with a large hairy creature Gavee had never seen standing behind it and shaking from fear. Next was a toad imp, a slimy creature with an odd odor and dead flies stuck to its creamy, light blue body. Its long black tongue wiped its right eyeball, then it removed a dead fly from its arm, slipping back into its enormous mouth. Gavee and Bahg had dealt with this creature in Eden's pirate city. It smiled and winked at the masura, and Gavee shook his head, and then it noticed Datta. Its eyes grew larger in fear.

"You owe me something, Geèm," she said.

The toad imp began speaking when the lizard interrupted.

"The three masuras run last. They get Lorg!" It garbled a laugh.

The lizard grabbed Dal and yanked him to the rear. It stepped to the double doors and waited.

"What is a Lorg?" asked Dal through chattering teeth.

"We get to find out together," said Datta. "Hoping for the brendentók."

"Stay within us. We'll find a way," said Gavee.

"Silence!" snapped the grangrul.

The horn thundered in the corridor, and the rush from the crowd surrounded them as the wooden double doors opened to the arena. The goblin hesitated, and the guard shoved it past the double doors. It slammed them shut, snapped its whip, and the line stepped forward. The walls shuddered from the cheers and rumbled as the masses watched another victim fight for their life. Dal's body shook, and Gavee tried to ease the masura.

Datta winked at Dal. "I was once a runner here before and fought in this place. We can escape."

"I trust you," Dal said, "but I'm still scared."

Datta nodded and stood. Gavee observed the masura's face turn furious, and concentration built in her thoughts.

"We will use the dragon," she whispered.

"How?" he asked.

"Once it's released, force it to follow and create a wide pattern. Make it gain momentum," answered Datta.

"I don't understand?" asked Gavee.

With the double doors opening, the dome fell silent, hands shielding against the brightness. The next in line entered, and they moved ahead. The cheering erupted and then faded when the doors opened.

"Quick kill!" hissed the lizard.

Geèm turned and smiled at the masuras, then disappeared into thin air. The lizard folk snapped its long neck from side to side, and Gavee stared at Datta.

"Where?" confused the lizard.

Gavee shrugged, and the creature hissed, stepping into the dome. The spectators booed at its appearance, and it growled. It twirled a pointy finger in the air, and guards scoured the dirt floor. As the toad imp disrupted the planned event, the attendees littered the field where the grangrul patrolled. A sharp whistle sounded, causing the lizards to lift their heads from their vantage point above the entrance before returning to their places. The captor snapped its whip. Like a thunderclap, the sound cracked, and the captor pointed to the masuras.

"Your turn!"

The audience erupted, and the booming rose in tempo, shaking the walls and rattling the doors.

"Now, runners!" the grangrul snapped the whip.

Gavee grabbed Dal's hand, squeezing it tight and pulling him into the light beyond the doors. They climbed several dirt steps with the grangrul jabbing its stick into Gavee's back. They stood outside the entrance, and the crowd hissed, booed, and chanted until it broke into an annoying pitch. The mixed group flew more than on the practice run, and Datta gave a blank stare to Gavee.

"I've never seen it this full," said Datta. "The arena is different."

The workers tied the rows into three sections, and the stadium rolled from left to right as if it moved outward. The dead forest included more trees, and the hill lay in the center, towering higher and just under the dome.

Dal pointed up.

"They have lightning?" questioned Gavee.

Each ledge had three grangrul holding massive rods with a weird charge coming from their tips. The small lightning bolts bounced to the edge, and Gavee glanced at Datta.

"New?" he asked.

"They have the wizard helping," said Datta.

Distant ledges echoed the rods' effects, resonating within the dome. Blinded by the flash, an echo rounded the arena. As the spectators cheered, the lizards lifted the rods into place. The wooden benches resounded from the stadium goers, and the excitement built into a deafening roar. The hungry hordes' bloodlust broke when a whistle blast echoed.

Datta did not wait and lifted. "Here come the hawks! Use the stones to knock them out and reach the flag!"

"What about the dragon?" asked Gavee.

"It comes in runs, but not the first," answered Datta.

"Runs?" asked Gavee.

"There could be several! After all, we killed a few training birds!"

She zipped into the trees, and Gavee helped Dal. "Let's find you a hiding spot until we kill these things."

"I'm not afraid."

The lad picked up a large stone and clamped his teeth in anger. Gavee grinned at the notion, and the pair darted low into the trees. The devil hawks came from the distant hill with the leader moving faster than Gavee expected, dipping and rising, already in the dead forest. The group leader released a resounding yell, and the crowd roared.

Gavee took Dal's hand, and they dug deeper into the dead forest, catching the devil hawk's eye.

***

Datta perched on the massive hill, waiting for a pattern to show, when the leader veered and headed to the masuras. The birds split, and Datta recognized the formation as they angled to move the masura in their direction. She moved to the second group.

The female masura ascended high above the trees, sending her whistle and surprising the group. They staggered in flight, confused, until they aimed for Datta. She turned right, observing the archers preparing their arrows. While searching for the devil hawks, the masura eased her wings.

The horned birds sped faster, and the thunderblood stretched her wings, veering to the archers, reaching them more quickly than they expected. The lizards released their rounds after she passed, still hitting a target, as the many devil hawks fell, leaving the small flock vulnerable.

Datta swooped to the ground, found a long, dead branch in the open center, and readied for the horned birds.

The small group's eyes burned red, with horns aimed at their prey.

She floated with the broken tree limb as they approached. Several swings met the hawk's arrival, cracking the birds and distracting those avoiding the melee.

The strategy worked, allowing the birds to separate and giving them a chance to attack each masura.

The whistle blew, and the far door swung open.

* * *

Gavee waited to see what emerged when the surprise enemy floated through and into the arena.

The male masura was taller than Gavee, with a visible scar cut across his bald head and a patch covering his left eye. He gripped metal whips in both hands, and sparks sent a charge under their snap. The spectators roared and then chanted until the sound filled the arena.

"Torëk! Torëk! Torëk!"

The mystery masura resonated with a growl, and the circle thundered. The remaining devil hawks darted through the decaying forest and settled on a perch.

Datta landed next to Gavee. "I know him."

"You know him?" questioned Gavee.

"I caused the patch."

Gavee snapped at Datta, and she showed concern.

She said, "I thought he had died during my escape. I was unaware he was still alive."

"Is he going to be happy to see you?"

"We'll find out."

Datta drove her wings down and towered high above the dead forest with the giant rocky hill behind.

Gavee waited for the distant masura's reaction when he cracked his whip, roared, and pointed to Datta. The thunderblood continued to hold the broken branch when she snarled and flew for the masura. He followed, cracking his whip and sending the arena louder in their continued "Torëk" chant. The masuras' attack saw Datta dodge a whip, then use a branch to catch another.

"There's our answer," said Gavee.

He searched again.

"Dal, see the hole between the large rocks?"

The lad nodded.

"Go inside and stay low. I need to help Datta."

Dal leaped, but Gavee grabbed an arm. "No, climb down from the tree and stay low. We ensure no one observes the movement. Do you understand?"

"I do."

The masura climbed downward through each limb.

"Faster," whispered Gavee.

The boy reacted to the demand, scaled the trunk, and ran to the hole. Gavee immediately sent his wings hard into the air. Datta continued to block the blows, and the broken limb became smaller with each direct hit. Torëk and Datta hovered in front of each other, with the male snapping the weapons. Gavee reached them and hovered in front of Datta and the stranger.

"I heard they captured a female masura," said Torëk.

"You were dead. I saw you fall," shocked Datta.

Torëk snapped the whip.

"And yet, you chose not to return and retrieve me."

Tears rolled down Datta's cheeks.

"I couldn't return. The grangrul had you before I could reach the gate, and it had closed. I had to keep moving."

"Together, you said."

"I tried! There was no way inside, and I thought your body was lifeless. You told me, if you fall, go on and find my way!"

The onlookers became restless about the stutter in the fight.

Torëk surveyed his surroundings, and anger seemed to take hold.

Gavee raised the branch and deflected a hit. The masura snapped the second whip and yanked the branch from his grip. The fury deepened within Torëk, and Datta pulled Gavee away from the masura.

"It's between us, not him," she growled.

Torëk snapped the metal whips.

"Why did you return?" he groaned.

"I was captured."

"Not true."

"Things are happening beyond the Lower Realm, and this masura is needed to help end it."

He snapped his whip, and the arena boomed. Silence fell over the stadium as the chanting ended. The whistle blew, causing the devil hawks to exit through the opened door. A siren blasted and arrows arched toward the masuras, hitting Torëk in the leg. He howled from the hit and, in one motion, snapped it clean and removed the shaft.

"Follow me!" he yelled.

Arrows arced above the flying prisoners. Some lit with its flame hitting the dried forest, and small fires building in the shrubs. Torëk moved, and Gavee recognized the flight pattern. He expected each move, and they curled into a protected rock formation. Upon landing, Torëk dropped Gavee with a hit to the face. He grabbed Datta by the throat and slammed her against the stone.

"I should kill you."

She clutched a hand and tried to fight. Her wings remained pinned, and Gavee lay stunned on the ground.

"I didn't."

"They beat me for days."

Datta wept. The arrows ended, and a loud horn blew, causing Torëk to drop Datta.

"The dragon is coming," growled Torëk.

Datta coughed from the release, and Gavee struggled to stand.

"We must find Dal," said Gavee.

The arena returned to life when a reverberating thunder vibrated the rocks. The beast roared again, and Datta's eyes widened at the power behind its call.

Torëk pulled the whips from his side and peered about the rocks.

Gavee jumped to the other side and watched the stands as their cheers remained on the distant beast. He worried about Dal and waited for the creature to show its flight.

"Datta, you mentioned a plan?" questioned Gavee.

The masura shook off the strangle and Gavee raised her from the ground.

"We use its strength to bust through the dome roof," she coughed.

Torëk eyed the dome, then once more at Datta.

"Force the dragon to fly into the roof?"

"It's the only way."

"How?" questioned Gavee. "Dragons have intelligence."

"It is a brendentók, the lowest species in the dragon lineages," said Torëk. "It's going to follow like a pet."

"How?" Gavee asked Datta.

"I'll explain at another time. We should use the hill, forcing it to circle and gain momentum. We trail it higher until the top and send it through the ceiling," said Torëk.

"You are helping us?" questioned Datta.

"No, I'm helping myself," said Torëk.

"Dal?" questioned Gavee.

"Bring him higher, then you jump in and distract the beast," said Torëk.

Gavee nodded. Torëk searched once more for the dragon.

"It's on the move."

"Where?" asked Datta.

"It hovers at the main gate. The lizards with poles appear nervous, and we may use them to aggravate the beast and cause it to fly faster," said Torëk.

"Are you with us?" questioned Datta.

"They shot me with an arrow. If I return, I'm dead," answered Torëk.

"I'll get Dal to a higher spot," said Gavee.

"Time to escape," said Torëk.

"All of us," said Datta. "I shall bring your body with me if I must."

Torëk did not respond to the gesture, just said, "Let's go."

"It's time," said Datta.

The female masura instantly pushed into the sky, disappearing. Torëk copied Datta's lead and left Gavee alone.

Gavee searched below and could not remember where Dal had found the hole.

"Dal? Dal!"

The lad popped out his head, and the dragon thundered into the arena.

Datta and Torëk circled the far dead forest edge, still smoking from the fire.

The dragon continued its hover near the gate, with the grangrul using their prods to repel it. They cursed the beast and blew their whistles to attack.

"Here, now!" yelled Gavee. "Keep your wings in!"

Dal nodded and crawled from the spot where the rippled dragon flames drowned out the audience. The brendentók chased Datta and Torëk across the tree line, bursting the branch tips. Angered by the trail, the beast charged harder to catch its prey. The three broke past the rocky hill and disappeared beyond Gavee's vision.

"Fly now!"

Dal did not wait and lifted enough to use his feet to pull up to Gavee.

Gavee hoisted Dal higher onto the rocks.

Spectators cheered as the dragon roared, and Datta and Torëk performed a low, ground-level swoop from the distance. The lizards reached out with the charged prods, keeping the brendentók from attacking the crowd and on pace for the chase. As he looked away from Torëk, the cheering crowd caught Gavee's attention. The lizards lined the walls, hissing and growling at the entertainment, and the mixed attendees screamed, trading fares on each dragon miss and masura gain. Datta began to rise and found Gavee with Dal.

"Draw it to the top!" she screamed.

Torëk and Datta drew the brendentók closer to the onlookers, and the dragon's scales flexed with a fire burst. The flames ripped across the lower bowl, taking out a grangrul tower with lizards jumping from the fire. The dragon's left wing snapped into an outlook, catapulting the lizard stationed there and slowing its momentum. Undeterred, Datta pressed on, her chase a continuous loop around the base of the hill. The dragon roared, and Gavee pulled Dal to the side.

"When we reach the top, hide and be ready to move when the top opens."

They climbed higher when an arrow just missed Gavee's hand. The masura reacted as archers fired, the dome now bristling with quills. Dal screamed.

An arrow had lodged in the lad's arm, another striking Gavee in the thigh.

The pair dropped, and the thunderblood pulled Dal behind several boulders.

The audience roared at the hit, and the dragon belched flames to the cheers. Datta returned to find the brendentók reaching the dead forest and blasting the already blackened trees.

Torëk veered to the left and hung close to the wall, remaining alert and waiting for the dragon. Then he plunged toward the floor, gaining speed and causing the brendentók to flap harder and faster. Arrows shot from the ledges as the dragon reached the small clearing, headed for the masuras, and then Torëk rose above the lizards. The shots fell short, landing amongst the onlookers and taking out their own.

Chaos hit the seats as lizards began cowering or running into each other, trying to avoid the arrows. The dragon's speed found its way, reaching short of its prey, when it shot flames, just missing their talons. The fire struck the onlookers, bringing screams and growls as they fought to escape. Torëk looked behind him with a grin, knowing the conduct would mean the end if he did not break free. Datta stayed tight with him as the two remained several paces ahead. The beast continued its aimless display, setting the seats ablaze and forcing the grangrul on the ledges to aim for their destructor.

"Gavee!" yelled Datta.

Gavee grabbed his thigh and hovered to watch the chaos in the stands. Datta disappeared behind the hill with Torëk and the dragon at full speed.

"Come on, Dal, we're there!" gritted Gavee.

The thunderblood ignored the pain and picked Dal up with his shoulders. They ascended to the top, reaching the mountain's apex and landing on its crest, monitoring the brendentók. When a giant horn blew, Datta saw the many creatures run to the exits in fear. The dragon continued circling the mountain and rising with each round.

"Now!" yelled Gavee

The thunderblood landed near the roof and awaited the dragon. They came to the edge when Datta and Torëk dropped into a ragged hole. The beast followed with its eyes burning red. The dragon roared, taking the focus off the distant masura. It ascended faster as the brendentók tore upward with the horn blaring in the background. The screams from the onlookers continued as the sounds carried to the dome top.

The massive creature's speed barreled through its fiery smoke when Gavee dropped and the beast crashed into the dome's roof. It tore through the mud ceiling, breaking the thin layer, and continued its flight. The smoke seeped through the opening, leaving the masuras hovering on opposite sides. Torëk did not say a word, just followed the dragon, as did Datta.

Gavee snatched Dal's hand and dragged him through the opening. Freedom awaited.

"We are free!" cried Dal. "Free!"

Chapter Sixteen

Shapía faced the black skeleton's brutal onslaught. Each attack was a grim dance of death, culminating in her lifeless form lying still amongst the dust and debris. The changes turned her skin ashen, and the bracers hardened on her arms. She awoke to two black skeleton attackers on a more massive rock formation. The rebirth landed on a different stone platform, and the bracers offered a sword and shield to fend off the foe.

Turning aside the first spear, the warrior sent it into the abyss, leaving it defenseless. The second chattered its teeth and ran for the masura with its battleaxe. She parried the strike and spun, dropping its arm.

Another skeleton seized her and pinned her arms as a second attacked. Shapía dropped, allowing the weapon to swing through, and lopped off the skeleton's head. It shattered into dust, and the masura brought down the last standing with a stroke against its legs. The possessed continued to swing its weapon from its broken position when Shapía kicked it beyond the rock. The new seer stood with its head rolling off and dissolving into ash.

"How many more?"

Her voice echoed, boomeranged, and surprised the masura. For the first time, a sound filled the space.

"Sattva! Sattva!"

Two skeletons rose from the stone face in the distant rock and chattered their teeth. She lowered the bracers and removed the weapons.

"No more!"

She turned away, and the spear pierced through, causing her to fall to her knees. The blood rushed in and filled her throat as she gurgled, unable to speak. Death claimed the mind once more. The blackness turned white, and Sattva's glass body walked forward in her saffron robe into floating clouds.

"What is the point? Dying repeatedly. What have I learned?"

"You have learned how to use your saktis in many forms."

"Why death? Why am I forced to endure such painful deaths?"

"All death is painful, and each molt has past effects, binding you to this plane. Its power shall continue to grow within and help you master the saktis."

"Binds me?"

"Yes, to be a seer of seers, you are bound to an energy plane greater than the one you partake in, giving you power and abilities. It is the way."

Her mind went blank, and she woke again, landing on an enormous rock not yet encountered, surrounded by five skeletons. The electric sword and shield snapped against the charged air, and the fury in her eyes burned red. She now saw the foe as demons through her new view, with entire bodies and gnashing teeth.

"Come, you filth," she growled.

The twirling sword popped, and the long shield exposed her charged eyes.

"Aza is not pleased!" the towering demigod cursed. "You come to our plane and demand to be greater than us!"

"I demand nothing! I sense nothing!"

Shapía beat her sword against the sparking shield.

The five beasts emerged, and Shapía defended two quick hits, jumping from the third and rolling from the last two swings. They sank into the stone and then reappeared behind her before she could react. The rock, black sky, and rock again twirled in front of her vision, then she landed, looking up at her own headless torso. She lost her breath, her ashen wings folding as she dropped to the rock. She blinked, and darkness took hold.

Sattva's voice pounded forward. "Weapons are a fool's game. The power you desire originates in the energy etched into the body and the saktis. Use its force to suffocate the foe and crush their attack."

Shapía sensed her awareness drift backward until the white faded to black, and then she materialized on a floating boulder. She spun to discover herself alone on a long, slim stone, sailing through the clouds. The wind pushed her hair, but she felt no sensation as the clouds cleared, when the rock settled against a larger stone. It held a carved staircase leading up beyond sight.

The masura approached the stairs, and the traveling stone dropped. Each step did the same as she climbed to the top, where a female in a black dress sat on her knees and slumped to the floor, only showing her ebon hair. Four thick chains bolted to four different distant rocks bound the motionless being slumped in the center of an etched circular glyph. The etching had five layers, with each disc section slowly rotating in opposite directions. The rock's grinding vibrated the stone.

Shapía readied the bracers into a shield and sword.

"Your chosen weapon is fated to fail." His voice was dark, with a sinister smirk accompanying it.

As the clouds dispersed, a red aura gathered against the darkening sky. Shapía dropped her arms down, and the static weapons disappeared.

"Find the strength to defeat the creature bound before the altar." The dark voice echoed, and the female screamed in pain as she floated to a hover above the rotating discs with the chains pulling tight. Tiny invisible strings pulled her hair in many directions and pulled her face forward, leaving her skin ashen and her eyes black. The mouth jawed with no words, and the shackles tightened at the wrists, exposing the black blood beginning to ooze from the wounds.

"Guru Sattva, come to me!" said Shapía.

The distant fiery red bellowed, and a rumble reverberated near the floating elevation.

"There are two others—sisters, like this one. Your plane depends on you to bring them to me and end their campaign."

"Who are you?"

"I am the keeper, the creator of the plane, and I give you its power."

"Where is Guru Sattva? I do not trust you!"

"Trust in me, my Seer. The energy from this plane is in your control."

Shapía observed the slow rotation and stepped onto the rotating disc, stopping its cycle. The witch's eyes stared into the beyond, body tense and rigid.

"Who is this?" Shapía asked.

"She is one of three demigods conjured in this plane as invokers to sustain its energy, but they betrayed me and moved beyond. My brother, Nathe, trapped and locked away the sisters, draining the plane of their powers. Something freed one and unknowingly freed the others, but not enough to return."

"And yet here she is?" confused Shapía.

A boom rattled, and the witch's face and body shuttered and shifted.

"Guru Lin!"

The woman's eyes held torment and pain, with skin remaining taut against the hidden pull.

"Help. Me." The words struggled through a dry mouth, and the agony filled the tears now falling.

"Release her! Sattva!" screamed Shapía.

"She shall be released when you return the sisters to me. I grant you the source to conjure the might from this plane and have it flow through your veins."

The rock gave way beneath her, leaving Shapía suspended before a red, rippling face in the darkness. A black wisp floated forward and touched her forehead. The surge jolted her body, and the pain shot across the bones. The blackness held tight, then red and orange until it all darkened.

She settled on the small, floating stone after the blackness slipped away, as it had in the seven previous deaths. The darkness remained, with a massive volcano floating among a series of rocks, spewing lava and falling into the abyss. Five demigods remained between the breaks in the flow, waiting for the seer to return from the in-between.

Shapía held out the bracers and studied the markings leading to the gems. The force surged through the bracers and charged her senses to the surroundings.

"Aza has granted you this ability, and we intend to reveal its source," thundered the tallest being.

Shapía attempted to move, but remained locked to the stone. The black beast on the far left grew a blue flame in its black claw, sending it into the masura's chest. Her wings ignited with a bright blue as the blaze engulfed her. The next black beast held a bright red flame, sending it into her chest, and her vision brightened to a glowing ruby. A purple flame erupted from the rightmost creature, shooting into her left bracer as the gems sparked from the surge, causing her hand to clench. The fourth beast formed both claws, sending a green flame into the right bracer, sparking the gems and causing a fist.

With its massive arms raised, the final giant beast cursed and grew a bright white flame. It growled out and sent an enormous fire into Shapía. The white light doused the other flames and seared her skin. She screamed in pain as markings appeared on her face and body. The sigils squirmed, brightened, and inked into the skin. She could perceive each one with a voice echoing in her ears, giving it command and control to conjure the strength to defeat a foe. The buzzing became louder, and awareness disappeared, dropping into silence.

"Shapía."

"Shapía."

The voice echoed, and she struggled to wake from the dream.

"Shapía."

Guru Sattva pressed a towel to her forehead, cooling the heat. The masura's dizziness did not fade as she raised her arm to the light.

"Wake, My Seer."

The once glass figure, now flesh, smiled through brown eyes, and the female masura flapped her wings, cooling the new seer of seers.

Shapía coughed and struggled to sit with Sattva, smiling and keeping her down, wiping her forehead.

"Mother Lin is in trouble," panicked Shapía.

"Where did you see her?" asked Sattva.

"Why did you leave me?" moaned Shapía.

"I am expelled from Aza's side, and he stripped me of my powers."

Sattva rose to her feet, and Shapía noticed the brown wings draped to the floor, along with the white robe. The female set the cup on a table and stared at the wooden floor.

"Aza has betrayed me. He has betrayed the Order."

Shapía removed the sheet, revealing the many sigils tattooed over her naked body. The bracers lay on a chair alongside her new warrior items, and confusion played.

"Why am I naked?"

Sattva grabbed the saffron robe and handed it to Shapía.

"This cooled you down. Your body heat tightened the leather around your skin."

Shapía donned the robe and poured a fresh cup of mead, downing the sweet nectar. They remained in Sattva's quarters, and the masura held worry and concern, keeping her gaze always down when speaking.

"I've lost my powers," lamented Sattva.

"Aza gave them to me to locate the witches and return them to his world. He holds Lin prisoner until I succeed in the quest."

Shapía poured another cup and downed it. She placed a finger on the repeated black-inked markings. The shape was like the common tongue capital F with a parallel line atop, going past the straight line, then curled, and the centerline curled like a tail. She had never seen such a symbol and panicked. Shapía approached the tall mirror and dropped the robe with the markings covering her torso, legs, arms, and face. Her skin was pure white, her talons and feet were black, and her wings were similar to her skin. Her hair remained brown, with her irises red. The view unnerved her, and she looked away from the mirror.

"You remain in the flesh. Consider it a gift," said Sattva. "My figure bore me great pain."

Shapía returned to the mirror and raised her hand to her face, sliding it down her body. The markings disappeared, and the skin returned to normal, along with the wings' brown and eyes' green. Reflecting on the old thought, she smirked at the realization that the practice would be a daily occurrence. She donned the warrior outfit and fastened the bracers. The soft leather had a natural texture, and she set the robe over the armor, hiding the apparel.

"You must continue to lead Horfa," said Shapía.

"In what regard? I hold no authority over it, only my knowledge."

"Knowledge is the most powerful tool you carry. They need to continue to believe in its existence. Otherwise, the islands may fall into disarray."

"Nothing here holds the islands to any cause. It is for the lost," said Sattva.

Shapía took some grapes and ate the vine.

"How quick we fall, Guru Sattva."

The guru dropped her white robe to reveal the sagging body, surprising Shapía, and she waited for the answer.

"My age is bound to reach my face soon enough. I am as old as the first age and fall as quickly as the second age arrives. I shall not reach the moon mid-flight or be able to lead Horfa anymore."

A tear dropped, and the elder shivered in the cold air. Shapía picked up the robe and draped it over the naked body. She hugged her tight as a daughter to a mother.

"You have given us all your love and commitment. The songs are to be grand upon your rise to the Great Hall, my great Guru."

Sattva pulled from Shapía.

"Rise to the Great Hall? We, holders of the seers, have no place in the Great Hall."

"Explain," said Shapía.

"The great hall is temporary for masuras living the masuran life. Everyone cycles through life, never staying for long. Its many books talk about how it's a great place to be, but temporary, and they return soon enough to continue their existence."

The sentiments resonated deeply, their truth striking her with the force of a physical blow.

"The seers become lucid," said Shapía.

"Yes, and walk among the Lucid plane, aiding the Great Hall but never joining it."

"Do you harbor sorrow?"

"Not sorrow, but concern for those in Horfa falling to either side of those planes. My death and Lin's disappearance may bring Horfa to a disturbing time."

"The cycle allows us to move with no burden on our shoulders."

Sattva walked to the table and eased into her seat. She took bread and dipped it into the bowl. The years descended from her expression, and Shapía saw life draining from the masura's wings.

"My home," said Shapía, "and there is Lin."

"Yes, Lin."

"She's being tortured."

"I know Aza's powers and the way the under god uses them. The painful tactics come and go. It's not constant. Most are for show to make you do his bidding."

"Why did you bring me there?"

"To end my torture."

The anger boiled within Shapía, and the sigils materialized from the mirage. "My life for yours?"

"Your mother died trying to search for a different way."

The older woman struggled to stand, her knees buckling.

"My time has come."

She rang a small bell, and several Horfa maidens emerged from the stairs, aiding the elder to a bed. The wings shrunk, and the older woman lay down as her hair turned gray and then disappeared.

"Your mother thought she ended the cycle. Find Aza's Bane and free yourself from the torture."

"Where do I even begin?"

"Go see Mulad in Mudra. He'll point the many ways."

Sattva paused.

"A choice must be made by you."

"How will I identify the correct one?" asked Shapía.

"You are the seer of seers, and each choice is correct. Go, my child. It is time."

Guru Sattva smiled, shut her eyes, and released her last breath.

The once great Horfa leader was no more, and her body crumbled to dust.

The maidens proceeded to the platform's edge and lamented the passing, sending the songs throughout Horfa as a memory. Shapía held on to the last words, watching the dust pick up into the breeze and float past the tree line. Thoughts of her mother and the death on the mountain by the dragons rushed into her vision.

"They have to know," she muttered.

The masura's thoughts drifted. She couldn't recall the duration of her journey to Aza's plane. The cloudy overcast settled on Bodhi, an odd event, with the many paying homage to Sattva. Shapía dropped her robes and shifted her appearance. The maidens did not notice, holding the tune, and she lifted, flying over the forest, listening to the lament filling the broken volcano. The concentration on getting to Mudra carried Shapía on a mission. Thoughts of Witch'Bane and her father surfaced, knowing that Aza's Bane will return to the mysterious realm to save them all.

The rain poured upon the island, and its sorrow filled the hearts. Shapía landed near the port and waited on the quiet street in front of the apothecary. Her memory reflected her first visit with Guru Lin to share health remedies. The idea of her gentle guru remaining a prisoner within the distant plane enraged her heart.

The transfer ship between Mudra and Ihandra remained idle in port as she reached the silent vessel and waited at the foot of its gangway.

"Captain?" she called out.

The door from the second deck room in the ship's stern castle opened, and an older human male with white hair and a beard walked forward with a limp. He studied the masura with wings deflecting the rain and reached the rail without a single drop falling into his appearance. The water cascaded around the invisible shield, and the elder removed his pipe and puffed into the lit tobacco.

"What may I do for the seer of seers?"

"I need to reach Mudra as fast as the wind."

"You want me to take the seer of seers away from Ihandra?"

The statement surprised Shapía.

"I cannot leave Ihandra?"

"I'm sure you could on your own, but if a simple boatman removes you, others should come to battle and return you to Horfa. Some may even kill you for the power."

"Kill me?"

"Guru Sattva mentioned you still hold simple thoughts on the role you've been born to."

"You spoke to Guru Sattva?"

"Oh, child, you have so much to learn."

"I intend to. However, I must proceed to Mudra."

"Mudra..." He frowned.

The older man puffed on the pipe and pulled a pocket watch, tending to its time.

"If we go, you must hide my vessel. Otherwise, we are doomed."

"Hide your ship?"

"Think about the gift. Once it's hidden, I'll take you."

The captain turned and walked back inside the cabin.

Shapía remained alone with the rain falling harder and contemplated the two giant masts.

"How do I hide it?"

The seer leaned against a wooden rail.

Things are not as they seem.

The idea rolled through her thoughts, concentrating on the floating vessel. Her gaze snapped wide, and her pupils turned bright purple. The blue flame formed in her cupped right hand, and thoughts descended onto Aza's plane. The ship's masts came into a blurred view, distracting the seer, and the blaze died down.

"I have these amazing powers but don't know how to use them," she groaned.

The rain came down harder, and she moved the loose hair stuck to her face.

"It is so effortless to hide my appearance. Let's try to hide the sails."

The seer created a flame, floated it just beyond, and then it sizzled against the water. She sighed and slumped against the stone wall.

The storm raged on. The seer couldn't conceal the sails. She had hidden smaller items with the thought filling her mind, and the vibration resonating through her bones, unable to act upon the more significant object.

The day turned into late afternoon, and the dim gray descended to dusk. The lament continued, and the docks remained empty, with light flickering within the captain's quarters.

Shapía paced in front of the craft and concentrated on the masts, absorbing the energy around it and sending it to no avail. She slumped against the cargo tied to the dock and allowed the rain to fall against her face. The lightning continued, bringing bright snapshots to the port, and she glanced at the wooden planks.

"The darkness allows us to sail," said the captain.

"I have not hidden the sails."

"I am aware. This is a skill the seer eventually needs. For now, the brewing storm shall do. Let's get you to Mudra."

The captain presented himself before her with an extended hand. The older man was taller and younger than she expected as he limped ahead onto the ship. Shapía followed as they both reached the ship's wheel, and the captain flicked a finger, dropping the sails and pulling in the lines from the port moorings. Unassisted, the captain sailed the boat from the dock into the tempest.

High waves worried the masura, as the seas rolled higher than the smaller sails. The night storm obscured the moonlight, and the battered ship remained stationary and did not progress south. Without a word, the captain's hands, calloused and strong, spun the wheel, releasing it from its hold. He grabbed it once again and guided them through the rain. The storm faded with the starlight piercing the clouds. The calm allowed Shapía to push the wings and wriggle free from the water.

"We need your magic, Seer."

"I'm doing my best." Snapped Shapía.

"I fear the alert triggering as we breach the clearing."

"Who is after us?"

He snapped his fingers, and several spirits materialized from below, mirages of their former selves as sailors, taking the wheel and hoisting the sails. The inhuman beings took notice of the seer and monitored the masura.

"Enough!" thundered the captain.

Re-centered on the work, the spirits heightened their attention.

The captain descended from the wheel and directed Shapía to follow as they moved to the bow. Overhead, the clouds continued their tumultuous dance, the distant, unseen lightning holding its breath before unleashing its fury.

"There are few who guide Horfa and understand Aza's might. We are guardians of its secrets and hoist Ihandra to its subtle hum."

The man produced a pipe, filled it with tobacco, lit it, and took a puff.

"My Sattva was the one with Lin, Mulad, Maitreya, and myself under the order to protect the islands as we must, with the force shifting, then snuffing out my love's life from the plane."

"My life for hers," moaned Shapía.

"Yes, but not by her choice."

He puffed circles from the pipe. "We don't have time for the stories, seer. Hide us."

"I know little about these abilities."

"Each holds an incantation. I carry a scroll for it."

The elder pulled a folded black parchment from his coat. Shapía unfolded the item, and it remained blank. The captain touched the center and spoke a word.

"Laever."

The black parchment sparked and popped, revealing gold letters in a confusing language, and Shapía looked at the man.

"I can't read it."

"Esrever," he spoke.

The letters drifted across the page and spun into the common tongue. The spelling appeared simple and easy to use.

"They do not function if you speak it in our tongue. I set the letters so you may begin learning which charm works, but read in their tongue to enforce its magic."

"Can you use these spells?"

"Those holding Aza's flame can call to the plane and invoke the spell."

The elder pointed to the third line.

"Each line gives what it shall perform and then the incantation."

He removed his pipe.

"Retreat to the shadow, including oneself, then its writ, red flame, seize the shadow and hide it from thy eyes."

He tapped the parchment, and the letters slid into their places.

"Now, try."

Shapía studied the third line and spoke each word, stumbling at first.

"Der emalf, ezies eht wodahs dna edih ti morf yht seye."

She looked at the man.

"The phrase is backward."

"Aye, if you are in Aza's plane, the scroll is readable. If you spoke Aza's tongue, it would be in his language. In time, they are to appear."

He lit the pipe with a match and looked to the fading clouds, with the moon appearing and stars sparkling. They slipped into the open sky when the ship sent a moaning boom, startling Shapía.

"We left port without notice, under the storm's shadow. The ship calls back home, requesting to be found. It tells who is aboard, and when the word *seer* lands in ears. Many would be on the hunt. You must invoke the red flame and hide this ship."

Shapía closed her eyes, and the image of Aza's beasts standing in front of the lava flow, each holding its flame. The red went into her chest, and her eyes burned. The thought raced through her mind, and the gem-inscribed flame upon her black leather chest protector sparkled red as she had a ruby-like stare.

"Now for the words," said the captain.

With an intuitive hold, the elder withdrew, and Shapía cupped both hands above her head, allowing a red flame to form. A low, resonant hum filled her ears as the conjuring incantation vibrated, the words a natural extension of the magic pulsing within her.

"Der emalf, ezies eht wodahs dna edih ti morf yht seye."

The vessel shuddered, and a shock wave came over the bow, flowing from midship to aft. The sky around pulsated, and no sound registered in their ears. Shapía lowered her thoughts with the flame in hand, and her gaze dropped as she sank to one knee. The energy drained from her body, and nausea filled her stomach. The elder placed a hand on her shoulder.

"Impressive work, Seer," he commended.

He winked and called out to his crew.

"Wheel master, keep Nathe's eyeing star to our starboard side. We shall sail to Mudra tonight and under Aza's guard. For the rest, I want a guard on all posts, for there is bound to be trouble tonight as we draw closer to port. With our lady's announcement, I am certain Malum knows the seer is hunting her."

The captain rubbed the railing, limped to the mid-stairs, and stood over the ship.

"Seer, prepare yourself for a rough journey ahead. You are no longer Shapía of Witch'Bane. You are the seer of seers, Aza's eyes. Your truth unfolds—starting now."

Shapía gazed at the black parchment, again blank, and at her bracers. The life she had was gone, and the inner force held an edge. She sensed its sting and gazed out across the moonlit sea.

"I need to learn to save the islands. Laever."

She tapped the parchment, and the golden letters came alive, sparking and revealing the inscription. She gasped as the confusing text revealed its true meaning.

"I read them without having to move them.

"Maybe I am the seer."

Chapter Seventeen

Asmodeus and his exercitus charged beyond the Raul River and into BataRaul. The surge overwhelmed the forest and overtook BataRaul, capturing the royal clan. He settled on a branch and could see Rhile in the far background cradling her belly. He hated her coming so close to the battles, but her warrior inside couldn't resist the action. Malum's spell had waned as he expected, allowing the etta to conquer forests in Asmodeus's name.

The exercitus filed the Bata masuras into the town square with the royals in the center. Queen Wunder held her young daughter, Princess Beatrice, with many male masuras circling to protect the female royals. King Bereet remained locked in a cocoon inside the king's quarters, and Prince Mahtri, the heir to the throne, remained missing. The black-eyed, purple-hued exercitus frightened the crying children, and the Bata clan gathered tighter.

Asmodeus and the Latuery flew in formation through the trees and settled on the terrace. Rhile offered her sword before the king bowed.

"My dear etta, raise your eyes so I may see into them," said the king.

"Indeed, Your Majesty," said Rhile.

"I believe Malum's spell has drifted, and my dearest has returned to me," he said.

"We are both healthy."

His reaction turned to concern. "You head into battle?" questioned the king.

"I handle the sword better than any other fighter," she said.

"Right, yet you battle for two," he said.

"Come and see the king of BataRaul. It's pleasing."

The etta grabbed the king's hand and entered the council hall where Bereet, the BataRaul head council, was bound to a chair. With a sneer, Asmodeus raised his battered, scarred face and scoffed at the Bata royal.

"Where's the king?" asked Asmodeus.

"In his roost," answered Rhile.

Asmodeus started for the king's quarters and stopped before the grand fireplace, where the BataRaul colors draped the room. He grabbed the tapestry and yanked it down, throwing it into the fire.

"They are no more."

He stepped into the bedroom to find King Bereet stuck inside a cocoon similar to his father's, with webbing throughout the room. Each strand reached the windows and crawled along the wooden floor, sinking into the cracks. The encasing throbbed with each breath taken, and the BataRaul king moaned in pain. Asmodeus touched the dark mesh, and the prisoner's body flailed in agony. He could feel the pain and revel in its energy.

"Mother's influence enriches everything it touches. How do I use her source?"

He released, and Bereet eased down to a long, drawn heartbeat.

Asmodeus met Rhile in the hall.

"Keep the head council alive. The miscreant needs to feed, and he'll be an excellent source."

"Queen and princess?" she asked.

"Keep them alive. We intend to use them to force the clan to join the exercitus."

"Your Highness, the great Malum has allowed them to unite with us without the queen's persuasion," said Rhile.

"I've seen the difference between those who enlist and those who die to enlist. Their fight is different. We keep them alive and force their hand to join. No more dead soldiers," demanded the king.

"How?" she asked.

"Fetch me the queen, her daughter, and a Bata citizen. We shall show her the correct path," said Asmodeus.

The guard left the council, grabbing the queen's restraints and pulling her along with the princess.

"What fine BataRaul citizen wishes to accompany the queen on the journey?" questioned Asmodeus from the upper deck to the crowd.

Two male royals stepped forward.

"Just need the one," said Asmodeus.

One rejoined the group.

"Come now, all three, please."

Asmodeus returned to the hall and approached the broken head council. With a smile, he ran a hand through his hair, lifting his head as the queen, regal and imposing, entered the room.

"You should look at your queen when she enters the hall."

Queen Wunder gasped at the head council's face, swollen from eye to eye and blood dripping from the mouth.

"You must excuse the mess, Your Majesty. The head council refuses to tell us where Mahtri is located, but I'm not worried. We'll get the information," said Asmodeus.

He dropped his head and sat in the king's chair.

"A fresh beginning is upon us, Queen Wunder, and your clan is part of its history. The chance to be at the start when the greatest Masuran clan was born."

"You're a murderer!" Queen Wunder spat.

Asmodeus removed his sword and shifted in the chair, dropping the tip onto the wooden floor. He spun the blade and stared at the ruby gem in the hilt.

"I am a conqueror, Madame. One who unites and does not split a family, which I believe you and your husband's family did many moons ago. Tearing apart the great Rauls and what was the word you used...? Oh yes, *murdered* families because they chose not to follow the great rift," said Asmodeus.

Asmodeus rose and sheathed the sword. A soldier gave him a goblet of mead after he snapped his fingers. He downed the vessel while silence filled the ears. Then Asmodeus slammed the metal goblet onto the table.

"I'm giving you a choice to save your daughter's life. You join us and become a member of the royal entourage, fulfilling your royal duties in Upper Asmodean and continuing to live a purposeful life. Or die and become a simple, mindless dolt, following orders and dying when I tell you to die."

He paced in front of the fireplace and then stopped, facing the queen.

"What say you, Madame?" he asked.

"I would not join you if you promised me a thousand lives and endless gold!"

Asmodeus shook his head and looked at Rhile for a moment.

"I expected this reaction, so I requested a volunteer to be the first to show you your chosen journey," said Asmodeus.

The male masura stood up straight and groaned at the words. "I shall die for my queen."

"If you insist, BataRaul duke, again, a choice is given, and it's your queen's final decision."

"BataRaul won't follow you, you evil *cur*!" screamed the queen.

"Oh, they're bound too, queen, but I wish not to spoil the surprise for the young princess."

Asmodeus winked at Beatrice and withdrew to Rhile.

"Bring in the necromancer," commanded Rhile.

A massive chain dropped to the wooden surface from the room above, and a guttural groan rippled down the stairs. Following the chain pull, staggered footsteps dragged across the surface. The Exercitus soldier pushed against a larger object with a pole. The unknown creature released a loud screech, forcing the prisoners to cover their ears and cower before the beast. In the wake of their battle with the necromancer, the Exercitus, with blackened eyes and wings, descended the stairs.

Terror washed over the queen's face, and fright covered the princess, forcing her to grab her mother's leg.

Against its captors, the beast thrashed, fighting restraints and spitting with each snarl. It towered with its hunched, hairy back and stumped wing arms. The once masura's face broadened. Missing a left eye and with skin black as coal, it snorted under its pig nose. The beast's torso, arms, and legs bulged from the extended muscles, and its feet held only two talons and bled from the nails. It roared at the fighting exercitus guard, holding the long pole against its enlarged neck.

Several guards fought the creature, pulling it toward the council center and waiting for their king. The beast thrashed and moaned when Asmodeus approached and extended an arm, calming the creature as it cowered in its stature.

"I, your compassionate king, once again, provide you with a pair of ways to enter the new kingdom. Volunteer on your own."

Asmodeus released his hold and withdrew to Rhile.

"Or volunteer in our method."

The king snapped fingers, commanding the beast to release a snarl, vibrating the wooden floors. It snatched the royal masura from his spot and bit into his side. As the beast recoiled its fanged maw, it came down onto the royal's neck, covering his head, and eliciting a scream of agony and terror, muffled by the beast's closed mouth. As the masura's screams slowed, the creature held on, wheezing and moaning. The male jerked a few times, then fell limp when the beast dropped its prey and withdrew from the scene.

Clutching her daughter, the queen cried as the lifeless BataRaul royal lay pale. She pulled away from the sight, and Asmodeus smirked.

"No, no, it is not over yet."

He snapped his fingers again, and the guards forced her to look at the lifeless masura. The mouth fumed as the body jerked. The gashes in its side and throat foamed, sealing the wounds. Its eyes popped wide, and it rose, turning to Asmodeus, its skin dulling to a grayish black. It came to attention, saying nothing, with its breath racing and growing without control. The king looked to Rhile, who pulled forth the small vial and stood before the queen.

"Your choice, Wunder. How do you wish to volunteer?"

The queen sobbed, and the young princess released her mother and grabbed the vial.

"I'm not afraid," said the young girl.

Before Her Majesty could react, she grabbed the vial and drank the serum. Wunder screamed at the action. Dropping to the floor, the princess lay listless, and the room went quiet.

Then her body jerked repeatedly, and she foamed at the mouth. The gurgling originated deep in the child, and she moaned in pain. Soon, her skin turned ashen, then gray, and finally black. The coal eyes popped open, and the once masura child stood and stuck out a hand.

"Come, Mother, do not be afraid." The voice echoed from her throat, and her breathing became labored.

"You're a monster! May Nathe bar you from the Great Hall!"

Asmodeus laughed. "I *am* the Great Hall."

Rhile held out the vial, and the BataRaul queen snatched and drank the serum. The queen collapsed, and Asmodeus moved to the balcony. He waited with the growing crowd as the BataRaul queen stepped to the front. Gasps filled the air below, and Asmodeus smiled.

"Your queen has volunteered to become a member of the one united masuran clan. I suggest you volunteer, or else we shall volunteer you for the service," said King Asmodeus.

"Accompany me, my family," said the queen. Wunder's voice echoed like her daughter's.

Beatrice stepped onto the balcony and stood alongside her mother.

"Be with us," Beatrice commanded her people.

The king snapped his fingers, and the exercitus guards pulled a vial from their cloaks and waited as the BataRaul clan joined their queen into the unknown and lost.

Asmodeus turned to Rhile. "Let us eat, and then we will conquer the beautiful dock just beyond."

King Asmodeus pointed to the Manawe wharf and gazed at the remote ships unloading their latest imports. The bustling Manawe city had been the primary Upper Realm docking station since the significant move away from Rath. The Manawes had been an ally to all masuras, never siding in disputes and keeping neutral during negotiations. Masura, elf, and man ran it, conjoining an agreement never owned by one being. The king stared at the trade and wanted control of it.

Rhile stood alongside him. "It is to be yours," she said.

"Once it is, we shall be at war with Breiv."

"And we shall win."

"With Malum's might, how could we not?" said Asmodeus.

"Let us eat, sire," said Rhile.

"All of us," said Asmodeus.

He caressed Rhile's belly, and the baby moved to the touch. The council hall returned to dining with the BataRaul king in his cocoon as a backdrop to the future. The once BataRaul royals served King Asmodeus and his etta as they ate alone, listening to the BataRaul members transform in the city square.

"Your army grows stronger, my King."

Asmodeus did not respond and continued to eat. With an Elite Exercitus guard by his side, he confidently snapped his fingers as he moved forward.

"Prepare them all to follow us into Manawe. We take the harbor today."

As the meal continued, the guard snapped to attention and delivered the message. The exercitus army awaited its king as the numbers grew into the thousands, filling the trees and the BataRaul beachhead. They finished the meal, and the king donned his battle garb with the violet Thunderbolt glistening in the midday light. He sensed Malum's power surge around the palm with its metal ring vibrating, propelling him to defeat an enemy.

The once BataRaul queen sat slumped on her throne with her head lowered and drool falling from her cracked lip. Beatrice served Rhile, aiding the pregnancy and providing Etta with a servant. Asmodeus downed his drink.

"The forces in the Lohr Mountains. Do they have the benndis prepared?"

"Aye, My King."

"Are they set to strike Manawe's south?"

"Indeed, My King. They stand ready and are about to attack once we leave Upper Asmodea."

"And the northern charge?"

"They are slower, and the benndis are not expected to reach the forest's edge until dusk."

Asmodeus groaned at the news. "We have arrows and slings at the ready?"

"Yes, I have received news that they arrived with the added troops."

"Good, and the ships?"

"We have two in dock, with three floating beyond sight, poised to move in once the south begins its attack."

Asmodeus stared into space, focusing on the Manawe siege. Striking such a port would start a war with elves and men, sending the alert through Breiv. The idea excited the king, and his body pulsed with the thought of the force overtaking the city would require. He held out his palm and drew forth a lilac orb. It possessed an energy mingled with Malum's and floated until it absorbed into King Bereet's cocoon. The jolt convulsed the once king's body, and the webbing strengthened its hold on its victim. Asmodeus grinned at the outcome.

"Send the word. We leave for Manawe."

Rhile pushed her aide aside and proceeded to the terrace, blowing the war horn herself. Similar horns rang out across the forest, and flyers flew off to start the war in Manawe.

The Elite Exercitus awaited the king as Rhile reached the balcony and lifted an arm. The troops became silent as Asmodeus grasped the handrail. His eyes sank to a dark violet, and skin took on a light violet hue, with the power filling his aura.

"Success remains with you, my Elite Guard! We are to be victorious. They fall to our greatness! Now, lead the path to the city. I am to be at your side as we breach the Sovereign Hall!"

The troops snapped to attention.

"Fly!" said Rhile.

The masuras filled the sky like locusts, devoid of emotion, lifeless behind their eyes yet ready to battle until their agonized breath ended. The king rose, and Rhile followed, pushing into the wind and darting across the water. Manawe was a short flight from the once BataRaul city, nestled along the waterfront. Benndis started the attack from afar by dropping explosives onto the city streets. The Asmodean ships raised their catapults in the harbor area, lighting the benndis and sending them into the city's many homes. As Asmodeus studied his army's endless flight, the distant ships approached the dock and sent their attack, while the city braced itself for the harbor conflict and the attack on the docked vessels.

Rhile sent another horn blast, echoed by additional horns, commanding the benndis to allow safe passage for the exercitus.

Arrows flew from hidden protections, and slings dropped from the flying fighters.

"Send a charge!" demanded the king.

The etta blasted the attack horn, its echo following the shore, and the struggle poured into the port city. Fire breached rooftops, and chaos covered the streets. Manawe flyers met the flight attack, and the sky battle reached over the water.

Asmodeus, Rhile, and the Elite flew to enter the fray. The swords clashed, and heads, arms, and bodies dropped to the water below, with the first Manawe fighter approaching the king. Asmodeus blocked the sword's lunge and twirled, allowing him to fall and return behind the soldier. The warrior was not an ordinary fighter and was prepared for the move, deflecting Asmodeus's sword.

When a second arrived, the king hovered in front of the soldiers, and they scowled at the Asmodean king.

Asmodeus elevated his left hand and built the purple orb, sending it into his enemy's eyes. The fighters screamed in terror, dropping in their flight, but catching themselves before hitting the ground, unable to end the terror. The orbs engulfed their heads, and they fought the scream filling their ears.

Asmodeus watched the magic snap their heads rhythmically when their eyes turned purple, and they hovered.

"Fight for me, my fresh soldiers! Protect me and send us into the city!"

The latest Exercitus Elite rose to the king and stood beyond his wings, ready to battle for his cause. Asmodeus extended his sword and curled an orb in his left palm, flying into the melee. He sent balls into Manawe fighters, turning them into purple-eyed exercitus, and they settled into formation behind their new king.

They barreled into Manawe, with elves falling to the arrows and necromancers charging the dead bodies, adding more to the fight. The siege surged when horns thundered beyond sight, and masuran flyers with silver arrows deluged the sky. Elves emerged from endless tunnel doorways appearing from the ground. And men thundered on horseback, meeting any foe on the run.

Asmodeus's enemies outnumbered his own, with the battle turning against Asmodea. The dead fighters hewed with ease against these new opponents, and Manawe's alarm echoed throughout the Upper Realm.

Rhile reached Asmodeus, surrounded by his warriors. "My King, we must get you beyond the dock and away."

"No, we push ahead and allow the necromancers to create our army as we fight!"

"Asmodeus!" Rhile thundered his name, and Asmodeus turned with surprise. "If you fall, we all fall."

The king, though angered, understood.

He withdrew his guard from the open lake. Then he watched the battle seesaw, with hidden Manawe warriors continuing to come from additional protection. In growing the exercitus, the necromancers remained strong.

*　*　*

Asmodeus held his position far past the fighting as the battle raged. The field reports flowed in, and street by street, the siege worked in their favor. His fighters did not tire and marched without worrying over a lifeless body. Malum's strike took its toll on Manawe, with dusk breaching the port city and the king's ship pulling into a dock. Rhile returned from her observation and landed on the ship's bridge.

"We circle the Sovereign Hall with the citizens barred to their homes, My King."

"Why have we not breached the hall?"

"There is no entrance, windows, or any access inside. It has become stonewalled."

"Stonewalled?" questioned Asmodeus.

"Yes, the hall is nothing but a stone pyramid."

"I wish to see this pyramid."

The king and Rhile flew with an additional guard at his side, poised to protect him. They charged over the Manawe streets with their gaslights lit, bringing life to the barren city. The stiff wind filled Asmodeus's wings as they soared toward the city center, and the three-story Sovereign Hall pyramid drew nearer. The dark building, lacking windows or doors, presented a stony facade, surprising Asmodeus. They landed atop a flat roof and studied the building.

"They walled themselves in?" asked Rhile.

"To do it so quickly?" wondered Asmodeus. "The elves have some magic in the hall."

"Do we need the hall?" questioned Rhile.

"Absolutely. The riches, trade routes, and detailed information about Breiv sit inside its vaults. We need its information."

"Then we shall get it, My King," said Rhile.

"Get me the map," demanded Asmodeus.

The Elite Guard created a large city map with streets and buildings shown and the Sovereign Hall in its center. Two guards held it steady while Asmodeus brought on a white orb, illuminating the map.

"Precisely as I suspected," said Asmodeus.

"There's an entrance into the Sovereign Hall?" asked Rhile.

"No, but a means of collecting what we are here to collect. I don't need the building, just its treasures."

Asmodeus tapped the map, and the guards stepped to the side.

"Call attention," demanded the king.

The etta blew the horn, and the exercitus filed in below, looking up to their masters. With a leg lifted on the building's edge, the king surveyed the bustling streets below. The mindless awaited their command and stopped at nothing to retrieve their king's desires. Asmodeus raised his left hand and allowed the purple orb to float in front of his mouth.

"The stone runs thick, withholding what is mine," his voice echoed. "We change course."

His voice reached each minion, and a soothing sensation washed over Rhile.

"Fetch me twelve benndis, leaving the catapults. Line the street with three and set a charge, allowing the street below to crumble. We set another three, and those shall yield us our reward."

He waved the orb away, and Rhile blew the horn.

"The tunnels below lead to the main underpass, separate from the hall. It is built within the elven caves of Lohr," Asmodeus said to Rhile. "Then, to the safe."

"Could the charge bring down the building we stand on?"

"No, it is built with the same stone and will hold. Map!"

The map returned, and Asmodeus elevated his palm to bring forth a green orb. It splashed against the map, with the streets and buildings disappearing, revealing tunnels and passageways leading to a large cave.

"Once we enter, we follow the slope downward, leading to the safe. There are traps, fighters, and other magical items the elves have put in place for protection."

"Could you not just send an orb in and destroy it all?"

"No, Malum's power is limited upon entering the tunnel. When what we seek is in my hands, Malum's strength becomes unstoppable."

He waved the map away.

"If they wall us out, we go under," said Asmodeus.

"Aye, My King."

Rhile sounded a horn. They could hear horses pulling large carts across the cobblestones. The line originated from the ships, and sledgehammers worked on the street's cobblestones. They made a trench to put the huge benndis in after removing the stone. As stillness settled upon the city, the crew arranged six, then three more, in a row.

Rhile signaled, and the troops retreated, with Asmodeus remaining on the overlooking building. He brought up his left palm, and a fire orb hovered. Pitching the lit ball into the stacked benndis, the king growled through gritted teeth. The items exploded with a sonic thunder rippling through the streets and dirt bursting higher than the buildings around the explosion.

Unmoving, the king waited, the thick dust a choking cloud around him, the smell of burned earth heavy in his nostrils.

In the new hole, a stone shell revealed the next target. The hidden passage foretold in the maps revealed but undamaged. Its solid state gave no avenue into cracks. When Asmodeus snapped his fingers, Rhile blew the horn, and three more benndis rolled into place, with workers running from the site and Asmodeus sending another lit orb into the weapons. The second explosion ripped into the stone, giving rise to a passage blocking both ends.

Rhile blew the horn, and workers dropped into the hole, pulling away the fallen rock to reveal the tunnel. Asmodeus and his entourage entered the tunnel and felt its cold air floating from the distant unknown, with blackness beyond sight. He pulled another, smaller map from his armor, detailing their path to the hidden vault.

"The path leads straight and then recedes down at an angle. It returns from some grand cavern to another passage, which falls in a twisted descent into a pool. The tunnel enters another open passage from the pool to the hidden vault."

"The elves built it?"

"No, the dwarves, but the elves maintain its many secrets, and I am certain it holds traps and death."

"What's in the vault, Your Majesty?"

"There is a stone necklace stolen from Malum, and it holds a force greater than any has ever seen."

"Have you seen it?"

"No one alive has seen it. Malum assures me I will know it."

The sound of distant foes digging their path from the Sovereign Hall's sealed passage came echoing forward. Asmodeus and Rhile turned to the fallen rock blocking the way into the hall.

"Prepare the fighters for what may pour from the hall. They're about to break through, and we must swarm into the building, killing all inside."

"And the path before us?"

"The Elite shall lead the charge with fighters behind and us within its center. We'll meet many things, my love, after we step in, but we will succeed."

"With Malum's ability within you, My King, I fear nothing ahead," said Rhile.

"I see no fear in any of us," said Asmodeus.

Chapter Eighteen

Fear hung heavy in the air as W.B., Datta, Dal, and Torëk picked their route through the rubble-strewn paths of the Shattered Mountain. They held on foot, giving them a chance to hide quickly when the devil hawks appeared.

The mountain range stood alone in a vast grassland, running far from the Lower Realm into the Eastern Realm. It would lead them to Eden, where Grunt and Crym would search for Dakii. The Shattered Mountain's name originated from the loose shale and stone covering its valley and both sides, and little to no life existed in its center. Gavee had trained in this mountain range and knew its hiding places well. The mountains soared into the clouds, all snowy, with a forest down below. The ravine contained a wet creek, giving fresh water, and many tunnels opening and falling daily due to the constant movement of the range.

Gavee remained in the lookout tree and ate berries he had collected before his turn at the lookout. A spot giving them the best view across the range. Datta landed behind and approached in silence, with W.B. maintaining his focus. The masuras did not speak until he broke the silence, keeping surveillance on the clear overlook.

"There is still some time remaining on my watch," he whispered.

"I'm hoping you've seen Crym and Grunt."

"Wasn't our meeting place Eden?" he asked.

"Yes, unless Dakii leaves."

The frustrated thunderblood brought his attention to Datta.

"How are we supposed to track them down?"

"They're to capture the keeper of the scrolls and bring him to these mountains," she answered.

"Why didn't you tell me? I could have been looking for them."

"I didn't think it prudent, W.B." Datta shrugged. "But the longer we remain within the mountain, we might as well look out for them."

"If they have Dakii, why not bring him to Witch'Bane or BataRaul?"

Datta sighed. "I've forgotten you've been locked away for many days."

Gavee turned his focus from the ravine. "What do you mean?" he asked.

"It means you're unaware of what Flued has done."

Gavee's mind raced, unsure how to respond.

"Flued's not the masura you think he was—or is," she said. "He's aligned himself with the evil plaguing both kings. He's thrown the Upper Realm into chaos, taking DasaRaul and soon BataRaul."

"What?"

Datta elaborated on Flued's wrath, the evil he'd become, and the danger all beings who live in Breiv now faced.

"He had you captured, W.B."

Gavee's eyes widened in shock, his breath catching in his throat.

"Yes, and Shapía," answered Datta.

"The grangrul enslaves her?" panicked Gavee.

"No, the Fens. Grunt and Crym had to locate me so I could get you out. You and Shapía are the only ones left alive who grasp Flued's twisted reasoning, and you alone have the resources to thwart his plans.

"If he's been planning the attack, I'm unaware and unable to know his mind. What has he done?" he asked.

"I received word before entering Bathhh that he murdered the DasaRaul royal family and paid the Fens to capture Bahg and Shapía, taking them in as workers. His next attack would be BataRaul, and there would be no means to stop his forces."

"My father?"

"Yes, and Shapía," she answered.

"I heard you, but the Fens are going to torture and kill Bahg."

"Why?" questioned Datta.

"I can't understand it either. He insisted that if we ever found ourselves between capture or death against the Fens, I'd end his life."

"Soon after they left Witch'Bane, they took both."

Gavee felt the lump in his throat grow, and a tear fell. Bahg would be dead, but the pain he would endure before death, he could not imagine.

"I will kill Flued," angered Gavee.

"His army has grown into a horde of the flying dead."

Gavee turned his head in disgust.

"He attacked Reflection?" mumbled Gavee.

"Yes, he's working with a sorceress. Flued has welcomed some evil into Witch'Bane, spreading through our forests. The fear is throughout Breiv, and the islands have taken notice."

"Good. If it's grown, as you say, we'll need help," said Gavee.

"Unless the scroll keeper has answers."

"I don't see a scroll ending an army," said Gavee.

"True, but it can stop a sorceress."

Gavee groaned at it all and then remained silent, staring throughout the ravine. The pair did not say another word. Instead, they focused on the trees. The afternoon drifted into evening, with darkness surrounding the mountain. Torëk arrived with Dal from the designated watch, explaining the situation to the male masura as they returned to the hollow within the tree boundary. Dal warmed in the heat, with a rabbit cooking over the flames.

"I'm hungry," said Datta.

"I'd be more comfortable if we ate among the trees," said Gavee.

"We need to keep the fire hidden. Besides, Dal is cold and not accustomed to being in the open," said Datta. "If you don't want to stay, go outside."

Gavee lowered his head.

"My apologies. I'm tired and hungry."

"Let's eat, W.B.," said Datta.

The thunderbloods shared a meal and sat in silence. Dal had fallen asleep with the flames' crackle echoing in the small cavern, and Gavee devoured the last tiny piece of rabbit.

Torëk eased into the hole and said, "There's a campfire up the ravine with a tontar."

"Crym!" Gavee and Datta blurted together, waking Dal.

"Show us!" demanded Datta.

The three returned to the lookout, and Torëk pointed to the flickering flames farther up the valley.

"Stay with Dal. We'll bring them to the cavern," said Gavee.

Torëk agreed, and the two masuras flew across the open air, using the thunderblood shadow flight. Through the trees they soared, reaching where an older fellow sat near the fire, stirring a pot. They looked at each other and then again at the man. With eyes on the surroundings, they crept closer. The sudden caw of a crow landed near Gavee.

"Why didn't you just greet me?" asked Gavee.

"This is for the best," said Crym, standing at the base of a tree. "Come down and say hello to the scroll keeper."

The group moved to the fire where the old fellow remained, not flinching from the unknown visitors. He was short and stocky, with a face holding more years than he wished to display, and burn marks on his left cheek. It marred his long white beard and cut short his mustache. His left eye was white, with the other black as coal. Hair, white, pulled into a tail. He wore a blue cloak, tattered at the ends, yet strong, resting on his shoulders. Rings placed on all his fingers and a small silver hoop in his nose. The small leather satchel hung on his right shoulder and fell under his right arm, with hand-rolled scrolls sticking from its top.

"We don't have enough for 'em," said the man.

"We've eaten," said Gavee as his stomach groaned.

"Earl of Witch'Bane, meet Dakii, the scroll keeper," said Crym.

Grunt shifted from being the crow and back to his weasel self when he tapped the man's shoes.

"Have some respect for the earl," said Grunt.

"All beings are equal in my sight and knowledge, weasel," said Dakii. "I bow to none, and none bows to me, except for an occasional demigod."

The older man snorted into a laugh and watched the flames.

Gavee kneeled on one knee. "Do you understand your purpose in being here?"

The fellow brought one eye up to Gavee. "I understand why I'm present. Do you?"

Gavee's shoulders grew heavy, and all around him except Dakii went black. The two stared at each other, and the older man smiled. The elder stood and walked out of sight, snapped his fingers, and Gavee jumped from the beyond. He was about to fall into the fire when Crym grabbed him and pulled the masura to his feet. Dakii remained seated and prodded the embers.

"What happened, Gavee?" questioned Datta.

The masura shook his head and pointed to Dakii. "Darkness grabbed me, then he and I stood alone."

"You push my friend into the in-between again, Scroll Keeper, and I'll conjure something your scrolls cannot defend," spat Crym.

"My name is not Scroll Keeper, you tontar oaf! I am just Dakii."

Grunt raised his cane to strike the man, but Gavee lowered his arm. "Easy, my friends. We need his help."

"Let's go to the cave and away from the open," said Datta.

"Yes, we have a cave, and others are joining our quest," said Gavee.

"We're moving? I just got this pot warm," cursed Dakii.

Crym removed a talisman from his cloak and blew into it, causing the pot to seal and shrink. "There, it ought to fit in your coat until we get to safety. Dakii and I shall follow your flight."

"As will I. It allows us to talk," said Gavee. "You and Grunt fly ahead. Crym and I will escort Dakii along the path."

Datta nodded, and Grunt shapeshifted into a crow as the pair flew into the dark. Dakii grunted as he doused the fire, grabbed his long walking stick, and stepped down the hill.

The old fellow moved faster than Gavee expected, both trying to keep in step, sliding on the loose rock. The man walked, looking over his shoulder and into the sky. They approached a gap, and Dakii dropped behind a large stone. Crym and Gavee looked at each other at his odd behavior and went to the man.

"Worries?" asked Gavee.

"Shhh, don't say my name, and get down before it sees us," stammered the man.

Crym dropped behind Dakii, surprising Gavee, and the masura followed, creeping to the rock to look over its edge.

"I sense its presence," said Crym.

"Who?" asked Gavee.

"It's a sinister elemental," answered Dakii.

"It has claimed the gap as its own. We would have walked into its trap if we had followed the path," said Crym.

"I would never have allowed us to enter such a simple trap," moaned Dakii.

"Let's go around it," whispered Gavee as he stood.

Crym pulled the masura down.

"It knows we're here, and it intends not to let us pass," said Crym.

"So, what do we do?" asked Gavee.

"We meet it," said Dakii.

The scroll keeper flipped his hood over his head, took both hands onto the walking stick, and twisted its center. The shaft grew larger until it became a staff with a blue orb slowly spinning at its top. He reached into his satchel and popped a red ball into his mouth. The fellow bit down and crunched until he swallowed its remains.

"Protection against the demis," said Dakii.

"The demis?" questioned Gavee.

"Demigods, you fool," said Dakii.

"What is the plan?" asked Crym.

"Shall Crym and I wait here?" questioned Gavee.

"No, it senses our presence. I sense its gaze upon us."

The older man dragged forward, and they followed onto a path as it dipped lower until the sides maintained a shale wall. The darkness grew thicker and the air colder as the passage zigzagged in many directions. Upon reaching the opening, a green glow flickered into view. Two shadowy figures stood in front of them in the cavern's echoing expanse, where glowing green moss cascaded from the high, damp ceiling. Dakii used his hand to stop Gavee and Crym.

"Show yourself!" demanded Dakii.

Silence endured.

Dakii placed a gem into a slot on his staff, and a yellow light emanated. The invisible barrier prevented the unknown from being revealed. He raised the staff, pushed it forward, and the light receded.

"Light, behold!" he said.

He popped the staff onto the stone floor, and the barrier cracked and sparked when it fell away. Gavee and Crym gasped at the images.

"That's us," said Gavee.

"This is a trick," growled Crym.

"Of course it's a trick, you fool. Now silence," angered Dakii.

The old fellow slid a hand down his beard and seemed to search for words.

"We wish to pass and disturb not a soul within these mountains. Please forgive our intrusion. Is there a price for safe passage?" asked Dakii.

"We talk only to the masura," said the shadow.

The old man growled at the notion and shook his head, looking again at Gavee. "Well, ask them," said the old man.

The thunderblood stepped forward. "Why did you permit our flight over earlier? After all, we flew past this point and now came back this way on foot?" he asked.

Dakii groaned. "It's not important."

"We wanted you to reach your group. It has been foretold," said the shadow Crym.

"What is foretold?" questioned Gavee.

"The scroll keeper knows it and is hiding his truth. Be wary until he tells it."

Gavee turned to the old man with a scowl, and Crym stepped closer to Dakii, placing a hand on his shoulder.

"Enough with the tricks. Show yourself, Mistress Crea!" demanded Dakii.

Echoing through the cavern, the man's voice filled the space as rattled shells came from the blackness. The drumbeat echoed, and the shadow creatures fell to a wisp. The green glow brightened, and a cluster of adobe buildings came into view as the road ahead climbed before dropping off the edge of the world. Distant dogs barking echoed through the stillness.

"The crowl," said Gavee. "When did they move here? Did you realize it was them?"

Gavee faced Dakii, the silence hanging heavily between them as the man remained silent. Crym came alongside Gavee.

"Things have changed, W.B.," said Crym. "Many are in hiding."

"But the village appears to have been here for a while," said Gavee.

The green humanoid beings lined their village with makeshift longbows, arrows, and wooden shields. The crowl possessed a slender build, taller than the masuras, and hair green, as was their torso. They lived in an ancient way, with shamans as leaders in their community. Gavee had had some encounters with the crowl before but had never met the shaman they called Crea.

"Bahg warned me of Crea," said Gavee.

Crym did not respond as a small group approached.

"Why the display?" angered Dakii.

"Do not come to my front door and question my ways," echoed a female voice.

The female voice spoke with a fine tone and intelligence.

"We have yet to be introduced to the Witch'Bane thunderblood, known as W.B. I am Crea, shaman and leader of the crowl. Welcome to our village. We have a feast waiting, so we may discuss your cousin."

Gavee gave a head bow. "Mistress Crea, leader of the crowl, I am unfamiliar with Flued's actions or the wrongdoings he has been committing for years."

The crowl group reached the three, and Crea wore a smile. "It is understood who is involved and who is going to prevent it."

"I'm still clueless about what he's done," said Gavee. "And even if I did, I don't think I have the power to end it."

"You hold power, W.B. The voice inside, the queen's sword, and Shapía's realization. It is all before us and must rid the pest from the island."

"We have others waiting for us," said Gavee.

"Yes, Datta and Grunt will be here soon."

"Dal and Torëk?"

"The unknown masura took the child after you left and headed toward Bathhh. I'm sorry he deceived you. We could not go after him. Our meeting is essential, and truths are to be discussed," said Crea.

Crea glared at the scroll keeper, who refused to look into her eyes and remained silent.

"Your captive would not have told you the truth, but I changed his plans," said the shaman. "Please follow us."

Gavee stuttered to move, with his mind on Dal. He wouldn't permit them to take the young masura to the bustling city and put him up for sale, not after showing him freedom.

"Torëk," said Gavee.

"We move forward, masura," said Crym.

He snapped from the image, and they all stepped onto the broken shale-covered ground. It was a tricky walk with talons, and Gavee wanted to fly over but remained on foot. The loose shale gave way to a smashed path and a better method of traversing when they reached a sizeable, uncovered eating area with many crowl feasting and staring at the visitors.

"Please partake of the food. It is plentiful," said Crea.

The shaman proceeded to a large table where servants placed the food in front of her, and other leaders sat around Crea. Gavee did not wait and devoured the endless fruit and meat at the buffet. Crym pulled the hungry masura away, and the thunderblood realized his mistake, composing his manners. They filled plates and sat at the far end of Crea when a crowl approached the shaman leader and spoke into her ear. She gave a nod, and several figures emerged from the homes.

"Datta," said Crym.

Datta and Grunt stood at the entrance. They met halfway.

"Torëk took Dal," said Datta.

"The shaman told us," angered Gavee.

"Why are the crowl here, this far from Jatta?" asked Datta.

"I have not asked, and the conversation has not gone past pleasantries. They offered the feast, and maybe we'll find the answers to it," said Crym.

"Has Dakii said anything?" asked Datta.

"No, it appears he had never planned to tell," said Gavee.

"How do we determine this?" asked Datta.

"The shaman Crea revealed it," said Gavee.

"This is Crea's clan?" questioned Datta.

"Yes, and I am concerned," said Crym. "The party seems anxious. We should return."

The feast continued with chatter amongst the group, not focused on outside information but idle conversation about simplicities and life. It continued for a period, with Dakii remaining to himself, saying little and keeping his eyes on his plate.

"For a talkative tail-spinner, you are quiet," interjected Crea.

The shaman caught the table's attention, and eyes landed on the keeper of the scrolls.

"I am at a feast I did not ask to attend, with a party I did not ask to partake in, and on an adventure I wish not to follow," said Dakii. "I also perceive your constant vibration upon my neck."

The crowl guard groaned at the disrespect and came to arms with swords. The shaman eased her guard, and they lowered their weapons.

"Yet here you are, on schedule and available to help our island," said Crea. "Do you wish for the scourge of Witch'Bane to be released and destroy the island you inhabit?"

"It matters not to me, for I answer to no one. I've lived many lives, surpassing those bringing the island to demise, and each time, my travels maintain their cursed course."

Crea gazed at Dakii, then snapped her fingers. Leaning in, the shaman whispered to the servant, who then left.

The table remained silent, with Datta continuing to eat and ignoring the conversation. The shaman smiled at the female masura.

"You ought to be hungry, Thunderblood."

"I am, Mistress. It has been a while since I had a wonderful gift such as this food," answered Datta.

"I am aware your homeland was destroyed by cruel means, Datta of Tryolic," said Crea.

Datta dropped the food onto her plate, and Gavee waited to understand the clan's name.

"Explain," worried Datta.

"Your name goes far and wide in Breiv, Masura, and when this chaos ends, we crowl would appreciate such a fine fighter and thunderblood in our clan."

Datta finished her drink and smiled. "I may consider it. My contract and association with BataRaul are ending. We must destroy the curse, and then I intend to decide where I land."

Mistress Crea returned a slight head bow, and Datta continued her meal. Crym followed, with Grunt reclining after his fill.

Gavee could not remove his eyes from Dakii, knowing the man could help the island, but his selfishness was against the idea.

The servant returned to Crea and placed a covered serving tray on the table.

"Scroll Keeper, what is your price to enter this war?" asked the mistress.

"More gold, silver, and gemstones than you could afford," he said.

"What if I hold something better than jewels and coins?" asked Crea.

The words raised the man's eyes from his plate, and curiosity filled his cheeks.

"You have my attention, Mistress."

"Before we reveal, I must have your sworn oath. You shall aid Witch'Bane's thunderblood in ending what Flued started."

Dakii raised his hand to his heart. "I promise, if the reveal is what I need," he said.

"No, I want your true oath, Scroll Keeper," said Crea.

The man's smile dropped to anger. "I shall once I see the payment and agree it is worthy."

She snapped her fingers, and the servant removed the cover to reveal a copper mask. It featured hollow eyes and an opening for the nose. Curled horns appeared at the top, and the mouth had fangs and a curled lip. The scroll keeper's eyes widened, and he released a small gasp.

"Mask of Lynul," mumbled Dakii. "My knowledge has Witch'Bane holding such an item. How did the crowl come into possession of it?"

"An agreement many cycles ago," she answered.

"And it is mine if I help this young masura?" he questioned.

"Correct. It belongs to you if you help end the evil," said Crea.

"Which evil?" he questioned.

"The one they call Malum," she answered.

The man studied the mask without finding an answer. He sighed, stood, turned, and left the party. They watched him walk further away, then Gavee shifted to Crea.

"Do we stop him?" he asked.

Dakii stopped just at the light's edge, and with his walking stick, he drew a large circle in the dirt, then a smaller one in the center, where he created a fire with his magic. He sat and waited, staring into the flames. The party looked back at Crea, and the shaman stood.

"Guests and warriors. Come with me."

Crea led them to the scroll keeper, where they all sat within the large circle and waited for the man to speak. Dakii spat the red ball from his cheek and dropped it into a pocket. He removed his hat, pulled a small leather sack from its brim, and opened it, pulling out gold dust. He sprinkled it onto the dirt, scooping and mixing it into a pile with his hands. Next, he removed a small flask from his coat and poured its contents into the mixture, forming a golden paste.

The elder grabbed a handful and smeared it on his face and beard. He invited the crowl shaman to do the same, and she followed until her green face disappeared behind the gold mud. Crea removed a long pipe from her deep green cloak, puffing on the object until smoke bellowed from its end.

"Each being who partakes in the journey covers their face as I do and joins the pact before the flames," said Crea.

Grunt and Datta grabbed a handful and covered their faces. Crym took two fingers, dipping them into the mixture and running two lines on his face. Gavee hesitated, but

Datta reassured him with a nod, and he smeared the mud across his cheeks, forehead, and chin. The crowl warriors followed suit, and the party sat in silence.

"Upon this pipe, bound by an ancient magic, the party remains entwined, their fates intertwined until the evil dissipates," said Crea.

Taking a deep inhale from the pipe, the shaman leader passed it to Dakii. The old man inhaled the smoke and handed it to Gavee as it passed around the circle. The group remained silent and stared into the flames. Soon, Gavee's head started spinning, and he tried to focus on Datta as she rested and gazed into nothing.

The fire roared, and the thunderblood jumped at the outburst when his vision turned green, and he experienced a hollow pit in his stomach, forcing him to lie down. Gavee floated down a tunnel and could hear a distant muttering. The remote light appeared into view as the green came back, and Crea sat inside the cave. She waved to him, and he lowered himself to a seated position.

"Where are we?" asked Gavee. His voice rippled.

"When you entered our village, I sensed another entity lurking outside your thoughts. We are in a safe space, beyond its reach, to discuss the gift you hold."

"Gift?"

"The green images, the mysterious voice in your head, and the daze you continue to fall into, do you not understand?"

"No, it's confusing."

"I am still unsure why the Esor Dragon did such an act. Your minds have been blended and are now one. I sense him around you and in search of your thoughts."

"Blended?"

"Yes, the Esor Dragons are not like other dragons. They live in a large community, building a hoard of treasures they share among the group. The docile volcano they call home is their city. It is quite an odd grouping for creatures who often prefer solitude and share nothing regarding treasure. In their oddity, they also hold a gift. The ability to blend their minds with other dragons. It allows them to hunt in packs, protect the treasures, and keep the community bonded."

"I'm not a dragon," muttered Gavee.

"It is unknown whether the dragons could blend outside their kind. I do not know how, but I can smell him."

"It has spoken to me," said Gavee.

"What did it say?" she asked.

"It said I would not understand, and it had to be done to save us all," he answered.

"What do the dragons have to do with the unknown evil?" she questioned.

"I am unsure. I could feel there is a connection, though."

"When the opportunity comes, I shall reveal an item to use in completing the riddle."

"Why not now?" questioned Gavee. "It may have the answer to end it."

"No, we need more information. Learn how to use the gift and reach out to the dragon to discover who and what they want. I am to be at your side," said Crea.

"You are coming?"

"Not to Bathhh."

"Bathhh?" questioned Gavee.

"You need to reclaim the queen's sword before taking on Flued," said Crea.

"The queen's sword?" questioned Gavee.

"Dakii holds the truth and history of your clan, the queen's sword, a weighty blade etched with ancient runes, and the raw, untamed power of your Witch'Bane generation."

The shaman pulled forth a glass onyx beetle sitting on her palm.

"When the moment is right, W.B., use it and conquer them all."

She handed Gavee the object, and the thunderblood studied its basic structure.

"How?"

"I'll explain when we must use it. The knowledge would place you in danger. For now, keep it safe," said Crea.

The shaman tapped his forehead with her long green finger, and his mind succumbed to sleep.

* * *

The black did not remain long before a piercing squeal awoke the masura. He found them all sleeping in the dim cave they had been using. Gavee searched around, hoping Dal was there, but the lad was gone. He clenched his fist, the betrayal burning in his gut as he thought back to the mountain, remembering the dragon's fiery breath and now Torëk's broken promise. He reached into his side pocket and pulled out the glass onyx beetle.

"I thought it was a dream," he mumbled.

He fixed his eyes on the cavern ceiling, trying to put the information together, but could not stop thinking of Dal. Where was his friend in Bathhh? He searched for the scroll keeper, finding the elderly man snoring in the corner. Gavee lamented, knowing he knew where the sword was and the best chance to find Dal. He realized he had to search for the young masura before stopping Flued. He could not tolerate his being enslaved or beaten one more time.

Chapter Nineteen

Shapía rested on a crate in Mudra's market. The sacred city did not bustle or bargain. Money, jewels, and metals carry no value with a kind aura in their gaze. She hid her identity as an old hag with an old, hooded robe covering her long nose and bulging eyes. With a cane, she shuffled her feet under the robe. She had escaped the ferry in time before Mudra protectors raided the vessel, seeking the seer. The aura she portrayed showed a dark tone with purples and grays, keeping most away. These colors would also prevent her from finding the information she needed to get beyond the protection.

The streets, buildings, and Mudra residents lived danger-free without cause for weapons or protection. It was a safe zone for those holding the aura of Nathe, the god of Breiv. Those having other auras could not stay without guardianship and permission. Shapía found it to be righteousness, and the overtone was an irritation. The pretend aura she carried became harder to maintain as the day moved forward, forcing her to remain within the shadows.

The day progressed with the streets never emptying of pretentious egos. Shapía reached a secluded alley and unrolled the black parchment.

"Laever," she said.

The golden words appeared, and she read them aloud.

"Der emalf, ezies eht wodahs dna edih em morf rieht seye."

The seer concentrated and shook off the old hag's appearance, transforming into a young human girl with a yellow aura. This fresh face and aura would allow her to gather food and drink. She wore a blue dress with black shoes and a blue bonnet covering her blond hair. She roamed the streets, peering inside the windows and gaining a proper understanding of the town.

"My mother has told me to avoid Deep Street," said the little girl to the flower shopkeeper.

"This is fortunate, my dear," said the elf, handing her a flower.

She took in the aroma with a grin.

"Where is it so I may stay clear? I'm afraid I'll go there by accident."

"No one goes there by accident, my young lass. Do you see the fireball hovering atop the tall tower?" The elf pointed.

"Yes."

"It's the entrance. I would remain far off and not cross the yellow path into the black, encircling our safety."

"Oh, I won't," she said.

The little girl skipped off and turned down a silent street.

"Esrever," she said, tapping the parchment.

The seer shifted to the hag, limping and leaning on the building wall for support. The act kept all prying eyes from interfering and allowed her to stay the course.

Turning another bend to the right, she reached the yellow path, where it met the black on its opposite side. The trodden path veered to the right and followed an alley with no light. She took it since it ran to the tower.

No door or other connection existed in the lone passage. Its cobblestones remained silent. The stone turned to an orange, dry clay, marking her clothing and footsteps. The alley ended at a square, the air heavy with wood smoke from the flaming tower, and with the city's hub visible in the distance between two diverging paths. Dark Street stood in front of her, and shifty characters hovered at its gate.

The seer released her cover, standing with bracers sparking. The tattooed sigils on her upper arms grabbed an orange glow, and her black body armor stamped with the Mighty Tree vibrated. Her black talons gripped the orange clay, and her bright white wings gave a white aura. She stepped into the square, and the unknown creatures at the gate hissed and slithered from sight. Shapía passed through the square and stepped under the tower when she experienced a small jolt from the invisible barrier.

She entered Dark Street, where the path turned to dirt, and small-lit shops lined both sides. It had a unique vibration, a darker sense with a dangerous aura and ever-watchful eyes.

The seer entered shop after shop and asked, "Does Aza's bane exist?"

Each time, an odd glare, and a finger pointed to the exit. It was a statement Sattva mentioned, and it required an answer. She searched for the being in Mudra who understood the answer and belonged to the Order safeguarding Ihandra. Her mother's death, Sattva's release, and Lin's capture showed her the Order understood the island was under attack. It came from Aza and the evil ravaging the Upper Realm.

She reached a building set apart from the others. It contained no light at its entry and a black door with no handle. The red placard with black lettering hid the letters, and Shapía struggled to read the words. A shimmering, almost invisible barrier of energy pulsed in front of the seer. She paused, sensing the powerful force, before breaching the plane between the other buildings.

"It's powerful," she said.

As the bracers' gems glowed with an inner light and the sigil ink deepened to a shadowy black, the seer stepped through the portal. It was the building, and she approached when the black lettering shifted and shimmered.

"The Order."

As the brick steps shifted, lowered, and stacked atop each other, the stairs ran down. The new entrance appeared below the door, and its redwood featured no doorknob or window to look inside. It popped open with a creak, and the aroma of cinnamon drifted past. Shapía pushed open the door, and the lights lit, showing a chamber on her left and a long corridor straight ahead ending at a wall. The marble floor would be tricky on the talons, and she hesitated to enter.

"Enter, seer of seers," said a male voice.

Shapía did not rush in and tried to use her abilities to see who called out. The pause caused a short man with pointed ears to pop his head from the chamber with a smile. He had a gap between his front teeth, an enormous nose, and dark green eyes with eyebrows curling at the ends. His long brown hair fell beyond the shoulders and onto an old brown tailcoat, tattered at the sleeves and frayed at its tail. The coat hid the off-colored laborer's shirt, which the elfmen straightened as he stood before Shapía.

She recognized the being as an elfman from the island of Róta. A mixed being between the Mountain Men and the Woodland Elves on Róta. She had spent time on that island while studying and had come across elfwoman as caretakers. Their beings were often servants and held a lesser position in society.

"Please come in, Sweet Great Seer. You are welcome at Master Mulad's home. We have dinner prepared for your stay," said the elfman.

He swung his arm out and fell into a full bow. The top hat rolled off his head, and his cheeks turned red.

"Excuse my clumsiness," he said, retrieving the dusty hat. "I would be honored if you followed me to the dining hall."

Shapía paused and studied the energy of the being, sensing his nervous but honest personality. This new power enabled her to perceive what she would step into when the man blushed.

"Great Seer, I am not here to hurt and trick you. You have my respect and admiration. It is an honor to stand in your presence."

She blushed as she realized she'd interrupted his private thoughts.

"Please forgive me. I am unfamiliar with your name, though you are familiar with mine," she said.

"My name is Ati, and I serve the Order. I am forever your humble servant and friend."

He smiled and bowed.

"Hello, Ati. Please lead the way."

The man's pointed ears wiggled with joy. He straightened his hat and proceeded along the corridor. Shapía stepped through the doorway and looked to her left, with a piano in its center, mirrors on the far wall, and a giant bar for entertaining against the right wall. The massive chandelier and its many candles lit the space, and an aroma of fresh flowers wafted as she moved past. At the corner, another corridor with stairs followed the left wall, and to the right was a massive space with a long dining table.

"Mulad likes to entertain, does he?" said Shapía.

"Master Mulad throws the best galas. Only the finest members attend."

"Members?"

Ati paused and looked behind with concern.

"I spoke too much. Please have a seat."

He gestured toward the far end where two places sat ready for a meal, a setting at the table with a tall chair and the other a masuran chair, allowing her wings to drape behind. Shapía settled and looked around, with Ati standing in the corner, waiting and remaining quiet.

"This is a beautiful room," said Shapía.

NESTED EVIL

Ati did not answer and kept his focus on the floor. She could sense the energy change to anxiousness. The table could fit twenty-five to a side, with six windows adorning the far wall and sconces with large, thick candles illuminating the space. A harp played a tune without its musician, and a sizable covered serving tray remained before her, waiting for its master. Shapía focused on the etched glassware with what appeared to be musical notes following the rim. A distant chime rang out, and Ati jumped straight up, placing a napkin on his forearm and breaking the silence.

"Master Mulad," announced Ati.

The tall, thin crowl entered the room, dressed in a long, bright blue robe with a brown rope as its belt. It glistened in the candlelight and matched Mulad's eyes. A smile came across his face, and he bowed before the sitting masura. Shapía moved to stand, and he cleared his throat, indicating she should remain seated. He clapped, and Ati removed the long robe, revealing a blue silk top and bottom with white foot coverings that clicked on the wood floor. Ati pulled out the seat, and Mulad took a seat, curling his sleeves. The thin green arms showed the blue veins and the pulse of his heart.

"I understand we are strangers, but I sense a familiarity, as if we've always been acquainted," he said.

The deep voice surprised Shapía, and the calmness the crowl maintained carried its own life, removing her reservation.

"I believe everyone's expectation of this seer of seers is beyond my abilities, and I do not apologize for it," said Shapía.

"It's as if the Book of Orders is being written before my ears and eyes, yet manifested during the first age of existence," said Mulad.

"I'm sorry?" confused Shapía.

Mulad snapped his fingers, jumping Ati and forcing the being to flee the chamber.

"Shall we eat and drink before I discuss things further?"

Ati returned with a dark bottle and poured it into Shapía's cup, then Mulad's.

"What am I drinking?"

"It is nectar," said Mulad, raising his glass for a toast.

Shapía stared into the purple drink and raised it.

"May I be the beacon you need to perceive the energy you invoke?"

Shapía groaned, taking a sip. The light and sweet drink offered tastes of purple grapes and red apples. She enjoyed the flavor, tossing back the cup and downing it, with Ati quick on the refill. Mulad settled as Ati removed the platter's gold cover, revealing a plate of differing venison portions, potatoes, greens, and bread. The host waited for the guest when she filled her plate and took in the smells. It reminded her stomach she had not eaten for many days, and hunger returned. She devoured the feast while a violin joined the harp.

"Are you familiar with the Order?" he asked.

"The Order?"

"So that is my position in it," he contemplated.

"I'm sorry?"

"Forgive me, Seer, I always wondered what my role would be when you arrived, and I believe it is knowledge."

Shapía smiled and raised the goblet.

"I need that!"

She extended the vessel, and Ati poured.

"The Five Islands' First Age created the Order. It was earlier than the masuras and after the thunderbloods," said Mulad.

Shapía lowered the goblet.

"I'm sorry, prior to the masuras? In my history, we created the Thunderbloods and forged the Five Islands."

"It is what you've been taught, but it is untrue. Five hundred years prior to the masuras, there were islands. The thunderbloods, from the beginning, kept peace and control over the banished."

"The banished?"

"Sorry, the three sisters."

"Something else left from our books," moaned Shapía.

"There is yet another within the Order with the history parchment, giving you the correct details. If the book says true, you shall meet him soon enough."

"What book?"

"The Book of the Order, our book, was written by a powerful oracle named Shaki. He foretold the history of the Five Islands, the Order's guidelines, and the hidden truth. The Order was created because the thunderbloods failed. They fell from the path and became mercenaries, spies, and thieves, putting the island in danger. The Order pulled together, putting an end to the sisters' return. We brought peace and stability, and when Nathe wanted more, he created the masuras."

Mulad raised his glass, and Ati poured.

"In the great book, Shaki placed a riddle explaining when the awakened age would begin, bringing true peace. It seems today is the day this riddle might have an answer."

Mulad raised his glass in a silent toast, smiled, and drank.

"Answer?" confused Shapía.

Mulad snapped his fingers, and Ati ran from the space. The two did not speak, waiting for the elfmen's return. Shapía continued to nibble at the feast, allowing her mind to return home. She had trouble imagining Flued doing these awful things.

"Your brother is just a muse, acting out what has been written," said Mulad.

"Stay out of my thoughts, please," she groaned.

"I am not in your thoughts, Seer. It would be an arduous task, and I am incapable of trying. Your thoughts are coming through to me. You must learn your powers."

"My thoughts are leaking?"

"In a way, they are loose. But without controlling it, anyone with the third eye would hear."

Ati returned, carrying a clay tablet with round divots lined in rows, covering both sides. Mulad placed the tablet in front of him, and Ati closed the door. The crowl snapped his fingers, and the candles puffed into darkness. The dark still held distant white lights from the four crystals hovering in the room's upper corners. Shapía had not noticed them before and wondered if they kept a watch on the space. Mulad touched a finger to the first divot, and a light orb popped from its location. It carried a volcano scene spewing its lava.

"Each ring contains a period in the Five Islands' past. The first is creating Ihandra and her great volcano."

Shapía marveled at the island view forming in front of her eyes. With a slight twitch, he withdrew his finger, and the orb dissolved, the silence returning to the room.

"The tablet appears to be full," said Shapía.

"Almost, Seer, this is how we recognize the awakened age is upon us."

He flipped the tablet over with space for the final three divots. He touched the clay, and it dipped in and rounded. A glowing yellow orb appeared with capacity for two additional circles.

"When the information in the ring has passed into history, the glow fades."

Mulad touched the third to last circle, and the illumination ceased.

"Two spaces left, Seer."

"How can you determine when to create the circle?" she was confused.

"The tablet calls to me, and I can see a red spot where a circle beckons to be made."

"Does it tell us what we are going to see tomorrow in the last circle?" asked Shapía.

He pressed his finger into the divot, and a small, pulsating orb emerged, its surface smooth and warm. The moment had Bahg fighting in the Fen forest alongside the hoods and tontars, pushing the Fens into the Mountains. The scene faded to smoke, and then the orb disappeared.

"Can it tell more?" she demanded.

"It reveals only the information. It contains a spell, and it has yet to be unbound."

"How do I know what to do next?"

"The orb before this contains the seer's arrival in Mudra and presiding in my abode," he said. "Beyond it, we return to the riddle."

Mulad flipped the tablet and returned to the first row, the ending circle. Words floated from the white cloud as the orb rose from his pressed finger.

"When the sister joined by blood returns, the awakened age appears. The land is to be filled with the walking dead, and the sisters are to reunite across the seas. The blood seer reveals it all and ends the chaos on the Five Islands. Peace abounds under the seer, and the blood outsider, owning the maps for an age, creates a new tablet."

Mulad removed his finger.

"The answer to the blood seer is you, Witch'Bane oracle, seer of seers."

He snapped his fingers, and the candles lit with a soft glow.

"It was assumed your mother was this seer when she took on the name Witch'Bane. In her quest as an Order holder, she found the actual truth. It released the single locked circle from the tablet, showing Phawa divulging who the blood seer was to Sattva. This circle was not released until you entered the city with Bahg."

Shapía's mind raced.

"You are the blood seer."

She pushed from the table and stood, walking to the table's end and staring at the lit crystal.

"You have many questions, and I won't have those answers," said Mulad.

"I've never trained to stop a witch or any force from saving the islands!" said Shapía.

"From the latest circle, it tells us Aza has shown you the power within, and you wear his markings."

The comment angered Shapía, forgetting her body had inked sigils.

"You need to understand how to use them," he said.

"Who'll teach me, you?"

"No, I'm not the teacher or the master," said Mulad.

"I'm your teacher," said Ati.

Shapía looked to Mulad, then again to the elfman.

"You are Mulad's servant," confused Shapía.

Mulad laughed. "Yes, but it makes him no less the master to awaken your mind," he said. "He, like me, had toiled long and hard to reach this moment."

"Seer of Seers, I awakened your mother, and I am here to awaken you," said Ati.

The elfman cupped his hand, and a white orb appeared.

"Through this light, we intend to awaken the sigils and your abilities in this plane," said Ati.

Shapía felt its warmth and averted her eyes.

"I'm to trust your word?" questioned Shapía. "I am not acquainted with either of you, and I refuse to go into the unknown with strangers."

Mulad turned the tablet and placed a finger in a circle, popping a white bubble. It swirled into colors until her mother appeared in the picture. She was young, and she cradled Flued in her arms. Ati and Mulad were sitting at the same table. Mulad snapped his fingers, and their voices echoed.

"I am not the blood seer?" questioned the queen.

"No, it's not you," answered Ati.

"Who is it? Which Witch'Bane?" she questioned.

"We are uncertain. The book does not show it," said Mulad.

"I married into this family to stop the carnage, and now I'm not the one." She sighed.

"You may still divert them from this danger," said Mulad. *"The Order needs you to be in the family."*

"Let's continue to cultivate your gifts, and when the blood one is born, I'll train them," said Ati.

"I am aware of the Order's needs, Mulad, and agree with Ati. Let us continue the search," said the queen.

Mulad removed his finger, and the image dropped.

"I wish to see where my cousin is," she demanded.

Mulad flipped the tablet and studied the last two divots. Shapía waited impatiently when Mulad smiled.

"Here he is," he answered.

The crowl placed its green bony finger into a divot, and the orb popped forward. An image of a crowl appeared, and Gavee remained next to her as they feasted. Mulad's eyes widened in surprise. Shapía withdrew with concern and mistrust.

"Seer of Seers, I am just the messenger and understand not why your cousin feasts with the head of my kind. I assure you, Mistress Crea is aligned with the Order and is working to stop your brother."

"Oh, Great Blood Seer, come, and we shall find your room for rest. We work together to gain access to your powers," said Ati.

"Rest? I cannot rest knowing my brother is destroying the island."

"In this rest, learn how to grasp the true cause of it all," said Ati.

The candles and crystals brightened, and Ati waited for the seer.

"I promise, Blood Seer, the rest is what you want," said Mulad.

Shapía released a sigh and stood.

"Take me."

"We shall see you in the morning," said Mulad.

The crowl stood and nodded to the elfman, who waved her on as he scurried into the hallway. The seer followed, studying the hall with mirrors on each side and the infinite loop. Ati followed the mirrors, plodding to each step until they reached the top.

"Yes, yes, there it is," he stammered.

The door creaked open to a spacious room with a bed fit for ten and a large roost in the left corner for those with wings. The walls contain a painted cherry tree mural and a path leading up a hill with a huge Bellow tree. It carried a tree loft, and a distant masura appeared to wave. The painting made Shapía uneasy.

The chamber had a door on its left, leading to an enormous bathroom with a ceramic tub. Shapía turned to Ati and a mirror on the wall. The mural was alive, and the masura stood at the path's base.

"His name is lost to the ages, but he has more history than I can tell. The explanation lies in your rest," said Ati.

"My senses tell me not to fall asleep, but my new way eases my concerns," said Shapía. "We have fruit on the golden table and cool water from the fountain."

He pointed to a large fountain cast into the stone wall with the goddess Ellebasi pouring from the jug.

"If you need anything, please ring this bell," he said.

He pointed to the small table beside the roost with a silver bell.

"I leave you, and please rest, so our training will be productive," he said.

The elfman proceeded to the door and closed it, then did something Shapía did not expect. He locked it. She listened to his boots walking quickly down the hallway before she could contest the idea. Shapía grabbed the bell and then stopped before ringing it.

"I have the power. Why am I still reacting in the old way?" she groaned.

She grabbed a golden goblet and placed it in the water, quenching her thirst. Juicy and delicious, the grapes caused her to snatch more than she turned to the mirror. Beside the path, the painted masura perched on a log, waving. The seer finished the remaining grapes and stared. The male masura waved her to enter the mirror, surprising Shapía. As the breeze blew, the tree swayed, and the masura's hair brushed his face. The living scene confused the seer when the sigil on the left arm vibrated. With a prickling sensation, the symbol's inked lines rose from her skin, and a voice, smooth as silk yet laced with steel, invaded her mind.

"To learn the future, you enter the disk."

"Why not?" She sighed, allowing her hand to break the surface. "Let's find out what this side holds for us."

The glass gave way like a wave in water, and its coolness grabbed her lungs. The wetness on her face forced her eyes shut. She pushed against the barrier, stumbling onto the grass. A gentle breeze carried distant birds and rustling rabbits and other creatures as they moved through the tall grasses in the fields. With the cherry tree fragrance and many wildflowers pleasing the senses, Shapía walked forward. The male masura waited with a smile.

"Hello, Seer of Seers, it is a good day," said the male.

"Where is this, and who are you?"

"This is the bardo, and my name is not important. You are important."

Shapía tried to use her senses, but something blocked her, and she noticed the bracers and warrior armor now gone, with her simple Witch'Bane robe replacing it.

"Your Aza protection shall return once you leave this plane. This existence is in-between, and these items are no good here. Nothing may manipulate my fracture."

"Why have you requested that I enter?"

"Come, let's go to the tree loft balcony and speak some truths."

He did not wait and walked up the path to the Bellow tree, then raised his wings to bring him to the tree loft's front. Shapía turned around, and the mirror was gone. Nothing but sky and rolling fields lay behind her. She had no choice but to lift and follow the masura. The front door remained ajar, and she entered a spacious open space. The large balcony, overlooking a great lake with fields stretching on either side and a cluster of trees on the far bank. Seated in a tall chair alongside a table, the man drank from a stein.

"Please join me," he said.

The view was breathtaking, and the comfort Shapía only found with her mother washed over her. With soft green eyes, brown hair falling to his shoulders, a simple maroon robe, and tall brown wings, the male masura appeared.

"What are we drinking?" she asked.

"A plain honey mead," he said.

She took a swig and found it to be her favorite.

"What is the purpose of our meeting?" she asked.

"I see the time in Aza's plane carries you," he grinned. "This is excellent. Time well spent, and now, a period for you to grasp the factual truth."

"Everyone keeps saying it. No one has shown it."

She downed the drink, and he poured another.

"You decide if you take Aza's direction. It leads to an ordinary existence for all beings on the Five Islands. Or you understand the blood in your veins and end Aza's reign."

"Who is Aza? I do not know what it signifies," she said. "I am in the dark about the actual truth and refuse to jump because others say to do it."

"Good, no one wants the seer of seers to do such an act."

The masura dropped his smile, and his stare drove through Shapía.

"There are four sisters who come from Aza's plane. They bring havoc wherever they may and destroy everything good. Aza did not expect them to turn on him as they had, since they were only to spy, not to follow their own desires. He showed the gods how to lock them away and promised to defend their islands."

"You said there are four? Aza and the great tablet speak of three."

"Aza, and the story with it, delivered the tablet. The fourth is exiled and is never spoken of or considered. She doesn't come from his plane. But she made a blood oath, and they intertwined the blood into hers, then into her brother's wife, and down to you."

"My father has a sister?" she panicked.

"Yes, Tora. She is banished to the southern tip of Breiv, in the land of the Ice King. With her, you will discover why they took the blood oath and how you are to free the islands."

Shapía stared at the lake and watched the ducks swim. The thought of an aunt living in exile and the endless amount of other information she has never been told. The memory of her recent imprisonment brought a shiver. Whispers formed in her head, and she concentrated on the muttering words.

"Stop," she said to the masura. "Talk without the mind."

"Go south and leave the fighting behind until you have Tora."

"But my skills are still short, and Ati is to train me in it."

"He already knows what needs to be done and is to lead you to where Tora lives. On this journey, you will master the powers Aza has given and how to remove his touch. This power starts where the sisters begin."

"You are Shaki."

Shapía surprised herself with the comment.

"I am, and you should know the true oracle. If you fail, the Order dies, the sisters roam free, and Aza imprisons you on his plane alongside Linn."

"Linn," she cried out.

"Yes, Guru Linn remains tortured and is going to be until you succeed or join her," he said.

The male masura stood and came to a hover, withdrawing, but staring at Shapía.

"Wait, I have more questions," she yelled.

Shaki didn't answer, and she drifted further, narrowing her focus on the surrounding scene until everything faded to black and then a voice.

"Madame Seer, it's time to wake. Madame Seer."

Shapía opened her eyes, and Ati stood with a robe covering his eyes.

She came off her roost and noticed she was naked.

"When do we leave?" She asked, putting on the robe.

"After we eat, we begin the voyage south, My Seer."

The elfman gave her a bow, and she smiled.

"We should eat and leave as soon as we can."

The elfman moved to the small table and poured a drink into the cup. Shapía ate, wondering about the words.

"Why does Mulad's tablet lie?" she questioned.

Ati smiled.

"There are members, and there are those who lead the Order. The leaders hide the one who could end this cycle."

"Why? Why are there so many secrets?"

"When Aza first arrived in our world, he promised greatness to those who befriended the god. Those beings became his spies and grew in power from him as they spun their stories to increase their position. The leaders saw this and banished the unblood sister to keep her safe."

"Tora is not a prisoner?"

"No, she is banished but is not a prisoner. She awaits your arrival," said Ati. "Your mother went to her, then was killed."

Ati's demeanor turned tense.

"Her death was unexpected, and I fear the reason."

"No more hiding, Ati. If you are here to assist me, you no longer hide," demanded Shapía.

"I am to be your honest guide. Anything further I say is unknown and speculation, not truth."

"But could be, so has to be shared."

The elfman took a deep breath and turned, staring into his reflection.

"It is believed your brother had your mother killed."

Shapía's mind could not grasp the words. She became sick, and panic took over her breathing.

"This is why I did not want to say it," said Ati.

He grabbed a towel, dropped it into the fountain, brought it to the seer, and placed it on her neck.

"How close to the truth is this?" angered Shapía.

"It remains unknown until we find Tora," he said.

"We must leave!"

"Soon," he said, removing the wet towel.

"Why soon? We need to go. The island needs us to go!"

"This is true, and the Order, the leaders, we need our seer to move strategically. Aza's spies will pursue if we rush south, placing Tora in danger."

"Mulad is a spy," she said.

"Yes, therefore I am here and play the servant's role."

"Why servant?"

"Only a servant would understand every move the master makes," he said.

"What do we do?"

"Eat, and we'll go visit Mulad. Follow my lead, and we will leave before the sun ends the day."

"My training is in how to lead the Order," said Shapía.

"Yes, and bring an end to Aza."

"I was once a simple princess with basic needs. Now, I end a god?"

"Not end, close his ability to reach us. He is a god. You do not have the power to take him down."

"Simple," she said.

He chuckled.

"You were never a simple princess, My Seer. I watched your power grow. Simple would never be your life."

"Now you sound like my mother," she said.

Chapter Twenty

The Elite emerged in front of a sealed passage as the fight behind continued to push into the Sovereign Hall. Asmodeus and Rhile remained within the center as the exercitus met each elvin fighter arriving underground. The push into the corridor halted, and Asmodeus read their minds.

"They discovered a rock wall blocking the way forward," he said.

The king lit the tunnel with an orange orb, showing the ceiling dipped lower and the walls closer. Asmodeus waved a hand, brushing the lost aside and reaching for the solid wall. Something melted the stone into the cave system. The masura closed his thoughts on the sounds, bringing Malum's energy and placing the metal ring onto the rock. Asmodeus moaned under the pressure, with his hand warming. The painful shards shooting through his gut, down his left arm, and into the ring forced him back. He snarled at the fight and raised his glowing purple eyes.

"I curse this rock and break its courage," his deep voice reverberated.

The stone cracked, crumbling at the broken lines and releasing a high-pitched squeal. Asmodeus fought back and pushed harder when the explosion flung the shards, blasting past him and decimating the exercitus fighters. But the route lay open, and a dim yellow light bounced around the passage.

"We need more fighters," said Rhile.

"They'll be here soon," said Asmodeus.

"What is this?" questioned Rhile.

"The Passage of Mirrors," he answered.

The wide corridor's walls and ceiling featured mirrors, leaving the surface in yellow marble. As the Elite Exercitus closed ranks behind their leader, the air crackled with anticipation.

Asmodeus's painful cry echoed as he jerked his hand away.

"The hidden magic is fighting back."

Two fighters approached, holding their battleaxes high and charging into the mirror. The initial hit bounced the axe back, lopping off the drone's head and rolling it to Asmodeus. The second arrived at it sideways, and the weapon ricocheted, landing in the fighter's gut. It did not scream, just fell to the marble surface, where blood pooled. Asmodeus groaned as two more advanced and entered the space with swords. The two creatures' talons slipped on the smooth floor, stepping through the blood. They stopped, pointed to an opening on the left, and disappeared as the tunnel thundered, closing the way. The route was gone.

Asmodeus entered the room and worked his senses to gain hold, yet the hall showed nothing and remained silent. His horrifying transformation was staring back at him in the mirror with the king's garb coal-black, wings deep lilac, and eyes glowing like amethysts. The masuran's skin was opaque, and talons were as black as a raven's.

His mind darkened with the exercitus' voices dwelling in his thoughts, and he fought to understand the section. Rhile appeared from behind and stood next to the king. Her beauty remained with dark purple armor, black wings, and lavender skin. Her eyes were all black, while her mind remained intact. The freedom from Malum's hold released her into the commingle.

The elite moved into the hall and hurried to locate the door. Some disappeared onto paths sealed behind them before being followed, while others worked to smash the mirrors without success. The room in chaos rumbled violently, and the hard rock reshaped, closing the outside.

"Enough," he said.

The drones froze and waited for their leader's command.

"Follow the passage straight. Find me the door!"

The Elite pushed, banged, and crawled on the walls, ceiling, and floor. As Asmodeus returned, he crushed the stone. In its place, he created a barrier preventing the way through from being closed. Rhile searched in the remote corner when the room rumbled, and a bright orb dropped from above, sending the mirrors into a blinding light. The reflections made the beings in the corridor drop to the ground, covering their sight.

Asmodeus stood with eyes closed when a loud hum vibrated and the Elite screamed in pain. The sounds coming from the drones surprised Asmodeus, and he tried to peek through the brightness. Peace suddenly zipped into the space after a short alarm blast. The fighters continued their struggle against the mirror.

Once more, the room rumbled, bringing its orb and returning the painful light across the room. The high-pitched squeal tormented the fighters.

"It's crushing my belly!" screamed Rhile.

"No!" said Asmodeus.

He lost his bearings, then kneeled as the noise echoed. The orb disappeared along with the noise, and Asmodeus ran to Rhile. She curled in the corner and directed his senses through his talons.

"There is a loose tile."

The king pressed a hand against the marble, vibrating until it shattered. The ground revealed a mechanism with several metal cogs and no handle to move it.

"Map," he said.

The ceiling's yellow sphere dropped, its light blinding the king, who kneeled as a squeal intensified into a wavering alarm. The masura expected the alarm to fade, but it never eased. He felt about placing the embedded ring on the largest cog, and it turned. The alarm heightened when a trapdoor opened on the deck, and a fighter fell. The signal ended with the light dimming and allowing his vision to return. Rhile remained curled on the floor.

"You cannot go any farther," he said.

"I follow my king," she said through a drawn breath. "I'm the leader of your army."

She tried to stand, but Asmodeus pushed her back, and she fell to a knee.

"My love, it's time for us to keep the heir to the throne safe." The king touched her stomach, and the pain eased. "If the alarm returns, slip down and stay safe from danger."

"There's no danger below?"

"I will post a sentry to ensure your safety."

Asmodeus rose, and two fighters leaped into the hole, landing on a wooden platform. He gave a wink and unfurled the map. "As the map has foretold, the platform is a safe location. Promise me. You will not follow."

Rhile held her tongue.

"Promise me!" he said.

"I promise not to follow and remain here," said Rhile through tears.

Asmodeus looked down and found glass steps falling into the distance. Each step could fit three masuras but was too thin for a foot, making the talons hang. No railing was present, and vines draped from overhead, just over each step. There was a glow to the downward passage, and the glass stairs sparkled. The enclosure remained too tight for flight, and the drop beneath the floating stairs contained glass shard spikes. Unable to free its human, the leading fighter lay pierced and still alive. The king stepped aside as an Elite placed a talon down on the first step, then the other, when a single tune echoed. As the glass step vanished, the warrior tumbled into a shower of razor-sharp shards. Shattering glass resounded, and the soldier fell to its death.

The missing stair reappeared when the tune's echo disappeared. Asmodeus sighed, put a hand on a vine, and lowered one foot. He pulled tight and put the other on the next step. The vines possessed a sap that stuck to his hands with each grab. They stuck to his wings and leather armor, too. The gluey substance hardened on his hands. The elite fighters followed the king step after step, trying not to put weight on their feet. Asmodeus got to the fourth step when a tune beckoned, and a fighter plunged to its death. He sensed his strength waning and quickened his pace. The sap thickened when the last three steps appeared in front of a hidden landing.

"Keep moving ahead!" he said.

The random tune played out with another fighter lost, and Asmodeus pushed faster. He reached the platform and cautiously stepped onto it, keeping his wings ready. The black wooden structure stood firm and extended into the darkness. The king could not see past the platform's end and awaited his fighters as they continued to pour down. Asmodeus instructed a soldier to move ahead. The drone grasped the hanging vine—and it curled and seized the fighter. Asmodeus looked up and watched new vines reach for the intruders.

At the end, the king crouched and saw six more glass steps that went down to a stone base. Asmodeus sliced off a vine that was ready to grab one of his drones. The creature squealed and reeled back into the darkness, leaving a gap. The masura hovered slightly, slicing through the living roots, searching for the ceiling. He sought to send an orb into the creature when the passage's magic blocked the powers. Asmodeus was angry at the block and cut down the vines. Screeches filled the darkness.

The king reached the next platform, stretching straight and ending at a stacked rock wall. He stepped onto the rock when both talons were sucked into the wet clay, bringing the wetness to his knees. He groaned at not having put his servants ahead and trudged forward.

The king explored the area, the scent of pine and damp earth filling his nostrils as he surveyed the landscape. The tight cavern gave no room to hover, and the extended surface held three masuras across. Asmodeus extended his left hand, and a yellow orb emerged, lighting the scene. The smooth, round stones stacked atop delivered no passage through and confused the king.

"Do we understand the riddle?" questioned Rhile.

He looked back in disgust.

"My place is at your side, not back there."

Asmodeus grunted.

"It's a dwarf door with a hidden keyhole, hidden somewhere amongst these stones."

The yellow orb brightened as Asmodeus moved near the wall. He tried to use his mind to solve the trick, yet it proved blank. The sphere fizzled, and the dark gave them nothing beyond their noses.

"My King…?" questioned Rhile.

"The way ahead controls all magic and destroys it," he said. "My vision, though, is not disrupted. I'll work the seams to locate the hidden door."

Smooth rocks, shaded purple, offered shadows and texture as he searched for a gap, running his hand up, down, and over. The tight stones did not move, and he arrived at the rocks in front of the clay when he realized it continued below the muck. As the masura searched in the wet clay for slippery stones, a small pebble dropped, causing several others to slide down and leave a gap at the top, eliciting a groan. The section revealed a steel door with the remaining stones locked in place.

"Where is it?" questioned Asmodeus.

His hands worked apart, fumbling in the dark and the cold mire. He persisted when a large boulder fell, with more to follow, revealing half the door. Asmodeus pulled the pile back and raised the yellow orb. Round rivets outlined the steel, creating a crisscross pattern lacking any keyhole. The king slammed the ball against the door, causing it to reverberate. The remaining stones tumbled and disappeared into the clay. Blue light illuminated the cavern, highlighting shining rivets and a large orange central indent. He ran his fingers over the different dents in the mark.

"Tell me your secret," said Asmodeus.

"Is it a stone?" asked Rhile.

Asmodeus snapped a smile.

"You're correct, my love."

He grabbed a rock and compared its size, understanding the difference. Rhile joined in the discovery, picking up countless rocks and comparing their sizes. The frustration boiled.

"It's taking more time than it should!"

The king stepped back as the drones advanced, tearing into the piled rocks. They sized and then discarded each one, repeating the pattern. Asmodeus kept a stern gaze, and Rhile joined the party when they found the needed rock. The placement upon the indent shuttered the door, and a seam rippled down the middle, popping it open. The tunnel continued under the same wet clay track, with a new opening in the distance.

Directed by a simple command, the fighters pushed down the hallway, the sound of their boots echoing as the exercitus followed in a powerful wave. He pulled his sword, and Rhile followed as they entered the next room. The chiseled tunnel seeped water, dripping and keeping the clay wet. As it rose to a base, the path became dense and more complex to push through. The darkened tunnel was warm, and the floor carried steam hovering just above it.

Under the heat, the wet clay hardened, adhering to everything it contacted. Asmodeus growled with its weight, and the dried cement fell from his clothing and talons. Malum's son held up his left hand and then dropped the hard rock from Rhile and the Elite fighters. They reached the doorway just past the cavern, and Asmodeus's purple eyes brightened to take in the vast cave.

"What do you see?" asked Rhile.

"It's filled with stalagmites and stalactites, with dead trees and stumps scattered across the bottom. It's odd to see such a mystery."

Asmodeus launched a yellow sphere into the air, bringing a dim light to illuminate the scene. Rhile gasped at the enormity of the endless dead trees.

"We must get into the trees. The trail is heating the longer we remain in place," said Rhile. "Our talons will sink into it again."

He pointed, and the exercitus flew into the space when the orb snapped and popped, fizzling out. The darkness caused the drones to crash into the dead limbs, dropping them to the hard floor. Asmodeus cursed and hurled a larger orb, keeping his hand steady on its location. The fighters poured into the area when arrows flew from the shadows.

"There!" said Rhile.

In a large stalactite, an opening appeared with two cave dwellers sending arrow after arrow into the space. Asmodeus and Rhile cut down the quills with simple strikes and jumped behind a stalagmite. The giant orb fizzled, and Asmodeus resisted the magic, keeping light over the cavern. Without hesitation, the exercitus flew past the barriers. The flight stayed short, dropping the fighters under a hidden attack.

"Cave dwellers protect the vault?" questioned Rhile.

"It holds the various items belonging to the Five Islands, and all intelligent beings have a stake in it. The one item we need to control the islands sits inside. All will protect it," groaned Asmodeus.

"But these humanoid types don't use gems or gold. They have no need for it," said Rhile.

"They fight for food and protection from the dwarves. This would really solidify a full allowance to the old cavern mines abandoned by the dwarves," said Asmodeus.

"Without Malum's power, how do we succeed, My King?"

"We fill the cave with our fighters."

The king waved them on, and the exercitus surged into the mysterious cavern. He struggled against the magic as it extinguished the yellow orbs. He protected the globe with arrows and blue glowing balls. The cave dweller's secret magic battled to vanquish the light. The flying masuras countered, sending arrows and attacking the endless hiding cave dwellers with swords. Asmodeus watched his fighters surge deeper into the war, pushing the humans from the entrance.

A darkening force met the yellow orb, suffocating its light from reaching below. He conjured a red sphere into the black as it bounced, exploded, and lit the dead trees.

"We will crush the living," said Asmodeus.

From the entrance, the two watched the fight unfold. The exercitus attacked each position, with cave dwellers and drones occupying the area. The king conjured orb after orb in distant corners, revealing the cave dwellers' iguana battle riders coming from side openings. Before he could comment, a force threw Rhile from her position, and she slid from sight. The king raised his sword and hovered, meeting two battle riders.

The iguanas hissed at the floating masura when an arrow slipped past his cheek. Asmodeus's anger caused him to create an air concussion, throwing the seated riders and breaking the iguana's legs. Arcing and fighting the pain, the screaming beasts lashed their tails against the stalagmites, causing chaos. The king smiled when a blow landed from the side, and a cave dweller launched them both into a tree.

The air forced from his lungs caused the masura to remain on all fours when a cave dweller kicked his ribs, and he rolled. Ignoring the searing pain in his side, the king roared and leaped forward, sword raised high. It caught the cave dweller off guard, and the blade slid into the humanoid's chest. Several exercitus circled their leader and fought back additional battle riders and cave dwellers on foot.

"Rhile?" screamed Asmodeus.

The battle raged in the countless shadows of the dim cave, then the yellow orb fizzled out. Asmodeus's dark vision materialized clean, and the many entrances into the cave showed. He directed fighters to the openings to meet their foes before entering, as he remained on foot. The king searched for Rhile through the broken and dead trees, with dead masuras and cave dwellers strewn upon the cavern surface.

He propelled two large white orbs into the cavern ceiling, where they attached to the rock and popped out more, dancing on the cave ceiling. It brought a brilliant light into the shadows, causing the cave dweller to cower and fight the blindness. The fire continued its jump from tree to tree, and the water on the floor sizzled into steam. The advantage swayed the invaders.

"Close the holes!" said Asmodeus.

From the entrances, the army carved a passage, using white orbs to contain the cave dwellers in the tunnels. The fight slowed, the remaining cave dweller dying as the battle waned and the dead cave dweller joined the exercitus. In the bright light, the gigantic design unfolded, and Asmodeus hovered above the trees and stalagmites, his shadow stretching long and distorted across the cavern surface.

"Rhile!"

She did not answer as the carnage below appeared. The fortress's destruction was immense, and the burning wood permeated the senses. While he searched for the vault's gateway, the drones searched for his commander and any living enemy. The exercitus hewed the standing trees and stalagmites, roaring like a hurricane, and Asmodeus flew to the opposite wall.

"They found her," he said.

The fighters flew to the king, with Rhile holding her bloody side. He met them and helped her, placing his left hand over the gashing wound.

"The iguana's fangs ripped into me," she said.

Asmodeus's eyes widened at the words. The battle iguana's saliva contained poison and would swell the brain until it exploded. He concentrated on the wound, and the blood pooled beside her on the ground. The poison was deep, and he could taste it in his mouth. Malum's son placed his right hand on Rhile's belly and fought the virus back from his child.

Rhile moaned in agony as Asmodeus sensed his mother's power surge through him, crushing the evil liquid. The black mass oozed, and he grumbled at the power conjured to take it out. They both slumped to the side and lay against the hard surface, staring at the bright ceiling.

"We need to uncover the portal," he said.

Rhile stood with armor torn and her side wound gone.

"Does it show a design?" she asked.

"No, hew it all down."

As the king wished, the two masuras rose, wings flapping, to hover over the scurrying fighters. The exercitus soldiers poured in, and havoc descended upon the cave lair. With a burst of exploding stalagmites across the ground, the many openings from the dark sealed shut. The dust rose and settled above their heads when Asmodeus took to the center. He hovered in front of a tall, broken stalagmite and a gaping hole dropping into the black. Rhile reached the king, and he released a yellow orb down. The light sparked in the calcium deposits and blinded the many fighters as it ended.

"Another muddy surface," said Rhile.

A fighter dropped into the hole. It landed in the mire and sank to its chest. The soldier moved beyond their vision, and another dropped in, repeating the action. Fighters followed, vanishing into the gloom.

"We should have had a report by now," said Rhile.

"Many secrets are kept within this vast, uneasy space," Asmodeus replied.

With a rumble, the room shook, and a mud wave poured past the opening. The violent ooze swayed in different directions as it curled below the drop-in.

"They found another opening," said Asmodeus.

He snapped to wings with Rhile, and they landed in the distance, where another stalagmite opened to the mud wave below.

An Elite fighter appeared and displayed the map before his king. "We're at the end of the next path."

"I want a full attack on the stairs. If we don't find another opening, we'll make one," said Asmodeus.

The exercitus swarmed the entrance into the cavern and crushed the many stalagmites, downing the tall spirals until they lay in ruin. Asmodeus channeled more power to the scouring orbs to find an opening and uncover a way down. It proved fruitless, with mound after mound piling and nothing to show for the destruction. Asmodeus pointed to the stairs leading down from the entry, and the drones tore into the base.

"We'll exit, and if the map holds, it'll drop us onto the final vault's route."

The fighters smashed hands, feet, and swords, digging and pushing the dirt base from the pit.

"My king, please excuse my ignorance. I don't understand," said Rhile. "How do the Sovereign Hall keepers reach the vault? Why isn't there an easier way?"

"One keeper controls the vault, with its knowledge surpassing Malum's. The items in the vault are brought to the hall and provided with a signature. We are going to the vault."

"Signature?"

"Another mystery. Witch'Bane has a ban on hall access. An action invoked by Rath."

"How do they hold so much control over the clans?"

"They are the ancient ones who were selected as the Masuran representatives for the hall."

"Those righteous fools," she said.

"I was tasked with lifting the embargo several years ago and was led to believe it might be removed. When I arrived to understand our signature, I was turned out and banned. Word reached my father before I could get home, and embarrassment covered his face. He threatened to usurp the throne and give it to Shapía."

"You never spoke about it?"

"It is mine to bear. Malum's blood oath and commitment drove me to pursue an alternative course concerning the island's truth. It opened my mind to its possibilities."

The gaping hole widened until the wall ended, with the rolling mud no longer bouncing from side to side. It remained on a pattern toward an unseen course beyond the void. Asmodeus eased his head into the gap and sent two orbs floating until they settled above the following opening. He stood and grabbed the map, following the turns downward.

"The ensuing direction spins and descends, carrying the mud. I don't want the mother to the throne to follow, but she won't heed the king's request, so I'll do the next best thing."

"And this is?" questioned Rhile.

"We'll drop into the muck and allow it to carry us through the passage with you in front. I will protect you and our child."

Asmodeus conjured several orbs and launched them into the passage, giving light and foresight. The drones dropped into the ooze, allowing the flow to take them when Asmodeus clutched Rhile's hand. It dragged them on, unable to reach the bottom with their feet, trying to keep their heads above the pulling mud. Asmodeus pulled Rhile in front, and they bobbed through the passage.

It contained a tight space with Rhile sitting within Asmodeus's legs as he bounced more orbs off the top, ensuring a complete view. The path gave them a bottom to rest on and stability with their hands. As they approached the leading bend, the walls and ceiling carried sharp points, like thorns sticking from a stem. Rhile took the first, screaming from the cuts when Asmodeus felt the strong points slice into his flesh. They encountered fighters pierced and stuck in the flow, causing the others to form a dam. Rhile screamed at the oncoming soldiers when Asmodeus set a red sphere into the pileup, exploding and forcing the clog to be free. The muddy flow destroyed the spikes and killed the fighters, clearing the way ahead.

The leader drifted red orbs ahead, breaking up the spikes and giving a better slide. Their speed increased with the free flow and thick clay, moving them faster than they could control. It spun them up the bumpy wall and placed Asmodeus in front, with them sitting back-to-back. The light orbs remained in place, keeping the darkness back as the mud rose and floated head-high. Rhile pulled around and clung to Asmodeus. The overhead skimmed just above, and the orbs disappeared underneath the flow, dropping them into darkness.

The masuras tried using their wings to fight the pull and struggled under the clay's weight. Asmodeus outstretched his arms to slow their descent and pushed against the smooth walls. The last bend flung them hard against the wall, and the distant light came on fast, throwing them from the tunnel. The two tumbled and made a hard right, coughing out the muddy water.

They lay on soft grass with a light filling the area as if the sun hung in the sky behind a few clouds. Bellow trees pocketed the massive area with a small lea farther on from it. They sat covered in drying mud and marveled at the beautiful sight. Before them, a sandy trail cut through the countless trees and settled upon a stream, stretched into the enormous cave. The trail continued on the distant side and ended in front of a waterfall, filling a large pool.

Out of their sight, the stream flowed into a tunnel, disappearing under a rock wall. The walls and ceiling sparkled in the hidden light source. Flowers filled past the trees and alongside the flowing stream banks, onto the hanging cliffs and decorated the waterfall's sides.

"Where's the vault?" asked Rhile.

"The path ends at the falls. It is beyond the water."

The exercitus continued to pour behind until they sucked under the cave wall. The party moved into the trees and followed the path when the flowers ejected spores into the air, and the endless particles fell like snow, with the drones dropping from the sweet smell. Asmodeus suppressed his breath when Rhile dropped to her knees and grabbed her throat.

"My throat is burning." She gasped for air.

Asmodeus did not answer but created an orb filled with air. It slipped over her head and allowed Rhile to breathe fresh air. He made more orbs for his Elite, encircling their heads and allowing his fighters to continue the mission.

The king and his followers stepped onto the sand, kicking grime from their talons and working the mess off their wings. They reached the water's edge, and Rhile dipped a hand in the cool, flowing stream, allowing it to wash the dried dirt.

"It's a natural spring, My King."

The clear water showed a shallow bed, with the drones entering first and coming knee deep. Asmodeus and Rhile followed, washing the thick mud as the others followed, turning the clear water brown. The king snapped his fingers, and the fighters tried to enter the falls, getting kicked back, popping their orbs, and ending their walking dead lives. The fighters scoured the rocks and climbed higher, with some taking flight and reaching the top.

"We must stop the water flow!" said Asmodeus.

The exercitus obeyed their king and piled the rocks to slow the water. After some time, the fast flow became a trickle, revealing the hidden vault. Reflecting in the sparkling water, the golden door, lacking a handle, spurred the soldiers to work harder, diverting the flow. The entry was free from the falling water when Asmodeus began for the door and Rhile pulled him back. The leader snapped her fingers, and the elite approached the door.

Despite the masuras' mindless efforts to push, slip blades into crevices, and lift the door, it remained firmly shut.

Asmodeus approached with Rhile pulling on his arm. The king eased her hand and stood in front of it. The gold shimmered in the faint light, and Asmodeus was driven to touch its beauty. With the touch, the gold disappeared, and an opening appeared. The king stood back as the first warrior approached. The drone masura proceeded into the space when it evaporated in a loud snap. Another drone moved in and jumped into the passage when it, too, vanished in a loud pop.

"It must be me," said Asmodeus.

The king took a breath and seized Malum's energy. He paused, then reached out his hand, placing it in the void. Nothing occurred. He found the entrance open. Asmodeus entered an extensive circular room with walls and ceiling covered in mirrors. The surface had a leather-like texture with the talon tips lightly gripping it, and a golden banister around the walls prevented touching the mirrors.

Footsteps approached on a marble floor as a light source reflected in the mirror, darkening the room. The creature's figure grew prominent, dimming the light source with its stature. With a snap of the shadow's fingers, mirrored reflections showed a circular gold wall where an elder crowl waited for the king behind a counter. The old being had a monocle in the right eye, a golden vest, and long gold fabric sleeves. It flipped through an enormous book and dipped a quill into an ink jar.

"What is your business?" asked the crowl.

Asmodeus remained in his spot near the door.

"I'm here for the Mazerth Stone."

The crowl looked up from his parchment and placed the quill into the jar.

"You are not its keeper."

"I am. My name is King Flued, keeper of Witch'Bane and rightful Mazerth owner."

"Witch'Bane does not own the Mazerth. The thunderblood protects it, and no one outside the guild has access but the one," said the crowl.

"One? Who's the one?" questioned Asmodeus.

"This knowledge transcends your station, Witch'Bane prince."

The words charged the new king. He went to grab the creature, but the image slipped through his fingers. The crowl remained still.

"I will bring down the hall and its vault until I have the jewel in my possession!"

It laughed. "If you must, odd king. Malum's power has no strength here, and any orb you conjure will fizzle."

Asmodeus raised his left hand, forming a silver orb and sending its energy into the mirror. The static ball bounced and ricocheted within the room until it indeed fizzled.

The crowl closed his book and placed it under his arm. "Our business is done."

The being snapped his fingers, and the room fell dark, then low light and the gold walls reappeared. Asmodeus stepped out of the room and approached Rhile.

"I want it all destroyed. It is the last time any being mocks me. Burn everything as you go until nothing remains."

"As you wish, My King," she said with a smile.

"The Sovereign Hall will bend its knee," he cursed.

Chapter Twenty-One

Crea and the crowl's send-off party was a magnificent spectacle, a vibrant swirl of color, sound, and celebration. With satisfied bellies, sharpened weapons, and travel packs packed, they were prepared to journey to Bathhh. They took rest in a hollow at the Shattered Mountains' southern edge. Dusk filled the area with the Lower Realms open, lea darkening, and Gavee uncomfortable.

Dakii continued alone in a far corner, facing the wall and mumbling in a low growl. The scroll keeper kept to himself after the fire pact, his demeanor and grumpy composure changing to determination and concentration. Crym toiled with the flames, keeping the smoke venting to the hollow's backside, and Gavee stared at the skill, wanting to learn it. Grunt returned with the next meal, and Datta perched atop the outside boulder, keeping watch.

Over the flames roasted the hares the shapeshifter had caught, and Gavee's stomach groaned with anticipation. The flight to the mountain edge took the day, with the scroll keeper riding within his cloud, hiding what he conjured from the many scrolls. The unknown human had several secrets and kept them out of sight. Grunt settled next to Gavee and took a drink from his flask.

"The nectar the crowl gave to the group is marvelous," said Grunt.

"Be careful. It has enough mead to blur your thoughts," said Gavee.

Grunt groaned. "Some days, Masura, you're exhausting."

Datta floated into the camp, grabbed the cooked meal, and returned to her post. Crym pushed the soft soil against a stone and relaxed in the warmth. Gavee grabbed the cooked meat and followed Datta, wanting fresh air. The two masuras stared into the starry night, eating and focusing on the beyond.

"I believe I've betrayed our Order," said Gavee.

"How?" questioned Datta.

"Flued. I thought I was close enough to him. I should have sensed or understood his malicious actions."

"He outsmarted your father. The greatest thunderblood."

"Yes, this concerns me."

Datta brought her attention to Gavee. "Do you think Bahg knew?"

"My love for him says no, but he's the greatest thunderblood. His senses and abilities are beyond even the best thunderblood. How could it all be masked so well that he sensed nothing? Or the queen, a great oracle. How did she not know or sense these changes to our island?"

"The evil force controls Flued, and its strength can hide any betrayal. It found a weakness in your cousin and is using him for its movement," said Datta.

"Why do you think Flued did it? What would this evil want from the masuras?" questioned Gavee.

"This is something to understand or find later."

"I still hold the blame. I was to take over Witch'Bane thunderblood in the next cycle. The masuran way is the primary rule and guide for the guild. Understanding the shifts in the energy around ourselves and our clans is necessary. In the observance of subtle things, I missed it all," said Gavee.

"The guild," said Datta. "I forgot."

"I haven't, and there is to be an inquiry."

"Let's destroy the malevolence and show the inquiry your place in it. As a united front, the investigations of how and why should show the evil escaped the guild. How do the Upper Realm clans have a memorial and not know this wickedness lurked in the shadows?"

"Someone should have seen it," said Gavee.

"Exactly. It slipped past all of us, and the guild should look at itself first."

"What if it didn't slip?" questioned Gavee.

Datta did not answer.

"It is all unknown," said Gavee.

"It'll all unveil once we reclaim the Upper Realm," said Datta.

"Let's hope," said Gavee. "Let's hope.

The pair went into the night and observed the stars' movement throughout the heavens. Thoughts of Bathhh swirled in Gavee's head when Grunt emerged from the hollow.

"The scroll keeper wishes you both to sit by the fire."

"A watch is required," said Datta.

"I'm to replace you," groaned Grunt.

"So, the human gets to dictate our patrol?" angered Gavee.

"Where's Crym?" asked Datta.

"Hard to explain. You need to go inside," said Grunt. "Dakii requires the masuras."

"Let's go," said Datta.

Gavee, hesitant, trailed behind as Grunt assumed responsibility for the post. They entered the void where Crym sat on the far right, leaning against the wall. His small flame burned deep orange and emitted thick black smoke. It snapped and popped with the tontar speaking in his tongue and a rumble settling around the rock circle. Behind him, the rock wall had sigils glowing bright red, popping and snapping.

Dakii stood in a robe with an oversized hood as the blue flames flicked the air, waiting for the masuras. Strange solid black stones encircled the fire and the scroll keeper. Two larger sitting stones facing Dakii awaited the masuras.

"Enter the fire, for there is much to discuss. Ignore the conjuring in the corner. The circle shall not allow others to enter," said Dakii with a heavy groan.

The masuras hesitated and looked at the tontar, remaining focused on his fire with strange moans and curling cries coming from its center. His eyes, glowing bright red, and his once-sloped horns stood straight upon his head. The acrid smell of burning coal stung the air as his tail hooked onto an unfamiliar symbol etched deep within the cavern wall.

"Enter," demanded Dakii.

The thunderblood masuras placed a fist upon their hearts, calling for the guild's protection and shifting their minds to the warriors' senses. Gavee felt the energy field as he entered and became enveloped by its protection. The masuras sat on the stones when Dakii reached inside his robe and tossed dust into the flames, jetting them into the ceiling and causing the space to darken to the blaze. The man unfurled a scroll and began a chant.

"Kers ben foul, Kers ben flay, Kers ben show a flaming way."

The fire pitched in a twirl, causing a wind to gush as it blew warmth onto Gavee's face. It bounced off the ceiling and slammed again into the center, creating a calm flame burning crimson red. He looked to Datta, who lingered in a spell, and Dakii read from the scroll.

"The path before you is not what you seek, yet it is, what is to come," said the keeper.

"Great, another riddle I don't understand," said Gavee.

Dakii lowered the scroll. "It's simple, Masura. What you thought was your path is not the way. You will see an alternative path while on this current path."

Gavee shrugged. "Okay, so then what?"

"Youth," moaned Dakii, "the universe will direct you in this manner."

"Where do I go from here?" asked Gavee.

Dakii studied the scroll. "Bathhh is the way. We must return what is rightfully yours."

"The queen's sword," answered Gavee.

"Your sword," said Dakii. "It belongs to the living. You must retrieve it."

With a flick of his wrist, the scroll keeper tossed several crystals into the fire, watching them pop and fizzle, sending sparks into the air. The flames turned green and then orange and back to green.

"The one who fused your mind is calling. Time to answer," said Dakii.

"Who is it? I have yet to understand," said Gavee.

"The one who killed your queen," answered Dakii.

Before Gavee could ask more, the man tossed in another crystal, and it exploded. Gavee's head swam, and his body collapsed. Soon, a tiny light popped into the far darkness and grew until the green sky appeared. He landed inside an enormous cavern when its green hue dissipated, and light from the unknown brought the total size into view. From the shadows appeared a giant dragon, and Gavee found he remained still and at ease. He sensed this presence and grew comfortable with the giant creature.

"Trogan," he said.

"It is I, Masura."

"Why did you do it?"

The dragon approached and towered over Gavee. Trogan paced the space, dropping small fireballs into crafted firepits. It created a circle around them, and Trogan settled on a worn stoop.

"It had to be done because we trusted Flued."

"Flued?" confused Gavee.

"My world's complexity led my family to despair. After a millennium of Esor's leadership, a challenge to our rule has come forth. My father, killed during the Great Masuran War, left my family vulnerable, and my mother, Queen Trea, stepped into his place. She rules with greatness, but this new challenge has soured our alliance inside Esor. This drove my mother to find others for help."

"Flued."

"Yes, we received information that he had conjured a force beyond our dimension. He appeared through the portal we maintain in our silent hall and expressed support for our future. The queen took an elixir, creating a connection to Flued. It worked for a decade until it turned on her, creating a cocoon where she remains in turmoil. We are now in even more danger, and my mother rages in agony."

"A decade? My cousin sided with evil for a decade. How did we miss it?" angered Gavee.

"What I learned in the war is your kind creates a world, not from truth. It lies to stand itself up higher than the surrounding beings."

"Its plans bring destruction to our island," said Gavee.

"When I sent a dedicated warrior through the portal, she returned in horror and said we must meet Flued at the Crescent Mountains, where he intends to tell us what is necessary to free the queen."

"Why did you kill her?"

"Flued demanded we gain your queen's sword."

"Lonn?" confused Gavee.

"Yes, it holds the capacity to liberate my mother. I arrived to discuss its use, but the Witch'Bane guardians who escorted the queen did not understand my arrival. We had to remove them and wait to talk to your queen. When you both fled, it became clear Flued's trust was a ruse. If the queen had not attacked, she would be alive today."

"It's *our* fault?" angered Gavee.

"No, masura, I'm explaining the events. My required escorts were not in favor of my family and believed we were there to kill Queen Phawa. Upon her killing, they returned and reported on the royalty's death. I lingered behind to get Witch'Bane's assistance and found the one way we could connect."

"The fusion," said Gavee.

"My goal was not to kill for the sword. I was there to seek aid."

"I had the sword. Why not just take it?"

"As I looked at the sword, I imagined the destruction it would cause, the cries of my people echoing in my ears. The Witch'Bane queen's death would cause war. I had to hide our presence and leave you alive, ensuring no one would believe we killed your queen. Her disappearance would be unknown. Her blade remaining in your hands, and you alive, would forever be questioned."

"You destroyed my life!"

"You would do the same for your clan."

Gavee went to pull his sword and found himself weaponless.

"You're in my mind, masura. There is no retaliation today."

"Release me!"

"I cannot and refuse to until we free my mother."

Gavee tried to walk and found a force keeping him within the circle.

"There is no exit."

His shoulders slumped. "What do you want from me?"

"I require the queen's sword."

"I don't have it. The grangrul took the sword and sold it to the wizard, who controls Bathhh."

The dragon groaned. "Stanton."

"What?" questioned Gavee.

"The wizard's name is Stanton."

"I know the wizard," said Gavee.

"He partners with another, who is the pirate king from Razuin Bay."

"Yes, the wizard Myst," continued Gavee.

"The pirate king is in Lotrs, which charges but one wizard to bring down."

"We?"

"Yes, I shall be a great help with our fusion. Once you get to the city, I can direct you to the sword."

"How?"

"You carry the dragon sense. It shall bring gold, silver, and endless gems. The queen's sword is silver from the dwarf city of Dohum, something sensitive to our senses. We'll sniff it out."

"What other senses have I received from you?" asked Gavee.

"Insight. Knowing when someone is lying, tricking, or telling a tale. And one more."

Trogan blew through the flames, extinguishing their light and sending the cave into darkness. Gavee blinked in the black as the green hue returned, and he could see the dragon and the cave.

"Now the darkness is not so dark," said Trogan.

"I intend to assist after I find my father and free my king."

"We are short on time, Thunderblood. It has to be done before the Call of Esor."

"I need to understand why Flued awakened the evil on our island."

"In time, we're to find the answer. The Call of Esor is coming. For now, my mother must be freed. She must present herself to our city and discuss the upcoming gathering. If she does not attend, turmoil may come over the mountain, creating a civil war reaching beyond Esor. The island may be in danger," said Trogan.

"You killed my queen! I don't have to assist you. I am not obliged to you!"

"True, but you must bring the dragons to help fight what Flued created in your forest. It is greater than you have ever seen. Even the mighty Bahg is doomed to fail in the task."

Gavee gritted. "When is the meeting?"

"This is not a meeting, masura. It is a calling and is greater than anything you have ever witnessed. It is the longest night when the snow and ice are on the mountaintops. The Esor Dragons and the dragons from Rivertop and Beacon come to see the ruling dragons. Each dragon city has its own. If my mother is not there, they will kill me, my son, my sister, and her son. Our family has ruled too long to break in this manner."

"How do I contact you?"

"Say my name, and I will hear."

"I'll want your help with the wizard."

"You have my skills and senses to retrieve what is yours and end it all."

Gavee stared at Trogan.

"You have my sword," said Gavee.

"A pact we have, and I shall hold you to your word," said Trogan.

Before Gavee could answer, the cave slid to black, and he could hear Datta calling his name. He woke with Datta shaking him and Crym holding a small flame in his left hand over his forehead.

"What's wrong?" asked Gavee.

"What's wrong?" confused Datta. "You've been in a heavy sleep for eight days!"

"Eight days?" confused Gavee.

He tried to sit, then stood when his legs gave in and folded.

"Hold on, masura," said Crym. "You require some nutrients before moving."

Grunt brought over soup and honey mead. Gavee finished his drink, and his stomach ached for food. He grabbed the bowl when Datta snatched it from his hands.

"Slow down, W.B., too quick, and you'll be sick."

Gavee grabbed the bowl and took a sip. The warm broth was soothing, and his stomach pangs dissipated.

"I've been asleep for eight days?"

"Yes, I've been worried. Last night was the worst with you thrashing and crying out," said Grunt.

"Do you remember anything?" asked Datta.

"Yes, after the fire with Dakii, I had another encounter," said Gavee.

"Fire with Dakii?" questioned Datta.

The group looked at the old man sitting with his back to them.

"What fire, old man?" yelled Crym.

"What do you mean, what fire?" confused Gavee. "When Grunt reached the watch, we moved into the hollow where Crym was in the corner with his fire, and Dakii waited at the larger pit."

"Gavee, you've been asleep since we arrived."

Dakii rose and joined the group.

"The Witch'Bane thunderblood has been given the information he requires to win the war. It belongs to him alone, and if he understands my words, it shall be kept to his chest."

Gavee stared at the scroll keeper's blue eyes and swirled on the words. The information would bring questions, mistrust, and confusion. He stood and downed the broth.

"He's correct. I cannot share what I've seen or heard. Trust is what I demand from you as my traveling companions. We have to get to Bathhh."

"And Dal," said Grunt.

"I'll find Torëk and Dal. He's my responsibility," angered Datta.

"With the thunderblood code, you have my trust," said Crym.

"I'll follow you everywhere," said Grunt.

"I'm tied to this party until the end," said Dakii.

"Scroll Keeper, you and I need to talk regarding your tactics," said Gavee.

"Here forward, no more tricks, Witch'Bane," said Dakii.

"Don't trust it," said Crym.

"Never," replied Gavee. "Mistrust is how we get more answers from this keeper."

* * *

Shapía sat with her back against the cold stone wall. She found a room at Mulad's place where she could sit in peace without interruption. Her mind tried to drift as she pulled it back to the center of her stare. A trick she learned from Shaki when meditation was in order. The seer knew she was deep in her position when the sigils on her body squirmed. The tingle was something she still struggled to adjust to.

She kept her eyes focused on the room's center tile when she felt a rush take over her body and the pull was on. Flashes of many colors went flickering across her sight. With her body feeling light, she could feel she was traveling through the portal. Soon she would reach Aza's plane and wondered why she was being called back.

The multicolored stream soon turned gray, and she floated her way to a floating black stone. She eased her talons down and waited for Aza. The stone she rested upon floated to another, and she had the urge to keep moving. There was a calling from within, and she could sense it drew her to Aza. She stepped onto the longest floating stone she had come across, where an etched pathway directed her position.

The seer kept her eyes ahead with the clouds now floating through the path, obscuring much of it when the stone rumbled and shook, almost causing the masura to fall off the tight path. Her talons dug in deep as the clouds became darker and thicker. The smell of ash and fire filtered in when the smoke dissipated, and Aza stood waiting. The god towered over her being, with his eyes silver-blue, his torso a stony black, and his arms and legs gray, as were his massive hands. He held a trident.

"Seer, why is Malum remaining in your plane?" asked Aza.

"I am still learning my abilities, and it is not simple," she answered.

"Do you forget?" he said, pointing.

Imaginary strings pulled all of Guru Lin's hair, fingers, toes, legs, and arms, stretching her out. Pain lingered in her eyes, with her mouth foaming as she gritted her teeth.

"Do you want to help this innocent child?" he asked.

"Oh, Great One, could you not free her from the torture and just hold her here until I return with Malum? Does this require her pain?" asked Shapía.

"It does, and she remains until you do my bidding. Or maybe you are not the Great Seer? Maybe it was a mistake," said Aza.

"I will get Malum and bring her back," said Shapía. "It was not a mistake."

"Maybe these will remind you of this place," he said.

He pointed to a far stone and raised his hand. From within the black rock, four black skeletons rose. They chattered with their teeth, with two holding black swords and the others holding black battle axes. Shapía said nothing and felt her bracers vibrate on her forearms. She formed a charged sword, glowing bright white, and an electric shield with its edges spitting electricity.

"If you die, there is no coming back this time, Seer," said Aza.

The being disappeared into a black cloud as it swarmed his body. Shapía growled at the words.

"Come, you filth! This will be quick. I do not have time for games! I must save my guru!" she thundered.

* * *

Asmodeus settled on his throne when his name echoed from the portal.

"Asmodeus, come!" squealed Malum.

He moaned at the cackle and shook his head.

"Just a minute's peace," he said. "But she will not give it until I do."

The king made his way through the portal as the massive cavern came into full light. He paused at its enormity, with it growing even since his last visit. Malum's home or castle was larger than the king's tree with its base three oak trees in length. Dwarves continued to chisel away, with the purple glow now bright and vibrant. The massive crack in the ground caused by Flame remained lit as it circled around her castle like a moat.

Each step leading down from the portal had sigils etched in it, and he could feel its magic. The bridge across had two exercitus guards posted, and he wondered who would visit. Malum sat in a chair on her front lanai, surprising Asmodeus while a servant poured a drink sitting on a small table. There was a chair on its opposite side.

"Come," she said.

The energy from the sigils traveled his spine with each step. It made him nauseous, but he continued past the guards and across the stone bridge to her location. As he approached, Malum drank from her cup while the servant poured a drink for the king. He sat in the stone masuran chair with a purple pillow to rest his bottom on. The scene was an odd occasion.

"Mother," he said.

He drank the sweet nectar.

"I see you failed yet again," she said.

The words made Asmodeus grit his teeth.

"I expected it," she continued. "Maybe you do not fit the King of Kings stature. Maybe you are more of a second in command being."

The witch drank her full cup and placed it on the table. Asmodeus held his tongue and finished his drink.

"Is this why you summoned me?" he asked.

"Yes, and we have another pressing need," she answered. "It seems the crowls have chosen a side."

"Who are they with?" he asked.

"Your cousin has made his way into their camp. There was a meeting."

"How?" he asked.

"We have spies in every corner of this island," she answered.

"He escaped," muttered Asmodeus.

"It seems," Malum angered.

"Send the exercitus to wipe them out," said Asmodeus.

"They have moved, and our spies do not know where," answered Malum. "We need Esor."

"The prince refuses to meet with me. He is angry about the placement of his queen. I knew it was too early to send her into the cocoon," he said.

"She is exactly where and how we need her. Besides, they hunt for the sword," said Malum.

"Where is it?" he asked.

"It may be back with your cousin," said Malum.

"May?" he questioned.

Malum ignored the question.

"The elvin queen in Dulisar has agreed to meet with you," she said.

"It's a trap," he said.

"Undoubtedly so, but you will attend as she offers us a truce," said Malum.

"I will kill her," he said.

"You try, and they will have your head before you realize it is gone," angered Malum. "You will receive this gift for the truce, then leave her alive. If you go against my wishes, I will have you slowly burned in Flames fire. You are, after all, replaceable."

Asmodeus remained silent.

"Do we understand?" she asked.

"Yes, I will do your bidding once again."

"Mother?" she insisted.

"Yes, Mother," he repeated.

"Go. You'll meet her in Manawe. The guards will show you the place."

He left her side, walking across the bridge and making his way to the stairs. The sigils squirmed with each step until he pushed through the portal. The king reached his balcony and paused.

"This is my kingdom, not hers. I go where and when I am ready," he said. "It is time to keep her in her domain and away from mine. It is time to put in the next steps for my empire."

COMING SOON

Coming *JUNE 2026*!

'The Scourge of Witch'Bane', Book Two - '*Wretched Evil*'

Come visit our website – mjgrothoff.com

Maps

For the island maps, please visit our website!

Island Maps

www.ingramcontent.com/pod-product-compliance
Lightning Source LLC
LaVergne TN
LVHW012034070526
838202LV00056B/5491